HERS BY REQUEST

KAREN ANN DELL

SOUL MATE PUBLISHING

New York

HERS BY REQUEST

KAREN ANN DELL

Cover Design by Ramona Lockwood

Published in the United States of America by
Soul Mate Publishing
P.O. Box 24
Macedon, New York, 14502

ISBN-13: 978-1-61935-647-4
e-book ISBN-13: ISBN: 978-1-61935-456-2

www.SoulMatePublishing.com

This book is dedicated to my brother,

who has always been the man

upon whom I model my heroes.

While certainly not flawless,

he is admirable in many respects -

especially in kindness

to his younger sibling.

CHAPTER 1

Devlyn MacMurphy's procrastination had paved his personal road to hell for the three weeks since his discharge from Walter Reed. Granted, the purchase of WMES, a small indie radio station on Maryland's eastern shore, had taken up considerable amounts of his time, but that wasn't the reason he had put off finding Danny's fiancée, Amanda Adams.

Eight months had passed since his friend's death and it was past time to keep the promise he'd made. He needed to find Amanda, make sure she was okay financially and emotionally. If she wasn't, he'd do his damnedest to fix it.

It was the very least he could do, considering he was the one who'd gotten Danny killed.

Last night in the wee hours while he played his music and kept his on-air comments to a minimum, Dev had gone through the Annapolis phone book and made a list of possible addresses for Amanda Adams. Finished with his shift at seven a.m., he grabbed a cup of coffee and with the same enthusiasm he would have displayed stepping in front of a firing squad, he dialed the first number.

On call number seven Rosemary, his middle-aged receptionist, her short, dark hair a mass of springy curls, poked her head in the doorway to say good morning. Seeing him on the phone, she retrieved his empty mug, returning in a few minutes with a refill. He nodded his thanks and continued down the list. On call number fifteen he hit pay dirt and almost spilled the fresh cup of hot coffee down the front of his shirt.

Amanda had sublet her apartment in Annapolis. The young woman now living there was happy to give him Amanda's new address. He sat staring at it for a few minutes, stunned to discover Amanda Adams now lived in Blue Point Cove, Maryland.

All these months he'd thought she lived in Annapolis, a safe distance away. Now he knew she was close enough that he could have accidentally run into her in the grocery store or at a gas pump. Hell, she might even listen to his radio station. He frowned, tore the slip of paper from his notepad, and tossed his pen on the desk. Crap. One more excuse shot to hell.

He grabbed his old Army jacket and told Rosemary he'd be back in a few hours. He'd drive through Blue Point Cove, just to look around. See firsthand how big the town was. Maybe . . . maybe, he'd drive by Gull Wing Lane, past the address on the piece of paper tucked in his shirt pocket. A little reconnaissance couldn't hurt.

Amanda settled into her ancient Honda Civic, crossed her fingers, and turned the key. The engine coughed to life and she breathed a sigh of relief. She glanced at the gallery where Zoe, artist and owner, rearranged some watercolors in the front window. Her friend looked worried—and rightly so, after the bad news Amanda had just delivered. If Zoe's cash flow didn't improve, there was a good chance she would have to close the Silvercreek Gallery.

As she pulled away from the curb, the screech of tires and irate blare of a horn made her stomp on the brakes and whip her head around in panic.

Despite the noise, the impact itself felt almost gentle. The bumper of a large dark green SUV kissed the front fender of her car just behind the headlight.

Eyes wide, her gaze traveled over the mountainous hood to the windshield where an incredibly handsome man, square jaw clenched, threw up his hands in disgust. She bit her lip and winced. He backed his car away then got out to survey the damage, casting an annoyed glance at her on the way by her door. She shut the engine off and got out.

Before she could begin an apology, he straightened from inspecting the dent and said, "You always pull out into traffic without looking first? Or were you shooting for the 'dumb woman driver award'?"

"Well, no, I—"

"You're damn lucky I've got good brakes, lady, or you'd be on the hook for a major repair bill."

Annoyed at his attitude, Amanda reminded herself that she was at fault and swallowed her caustic reply. "I'm so sorry! I'm completely to blame." She fished in her purse for her wallet and handed him her insurance card. "Are you okay? And your car, is there much damage?"

Zoe appeared at her elbow. "Mandy, are you all right? I saw the whole thing through the window. I thought you were going to get squashed by that big SUV." She spun on the man. "You were going too fast through this shopping district. Don't you read the speed limit signs?"

"Zoe, stop. It was my fault, not his. He must have been in the blind spot of my rearview mirror, but that's no excuse."

She returned her attention to the tall man. A thick lock of dark brown hair had fallen across his wide forehead and his jaw was shadowed with a day's growth of beard.

"I apologize again and I'll be happy to pay for any repairs your vehicle needs." The wind whipped strands of hair across her face and she swiped at them.

Dev's irritation subsided enough to let him take a closer look at the tall, slender blond in gray slacks and black pea coat. His heart skipped a beat then ran double-time to make up for it.

Fate was having a real belly laugh at his expense.

Without doubt it was Amanda, his best friend's—former

best friend's—fiancée.

Sweet Jesus, she was beautiful. The picture Danny had always carried didn't do her justice. Tendrils of hair the color of liquid sunlight curled around a heart-shaped face, the rest tied back in a braid. Her delicate features were enhanced by flawless ivory skin, and her incredible gray eyes, wide-set and luminous, were the kind that could look into your soul and discover everything you wanted to hide.

With the woman standing two feet away looking like every man's wet dream, his courage failed him. No way was he ready for introductions.

"There's no damage to my car, A . . . Miss." The bumper of his behemoth didn't even have a scratch. Her smaller car had taken all the damage. "As far as I'm concerned there's no need to file an accident report. You can probably have that dent popped back out at a good body shop. Shouldn't cost you much. Probably a lot less than whatever your deductible is."

"That's very kind of you, Mister . . .?"

"MacMurphy. Don't mention it. Just remember to look around next time."

"Oh, I will, believe me. And thank you for being so understanding." She smiled and offered her hand. "My name is Amanda Adams, by the way. In case you discover later that there's any problem with your car, here's my business card."

He stashed the card in his shirt pocket, nodded brusquely, and climbed back behind the wheel, escape his first priority.

Oh yeah, Fate was having a field day.

Because despite all of his guilt, and a burgeoning sense of betrayal, he found himself undeniably attracted to his dead friend's fiancée.

No more worries about paving that road. He had arrived. This must be Hell.

Amanda watched the SUV drive away. At the town's only traffic light the handsome stranger made a left toward Easton.

Zoe tugged on her sleeve. “You sure you’re okay?”

“Oh, I’m fine, Zoe, really. Considering that the accident was totally my fault that guy was pretty reasonable. When he first got out of his car he wore such a scowl, I was afraid he was going to read me the riot act.”

“Not if I had anything to say about it,” her friend huffed.

Amanda grinned. “Yeah, it was like watching a Chihuahua challenging a Great Dane. He was at least six-two and you barely clear five-feet-three.”

But that six-foot-two-inch frame was wide-shouldered, slim-hipped, and well-muscled. Once he lost the frown, his arresting good looks made her forget his abrasive comments. All in all, a very nice male specimen.

Not that she cared.

“Yeah, but he was one hot mess, don’t you think?” Zoe elbowed her in the ribs.

“Objectively speaking, I’d have to agree with you. Are you looking to find a replacement for Jeff?” Amanda chuckled.

“No, you fool. I was sizing him up for *you*.”

“Well, don’t waste your time. I’m not interested. What you should be considering is the event planning business I suggested earlier.”

“I know, I know. I can’t give up now that Jeff convinced Russell Manheim to do a major show here. Having a top-notch artist offer us an exclusive showing of his work won’t mean diddly if I can’t put together enough money for decent advertising. After all the work Jeff and I put into this place my bank account is on life-support and my credit cards are merely useless squares of plastic. We only need a few thousand dollars, but it might as well be a few million.”

The irony of their situation wasn’t lost on Amanda. The second late notice on her student loan payment had come yesterday afternoon. They were both in the same boat and it was taking on water faster than either of them could bail.

"Well, the budget for Mrs. Wyndham's party floored me. She and the Admiral have a lot of high-level brass in their circle of friends and she's sparing no expense. Someone is going to make a ton of money doing this party and I figured it might as well be the two of us."

She'd hoped her friend would be more enthusiastic about the idea since it seemed such a perfect fit for them. She was an expert at organization and number crunching. Zoe was creative, ingenious, and had a flair for the dramatic. Together, she thought they'd make an awesome team.

"Think about it, Zoe. I'd hate to see you close this place." She gave her a quick hug. "Call me soon and we'll do dinner, okay?"

"Sure thing," Zoe mumbled, lost in thought.

Amanda got back in her car. Stroking the steering wheel, she crooned, "Okay baby, I know you had a little scare and a nasty bump but don't let it throw you. We'll get you fixed up—someday soon." She turned the key and obediently the little car started right up. Thank goodness. Cause that little dent was going to be there for quite a while.

CHAPTER 2

The second hand made its jerky approach to twelve on the wall clock and Dev took a swallow from the half-full glass of amber liquid next to the microphone. The short news feed from the network would end at precisely eleven-oh-five.

Andy Phelps, the seven p.m. to eleven p.m. announcer, passed in front of the studio's glass window and tossed him a semi-salute on his way out. Shoulder-length dirty-blond hair straggled around his face and he wore his usual attire—faded plaid flannel shirt, ripped-at-the knee jeans, dark blue hoodie, and shit-kickers. Dev tried to remember what he'd looked like in uniform. The fresh-faced, buzz-cut youth in fatigues was long gone after eighteen months in Iraq.

Dev blew out a breath. Who was he kidding? He was no better. He just kept his disarray on the inside, hidden from the casual observer.

Three. Two. One.

He acknowledged the 'go' sign from the engineer in the control room and flipped the switch on the mike.

"Good evening, ladies and gentlemen, lovers and loners, you're listening to the Friday edition of Dev's Dream Machine on WMES, 89.9 on your FM dial. Sit back and relax or snuggle up with your honey and come along with me. Back to the days when music was synonymous with the words Big Band. When vocalists were called crooners and had names like Ella, Frank, and Bing, and Hollywood was making musicals, lots of musicals—so that Fred and Ginger could wow you with their fancy footwork and leave you itching to get your partner in your arms on a dance floor.

I'm going to open tonight's time travel with Woody Herman's rendition of Skylark. Eleven to midnight is our 'by request' hour and the phone lines are open. I'm waiting for your call, so dial 888-555-WMES and let me know what you'd like to hear."

The other shifts played top forty hits mixed with a judicious amount of golden oldies. Since he was the boss, he indulged himself for one hour on Friday nights to play the music he loved. Big band hits, classics from Gershwin, Ellington, Cole Porter, and jazz featuring Stan Getz, George Shearing, and Johnny Coltrane, among others. He figured since he took the whole eight hours of the most unpopular shift he was entitled to his eccentricities. Turned out a lot of his listeners liked his choices and his 'by request' hour was the result of their frequent calls. Most evenings the phone lines stayed lit the entire hour.

Settling in for the night, Dev took another cautious sip of Jack Daniels—it had to last till morning—and tried to rub the ache out of his left arm. The Jack was another perk of ownership. No one else would dare bring alcohol into the studio. But it beat taking the pain medicine so many other veterans got hooked on while they recovered.

He flicked the mike off and swiveled his chair around to sort through the stack of CDs he'd chosen for tonight's show. Andy had left the studio a mess, the remnants of his McDonald's dinner spread across the back table, the mostly-empty drink container serving as an ashtray with several butts—not all cigarettes—floating at the bottom, and his own selection of CDs scattered haphazardly among the debris. Dev picked up the CDs then swept everything else into the trashcan under the desk.

As the new owner, he made the rules, and although he was willing to cut his little band of misfits a lot of slack, this time Andy had crossed the line. He was due for a "Come to Jesus" meeting in the near future. Dev rubbed his left elbow, an unconscious habit he'd picked up even though it did little to ease the almost constant pain in that joint.

Amanda snuggled under the two quilts and a blanket she had layered on the bed. After sunset, the electric baseboard heaters lost the battle with the cold drafts sneaking in around the windows. She had better pick up some caulk this week at the local hardware store. January in Blue Point Cove wasn't merely chilly, it was downright cold.

She slipped an arm out from under the covers and turned up the volume on her radio. "Don't Get Around Much Anymore", a tune composed by the great Duke Ellington was playing. The song lyrics so matched her life they brought tears to her eyes.

It had been eight months since Danny had died in Iraq, and the pain of losing her fiancé was still fresh. She missed him so badly it seemed like she had lost two men, her lover and her best friend. Countless times over the past months she'd be in the middle of her day when something caught her attention and she'd think, *I have to tell Danny about this*— only to feel the renewed pain of his absence tear at her heart all over again.

That cliché about time healing all wounds was crap. How long would it take before she stopped crying herself to sleep every night? Months? Years?

The song ended and the deejay came back on.

"Let's switch to a tune with a happier outlook and a more upbeat style, 'Walking My Baby Back Home', by Nat King Cole. Remember, we still have another thirty minutes in this request hour, so call me, I'm waiting to play something especially for you."

As she had done several times in the past few weeks, she picked up the phone and dialed the toll-free number.

"Thanks for calling Dev's Dream Machine. What can I play for you tonight?"

"Could you please play 'Someone To Watch Over Me'?"

There was a short pause on the other end before the deejay acknowledged her request. "That must be a favorite of yours. You've called in and asked for it a few times."

Darn. This guy was keeping track? She winced as heat crept up her neck. Up to now she'd felt safely anonymous with her calls. "Yes, I have. Is it a problem?"

"Not at all. If that's what you want to hear, that's what I want to play for you. You can call in and ask for it every Friday if you want."

A ghost of a smile twitched her lips at the kindness in his reply. This man had the perfect voice for his job, she decided. Warm, deep, intimate—just right for late at night when a person could imagine he was speaking only to them. Tonight his voice sounded strangely familiar. She shrugged it off. After all, she'd listened to this station for weeks now, and her favorite show was the Friday night request hour he called Dev's Dream Machine.

"How did you know it was the same person?" She tugged the quilts up to her ears to thwart the cold draft trying to sneak down her neck.

"I have a good ear for voices."

"You have a good voice for the ears, too. I bet your friends told you to become a deejay by the time you were in high school."

He chuckled. "Actually, no. Back then I was a player, not a talker."

Amanda got quiet, not sure what kind of 'player' he was referring to. The silence lasted a few seconds too long to be comfortable. "Well, thanks for playing my song. I'm a big fan of this format. Not many stations play this kind of music nowadays."

"Glad you enjoy it. Can I dedicate your song to anyone in particular?"

"No. He'll know it's for him. Thanks again." Her voice caught and almost broke as a fresh wave of loneliness swamped her.

"You're welcome. Call anyti—"

She hung up before he finished, afraid a sob might escape and be heard over the line.

The very next selection was Ella Fitzgerald singing her request. She blotted her tears on the sheet and lay in the dark, remembering the days in junior high when the taunts of the other students were especially brutal and Danny's unflagging support kept her from sinking in a sea of misery. It had been their song ever since, and listening to it somehow made her feel he was still looking out for her.

Dev of the Dream Machine followed it with "For All We Know", which sent a fresh torrent of her tears dampening the covers. She knew it was just a coincidence, but the man certainly knew how to string a couple of songs together for maximum impact. She listened for the remainder of the hour, then, exhausted by the emotional release, fell asleep to the sound of a stranger with a voice as dark as a moonless night and as soft and warm as her favorite cashmere sweater.

The following morning, coolly professional in her charcoal gray pinstripe suit, Amanda rang the doorbell. She'd convinced Zoe to give her plan a try. Now she silently prayed for success. Zoe hovered behind, her pressed jeans, white button-down oxford shirt, and herringbone blazer as businesslike as her eclectic wardrobe allowed.

The door opened to reveal a slender, attractive woman in her early sixties.

"Hello, Mrs. Wyndham. Thank you so much for meeting with us."

"No need to thank me, dear. I'm grateful for any distraction when I'm down here this time of year." She stepped back, opening the door wide. "Come in, come in, ladies." She huffed out a breath and shivered. "How the Admiral can stand to go fishing in these temperatures is beyond me. I should have stayed in town and let the man fend for himself, but he might have starved to death." She smiled ruefully and motioned them forward. "Men. Can't live with them, can't shoot them." She chuckled at her own humor, then morphed quickly back into the proper hostess.

"Mrs. Wyndham, I'd like to introduce you to my partner, Zoe Silvercreek," Amanda began. "She owns the Silvercreek Gallery down town, so you may have seen her there."

"I believe I have, though I must admit I've not been in the gallery in quite some time."

She led them from the spacious foyer to a large living room with a high, beamed ceiling, whitewashed planked walls, and a panoramic view of the bay through a series of French doors that opened onto an enormous deck. Nautical memorabilia was scattered throughout the room and multiple sectionals in shades of blue provided enough seating for a large gathering.

"Mrs. Wyndham, this room is beautiful," Zoe exclaimed.

"Why, thank you, dear. I wish I could take credit for it, but I hired a decorator and let him have his way with me." She winked conspiratorially. "I mean with the room, of course." She switched from coquette to jet-set so fast Amanda had trouble deciding how to react. She shot Zoe a wide-eyed look and tried a noncommittal smile.

Mrs. Wyndham gestured toward the sectional in front of the fireplace. "Please, make yourselves comfortable while I get us some tea." She disappeared in the direction of the kitchen.

Zoe put her hands out toward the fire. "Lord, I'm so nervous my hands are like ice. How did I let you talk me into this?"

"I think your balance sheet did most of the persuading. Let me do the talking unless she asks you something directly. She's always been very friendly and easy-going when I've met with her to do their books."

"Great. You talk. I'll just sit here and try to look professional." She sat primly on the edge of the sofa and clasped her hands in her lap.

Mrs. Wyndham returned pushing a glass teacart with a full tea service and a tiered server filled with several types of pastries and tiny sandwiches. "Now, ladies, help yourselves and tell me what brings you to see me today." She poured a cup of fragrant oolong and handed it to Zoe who bobbled it but recovered without spilling any on herself or the sofa. She rolled her eyes at her friend in dismay.

Amanda quickly spoke up, drawing Mrs. Wyndham's attention. "Last week when I was here working on your books, you mentioned that you wanted to throw a seventy-fifth birthday party for your husband, and we were wondering if you had hired someone to handle the preparations yet." She accepted her cup of tea and a linen napkin.

"No. Not yet. It will be quite a bit of work and I didn't feel there was anyone locally who could handle it. Why? Do you have someone in mind?"

Amanda set her cup down and straightened her shoulders. "Actually, Zoe and I have been thinking of starting an event planning business for several months"—she crossed her fingers against the slight exaggeration—"and we'd like to apply for the job."

"Oh my dear, I don't know . . ." The woman shook her head slowly.

"Mrs. Wyndham, we know we don't have experience or former clients who could give us references, but we have enthusiasm, talent, and excellent organizational abilities. Zoe is imaginative, artistic, and capable of creating whatever ambiance you want for your party. My skills lie in the financial and detail-oriented side of the business, and together I know we can produce an event your guests will talk about for years to come."

Amanda studied the woman who even in the dead of winter in a sleepy resort town, was fully made-up, every strand of silver hair styled to within an inch of its life, and capable of producing 'high tea' on a moment's notice. There was no doubt in her mind that if they got this job their company would be on its way to success.

"Well, Miss Adams, I appreciate your enthusiasm, but I think this affair might be just a little too large for your first attempt. The guest list would be extensive and I'm sure you understand that their social status would demand the highest standards in every aspect of the event. Taking a chance on a couple of unknowns would be a very risky proposition." Mrs. Wyndham sipped her tea, her frown clearly indicating her reluctance to hire two untried young women.

Not willing to give up so easily, Amanda poured the maximum amount of gentle persuasion into her next few words.

"Mrs. Wyndham, would you at least let us work up a proposal and take a look at what we can do? The opportunity would be a valuable learning experience for us, and who knows? We may even surprise you."

Mrs. Wyndham sighed deeply. "All right, young lady, you've twisted my arm. Against my better judgment, I'll look at your proposal. But don't get your hopes up," she added quickly. "My standards are high. I won't accept inferior work, regardless of my willingness to support local talent."

"Thank you, Ma'am. You won't regret it." Zoe hadn't said much during Amanda's little speech, but the absolute confidence with which she said those words was unmistakable, and Mrs. Wyndham gave her a nod and a fleeting smile.

By the time she climbed into her car, Amanda's professional façade was wearing thin. At least Mrs. Wyndham hadn't turned them down flat. There was still hope.

Zoe collapsed into the passenger's seat and slammed the door. She heaved a sigh as she clicked the seatbelt. "Sorry, Mandy, I totally blew our chance to become Blue Point Cove's premiere event planning service. I told you I wasn't any good at this kind of thing."

"Don't be silly, Zo. And don't be so quick to give up."

Amanda put the car in reverse and swung it around to head down the long, curving driveway.

"Okay, so our first interview could have gone better, but Orville and Wilbur didn't get airborne their first try either. We just have to come up with a concept that is so imaginative, outlined in a proposal that is so precise and detailed, that Mrs. Wyndham will have no choice but to hire us to make it a reality."

Zoe raised a single eyebrow. "Right. No problem."

"I'd say no problem the two of us can't solve with the judicious application of brains and hard work." Amanda gave a decisive nod to her friend. "Nobody said this was going to be easy. But your first painting wasn't a masterpiece either, was it?"

"Are you kidding? I painted over it three times and finally took a palette knife to it to put it out of its misery." Zoe laughed at the memory. "Okay, partner, I'm still on board. What's our next move?"

"Pizza and brainstorming. Here, after you close the gallery tonight. I have an eight-dollar bottle of Chianti that I'm hoping will spark our creativity." She angled to the curb in front of the gallery and Zoe hopped out, her enthusiasm restored. She slammed the door, took a step away, then turned around and tapped on the window.

Amanda leaned over and cranked it down. “What?”

“I just want you to know how happy I am to be working with you. You’re the perfect foil for my lack of self-confidence.” She grinned and whirled away to the gallery door. “See you around six.” She waved and went inside.

Amanda rolled the window up. *We are a good team*, she thought, already setting up spreadsheets in her head for food, drinks, entertainment, and prop rentals.

Now all they had to do was come up with that irresistible idea.

CHAPTER 3

Amanda took a sip of her wine and straightened the yellow legal pad, her freshly sharpened pencil poised above it. She and Zoe had finished the pizza but so far no fantastic ideas for the Admiral's birthday bash had made it onto the paper.

"Okay, we've decided both a nautical theme or a sportsman theme are too easy, and too clichéd," Amanda said. "Let's see, this is his seventy-fifth birthday so that means he was born in nineteen thirty-three."

"So," Zoe mused, "when you're seventy-five and looking back, what's the time you *want* to remember?" She spread her arms, palms up, as though the answer was obvious. "When you were a teenager, spreading your wings and discovering girls. So let's look at the late forties and early fifties."

"Okay." Amanda concentrated. "World War II ends, prosperity increases, Hollywood is full of glamorous movie stars making big-budget musicals, and the kids are listening to swing, jazz, and big bands. A much happier time I bet the Admiral could get very nostalgic about." She sat back, her eyes sparkling. "What do you think?"

Zoe nodded her head and grinned. "I'm liking this idea. We can go with the big glam of that era. Those social high-brows love to dress up and have the champagne flow like water."

"And, oh my God, Zo, the music from back then? It's fabulous. I'll find a group who can play those songs. Maybe

I can get in touch with that deejay from WMES, too. He could either deejay the whole thing or give the band some breaks if Mrs. Wyndham insists on live music." She beamed at her friend and clinked their glasses together. "See? I knew you'd be great at this."

Zoe started scribbling on her tablet. "We'll need the main room and dining room inside, the big deck up by the house for the tables and the pavilion down by the water for dancing."

"And fairy lights. Lots of fairy lights," Amanda said dreamily. "I wonder if there will be a full moon that night?"

"Hey, romance girl. Back to reality. You need to be figuring out how much this will cost, not the phase of the moon."

Amanda snapped out of her daydream. "Right. I'm on it. Rental tables, chairs, linens, tableware, glasses. Food. Booze. Serving help, bartenders, valet service." The legal pad started to fill. "Thank God she doesn't want a sit-down dinner. Canapés and finger food will provide more variety and cost less."

They stared at each other, the enormity of the undertaking starting to register.

Zoe gulped the last of her wine and jumped up. "You gotta go. My head's exploding with ideas and I have to get to my drawing pads."

"Okay. Let's plan to get together again Saturday night and compare notes. I'll want at least a rough idea of what you'll need for decorating by then."

"Deal." Zoe grabbed her pad as Amanda headed for the door. "Hey, what are we calling this business, anyway?"

"A to Z Enterprises?"

Zoe grinned and slapped a high-five. "Perfect."

Amanda sat in her car as Zoe's energy drained from her. She'd thought Mrs. Wyndham's budget was huge when she first heard it. Now she wondered how they'd ever stretch it enough to cover their expenses and leave a decent profit for them to split.

Dev sat in the studio watching the clock. Only ten minutes left in his 'request' hour. Seemed like his frequent caller wasn't going to check in tonight. Probably just as well. No point in—

A light appeared on the call-in lines. He watched the little button blink for a second then took a slow breath and punched it.

"Dev's Dream machine. What can I play for you tonight?"

"Would you please play 'My Funny Valentine'?"

Yep, it was her. But not the request he'd expected.

His gut relaxed. "Sure thing. Is it for anyone special?"

"It is. Dedicate it to Frank from Amanda, please?"

He caught the wobble in her voice, and was that sniffling he heard on the other end? Shit.

He wanted to keep her on the line, but not crying, so he added, "You've got great taste in music, Amanda. I'm surprised someone your age is so into the big band era."

She cleared her throat and gave a half-hearted chuckle. "How old do you think I am?"

Oops. This tiptoeing around knowledge he wasn't supposed to have made a conversation with Amanda a virtual minefield.

"I'm good with voices, remember? Hmm. No way you could be thirty. If I had to guess," which he didn't, "I'd say you were no more than twenty-five." Underestimating a woman's age was always a good thing, right?

"Close. I'll give you two points for that answer, Mr. Dream Machine. And my taste in music comes from my dad. He played tenor sax. 'Funny Valentine' was his song for me."

His last selection was about to end. “Hold on for a sec, Amanda. I’ll be right back.”

“No. That’s okay. I know you’re—”

He pushed the hold button and cut her off, praying she had better phone etiquette than he, and wouldn’t hang up on him while he cued up the next song. Two seconds to think and he had “You Don’t Know Me” in the player. Would she make any connection? Probably not. He wasn’t sure he wanted her to, anyway.

Her line still blinked. He picked up again.

“Hey, I’m back. Thanks for holding.”

“You’re welcome, but I know you must want to keep your phone lines open for other requests.”

He glanced up at the clock and smiled. “Not really. You were the last caller for the hour. No more requests tonight.”

How long could he keep her on the line?

“Did your Dad play professionally?”

This time the smile in her voice came clearly through the phone. “Oh yeah. When he was younger he played backup for some pretty well-known bands. By the time I came along, he’d been playing with the same combo for years all around Annapolis and even D.C. sometimes.”

“No wonder you’re so into this music, then. Any other particular favorite I can play for you tonight?” *Please, please do not ask for “Someone to Watch Over Me”.*

“Oh my. So many to choose from. How about ‘In The Mood’?”

“Nice choice. I’ll cue it up right after your first request.”

“Thanks . . .?”

“Dev.”

“Dev,” she repeated. “I really have to go now. It’s been nice talking with you.”

“You too, Amanda. Call again. Anytime.”

He cradled the handset, leaned back in his chair and took

a thoughtful sip of Jack Daniels. One accident, two one-minute phone calls, and already the beautiful Ms. Adams enchanted him.

"My Funny Valentine" began to play and Amanda's eyes misted up. The night he disappeared, her dad was supposed to come here to the cottage after work, checking that the beach house had survived the winter and was ready for their summer stay. But there was no indication he had finished the trip. When the police investigated after her mother's missing person report, the place appeared undisturbed since they had closed it up the previous fall.

What happened to you, Dad? I still miss you so much.

The song ended and, true to his word, Dev played her second request. The upbeat song dispelled her sadness. Gratefully she swayed to the beat and sang along with the Andrews Sisters.

I wonder how old Dev is? She wasn't as good at guessing ages as Mr. Dream Machine. With a voice as smooth as fifty-year-old cognac, she figured he had to be in his forties at least. Probably even older considering his love affair with music from the forties and fifties.

Funny how your imagination pictured someone when you had only their voice to go by. Josh Lucas? Harry Connick, Jr.? No, someone a bit older. Pierce Brosnan? Mmm, yum. She laughed at herself. The guy was probably fifty and balding, with a paunch that spilled over his belt.

She turned off the light and snuggled down in bed. That voice of his sure warmed up her insides though.

Amanda parked in front of the red brick building. About two hundred yards behind it stood a tall metal tower with an antenna array on the top. A sign next to the door identified it as WMES.

She'd come early knowing Dev's shift ended at seven a.m. Hopefully he didn't run out the door as soon as he was off the air.

Inside, the front office was small and dimly lit by the morning light filtering in through half-closed blinds. The lack of overhead lighting helped to disguise furniture that had seen better days. Amanda's hopes improved. Perhaps this deejay wasn't beyond her budget after all.

No one sat at the receptionist's desk, so she tiptoed past and peeked through the doorway that led to the rest of the building. The long hall had a couple of doors on the left and a glassed-in studio on the right.

"Hello? Is anybody here?" she called softly, taking a few cautious steps toward the first doorway. She heard the scrape of a chair and froze, considering a dash back to the waiting room. Indecision kept her rooted to the spot at first, then as a man stepped into the hall, surprise continued to hold her in place.

The owner of the green SUV stared back, speechless, his own surprise mirroring hers.

The long legs of his six-foot-two frame were wrapped in denim worn soft enough to outline his thighs nicely. He wore a long-sleeved white dress shirt open at the neck and casually stuffed his left hand in his pocket, bracing his right forearm high against the door jamb while he shook his head slowly. His dark brown hair curled slightly over his collar, a thick wave of it falling across his high forehead. Green eyes, the color of the bay before a storm, regarded her with an expression she couldn't fathom.

Embarrassment sent heat to her cheeks and the urge to flee almost had her turning around. Instead, she angled her chin up a notch.

"I'm sorry to intrude. I'm here to see Dev. The late-night deejay? There wasn't anyone out front, so I . . ." *Thought*

I'd stand here and blither like an idiot. She pointed over her shoulder. "I'll just go back out there and wait."

"I'm Dev MacMurphy, Miss Adams. What can I do for you?"

His deep, mellow voice rolled around her like a hug and had her smiling at him like an old friend. She walked closer and offered her hand. "Hi. I thought your voice sounded more familiar the last few times I listened to your show."

His sensual mouth curved in a smile as he shook her hand, his grip firm and warm. "Miss Adams, it is a pleasure to see you again. Had I known you were one of my frequent callers the other day, I wouldn't have been in such a hurry to leave."

"Oh, I am truly sorry about that. You must think I'm an idiot. I'm usually a good driver. I was just juggling too many mental balls at the time. Which is no excuse, I know. I'm glad you have fast reflexes."

Shut up, Amanda. You're running on like a star-struck teenager.

He gestured her into his office. "Have a seat, Amanda. What brings you here so early in the morning?" He dropped into a chair behind the massive wooden desk topped with stacks of neatly arranged paperwork.

She sat, mentally comparing the reality of him with her imagined version—fat, fifty, and balding. Wow, was she ever off. Tall, young, and hunky. She blinked. "I'm sorry. What did you say?"

"I wondered why you were here," he said, his eyes wary.

"Of course." She couldn't get over how perfectly sculpted his nose was or how the dark shadow over his unshaven chin made him appear a little dangerous. Dangerous . . . and sexy.

Stupid woman. Do you want him to think you're a fool? She ordered herself to ignore the physical package and concentrate on the professional inside.

"I was hoping I might be able to hire you as a deejay for an event I'm planning. I wasn't sure if I should ask you directly or if I should go through the station's General Manager. Since I knew your shift ended at seven, I thought maybe I could catch you before you went home."

He appeared to be at a loss for words and spent several seconds studying the top of his desk. Maybe this was an unusual request. "Okay, should I have discussed this with your boss first? I admit I'm kind of new to this, so if I stepped on somebody's toes or . . ."

"No, you're fine." He held up his hand to stop her babbling. "In this case, anyway, since I am the General Manager. And the owner. And the janitor too, for that matter." He leaned back in his chair, studying her with those bottle-green eyes. "Exactly what sort of event is this you're talking about?"

"My potential client, Mrs. Wyndham, is planning an elaborate seventy-fifth birthday party for her husband. Being the wealthiest woman in our little seaside community, she's pulling out all the stops, and my partner, Zoe, and I hope to win the contract to produce it. Our theme is to re-create the glamour of the late forties and early fifties, when the Admiral was a young man and the world was his oyster, so to speak."

She stopped talking to allow him to make a comment, but he appeared totally engrossed in what she had to say, his gaze never leaving her face as he waited for her to continue.

"We'll contact a couple of local bands who have the kind of repertoire we need, but my hope was that you might fill in as a deejay during their breaks. So there would be continuous music for dancing . . ." Her voice trailed off as he shook his head.

"I don't do that sort of thing. Besides, I have a standing gig here every night, and I'm assuming this is an evening affair you're talking about."

She bit her lip, her disappointment somehow sharper than she'd expected it to be. She hadn't held out much hope during the drive here, but as soon as she saw him, she knew he'd be perfect. And she wanted him. For the job, she added to herself sternly. She wanted him for the job. She felt her bottom lip edging out in a pout.

"Isn't there anything I can do to change your mind?" she pleaded. She had no idea what she could offer him. It didn't appear to be a money problem. He hadn't even asked what she would be willing to pay for his services, so even if she had more room in her budget it wouldn't matter. If it was only the timing conflict . . . "Couldn't you get one of the other deejays to cover for you for a couple of hours? We expect the party to wind down by one a.m., so you could be back here by two for the rest of your shift." Of course that would make it a pretty long workday for him but he should be able to handle it. He couldn't be older than thirty, thirty-five, tops.

The phone on his desk rang, startling them both.

"Excuse me," he said as he picked up the handset. "WMES radio, may I help you?" He listened a minute, his expressive mouth flattening into a grim line. "Listen, Mr. Coghill, I can't put this off any longer. I've stayed here three times to meet with you and you've had some reason to cancel every time. And at the last minute, I might add. So let's agree that you don't need my business and I'll find someone else to do the work." He listened again, the phone propped between his shoulder and ear, drumming his fingers on the desktop. "No, no more appointments, Mr. Coghill. Three strikes are enough for anyone. Good-bye."

"Sorry. Where were we?"

She watched him mentally shift gears to focus on her again. And focus was the correct term to describe the full force of his attention. It reminded her of an experiment her dad had shown her one sunny afternoon, using her eyeglasses and a scrap of paper. She wouldn't have been surprised if she had started to smolder from the intensity of his gaze. She met that intensity with a knowing smile.

She might have some leverage after all.

When she'd first arrived, Dev was afraid Amanda had found him out and was here to condemn him for killing her fiancé. Instead, she turned on a fifty-megawatt smile, greeted him like a long-lost friend, and he started to sweat for a completely different reason.

Her slender hand in his had sent an electrical jolt up his arm that shorted out half of his brain cells. He'd missed most of her explanation for coming to see him, his remaining neurons being too preoccupied by the graceful way she crossed her legs when she sat and the fluid cling of her deep purple blouse. The neckline was the draped kind and he wanted to do something to make her lean toward him so he . . . Shit! He'd jerked his mind up from the gutter and tried to concentrate.

The phone call from Coghill had given him a chance to regroup. The dirt bag had blown off their appointment for the third time and he'd had it with the guy's attitude. The satisfaction of firing him was fleeting, though, since he now had to find a new accountant and bring him up to speed a.s.a.p. At least his anger had burned through the haze of desire surrounding Amanda Adams and enabled him to respond to her like an adult instead of a fifteen-year-old caught in the throes of a raging hormonal storm.

"I couldn't help overhearing," she said. "You seem to be in need of an accountant?"

The feline smile on her face was so smug he expected to see yellow feathers littered across the top of his desk. "I beg your pardon?"

"Mr. Coghill? The man you just fired over the phone? He was your accountant, correct?" She tilted her head to the side, nodding a little to encourage him to confirm her guess, like a school teacher with a reluctant student.

"How did you know?"

He watched her toy with the idea of keeping him guessing, then she said, "His name comes after mine in the yellow pages. There are only about half a dozen accounting firms in this little community."

She grinned and his heart took another hit, forcing him to smile back into eyes that had taken on a lavender tint. His decision not to reveal his identity, made in the first thirty seconds as she stood at the end of the hall and stared at him in surprise, forced him to ask about things he already knew.

"So, you're an accountant, then?"

"Yep. Bonded and certified. I don't suppose I could interest you in my services, by any chance?" She worried her bottom lip with small white teeth and rounded her eyes in pretended innocence.

Dev pushed his chair back against the wall to increase the space he would have to cover before he could snatch her out of her seat and taste her now slightly swollen lower lip. If he was going to use distance as a defense, he'd better get the hell out of the building. He took his left hand out of his pocket, the thin glove covering the mutilated digits a graphic reminder to stay away from temptation.

"Why do I have the feeling that hiring you as my accountant will have some unwanted strings attached?" He kept his left hand in his lap, unready to deal with the inevitable questions its visibility would provoke.

"Strings? No. I'd like to think of them as ribbons tying up a nice, neat, win-win package for both of us."

She leaned forward in her chair.

Dev heard a faint echo of his father's voice saying, "*Be careful what you wish for . . .*"

CHAPTER 4

"All right, Ms. Adams. Let's talk turkey. I need someone to set up my books, make sure I'm following state and federal payroll laws, and figure out how much income I need each month to break even. Then there's always income tax stuff. I'm completely at a loss in that department."

She beamed and he could tell she had already tied a big fat bow with those ribbons. This was going to cost him. In more ways than one.

"First of all, please use Amanda. After my calls to your request line Ms. Adams seems unnecessarily formal at this point, don't you agree?"

He nodded, hoping she didn't notice how her reference to their late-night phone calls affected him. She quoted him her hourly rate, and when he raised an eyebrow, she was ready with a package deal for the year, which included a substantial discount for the first quarter if he would agree to deejay her party.

He had used a good chunk of his Aunt Edith's bequest to buy the station and supplement its income to pay his employees, and he wanted to increase profits before that money was exhausted. Especially since his father showed no signs of releasing his trust fund in the near future. While he worked on doubling the station's advertising revenue, Amanda's discount would come in handy. And helping her to succeed was part of what he'd promised Danny.

The idea that she would have to spend more time at the station with him while she set up his books and made sure the IRS wouldn't haul him off to jail, had absolutely nothing to do with his decision to hire her. He told himself he was only keeping his promise. He expected his pants to ignite any second from the magnitude of the lies he was telling by omission. What difference did it make? It was just one more reason for his eventual consignment to a fiery afterlife.

"As you probably guessed from my conversation with Mr. Coghill, I'm in need of your help right away. I have last years' invoices and payroll records but since I only bought this station recently, I'm not at all sure about how the whole tax calculation thing is supposed to go when I file in April."

"I see. Well, in that case, you're right. We need to get working on this soon. I'll need to see all the paperwork you have for the last six months of last year and get that sorted out. Then I can set up your books for this year. Your first quarter tax reports for this year won't be due until April 30, but the corporate return for last year will be due by March fifteenth."

"You mean April fifteenth, don't you?"

"No. Corporate tax returns are due March fifteenth. You're thinking of personal tax returns." She gave him a smile to soften her correction.

"Ah. I see Mr. Coghill was less than informative on several topics. I've never filed corporate tax returns before."

"But you have incorporated, right?" she asked a little sharply.

"I have," he assured her, and saw her visibly relax. He'd only done it because the lawyer handling the sale told him he should. Guess it was a good idea.

"Well, now you have someone who'll tell you everything you need to know in plenty of time. But I'm sorry to tell you that I'll need a fair amount of your time over the next week or two in order to get things completed on time."

She opened her Day-Timer and started jotting notes, a tiny frown marring the perfection of her delicately arched brows. She trapped her lower lip between her teeth as she concentrated, a habit he found compellingly sexy.

"I hope that won't be a . . ." She glanced up to catch him staring at her mouth and seemed to lose her train of thought. ". . . a problem?"

"No problem, Amanda. I'll devote as much time as you need to get everything set up properly. Other than when I'm on the air, my time is all yours." He held her gaze as this last statement brought faint color to her cheeks. "Will this interfere with your other plans?"

"Other plans?" She tilted her head.

"The party you're preparing for?" he prompted, keeping the satisfaction he felt at her confusion hidden. He liked the idea he could put a little ripple in the calm, professional aura that surrounded her. He couldn't resist another glance at her lips and watched the tip of her tongue slip out to moisten the lower one in response.

"Oh, the party. Yes. I mean, no. No, I can handle your company's work as well as the party preparations. Assuming we get the job," she conceded. "Once we do, I'll have to go over what you'll need from us for your set-up." Her smile was pure mischief. "For that, my time will be all *yours*." Then she turned serious. "You haven't told me what you'll charge to deejay our party."

"You mean the discount you offered on my first quarter accounting fee isn't my compensation for doing your gig?"

"Oh no. That's just a little added incentive to convince you to say yes. We would still expect to pay you. On the other hand, my budget is fairly limited, so I'm willing to throw in considerable amounts of my time working on your books for free to sweeten the pot. Cash is what I'm short on, so please take that into consideration when calculating your fee."

Her hopeful, and very persuasive, smile almost had him offering to pay her for the chance to work her party. He doubted many men resisted any request from this siren in a suit.

"Don't worry, Amanda, my fee will be very reasonable. You'll have no trouble paying it." His concentration on her mouth might lead her to think his fee could be taken in kisses. A method of payment he was suddenly highly in favor of. He saw her eyes narrow the tiniest bit and her chin come up. Oops, too much attention paid to those luscious lips. She flattened them into a determined line and he knew he'd better get a grip.

"Mr. MacMurphy, I want—"

"Dev," he interrupted. Her hesitation told him she was suddenly unsure whether being on a first-name basis was a good idea.

"Dev," she conceded. She took a breath. "I want to, um . . ."

"Yes? You want to . . .?"

"I want to keep our agreement completely professional," she declared, this time tearing her gaze from his mouth and meeting his eyes.

"Absolutely, Amanda. I couldn't agree more," he assured her. "I haven't done this deejay business at a party before. I'll have to do a bit of research before I can quote you a fee."

"Oh. Of course." She bit at her lower lip again.

He could tell she wasn't sure whether his intense interest in her lips was real or her imagination.

"Certainly. Well, then, you do your research and when we meet again, you can tell me what you decide."

"Sounds good. When would you like to get together next?"

"If you have last year's ledgers handy, I can take them with me today, go over them at home the next few days, and meet with you again on Friday."

"Hmm. Ledgers?"

"Yes. You know, last year's books."

He pointed behind her to a small conference table where five cardboard boxes sat like islands surrounded by a sea of paper. Bills, receipts, purchase orders, and other assorted scraps of multicolored paper, including several napkins with figures scribbled haphazardly across them, covered every available inch of the tabletop.

She turned, then stood slowly. Her mouth fell open.

"Please tell me you're kidding. That's a joke, right?" She jerked her head toward the document disaster.

He had the grace to look chagrined. "No. That's the real deal. I've been sorting through it, trying to separate it into categories. Then I was going to order each pile by date . . ." He broke off, cowed by her expression of total disbelief. Okay, so graduating cum laude from the New England Conservatory of Music didn't include business savvy with the diploma. He'd been winging it, hoping that bastard Coghill would sort everything out.

She stared at him for a few more seconds, both hands covering her mouth. Her shoulders started to shake, then the laughter she couldn't hold back erupted. He found himself grinning in response, then chuckling and finally giving in and howling with mirth right along with her. For a few minutes they were convulsed, helpless to stop, tears leaking from both of their eyes.

Finally, she got herself together enough to say, "Now I understand why Mr. Coghill kept missing his appointments."

That set them both off again. She had to sit down eventually, out of breath, but unable to stop smiling at him.

"I—" he began.

She put her hand up. "Don't. Give me a chance to catch my breath or we'll be calling nine-one-one." She fished in her purse.

He opened his desk drawer, produced a box of tissues, and offered it to her. Her glance fell on his glove-covered hand and she looked him a question.

His hilarity evaporated like drops of sweat in the Iraqi desert.

"Explosion," he bit out, the paucity of details meant to close the subject to further discussion.

"Oh my." Her eyes darkened to smoke. "What happened?"

"War."

"Oh. I see."

He hoped to hell she didn't.

"I'm sorry." There was regret but no pity in the steady regard of those gray eyes.

"Don't be." *I deserved this and a whole lot more.*

She seemed surprised at that reply but politely responded to his terse comments by changing the subject. She gestured to the sea of paperwork behind her.

"Well, I think I may have to deal with this here rather than take it home."

"Yeah." He surveyed the conference table. "I guess I should have given you fair warning before you quoted me your fee. I think I'll just waive my deejay pay, unless you think that isn't fair compensation for the extra work you'll have to do."

Then again, maybe she wouldn't even want him to do the party now that she'd seen his messed-up hand. Good thing he had a long-sleeved shirt and his glove on. She might have thrown up, or fainted, if she saw the ravages of the burn scars from his shoulder to his fingers. The ever-present ache and tingle in his forearm intensified. He shoved it to the back of his mind. *Let's get this over with as quickly as possible.*

"Amanda, don't feel any obligation about the party. I completely understand if you'd rather find someone else. In fact, let me talk to a couple of the other announcers here and see if one of them would be willing to do it."

"Why would I want someone else?"

She appeared honestly puzzled. Did he have to actually spell it out? He made a gesture toward his left hand.

She studied his arm more closely. "Are you trying to tell me that you *can't* do the job? Or that you don't *want* to do it? Because I would rather have you than anyone else."

"No. I can do it. I just wanted to be sure you . . ."

"Still wanted you? Oh yes, I still want you," she said emphatically, clearly unimpressed by his perceived handicap.

"Okay, then. I'm your man," he affirmed.

They both listened to the mental echoes of those sentences and found somewhere else to stare for a few seconds.

"I'll get started on Project Paperwork tomorrow, if that's okay. I have other work scheduled for today."

"Of course. I'll be here until about three. Then I usually try to grab a few hours' sleep before I come back for my tour. You can come . . . anytime. Whenever it's convenient."

She stood and gathered up her coat. "I'll probably be here early. There's a lot of work to do." She rolled her eyes and her lips twitched with the effort not to laugh again.

He came around the desk and took her coat, holding it so she could slip her arms inside. He couldn't resist brushing the side of her neck with his fingers and felt the electricity sizzle up his arm.

"Thanks."

Was there a little wobble in that word? Her eyes seemed wider, brighter, almost silvery as she held out her hand to him. "See you tomorrow, then."

He clasped hers gently but firmly, foolishly grateful his left hand was the injured one, not his right. "Tomorrow," he agreed.

He walked her to his office door and watched the sway of her hips as she went down the hall. Slender and graceful, she had curves in all the right places and a pair of long perfect legs that would wrap around a man with the promise of heaven in their embrace. His jeans got so tight he could feel his heartbeat against the zipper.

He would see her again tomorrow.

How long had it been since he anticipated something—anything—with pleasure? So long he couldn't remember. Since before . . . before he'd killed his best friend.

Reality crashed down on his anticipation like a cinder block on a soap bubble.

On the drive home Amanda congratulated herself on the acquisition of another client.

Blue Point Cove was a small town with a resident population of about eleven hundred. During the summer months tourism swelled the numbers to three times that, but between Labor Day and Memorial Day the sleepy community on the lower Chesapeake Bay settled back into obscurity. With the town empty of tourists, those winter months were lean, frugal times.

So far she had only a handful of accounting clients, so the next winter would be a struggle unless she found another way to supplement her income. Landing this job with Zoe would be an answer to both of their prayers.

When her mom had remarried she'd given Amanda the cottage. That put her one step up from Zoe. At least she didn't have to pay a mortgage. Food, utilities, insurance, and gasoline all added up, though. To say nothing of her student loan. That bill loomed over her every month like a carrion crow, ready to extract its payment in flesh.

She parked in the gravel area in front of the building whose weathered clapboards matched the gray wings of the sea gulls circling overhead. Unlike the Wyndham's "Cottage", her home deserved the name. Two bedrooms, one bath, and a kitchen, dining, living room combo made a small footprint nestled on one of the tiny inlets around the cove. A short dock led to the water, so shallow here that only boats with very low draughts could tie up safely.

She loved "The Last Call", as her father had named it, probably because he had loved it, too. She and her dad had shared a special closeness when she was growing up. Until the fateful summer of her eleventh year when one evening he left for work and never came back.

She dropped the day's mail on the dining table and took her laptop into the second bedroom, which did double-duty as her office. The machine was old, weighed a ton, and had a battery that barely lasted two hours—if she didn't stress it too much. She plugged it in and hooked-up her modem. No Wi-Fi out here in the boonies. No fast, broadband service either. Blue Point Cove was a good five years behind the rest of the modern world, a condition the tourists often found charming. As a businesswoman, she'd prefer a little less charm and a bit more speed.

The connection established, Amanda set the machine to download her email and went back to the kitchen to reheat the remnants of this morning's coffee. She changed into sweats then laced a mug of hot coffee liberally with French vanilla creamer and walked down the short dock to the water.

During the summer, sleek little motorboats raced down the center of the channel towing skiers, their boom-boxes blaring the Black Eyed Peas or Cold Play loud enough to be heard over the whine of the outboards. In the chill of late January the water was still as glass and the silence a blessing. She remembered how quiet it was twenty years ago when her parents first brought her here. Now the long summer days were punctuated with the sounds of teenage laughter, rock, pop, and hip-hop. She was glad to have a few more months of solitude before the onslaught.

Amanda removed the elastic from her braid and ran her fingers through the strands, shaking her head to let the loosened tresses cascade down her back. A noisy flock of seagulls wheeled overhead and turned toward the sea. The sun was about to extinguish itself in the waters of the bay and a breeze set goose bumps chasing up her arms. She hurried back to the relative warmth of her kitchen, refilled her coffee, and went to check her email.

There was a short note from her mom about plans to visit Annapolis in the spring. She and Amanda's step-dad lived in San Diego now and enjoyed perfect weather three hundred twenty-five days a year. Amanda was happy for her. Jack was a nice guy and they were well-suited to each other.

She checked the clipping services she subscribed to in the off chance that one had posted something new about her father's disappearance. As usual there was no news on that front. Maybe living here full time would give her a chance to do more digging—not that she expected some long undiscovered clue to drop into her lap. But, you never knew. She felt closer to her dad here than anywhere else. With the two men she'd loved and lost watching over her, maybe her luck would change.

CHAPTER 5

Amanda had her spreadsheets up on the laptop, adding the costs of items she had priced so far while Zoe sat, cross-legged, on the twin bed next to Amanda's desk. Sketches covered the bedspread. One of the great things about her friend's talent was her ability to show prospective clients how the setting for their event would appear. For those with poor visualization these illustrations could make the difference between acceptance of their proposal and a pass.

"I checked with the local VFW hall about renting their tables and chairs. They'd never done that before but were willing to make some money. They gave us a great deal, especially after I told them we might need to do this again, many times, in the future. They were willing to throw in tablecloths for free but their tablecloths won't do. Too many stains. I'll check in Easton or Waldorf and see if I can find covers for the chairs there too. Do you have specific colors in mind or should I go with white?"

"We're going formal with this—well, not actually white tie and tails, though I'd love that, but dressy, so I'm keeping the theme to black and white. I'll use splashes of color—red mostly—to add some zing." She sorted through her drawings. "White floor-length tablecloths with black toppers. That might mean you could use the VFW linens on the bottoms if we get the black toppers elsewhere."

Amanda nodded. "Good idea." Another money saver.

"I did want to get red carpet runners down the walkway to the pavilion and for most of the deck so the women won't be catching their heels in the boards. We'll need a portable dance floor for the pavilion too."

"I'd planned on the dance floor but will have to check on the carpet. We'll need to measure the walkway and pavilion before I get an accurate quote, but I'll guesstimate for our proposal. I have prices for glassware and cutlery and alcohol already. I've calculated costs for wait staff and a dishwasher. And I'm still working on finding two bartenders. Staffing this first time around will be a bear. Once we've done a few events we'll have accumulated a roster of helpers we can call on."

"Have you found a band yet?"

"I've got two possibilities. I'm just praying one of them isn't already booked for that Saturday. Dev has already agreed to deejay in between sets."

Zoe frowned. "Dev?"

"The deejay at the radio station. I talked to him on Monday. He not only agreed to do the party, he hired me as his accountant as well."

"Well, that's nice. I don't suppose—" Zoe eyed her friend closely. "Are you blushing?"

"Of course not." Amanda busied herself with annotating her spreadsheets.

"Really? You could've fooled me."

Her friend was worse than a barnacle. Once she got interested in something there was no prying her away from it until she was satisfied. Redirection rarely worked, but Amanda gave it her best shot anyway. She picked up one of Zoe's drawings. "This will knock Mrs. W's socks off, Zoe. If we don't win this bid it won't be for lack of effort on your part. Are we taking all of your illustrations tomorrow?"

"Mmm, three I think. The main deck, the pavilion, and a close-up of a table setting." She separated the corresponding drawings from of the assortment on the bed. "So, how hard was it to convince the radio man to do our party?"

Yeah, no dice on the distraction.

"Not too hard at all really. Did I mention that he is the guy from my accident?"

"No kidding?"

"Yeah. Turns out he's in desperate need of an accountant so I leveraged my talents in that department to convince him to help us out. You'll like him, Zoe, after you spend a little time around him. He got injured in Iraq and has only been out of the hospital for a month or so. He actually owns the radio station now."

As soon as she said the word *Iraq* she saw Zoe flinch and knew she'd drop the subject of Dev like a live grenade. Ever since Amanda had told her about Danny dying over there, Zoe avoided any conversations about the war. For once Amanda was grateful for her friend's restraint, though she usually was okay with talking about Danny. He was gone but certainly not forgotten, and she didn't want him to be relegated to the past and only spoken of in whispers around her. He was, and always would be, her hero.

Amanda parked in front of the Silvercreek Gallery, debating whether to shut the car off and risk not being able to start it again or keep it running and use up what little gas she had left. Believe, she admonished herself, and turned the key. Trim and sleek in her navy pantsuit, she entered the gallery, the tinkle of the little bell over the door drowned out by the raised voices coming from the back.

"I told you, Jeff, it's not happening this afternoon. Don't ask me again."

"Aw, come on, Babe."

A lithe Lothario in tattered, clay-splattered jeans and an Eagles T-shirt leaned against the counter. His tousled brown hair, full lips, and smoldering eyes put Amanda in mind of a satyr.

"Just an hour or so. I won't be long, I promise." He reached out and tucked a strand of Zoe's waist-length mink brown hair behind her ear. "I'll keep the studio really warm, put on that music you like. . ."

Zoe batted his hand away. "What part of 'no' don't you understand? For the last time, I will not pose in the nude for you today. I have too much to do."

She glanced up and saw Amanda trying not to smile as she pretended an interest in one of Jeff's sea-life sculptures.

"I gotta go. Which means you have to go, too. I'm locking up for an hour to . . ." She mumbled, " . . . to run an errand."

Jeff straightened away from the glass case. "Okay, Sweet Cheeks, we'll finish this discussion later." He brushed a thumb over her high, delicate cheekbone and turned to leave.

"The discussion *is* finished," Zoe declared to his retreating back. She rolled her eyes and huffed.

"Hi, Beautiful." He winked at Amanda on his way out the door.

"He seems pretty determined." Amanda couldn't hide a grin.

Zoe's dark brown eyes flashed with annoyance. "I love the man to death, but when he gets a wild hair about seeing me naked, I'm supposed to drop everything and strip so he can do sketches for the secret project he won't let me see. It's not like he doesn't see me naked every night in bed, for pity's sake."

"True enough. But I'm sure he's distracted by other things then. Besides, anybody with that kind of persistence deserves a reward every now and then."

"The only reward he's getting from me this afternoon is a swift kick." She drew three twenty-by-thirty-inch illustration boards from behind the counter. Each displayed one of Zoe's design concepts for the party.

"Wow, Zoe, these are amazing."

Amanda held up the one of the deck. Tables dressed in white linens with black toppers were scattered across the area. Centerpieces of crystal hurricanes surrounded by dramatic red amaryllis nestled in beds of needlepoint ivy graced each table, while garlands of ivy twined with tiny white lights wrapped around the deck railings. A white tent at one end would showcase the five-piece band, while its mirror image at the other would house the bar. Both would be outlined in more ivy and white-lighted garlands. A red carpet continued down the boardwalk to the pavilion by the water where a portable dance floor would cover the decking. Again garlands of ivy and white lights would drape posts and railings and pots of red amaryllis would provide splashes of color. As it turned out, Mother Nature would cooperate and supply them with a full moon—free of charge.

"You have done a wonderful job on these, partner." Amanda gave Zoe a hug. "You may not be a smooth talker but these pictures are worth more than a thousand words. Mrs. Wyndham is going to be blown away."

"I hope so."

Me, too. I'm already ten days late on my student loan payment and the government has absolutely no sense of humor about these things.

Zoe played nervously with the ties on her white peasant blouse. They had decided to play up their differences to accentuate their respective talents. Amanda, ever the professional, her blond hair in a neat French twist, her navy suit unadorned, would exemplify organization, attention to detail, and planning. Zoe, in a long denim skirt, poet-sleeved white blouse and snug black vest, her long straight hair a river of glossy brown down her back, silver hoops in her ears, would provide the contrast of artistic talent, imaginative design, and a flair for the dramatic.

Amanda had her laptop, complete with PowerPoint presentation and spreadsheets plus hard copies of all the estimates to leave with Mrs. Wyndham. Zoe had her beautiful illustrations. They were as ready as they were going to get.

Amanda's little blue Civic stuttered a few times before the engine caught but finally cooperated and they arrived at the Wyndham 'Cottage' exactly on time. A shiny white mini-van was already in the driveway. 'Call Us For An Affair To Remember' was lettered in gold on the back and sides.

Amanda's eyes narrowed and her pulse quickened. She parked far enough to the side to allow room for the van to get by which let her heels sink into the soft dirt when she got out. Annoyed, she grabbed her briefcase while Zoe retrieved her illustrations from the back.

Before they climbed the steps to the entrance, the door opened and a woman wearing a smartly tailored black suit stepped out, followed by a younger man who pulled a wheeled metal case and had a collapsible easel tucked under one arm.

The woman turned back to Mrs. Wyndham and offered her hand. "Thank you so much for this opportunity, Mrs. Wyndham. You won't regret it. I'll keep in touch."

She started down the steps, the young man following her like a puppy on a leash. When she passed Amanda, she regarded the tired but trusty Civic and smirked.

Amanda restrained a very unladylike urge to trip her and heard Zoe mutter, "Bitch" under her breath. She pasted a confident smile on her face and squared her shoulders as Zoe followed her up the steps.

As usual, Mrs. Wyndham was impeccably dressed, her silver hair stylishly cut to accentuate her patrician features. She smiled and invited them in. This time she led them into the dining room where one end of the table had a number of brochures spread out upon it. Next to them was a contract that Amanda could see was unsigned. Adept at reading figures upside down from working across a desk from her clients, she managed to check the total on the bottom line as she walked by. The bid was significantly higher than theirs and she wondered what the rival company had promised to justify the cost.

Mrs. Wyndham offered them seats at the opposite end of the table.

"Amanda, Zoe, I appreciate your promptness. My earlier appointment arrived late, so you've already made a point in your favor. As you can see, I've been requesting bids from other event specialists—doing my due diligence, if you will. While my husband has left most of the arrangements in my hands, he has given me a budget." A little quirk of her mouth indicated some annoyance with her husband's monetary restrictions. "I intend to comparison shop to see who will give me the best value for my money."

She sat down at the head of the table and glanced at the gold Rolex on her wrist, then awarded them pleasant smile. "All right, ladies. You asked for an opportunity to do a presentation. Let's see what you can do."

Amanda opened her laptop and spun it around to face Mrs. Wyndham. Crossing her fingers behind her back, she clicked on the icon to open the PowerPoint presentation.

Amanda began with their main concept—the glamorous late forties—when the Admiral was a young man facing a future full of promise. Using Zoe's beautiful illustrations to set the scene, Amanda played up the magic of Hollywood glitz and glamour, plus the music of a live band, to transform The Cottage into an open-air nightclub so posh no one would be surprised if they saw Fred Astaire on the dance floor or Ella Fitzgerald at the microphone.

Then she walked through a detailed timetable from set-up to clean-up. Every conceivable item, from toothpicks for the hors d'oeuvres to the 200 cubic feet of pine bark mulch they would use to create a parking area for thirty-plus cars, was included on one of Amanda's spreadsheets. For the next thirty minutes, Amanda covered the personnel she intended to hire. Every person, every item, had a price range and when she totaled the entire package, she used the high-end figure to give herself some bargaining room if Mrs. Wyndham felt the estimate was too high. Her cost was still lower than the amount she had read on the other company's contract.

As the last slide of the PowerPoint presentation faded from the screen, Amanda opened her briefcase and retrieved the printed version of her proposal along with the contract. She laid them in front of Mrs. Wyndham.

"Are there any questions I can answer for you, Ma'am?"

Mrs. Wyndham raised a single eyebrow. "I don't believe you ladies have been completely honest with me."

Before either of them could voice a protest, she smiled. "It's hard for me to believe you could have produced such an exceptional presentation on your first attempt. I am impressed. I am very impressed. I do have a few questions, however."

Amanda managed to hide her exultation at Mrs. Wyndham's praise, schooling her expression to one of polite interest in the woman's questions. Across the table, Zoe's excitement was almost palpable.

"Yes, Ma'am?"

"The band you intend to hire? How did you find them? I hope it's not some young rock group who've agreed to play music from that era on their electric guitars and blast the guests with over-amplified percussion."

"No, Ma'am. It's not a rock group. I asked one of the men from my dad's old group for suggestions. They gave me a few names and I've checked their credentials. The five-man group I intend to use have an extensive repertoire of songs from the forties and fifties."

Mrs. Wyndham nodded, but her expression was bit regretful. "It's such a shame your father's group has stopped performing. They were wonderful."

"You heard my dad's quintet play?" Amanda couldn't hide her surprise.

"Oh, yes, dear. The Admiral and I attended an affair in Annapolis where they played. They were so good." She sighed and rolled her eyes. "Your father in particular. When he put his lips on that saxophone, he was amazing. Every woman in the room was riveted. He was so handsome, you know. By the time he finished playing all of us ladies were 'In The Mood'." She winked at the play on words. "After that, the Admiral and I often went to that little club downtown where his combo played regularly." She reached out and patted Amanda's hand. "His disappearance was such a tragedy. I'm sure it must have been terribly hard on you and your mother. You were quite young as I recall."

"Yes, Ma'am." Amanda had to fight to keep her eyes from tearing up. The older woman's praise for her father's playing was unexpected but heartwarming. "I was eleven. I still miss him." Squelching the sadness that always came when she talked about her father, Amanda finished, "I'm glad you got to hear him play, though."

"Yes, well." Mrs. Wyndham directed the conversation back to the matter at hand. She steepled her hands in front of her face and tapped her lips with the index fingers while she held an internal debate. "First, I love the theme you've chosen. So far the others all went with a nautical one—for obvious reasons. So unimaginative. Second, and I guess this would be first on my husband's list, your pricing is reasonable enough that I might upgrade some of the menu items and still stay within the *budget*." Again she made a disparaging face at the word. She glanced from Amanda to Zoe. "I hope your execution is as good as your planning, ladies, because

I believe your proposal is the best. Congratulations. You've just landed your first job as event planners."

Stay cool. Be professional. Don't blow it now. But inside she was jumping up and down like a five-year-old who'd been told she was going to Disneyland. She knew Zoe must be struggling to maintain her poise as well and refrained from even glancing in her direction.

"Thank you so much, Mrs. Wyndham. You won't regret it." Amanda gloated internally at her repetition of the other event planner's words. She slid the contract in front of her new client and offered a pen. "If you'll sign here, please? I'll have this copied and back to you within twenty-four hours. Then we'll need a deposit so we can begin to order supplies. Oh, and I'll need to arrange some time to take accurate measurements of the outside spaces and to go over the menu with you if you plan on making some changes there."

Mrs. Wyndham signed the contract with a flourish. "Certainly, dear. I need to get back to Annapolis by the end of next week, so I'd like to get the details firmed up as soon as possible. I'll check my calendar and call you to set up the schedule."

They made it to the end of the Wyndham's winding driveway before Amanda had to stop and cheer. Laughing and hugging, they congratulated each other. Instead of turning back toward town, Amanda pointed the car in the other direction and followed the winding road toward the turn off to her house. The ins and outs of the shoreline had the trip taking ten minutes, even though, as the crow flew, it was less than a mile from Mrs. Wyndham's home to hers.

"We have to celebrate," she announced. "This is too momentous an occasion to let go by without at least a toast." She waggled her eyebrows like Groucho Marx and whispered conspiratorially, "I bought champagne."

"You were that sure?"

"You gotta believe, Zo. I'm convinced that believing you can do something is more than half the battle." She shrugged. "I believed. I bought. It worked." She parked in front of her little house, happier than she'd been in months. Maybe her dad had been watching over her. It seemed more than just coincidence that Mrs. Wyndham had brought up having met him. She sent up a silent prayer. *Thanks, Dad.*

CHAPTER 6

Dev had not been able to sleep all afternoon, Monday's meeting with Amanda playing over and over behind closed eyelids.

He should never have agreed to do her party gig. Should never have hired her as his accountant. At least not without full disclosure. The more interaction he had with the woman the more difficult it would be to come clean and tell her who he was. At which point he had no doubt she would banish him from her life forever.

He'd tossed and turned for two hours, before he'd given up and taken a shower, then stripped the tangled, sweaty sheets from his Murphy bed. He put clean linens on and folded it away.

He'd never been a particularly neat guy, but the tiny studio apartment forced him to clean up after himself or there would be no place to sit or walk around without tripping. Dressed, he opened the heavy drapes he used to block the daylight. The watery winter sun washed the walls and cast pewter shadows into the corners. It was only after his meeting with Amanda, who brightened his office with her warmth and laughter, that he realized how drab and colorless his apartment—hell, his whole life—had become.

He'd figured he might as well use the time he should be sleeping to catch up on his laundry. Dev hated going to the town's only Laundromat where half the women with wild-eyed toddlers regarded a male washing clothes during the day with the scorn reserved for shiftless, jobless slackers, and the other half saw him as lunch. He generally started three loads then escaped to the diner down the street and drank coffee till it was time to move them to the dryers.

Now, watching the seconds tick away toward midnight, he finished the can of Red Bull he'd bought at the 7-Eleven along with a turkey sandwich. Hopefully it would help keep his exhaustion at bay till morning. He'd skip the pain-easing Jack Daniels tonight. The ever-present ache in his arm would help to keep him alert.

No request from Amanda tonight. He hadn't expected one. He faded out "Take the 'A' Train" and into "The One I Love Belongs to Somebody Else".

Shit. Who was he kidding? He'd hoped Amanda would call with all the futile expectation of a high-school nerd waiting for the beautiful cheerleader to notice him. That was why he didn't tell her who he was when he'd had the chance. He'd wanted her to like him. And that wouldn't happen if she knew the role he'd played in Danny's death. Down the road, when the reckoning came, she would undoubtedly despise him, but then he knew that going in, so how much worse could it be if he waited a couple of weeks?

He'd pay her for the accounting work, which would help her out in the near term, and give her all the assistance he could with this party to get her second business off to a good start. That left only one thing on his promised list. Somehow during the next few months he had to encourage her to get past Danny and consider someone else to spend the rest of her life with. Someone who could appreciate not only her beauty, but her intelligence, kindness, and humor. The man would have to be damn near perfect to deserve her. Luckily finding the guy wasn't his job. He just had to convince her to start searching.

The light on the call-in line began to blink. Less than a minute to midnight. Dev punched the button.

"Dev's Dream Machine. You just made it under the wire. What can I play for you?"

"'Someone to Watch Over Me', please, Dev."

Ouch. She was back to that song again. He swore he could see a faint reflection of Danny's smiling face in the glass window of the broadcast booth.

"Sure thing, Amanda. Any dedication this time?"

"No. It's really for two people, and they'll know I'm thinking about them."

"Okay, you got it," he said, trying to sound the same as he would to any caller's request.

"Thanks, Dev," she murmured, the warmth in her voice demolishing his pitiful attempt to keep his distance. "Sorry I called so late. I've been working like crazy on to-do lists for the party, since we landed the job this afternoon." Her happiness bubbled through the phone. "The song request is kind of a thank you, but I wanted you to know I'm definitely going to need you."

And I'll be here for you. Whenever . . .

"Well then, I'd better do that research on my fee pretty quick. Congratulations on landing the client, Amanda."

"Thanks. Zoe and I are really pumped about this. Anyway, I don't want to take up any more of your time tonight. I'll see you at the station tomorrow around nine, okay?"

"I'll see you then."

"Good night."

"Good night, Amanda. Sleep tight." The vision of her in bed, her long blond hair spread out on the pillow and those perfect breasts peeking above the sheet had him hardening to the point of pain.

He cued up "Someone to Watch Over Me"—no surprise it was out and ready to go. Then he picked Cindy Walker's great tune, "You Don't Know Me" to follow it.

He checked the time. Nine hours to go. At least he was wide-awake now.

Amanda was a woman of her word. At nine-oh-one Rosemary buzzed him on the intercom. "Miss Adams here to see you, Dev."

"Send her on back, Rosemary."

Dev stood up as she came to the door.

Her cheeks were rosy from the crisp morning air and a few tendrils had already escaped from her neat French braid. She set down her briefcase and started to untie the belt on her camel hair coat.

He came around the desk to help her off with it and hung it on the coat rack next to his. He nodded toward the conference table, its surface now pristine except for the five boxes lined up down the middle. When she turned to inspect them, he took a few seconds to admire her endless legs in black tights and the rose-colored sweater dress that hugged every curve and barely made it to the middle of her thighs. Sweat broke out at his hairline as his eyes traveled over her perfectly sculpted derriere. The woman was going to kill him before he even got a chance to do her party gig.

"Wow. You sorted through all that paperwork since Wednesday?"

"Yeah, well, I had some free time." *Since I wasn't sleeping.* "I felt pretty bad blindsiding you with all that the other day. Rosemary helped me. I think that first box is already sorted by date. The others aren't . . . yet."

"You're wonderful. Thanks for the help." She slid the first box toward her and started to sort through it. "Okay, this appears to be purchase orders and receipts." She dropped the papers she'd scanned back in and went to the next one.

"Those are invoices we sent to our advertisers." His mouth quirked up at one corner. "As you can see, that's the shortest pile."

She gave him a smile. "By next year, it'll be a lot bigger. I have a couple of ideas on increasing your revenue." She moved down the table, inspecting the rest of the boxes.

By next year you'll be sorry you ever laid eyes on me. "I'll be glad to work on these other boxes—sorting them by date. And Rosemary can help today too."

"Oh, that will be great. Let's ask Rosemary to do the sorting by date on those last two boxes. I'd like you to go through this first one with me and tell me what invoices are for routine operating expenses and what are for big purchases that you would call capital expenditures."

"No problem. Would you like a cup of coffee before we dive in?"

"Mmmm, no thanks. Maybe a bottle of water?" she suggested.

"I'm not sure we have any." He pressed the intercom button. "Rosemary, do we have any bottled water in the building?"

"Sure, Boss. I put a six pack in the fridge yesterday afternoon."

"Rosemary, you're amazing. Bring a bottle for Ms. Adams and forward the phones to my desk. You're going to be back here in the trenches with us this morning."

"Let me get my waders on, and I'll be right there," she said with a chuckle.

Amanda removed her laptop and charging cable from her briefcase and checked for a nearby outlet. The closest one was about a foot too far away from the table. "Do you have an extension cord? If I work off battery I'll be dead in the water in less than two hours."

"No extension cord, but don't worry." He picked up the end of the table and dragged it toward the outlet.

"Wait, I'll help—" Amanda started. Before she finished he'd moved it close enough to for her cable to reach.

Without a word, he took the cord from her and plugged it in.

"Thanks." She booted the laptop up while he arranged a pair of chairs close together.

He slid the box of papers over, sat down, and started to separate them as she requested.

Amanda took her cue from Dev's body language. Her offer of help had been a mistake. She wasn't trying to point out his handicap—hadn't even thought about it, honestly. She would have offered to help Arnold Schwarzenegger move the darn table. On the other hand, she ought to be more considerate of how he must feel. Too bad he was so touchy.

She had to remember this was a job, not a social occasion. Somehow those few times they'd spoken late at night made him seem much more a friend than he was. That voice of his was like a tractor beam, reeling her in, making her feel cozy and comfortable and welcomed into a private slice of the ether populated by just the two of them. Obviously his 'on air' persona was not the real Dev. She'd do well to keep that in mind.

Rosemary brought her a bottle of water and handed it to her with a wink. "The boss cracked the whip about these files yesterday, Ms. Adams, so I got as much done as I could by five when he came back and finished up. What shall I start on today?"

"Have you set up a filing cabinet for any of this yet?" Amanda didn't want to suggest any system that might conflict with what was already in place.

"Just the typical alphabetical kind," Rosemary replied.

"How about making one for the year and subdividing it into bills, advertising invoices, equipment purchases, that sort of thing. Keep correspondence and vendors under the system you already have, but anything you find that you think will be specific to last year's income or expenditures should be together in one place. That will make it easier for me to find if I have to cross-reference anything."

Rosemary nodded. "I'll start on this last box. It has mostly letters you won't need to bother with. That way I won't get in the way between you and the boss," she added with a sly smile.

She blithely ignored the glare Dev shot her and got to work at the other end of the table.

They worked in silence for a while sitting close enough that her arm occasionally brushed Dev's. The contact gave her a jolt every time, which she did her best to ignore. The faint aroma of his aftershave distracted her too. Its fresh, woodsy scent mixed with smell of clean linen from his starched white shirt. She realized he must have gone home after his shift and showered, shaved, and changed before she arrived.

Last Friday when she had dropped by unannounced his jaw was shadowed and his clothes were rumpled. Had he gone to the trouble of cleaning up just for her? How sweet, she thought, smiling to herself. Maybe that was what Rosemary's little smirk was about.

After about half an hour, Amanda came across an invoice for something she had no idea how to classify. Touching his arm to get his attention, she leaned toward him and held out the paper. "Can you tell me what this is for?"

He turned at her voice and she got her first real close up of his sea-green eyes, deep and mysterious and a bit haunted. Whoa, she said to herself. His eyes dropped to her mouth and she worried that she'd spoken aloud. She rustled the paper to get his attention transferred there so she could breathe again.

He glanced at the invoice.

"That's for a piece of equipment Mike said he needed to calibrate the antennas. I think that would fall under capital expenditures," Dev muttered. "At that price we'd better not be buying more than one of them."

He picked up a few other papers and handed them to her. "These are also what I'd consider capital expenditures. Mostly equipment I had to replace when I bought the place. We upgraded from turntables to CD players. I kept one turntable around in case we had to play an oldie that hadn't been re-mastered onto a CD or DVD yet."

"Okay, good." She tried to keep her expression merely pleasant but couldn't stop a smile. Darn, she really liked this guy and hoped her earlier *faux pas* wouldn't keep them from becoming friends. She'd bet he didn't have many.

When Danny was home on leave between tours, he'd talked with her about how some of his buddies had such a hard time at home after they were injured. Dev seemed relaxed and friendly on the air but even in the short time she'd spent in his company she sensed a certain solitary, withdrawn quality about him.

She forced her attention back to the present and she and Dev worked steadily till noon, when they took a break for lunch. She had planned on going out somewhere to pick up a sandwich but Rosemary called the sub shop a couple of miles down the road in a little strip mall.

"Bud's our lifeline around here," Dev explained. "We're so far out of town his is the only place close enough to deliver. Since we all order from him, he's willing to make the drive out here. Lucky for us his subs are pretty good." He handed her the short, hand-written menu. "It's not The Top of the Hub, but I'm buying, so knock yourself out."

The smile he sent her took five years off his face and the little twinkle in his eyes was almost mischievous. This more relaxed Dev gave her hope all was not lost as far as friendship was concerned. She grinned and effected a southern accent. "Why, you are too kind, suh. How can I evah repay you?" She batted her lashes at him.

He came back with a passable John Wayne drawl. "Well, Ma'am, I'm sure I'll think of somethin'. You aren't leaving town anytime soon, are yuh?"

That got them both laughing and Amanda heaved an internal sigh of relief. After she scanned the short menu, she ordered turkey and provolone on whole wheat. Dev chose roast beef and cheddar on rye. Rosemary went down the hall to see if Hank, the announcer doing the mid-day shift, wanted to order a sandwich too.

"What's the Top of the Hub?"

"A very nice restaurant in Boston. It's on the fifty-second floor of the Prudential Tower, so the view is terrific. Food's pretty good, too. It was only a few blocks from where I went to school."

"So, you're from Boston originally?" Amanda stood up and stretched to get the kinks out after sitting so long.

"No. I was born in Virginia, moved to New York when I was twelve. Went to college in Boston."

Shorter replies might mean he wanted her to steer clear of this topic for some reason. Maybe she was misinterpreting the signal, though. She'd give it one more try. "What school did you go to?"

The pause told her she'd been right. Still, it seemed a harmless question. She kept on, a friendly smile curving her lips.

"Let me guess. B U? No. Harvard? No." Little shakes of his head rejected each guess. "MIT?" That got her a bark of laughter.

"Do I look like a techie to you?"

"Well, you can't always go by appearances." She shrugged. "So tell me. Where?"

He sighed. "The New England Conservatory."

The way he said it sounded almost painful.

"Of Music?" she exclaimed. "You went to the New England Conservatory of Music," she repeated, to confirm she hadn't misunderstood. "Wow, I'm impressed. That school is really tough to get into. One of my friends from high school tried to get in there. She didn't make it, though. You must be a fantastic musician," she rattled on.

Then it hit her and she winced.

She couldn't keep her eyes from going to his injured hand. And wanted to sink through the floor. What an idiot! She closed her eyes, too mortified to meet his. "It's too much to hope for that you went there for voice, isn't it?"

"Yeah."

He swiveled around in his chair. “Piano. He gestured to include their surroundings. “But now I’m here. Providing music to a much larger audience.” He turned back around. “Nothing more than I deserved, anyway,” he mumbled under his breath.

Good God, what a tragedy. She was furious with herself for her thoughtlessness. She had to push it, didn’t she? Never did know when to leave well enough alone. Now what could she say? She reached out to him, but her hand slid off his arm as he stood up.

“Excuse me. I, uh, need to get some coffee,” he murmured and was out the door before she could say another word.

Well, guess that pretty much blew her chance to become his friend. Her heart ached for his loss. *Damn it, I hate war.*

CHAPTER 7

"Oh, Zoe, I can't believe I was so insensitive," Amanda groaned. "Really, my mother was right. Half the time I don't engage my brain before I open my mouth."

Zoe opened a new string of lights and grabbed a couple of needlepoint ivy garlands from the pile at her feet. She deftly began to embed the lights in the ivy. "I'm sure Mr. MacMurphy isn't going to hold it against you."

"He should, though. It was stupid to keep pushing when he obviously didn't want to talk about his alma mater. I have to get used to the idea that he's one of our wounded warriors. I think because I spoke with him on the phone a few times and he seemed so nice, and friendly and, and . . . well, normal, I don't picture him as injured. He wears a long-sleeved shirt and usually keeps his left hand in his pocket, so I don't really notice it. The rest of him is too distracting anyway," she murmured.

Zoe looked up sharply. "What do you mean by 'distracting'?"

Amanda felt her cheeks heat and she ducked her head to concentrate on twining the artificial ivy around the strings of tiny white lights. Her fingertips were red and swollen from tying them together with green floral wire. "How much more of this do we still have to make?"

"About five more miles," Zoe responded, "and don't try to change the subject. Tell me about the distracting part."

"Oh, well, he's quite tall and very nicely put together." *As in great ass.* "And he has dark green eyes that are real showstoppers, although they seem sad a lot of the time. He's got this clean, piney, sort of manly scent about him. It's very, um . . ."

"Sexy?"

"Well, I wouldn't say sexy, exactly. It's more, ah, kind of . . ." She finally gave up and finished, "Yeah, it's sexy. Must be one of those pheromone things. Makes me just want to rub up against him, and—" *lick him all over.* Amanda snapped her mouth shut, horrified at the direction her thoughts had taken.

"I need to meet this guy. Like, tomorrow," Zoe said with a huge smile. "Invite him over for dinner. I'll cook."

"You'll cook. *You'll* cook? Zoe, you don't cook. Ever. You and Jeff live on take-out and microwave dinners."

"Okay, then, *you* cook. Jeff will come too. That way—What's his name, again?"

"Dev."

"Right. That way Dev won't feel outnumbered by two women."

"No, no. Zo, hold on here a minute. I have no reason to invite him for dinner. Your curiosity doesn't count. After the way I embarrassed him today, I doubt if he would come anyway."

"Of course you have a reason to invite him, silly girl," Zoe prattled on. "We have to find out what facilities he'll need for his equipment." She stopped twining ivy and seemed very pleased with herself. "As a matter of fact, I think he should come with us over to Mrs. W's when we take our final measurements, so he can see the layout and make sure we have things set up right. We wouldn't want him to show up on party night and not have something essential."

"I suppose so. Ouch!" Amanda sucked her index finger where the floral wire had poked yet another hole. "Darn this wire. My fingers are so sore I can barely type as it is." She looped the finished length of garland over the makeshift rod they were using to keep it from tangling. "I need to get some alcohol."

"It's on the bottom shelf in the fridge," Zoe said.

"For my finger, Zo. Alcohol for my finger," Amanda chided, holding up the injured digit.

"Stick your finger in the glass after you pour the wine," Zoe retorted. "And I'll have a glass too, thank you very much."

"Why not?" Amanda chuckled, eyes heavenward. She took out the bottle of Pinot Grigio and poured two glasses, set one on the table next to Zoe and dropped back into her chair. "Okay, I'll ask Dev to come along to Mrs. Wyndham's—when he should be sleeping." She hiked her eyebrows up for emphasis. "So I doubt if he'll want to come for dinner or he'll have no time at all to sleep before he has to go on the air again."

"I think it's sweet the way you worry about him getting his rest." Zoe smirked.

"I'm not *worried* about him getting his rest." Amanda gave Zoe a narrow stare. "Don't start getting any ideas, Zo. Just because I can appreciate the hunky body and the gorgeous eyes and the subtle scent of spicy male, doesn't mean I have any interest in Mr. MacMurphy other than a purely business one."

"Oh, absolutely," Zoe agreed. "It just means you're still a living, breathing, fully functional female."

Amanda wasn't going to follow Zoe down that particular path so she circled back to the meal she had to decide on for the dinner. Sure that there would only be the three of them, she figured a casserole would be the best bet in case she had to stretch it to four. She had a nice chicken, broccoli, and cheddar recipe that would work, along with a salad and some crusty baguettes.

She leaned over and picked up another ivy garland. "It's a good thing you've got a nice big back room here at the gallery. Once we start stockpiling things that aren't rentals, we're going to need a fair amount of space for storage."

"Until Russell Manheim's pieces arrive, we'll have no problem with storage space." Zoe sighed.

She lived in the space above the gallery that Jeff had helped convert into a studio apartment. The skylights gave her plenty of natural light for her painting, and a back-to-back kitchen and bath acted as the divider between public and private areas. Now that Jeff had moved in semi-permanently the space was a bit more crowded, but he still kept his studio/apartment at the motel where he worked as *de facto* superintendent and handyman. It was good to keep their work spaces separated.

Zoe ordered Chinese from the Lotus Garden a few blocks over and they continued to work through dinner to finish up the ivy garlands. By nine-thirty, Amanda's fingers were begging for relief. She hung the last string of ivy and rubbed her sore hands.

"I'm heading home, Zo. Our meeting with Mrs. Wyndham is at two o'clock Friday afternoon, so I'll be by to pick you up around one-forty-five, okay? Dress down this time. I'm sure we'll be slogging around alongside the decks and walkways. We have to decide where to put the temporary parking area, too.

"Yeah." Zoe yawned. "Jeans, boots, sweatshirt, jacket. Got it." She walked Amanda through the darkened gallery to the front door. "Drive safe, Mandy. See you tomorrow," she said and gave her a quick hug. She waited to hear Amanda's little Civic sputter to life and drive away, then closed and locked the door.

Considering all the things Amanda carefully didn't say about her radio deejay, Zoe couldn't wait to meet Dev and find out what, if anything, was going on between them.

Blue Point Cove was a ghost town at ten o'clock at night in the off season. Amanda drove slowly once she was out of the center of town. Her car was the only vehicle on the sleepy streets. The winding road followed the ins and outs of the shoreline and there were no streetlights or sidewalks to mark the edges. She was glad she knew every little twist and turn by heart. Her headlights occasionally illuminated a pair of eyes from some nocturnal creature as she rounded a curve. Possums, raccoons, whatever, she'd be a basket case if she ever hit any animal, so she took her time. The friendly yellow glow from the porch light welcomed her home and she hurried inside, deciding a cup of chamomile tea would be just the ticket before bed.

While she heated the water, she turned on the radio and changed into flannel PJs. In the summer she usually wore a tank top and boxers to bed, but until she got the little cottage winterized she needed the extra warmth. She took her tea into the spare bedroom and checked her laptop for new email. Nothing but spam. She didn't have many friends and her mom generally emailed her only once or twice a week. She shut the laptop down, too tired to bother updating spreadsheets, and went into her bedroom.

Tomorrow she was due at the radio station at nine. So far Dev had been there each morning. She wondered if that was his normal schedule, then chided herself. Of course it was. He wasn't going to rearrange his life just to be there when she was. Now that they had sorted through all the invoices, he didn't need to stay while she worked on his tax returns and set up this year's books, but she found herself hoping he'd be there anyway.

She glanced over at the picture of Danny sitting on her dresser. He was wearing fatigues, standing in the shade of a solitary tree somewhere in Iraq, surrounded by flat ground—no grass, just dirt and rocks. He was smiling that wonderful smile of his, his blue eyes full of humor. He told her his buddy, Mac, had taken the picture, making him laugh over some faintly pornographic joke. She wished she could have seen Mac, too, because Danny had mentioned him often in his letters. He always seemed to be the one taking the pictures instead of being in them. Mac had been Danny's best friend. He hadn't been at the funeral, because he was still at Walter Reed recovering from the injuries he'd received in the same bombing that had killed Danny.

She kept that photograph on her dresser and studied it every morning and every night, because even after only eight months—was it nine, now?—she was starting to lose the sharp image she carried in her head. She wanted to remember every detail, every freckle, every hair, every laugh line around Danny's eyes, because that was all she'd ever have.

First her dad, then Danny. She would not love another man. Love was too risky. For any man who loved her, she was the kiss of death. And she couldn't bear another parting.

She would date, yes. She might even have an affair. She did still have a woman's needs and missed that sweet heat two bodies could make when they came together in passion. But love? No way. Not again.

A familiar voice pulled her away from the picture. She glanced at her bedside clock and a tiny smile curved her lips. Dev's Dream Machine was ready to take her wherever she wanted to go. She finished her tea and climbed under the covers, bringing the telephone close, content to listen for a while and hear what others requested. She let his voice flow over her like sun-warmed honey, thick and sweet, while she thought of what song she'd request tonight.

"Here's a request from a listener who'd rather not give a name. It's called 'Dream'. Remember, our call lines are open and I'm waiting to answer, so dial 888-555-WMES and tell me what you'd like to hear."

She couldn't resist his invitation and, triggered by the lyrics of the first song, she decided to request "Serenade in Blue". *I ought to put this number on speed dial* she thought as she tapped the buttons. Then the smooth, friendly voice was in her ear, lifting her spirits in spite of her melancholy mood.

"Hi, Dev, it's Amanda. Would you play 'Serenade in Blue', please?"

"Hello, Amanda. Nice to hear from you tonight. Good choice. I'll cue your request up next. Are you dedicating tonight?"

"No, not tonight. This one's for me."

"Okay, Honey, you've got it. And you can always call again, you know. I'll be here for a while."

"Maybe, Dev. But if I don't see you in the morning, I wanted to ask if you might be willing to come with Zoe and me to Mrs. Wyndham's house next week. Zoe thought it would be a good idea for you to see the area where we're thinking of setting you up to make sure it'll work for you."

"Sure. That's a good idea. But I'll be seeing you in the morning, anyway. Gotta run, Hon. Other calls are lighting up my board."

"Good night, Dev. See you in the morning." She hung up with the familiar warmth in her belly that his voice always caused. Much better than chamomile tea, actually. She listened to her request and the next selection was "Dream a Little Dream of Me". She didn't know if that was a request from someone else or Dev's choice, but once again she wondered at the sequencing of the songs he played. She could almost think he was selecting them especially for her. But that was ridiculous. He'd hardly tailor his show for her enjoyment. She was foolish to even entertain that idea.

True to March's reputation, a brisk wind was blowing the last of winter's leaves from their hiding places under low-hanging evergreen branches and whirling them in mini-cyclones around the open field behind the radio station. The tree line across the back of the field had taken on a hazy outline as spring coaxed new growth from the maples and sycamores.

Dev pushed back a thick lock of brown hair, which the persistent wind immediately flipped back across his forehead. His unbuttoned olive-green coat flapped open as a strong gust plastered the chambray shirt across the broad expanse of his chest. As usual, his left hand stayed tucked in his pocket as he listened to whatever Mike Kovak was saying.

Amanda watched out the window in the break room as the pair conferred at the base of the antenna tower. She sighed.

With two weeks of almost daily appearances at the radio station, her set-up work was nearly done. After Friday there would be no more hours spent at the conference table where she could glance surreptitiously over at Dev working at his desk, watching that same impudent lock of brown hair curl softly over his forehead. No more companionable lunches in the break room with Dev or Rosemary. No more friendly banter with Mike Kovak or Neal Taylor while they made coffee or grabbed a donut. Funny how quickly she'd begun to feel a member of this unique family.

She couldn't hear their conversation but Mike's gestures upward toward the antenna array, followed by pointing to the papers in his hand, left no doubt he was trying to explain a technical problem to Dev.

She had to smile at the intent expression on Dev's face. He tried to appear as though he understood Mike while he patiently waited for him to finish. But she knew he hadn't a clue what his chief engineer was talking about. Technical details were not Dev's forte. When he finished, Dev would nod and agree to whatever Mike said he needed to keep the station on the air and in the good graces of the FCC. Then he would come inside and ask her if there was any way they could afford whatever it was Mike had asked for. And she would do her damnedest to find a way to squeeze the money out of his overstretched budget.

She took a sip from her bottled water and turned to go back to the office. She jumped and let out an involuntary squeak of surprise at the sight of a man in a military uniform standing just inside the doorway.

"Sorry, Ma'am. Didn't mean to startle you," he apologized with a smile. "I'm Chris Majewski."

He offered his hand and Amanda hastily switched her water bottle so she could shake it. "Hello, Captain Majewski. My name is Amanda Adams. It's nice to meet you."

"The pleasure is all mine, Miss Adams." His smile widened and his blue eyes sharpened with interest. "I was just going to get a cup of coffee while I waited for Dev," he explained as he went to the coffee pot and got a mug from the shelf above it. "Rosemary said he was out in the back forty going over some technical problem with Mike." He added two packets of sugar and stirred his coffee as he gave Amanda a brief once-over.

From the comfortable way he moved around the room, Amanda could tell he was no stranger to the premises. "Are you a friend of Dev's from the Army, Captain Majewski?" The gold bars on his shoulders made his rank an easy call.

"I am. But, please, let's dispense with the military rank. Chris is fine. I had an early meeting in Annapolis or I would have been in civvies for this visit."

He took the mug of steaming coffee over to the small table and sat.

"Did Rosemary bring in any of her legendary blueberry muffins this morning?" He scanned the room hopefully, then pinned her with an expression of mock suspicion. "You've hidden them, haven't you?"

Amanda couldn't help but laugh at the twinkle of mischief in his summer-sky-blue eyes.

"If you think I'm giving up the location of the best blueberry muffins in Somerset County, you're mistaken," she said, then glanced pointedly at the tin on top of the refrigerator. "I'll never tell."

"I'm afraid you've met your match, Amanda," Dev said from the doorway. He watched the other man and gave a barely perceptible shake of his head. "Captain Majewski is a master at getting people to tell him everything he wants to know."

"Really, Chris? Are you an interrogator? Should I be worried?" She was sure Dev was joking but more than happy to follow his lead. "Will you pull my fingernails out one by one until I tell you where the muffins are hidden?"

"Nah, no bright lights or waterboarding from me. That's for the guys in black over in intelligence. I find asking politely usually gets me what I want to know." He swiveled in his chair to face Dev. "So tell me, my friend, how did you find this lovely lady and talk her into working here?"

Dev shrugged out of his coat and slung it over the back of a chair, shooting the other man a scowl.

"Actually, it was more the other way around," Amanda offered. "I wanted to hire him to do a deejay gig for a party and when I showed up here one morning out of the blue, I think I surprised him into agreeing."

She smiled at Dev and thought his cheeks reddened—or was it windburn?

"Don't let her fool you, Chris. She found out how desperate I was for an accountant and used that information ruthlessly to bend me to her will."

Dev's comments seemed almost serious compared to the lighthearted banter she and Chris had been sharing.

"She'll use any means to get what she wants. When she's determined, watch out," he concluded.

Amanda took that as a compliment and grinned proudly. "What can I say? I'm irresistible." She shrugged.

Chris glanced from Amanda to Dev. "And what she wanted was you?" he asked in amazement. "Give me a few minutes alone with her and I'll fix that." He chuckled.

Amanda gestured at the pot. “You want some coffee, Dev? Or a blueberry muffin?” She slid a sideways glance at Chris, who raised one eyebrow at her show of innocence.

“Well, I’m beginning to see the light,” he commented.

“Great song,” Amanda and Dev said in unison, then shared a smile.

She went to the refrigerator and brought back the tin of muffins. Then she poured Dev’s coffee in his World’s Best Boss mug and set it in front of him.

“Chris, I have to get back to work. My boss is a real slave-driver,” Amanda stage-whispered. “It was nice to meet you.” She retrieved her bottle of water and sauntered out the door. She was curious what Chris wanted to talk with Dev about, but too polite to eavesdrop. Still, she walked as slowly as she dared in hopes of catching a few sentences.

Dev’s reaction to Captain Majewski put her inquisitive nature on alert.

CHAPTER 8

Chris Majewski was a psychiatrist at Walter Reed and Dev had been one of his more spectacular failures. Which never stopped him from trying to help. Dev could shut him down temporarily but he'd never stay away for long.

He'd made the mistake of telling Captain Majewski his plans, and once he was discharged, Chris kept in touch by sending him other former soldiers who didn't have a job or a home to go back to. He figured the peace and quiet of the sparsely populated Eastern Shore might give them the chance to recover the balance Iraq or Afghanistan had beaten out of them. It made for an interesting crew, Dev had to give him that.

The one job Chris hadn't found anyone to fill was that of Business Manager. So Dev was saddled with it, which to his way of thinking, was barely one step above the Chief Engineer slot.

"What a lovely woman," Chris commented, judiciously selecting a blueberry muffin.

Dev was in no mood to discuss Amanda with his former shrink. He would have told him about meeting her eventually but he hadn't been ready yet. Too late now. He could already see the speculation in Chris' eyes. He had been pushing Dev for months to get in touch with Danny's fiancée, confident that the meeting would help resolve at least some of his massive survivor guilt. Dev was equally sure Amanda would despise him for the part he played in Danny's death. Now that he'd spent some time with her, he doubted she would accuse him of killing Danny outright—she had too much class for that—but inside she'd still blame him. And run as fast as she could in the other direction.

"Before you ask, no. She doesn't know who I am." Dev took a swallow of coffee and grimaced as it scalded his tongue.

"And she really just showed up here one day, searching for you?"

"Yeah. She listens to us." Dev tilted his head up toward the overhead speaker that constantly carried their live broadcast. He finally met Chris's eyes.

"I'd only found out she moved near here a couple of days before. Then I drove over to Blue Point Cove—that's where she lives—and damn near killed her with my car." His hands shook slightly so he put his coffee down and folded his arms across his chest.

Chris merely sat and waited.

"Cut the shrink crap," Dev muttered. "I hate it when you do that."

"Do what?"

"Just sit there without talking and wait for me to spill my guts. You're not my therapist anymore so you can lose the couch-side manner."

"Okay. So you just found out she lives close enough to call using two empty soup cans and a piece of string, but you drove over instead and tried to kill her with your car?"

"I didn't *try* to kill her. The accident was her fault. She pulled out in front of me without looking. Luckily the Rover has good brakes. After I got out of my truck, I realized who she was."

"So you went over to introduce yourself . . ."

"Actually she introduced herself first. I merely told her my name—which meant nothing to her—checked the damage, which was minor, thank God, and suggested we not involve the police in an accident report."

The hum of the refrigerator filled the room.

Dev took another slug of coffee and concentrated on the tabletop. Damned if Chris would get another word out of him on this subject.

Chris caved first on their silent tug-of-war.

"Okay, then let me ask you this. How long are you going to wait before you tell her who you really are?"

Dev's scowl would have made a lesser man back off. He had perfected it dealing with Iraqi rebels at numerous checkpoints.

"You do plan on telling her at some point, right?" Chris glanced at him over the rim of his cup as he sipped his coffee, his own bland expression perfected in hundreds of interviews with troubled, frightened, belligerent soldiers.

"Of course." Dev rocked his chair back on two legs. "I'm trying to help get her new business venture off to a good start. That, plus hiring her to do the station's books will give her a bit more financial security. Then I have to convince her to move on and find someone to replace Danny in her life."

He leveled the chair, and went over to the sink where he dumped the remains of his coffee and stared out the window. Without turning, he said, "You and I both know as soon as I tell her who I am, that will be the end of any kind of interaction between us."

"I'm not as sure about that as you are, Marconi, but I understand your caution. Is Amanda showing any signs of interest in other men? Do you know if she's dated anyone yet?"

Dev pivoted, rubbing his left arm and flexing the fingers in the thin glove he wore. He came back to the table and placed both hands flat on its surface, then leaned forward and narrowed his eyes. "Tell me, Chris, is your interest purely clinical or are you hoping for a date?"

"It's simple curiosity, Dev. No need to get your hackles up." He finished his blueberry muffin and brushed the crumbs from his fingers. "I really stopped by to see if I could interest you in another employee."

Dev rolled his eyes skyward. "What's the matter with this one? Please tell me he can at least get around under his own power and doesn't have any violent tendencies."

Chris cast a reproachful glance at Dev before he withdrew a sheaf of papers from his inside jacket pocket. "Physically he's fine. But you'd have to assign him an evening slot, for a while at least. Nights would be even better, if you'd be willing to give up part of your shift. He has a little difficulty with noise and daylight." Chris put his hand up to stop Dev's interruption. "He is coming along quite well, actually, or I wouldn't have suggested that you take him on. He needs some time to get his feet back under himself, that's all."

Chris Majewski was nothing if not discreet about his patients' histories and diagnoses. Dev took the paperwork and glanced through it. Lance Fisher, thirty-five, a sergeant, and the only survivor of a suicide bombing on the police station he and his men were protecting out in Zabul province. A fifteen-year veteran whose only skill before entering the Army was as a wide receiver on a Level II College Football team. He quit college to join the military and now here he was with PTSD and no marketable job skills—assuming you didn't count shooting people. Dev could relate.

"You bring him along with you?"

"Nah. Didn't want to get his hopes up until I spoke with you first."

Dev gave a half-smile and shook his head. "I appreciate your restraint, Dr. Freud." He blew out a breath. "Luckily for you I just happen to have an opening from three to seven a.m. Send him on down here and we'll see if we can work him into our little group."

Chris' smile dropped years off his face. "Wish I could get you to cut yourself a little slack, Marconi. You're a much better man than you give yourself credit for."

"No. I'm not. Be grateful for my guilt. It's the only reason I let you dump your hapless rejects on me."

He saw the change in Chris' expression, and closed his eyes. "Mike's right behind me, isn't he?"

Chris nodded. "Yep."

"It's okay, boss. I knew I was a reject when you hired me. And I'll always be grateful you gave me a chance anyway," Mike assured him.

He went straight to the sink and began washing up the mugs left in it. Clouds of steam rose from the scalding hot water. He brought a dishcloth over to the table and began to wipe up the crumbs Chris had left behind, giving him a disgusted snort.

Chris threw up his hands. "I know, I know. I'm a slob."

"You are," Mike agreed. "But you're in good company around here. They're all slobs."

"Mike, I'll take care of this. You don't always have to be the one who cleans up," Dev said. He regretted Mike had heard the way he referred to the men Chris had talked him into hiring. He didn't see them as rejects at all, really. He was only trying to jerk Chris's chain and get him off the topic of his own shortcomings.

"I've got this, boss," Mike replied. He glanced over at Chris. "You sending us another reject, Captain?" He purposely ignored Dev's frown but didn't hide his little smirk from Chris.

"I think I may have found someone to shorten Dev's all-night shift, Mike. I know I can count on you to give the guy a hand finding a place to stay. Maybe you could be roommates for a while till he gets settled in."

The horror on Mike's face had Chris back-pedaling quickly. "Or not. I just thought with opposite shifts you wouldn't be in each other's way much."

"I'll help him find a place, Captain, don't worry. This economy has lots of folks around here renting out rooms in their homes for some extra income. When's he starting?"

Mike asked Dev, who bounced the question over to Chris with a shrug.

"He'll be discharged from the hospital tomorrow. How soon can you work him into your schedule, Dev?"

"Pretty confident I'd say yes, weren't you? Humph. Might as well have him come on over right away unless he has something else he has to do. I'll ask Ed to show him the ropes for the next couple of days—"

Chris winced.

"Oh, right." Dev tried to figure out a plan but it wasn't going to be easy. "Well, hell, Chris, they aren't going to discharge him in the middle of the night. He's going to have to deal with some daylight till we find him a place to stay. I'll ask Ed to work late and go over procedures in the evening. Then I can start him with me until he's ready to solo."

Mike folded the dishcloth in three exactly equal sections, made sure the handles of the mugs were all pointing in the same direction on the shelf over the coffee pot, and came over to straighten the chairs at the table. "I'll check on a house that put a sign in the front window a few days ago about a room rental and see what they're asking. Maybe we can have him settled in by tomorrow or the day after."

He moved the salt and pepper shakers a half-inch further apart and Dev had no doubt they were aligned exactly along a north-south meridian and equidistant from both edges of the table. "Thanks, Mike. Let me know when you've got those test patterns on the antennas done and I'll sign off on the paperwork."

"Sure thing, boss."

Chris stood up and carefully set his chair opposite the one on the other side of the table. "I have to get back to the hospital, Dev. Thanks for helping out with Lance. I think you'll like him. And, ah, let me know how things go with A—"

"Yeah, I'll keep you posted," Dev interrupted.

“Right. Good to see you, Mike,” Chris finished as he headed toward the door.

“Likewise, Captain.” Mike nudged Chris’ chair two millimeters to the left.

Dev followed Chris down the hall and watched as he leaned into the doorway of his office.

“Nice meeting you, Amanda.”

Amanda glanced up from her laptop. “A pleasure to meet you too, Chris. Will we be seeing you again soon?”

Nice that she used the word “we”, Dev thought. As though she considered herself a member of their organization. Not so nice that she cared whether Chris stopped in again or not.

“Oh, I’m the prototypical bad penny,” Chris replied. “You never can tell when I’ll show up.” He shot Dev a look over his shoulder that was part amusement, part challenge. “Hang in there, Marconi.”

“Yeah. You drive safe, Doc.” Dev clapped Chris on the shoulder. “Roads can be dangerous around here.” He glanced over at Amanda in time to see her drum her fingers on the conference table and give him a dirty look. That was all it took to improve his mood one hundred percent.

CHAPTER 9

No. This couldn't be happening. Amanda turned the key in the ignition again and got the same result. Nothing. Not even a sputter. She checked to see if she'd left the lights on or the radio or . . . anything. She hadn't, yet somehow the battery was dead.

She pounded her hands on the steering wheel. She was supposed to pick Zoe up in fifteen minutes. And then turn back around and retrace her route to Mrs. Wyndham's house and get there by two o'clock. Not a chance she would make it now.

Zoe didn't own a car. Her living quarters above the gallery were right in the center of town and she walked anywhere she needed to go, or hitched a ride on the back of Jeff's motorcycle.

She hated to ask Dev for a favor but if he was going to meet them at the Wyndham's anyway, he was her next best bet. She dialed quickly but had her hopes dashed as the call went to voicemail. She left a message without much hope he'd get back to her in time to help. Damn, was nothing going to go right today?

Back inside, she grabbed the phone book to find the nearest car repair service. Maybe she could get a jump-start and still make it on time to Mrs. Wyndham's. She remembered the woman's remark about how the first event planner had been late. That was the company that *didn't* get the contract.

There were only two service stations in town. Amanda quickly dialed the number of the first one, and got a recording.

Drat. She hung up and called the second one. Thank God, a human voice answered the phone. She explained her problem and the man on the other end promised to have someone out to her house with jumper cables, just as soon as he got back from changing a flat tire for Mr. Abernathy. Shouldn't be more than thirty minutes.

Great. Perfect. She blew out a breath. She called Zoe next and explained her problem.

"Um, okay, let's try this," Zoe suggested. "Jeff was going to meet us there. I'll just ask him to stop and pick me up first. Then, after he drops me off he can come get you. At least one of us will be there on time. That should count for something."

Amanda wasn't thrilled at the thought of riding on the back of Jeff's Suzuki, especially the way he flew around corners on the thing, but desperate times called for desperate measures . . .

"Okay, Zoe. Tell Jeff I really appreciate the rescue. And call me when you get to Mrs. Wyndham's, please? That way I can relax a little. Meanwhile, I'm going to call Dev again and see if I can hitch a ride with him."

"Right. Hanging up to call Jeff," Zoe said. "I'll keep in touch."

"Kay. Bye."

On the second try, Dev picked up.

"Hi, Dev, it's Amanda." She tried to slow down because she sounded a little frantic even to herself. "I hate to bother you, but I've got to ask you for a big favor."

"Hi, Amanda."

She could hear the surprise in his voice, but he didn't miss a beat.

"What do you need?"

"I'm having car trouble and I don't want to be late to this appointment with Mrs. Wyndham. I was wondering if you have enough time to swing by my house and pick me up on your way there." She closed her eyes and crossed her fingers.

"No problem. I can be at your place in fifteen minutes. Will that be enough time?"

Just the sound of that perfect, soothing, wonderful voice was enough to calm her jangled nerves and slow her racing pulse. She blew out a long breath of relief. "Yes. That would be fine. Thank you so, so much. You're a real lifesaver, you know that?"

She heard him mumble something. "I'm sorry, I didn't quite catch that."

"It's nothing. I'll be there in a few minutes, all right?"

"Yes. Thank you again, Dev. I owe you one. Bye."

She hung up, then called Zoe to tell her of the altered plans. "Would you rather we came by and picked you up, Zoe?" she asked.

"No. Don't bother. Jeff is already on his way over here, so I'll go with him and meet you guys out there. No point in you two driving past Mrs. W's to get me then having to backtrack."

"Okay, Zo. See you there at two."

Amanda sighed. Thankfully she'd defrosted extra chicken tenders. She would definitely talk Dev into staying for dinner if she could. She owed him that and more for the rescue.

She called the service station back to say she'd be gone before their mechanic could get to her house, so she would wait till she got back to get a jump-start.

One glimpse in the mirror and she ran to the bathroom to brush her hair. She'd been running her hands through it in frustration and Dev would think she'd just gotten out of bed. A little lip gloss to replace what she had chewed off and she was set to go.

She stood on her front porch, dressed in jeans, a black turtle-neck sweater, high black boots, and her black pea coat when Dev pulled up a few minutes later. Slinging her leather satchel across her shoulder, she locked the door and climbed into his green Land Rover.

"Hi. You made it in record time. Thanks again for the rescue, Dev." She glared down at her little Civic, then over at him. "I'm afraid my little baby needs a new battery. If I could impose upon you for another favor, when we get back from Mrs. Wyndham's, could you give me a jump-start? Then I can drive into town and get a new battery."

"Sure. Buckle up now. You know there are some crazy drivers out there," he added with a wink.

Wearing an oatmeal fisherman's sweater over khakis and with that defiant lock of brown hair curling over his forehead, he generated a flash of heat that zinged through all her erogenous zones. Squelching those feelings, Amanda smacked him lightly on the shoulder. "You're never gonna let me forget that accident, are you?"

"Nope. Stuff like that lasts a lifetime."

She liked it when he laughed. It made him appear so much younger. If he got a chuckle out of her bad driving, he could bring it up every time they got together. He needed to lighten up more, anyway.

"And to think I was going to offer you dinner tonight," she said with a sigh.

"Really?"

His surprise was seemed so genuine it made her sad. Did he think he was so undeserving of any kindness?

"Really. I planned to make dinner for Zoe and Jeff, and we'd all like it if you could join us."

She could tell it made a difference that Zoe and Jeff were going to be there. His expression changed but she couldn't get a good enough read on his profile to tell what it meant. Maybe he was nervous about meeting new people. Probably overly self-conscious about his arm and hand.

Impulsively she reached over and put her hand on his leg and gave a little squeeze. "Please come. I know you haven't had much sleep today but I'd really like it if you could join us. Just consider it payback for giving me this ride."

"Is this where we turn?" His usual velvet voice sounded strangely rough.

Amanda peered at the street sign. Crooked Neck Road. She took her hand off his leg, suddenly worried he might get the wrong idea.

"Yep, this is the turn. It's about a half-mile up on the left."

They drove on in silence for a few minutes.

"So, will you come to dinner, then?" She couldn't stand the suspense any longer.

"You don't owe me anything for this ride," he told her with a quick glance in her direction. "Don't feel obligated. I'm glad to do it. It wasn't far out of my way anyhow."

"I don't feel obligated. I planned on inviting you even before I needed a ride. But I understand if you'd rather not."

She gazed out the window to hide her disappointment.

He wasn't coming to dinner. He wasn't going to be her friend. She'd botched that up the other day, and the best she could hope for from Dev MacMurphy was politeness.

Chivalry wasn't dead on Maryland's Eastern Shore. Dev might help a damsel-in-distress but there wasn't going to be any personal involvement connected with the deed. What a shame. She hadn't felt friendship toward a man other than Danny since she was . . . well, ever, actually. She could kick herself for accidentally calling attention to his war wounds back at the radio station when it was obvious he didn't want to talk about them. Now he probably figured that if he came to dinner she'd make another big deal out of his injury and embarrass him in front of her friends.

Dev knew it would be a struggle to keep a cool head when he'd gotten Amanda's phone call asking for his help.

He had just stepped out of the shower, where his fantasy of Amanda, naked and slippery with the soap he was rubbing all over her luscious body, did more to steam up his bathroom than the hot water he was using. Heavy and aching with the desire to pick her up and slide her onto his rock-hard erection, he twisted the hot water off and let the ice-cold result drown that dream.

Listening to her worried voice on the phone, it was easy to imagine her biting on that bottom lip and peeking up at him through her lashes, her eyes twin pools of twilight. And he was right back to ready, the cold water forgotten as his cock sprang to attention again. He'd cursed under his breath at his inability to stay in control.

When he pulled up in front of her little house, she stood on the porch waiting for him, so beautiful his heart stuttered for a beat or two. Her hair was loose around her shoulders, framing the face that lately haunted all his dreams. Those long, long legs in tight jeans and boots had him stiffening yet again and he shifted in the seat trying to ease the tightness in his pants. Christ, what was he doing here? Torquemada and the Spanish Inquisition couldn't have come up with torture like this.

When she climbed in and her fresh scent wafted across the cab, his deep breath was a reflex he couldn't control. Perfume? Shampoo? He had no idea what the scent was, but to him it was an aphrodisiac like no other. He kept his hands locked on the steering wheel or he knew he would reach out, slip his hand behind her neck, through all that gold, silken hair, and draw her close, the little 'O' of surprise on her mouth all the invitation he'd need to cover it with his own and feast on the soft lips he'd been dying to taste.

She'd asked for a jump-start when they got back from this meeting, and he swallowed his first response and managed a single word reply. Then he teased her about 'crazy drivers' and made her buckle up. She rewarded him with a girlie punch on his shoulder and a million-dollar smile that delighted him enough to make him laugh out loud. Her offer of dinner took him by surprise, but when she explained that she was having her friend, Zoe, and another guy over as well, he knew he'd leapt to the wrong conclusion.

Like she was going to invite him over for a cozy dinner for two. Yeah, that was going to happen. Right after he won the lottery. No, she was simply being kind to a lonely misfit she felt sorry for.

When she'd put her hand on his leg, he bit his tongue to stop his body's reaction and quickly distracted her by asking for directions. He wanted to be able to get out of the rover and walk without embarrassing himself. If she touched him again, he'd be toast.

CHAPTER 10

Old Lady Wyndham wasn't such an old lady after all. With a husband celebrating his seventy-fifth birthday, Dev didn't expect an attractive woman in her early sixties. Slim and well-preserved, Mrs. Wyndham could easily pass for a woman in her fifties. She had the carefully maintained appearance that spoke of frequent spa visits and a masseuse on retainer. If this was the first marriage for them, he suspected the Admiral had taken a fair amount of 'robbing the cradle' ribbing before they tied the knot.

Once Amanda introduced him, Mrs. Wyndham was gracious, charming, and happy to flirt a little as she showed them all through the living room to the deck.

Dev had a difficult time staying focused on the task at hand as he followed Amanda's long-legged stride down the walkway toward the pavilion overlooking the bay. The day had warmed up in the unpredictable way March had of changing its mind and Amanda had slipped out of her heavy pea-coat, unknowingly letting the close-fitting black turtleneck and snug jeans keep them both warm. The knee-high boots had him imagining her whipping out a riding crop to point out the placement of speakers and lighting. Visuals of horseback riding devolved into steamier fantasies where the animal plunging between her legs had only two legs but more than enough enthusiasm to have her panting with desire.

"Nice working for the rich ones, isn't it?" Jeff swung a leg over the railing of the pavilion and balanced on the narrow edge of decking on the other side.

“Hmm?” Dev snapped his attention away from Amanda and watched as Jeff held on with one hand while he examined the underside of the decking.

“I mean, it’s a nice set-up. The pavilion is already wired for electricity and sound. Did you notice the speakers up in the rafters? Must be hooked into the house’s audio, so I’m hoping you and the band can tap into that so we don’t have to run our own wiring down here.” He did a neat vault back over the railing and brushed his hands off. “It’s about a six-foot drop into the sea oats and saw grass, and I for one will be glad not to have to slog through it unrolling speaker wire, you know?”

“I’m with you there. I don’t know what kind of amplification they’ve got up at the house, but if the band doesn’t bring an amp with them, I’ve got one that will handle all the output we’ll need for this shindig.” He kept his eyes on Amanda while she and Zoe measured for the dance floor.

Amanda snapped the measuring tape shut and jotted down something in her notebook, then came over to join Dev and Jeff.

“Hi, Beautiful,” Jeff greeted her with a wink. “I hear you’re going to feed us all tonight.”

“Well, I’ve got to do something to pay you for all the help you’re giving us.”

The easy way Jeff called her beautiful set Dev’s teeth on edge. And the sparkle in Amanda’s eyes didn’t sit too well either. Could they be . . .? No. He couldn’t bear to think about it. Even if it would be good for her.

“Please change your mind and say you’ll join us,” Amanda coaxed, turning her warm, friendly gaze on him.

“Man, don’t miss out on her cooking,” Jeff encouraged him. “She can put some dynamite meals together.” He slung an arm over Zoe’s shoulders. “Unlike some other females I could name, who can’t make toast without burning it.”

So, Jeff had already eaten some of Amanda's home-cooked meals. How many? Dev knew he shouldn't, but when he opened his mouth, "Sure, I'll come. Sounds too good to pass up," came out in spite of his best intentions.

Amanda beamed at him. "Great. Oh, I'm so glad you changed your mind. We'll try to eat early so you have a chance to get in a couple hours of sleep before you have to work tonight."

"Nah. Sleep's overrated. Dinner with you beats a few hours in the sack any day." Unless, of course, she was in there with him. He held her gaze for a second, then turned to Jeff. "Let's get back to the house and check out the sound system."

"Yeah. Then we have to figure out where we're gonna park all those pricey cars."

They trooped back up the walkway to the main deck. Amanda asked Mrs. Wyndham where the sound system for the house was. She led them down a short hallway off the living room and into a media room furnished with theater seating and a huge projection screen. A small room at the back held a front-projection TV and the electronics for the audio system. Dev and Jeff were attracted like iron filings to a magnet and deep into audio-speak in thirty seconds.

Amanda and Zoe left the men to check out the sound system and went back outside.

"I know there's another driveway just a little further down the road from here," Amanda said. "The Wyndham's bought two pieces of property side-by-side when they decided to build here. I remember my dad talking about how one lot just wasn't big enough for Mrs. Wyndham's 'Grand Plan'."

They walked down the curved driveway and turned left to continue down the road. It dead-ended in a hundred yards or so, 'The Cottage' taking up most of the land ending at the tip of Blue Point Cove. A narrow, rutted driveway angled toward the water and another cottage, much like Amanda's, sat off to the side.

"They tore the house on the other property down so they could build theirs. As you can see, it took up most of this lot too. I remember they actually stayed in this little house while the big one was being built," Amanda reminisced.

"I bet that was a hoot." Zoe laughed.

They continued down the driveway and peeked in the window. White sheeting covered a few pieces of furniture, but most of the space was empty. The driveway disappeared around the side of the house and ended in front of a ramshackle shed almost completely overgrown with lantana vines and mossy plants.

"That must have been a garage in its better days," Zoe guessed.

"Or maybe a boat shed," Amanda added. She turned and went back around the house. "I think we could clear out enough space on either side of this driveway to park some cars. There are no big trees or shrubs, just a lot of vines and grasses. Once we get a weed-whacker in here and spread a few inches of mulch over the area, it ought to be good to go. At least for one night's parking."

Zoe dug through the ground cover with the toe of her boot to test the soil. "Feels pretty firm. As long as we don't have a week of rain right before the party, I think it'll do."

They walked back out to the road and turned toward the big house.

"So," Amanda said with studied casualness, "what do you think of Dev?"

"Woman, you need to snatch that man right up. He's a keeper." Zoe fanned herself. "And sexy as hell, too."

A little smile quirked Amanda's lips. "He's nice, isn't he?"

"Nice? He's nice? That's the best you can come up with?" Zoe huffed. "He's a fine specimen, and it's a damn shame he got injured like that. I bet he used to play a mean piano. Those long, slender, strong fingers and all." She slid a coy glance at Amanda. "Betcha those hands have *lots* of talent."

"Getting past the physical, which, I agree, is noteworthy, I'm glad you'll get to see what a genuinely nice guy he is at dinner tonight. You should see him at the radio station, Zoe. He's hired a bunch of veterans who all have some kind of problem and he's given them a place to work and recover without putting a lot of stress on them. They all worship him and he doesn't even know it."

"You seem pretty impressed yourself," Zoe commented, eyebrow arched.

"Don't read anything into it. I'm not . . . interested . . . in anything like that. And I don't want to fall in love again, anyway. Someday a fling, maybe, but no more love. I couldn't risk losing someone else I loved."

Zoe made a sad face. "Oh, honey, you don't want to spend the rest of your life alone? That would be a terrible waste. You'll feel differently in time. You'll see."

Amanda didn't bother contradicting her friend. Zoe wanted everyone to have a happily ever after, but that didn't happen in her life.

They walked back up the curving driveway to the house where Mrs. Wyndham was chatting with Dev and Jeff on the front porch. It was obvious she enjoyed the attention of two handsome males as she flashed a smile at one then the other.

"It appears these gentlemen have everything worked out as far as the music and lighting goes. I can see I made an excellent choice when I hired you and Zoe to manage this party," she said as Amanda and Zoe climbed the porch steps. "The Admiral will be pleased. He had plans to have the channel and approach to our dock dredged this spring but I made him wait until after the party. Who knows what kind of mess they'll leave behind, and I didn't want our guests having to deal with anything ugly or smelly on the big night.

Once he sees how professionally you're handling things, he'll finally stop grumbling about putting the dredging off."

"Why is he having the channel dredged?" Zoe asked.

Jeff looked smug and gave Mrs. Wyndham a little nudge with his elbow. "I bet your husband wants to buy a bigger boat."

"That's right" she said, rolling her eyes. "He said something about the draught not being deep enough for a fifty-eight foot Meridian. I'll admit the pictures he showed me are pretty but personally I think the boat we have is plenty big enough." She shrugged. "But then I'm not an Admiral who's used to being on battleships." She gave a resigned little chuckle. "At least we won't have to deal with that till the day after the party."

"Well, I think we have all the measurements we need for now, Mrs. Wyndham," Amanda said. "We will be hiring someone to clear the undergrowth on either side of the lane that goes back to the old house up the road. A few days before the party we'll spread a nice thick blanket of mulch there and use it to park your guests' cars."

"You won't need access to inside for anything else, then? Because we'll be going back to Annapolis the day after tomorrow and I wouldn't be able to come back for several weeks." Mrs. Wyndham glanced from one to the other of them for reassurance.

"No, I think we'll be fine," Amanda said. "I was hoping we could use the little house to store some things, though. The tables and chairs, some of the decorations and the carpeting will be delivered a week to ten days before the big event and that would be a perfect place to stash them till we start setting up. Would that be okay with you, Mrs. Wyndham?"

"I suppose so," she said after a little hesitation. Then her doubts seemed to vanish and she said brightly, "There's really nothing valuable in there. And it's not like I'm worried you'll make off with the family silver. Come inside,

Amanda, and I'll get you the key. You're right about it being an excellent staging area."

The other three waited on the porch as the afternoon shadows lengthened and the earlier warmth was dissipated by a brisk breeze off the bay.

Zoe shivered slightly. "Let's get going, Lover Boy," she said to Jeff. "I've a few things to do back at the gallery before dinner."

Jeff slipped on his leather jacket and made a mock bow. "Your chariot awaits, my Lady."

Zoe merely rolled her eyes.

"I'd be glad to drop you off if you'd be too cold on the bike," Dev offered.

But Jeff was quick to put a proprietary arm around Zoe's shoulders and walk her down the steps.

"No worries, mate. I like her to keep my back warm. We'll catch up with you at Amanda's later." He handed Zoe his helmet and swung his leg over the big bike. She took her place behind him and wrapped an arm around his waist.

"See you later," she said, the rest of her sentence drowned out by the noise as Jeff kicked the bike to life. She gave a little wave, then held on as they made a tight U-turn and sped off down the road.

"That girl has a lot more courage than I," Amanda said from behind Dev as she watched the pair disappear around a bend.

She'd retrieved her pea coat and satchel and tucked the key to the older house inside it.

"Let's hope there's enough time for you to give my car a jump," she said. "I want to get a new battery as quick as I can. Around here there isn't any public transportation to fall back on, so being car-less will be a major inconvenience."

He held her door as she got in, then went around to the driver's side. As she watched him climb into the driver's seat she realized she hadn't thought about his injury all afternoon. Hadn't even noticed it, really. She gave herself a mental pat on the back for not doing or saying anything that would bring attention to his injury.

"What are you smiling about?" He glanced over at her before he backed out of the driveway.

"Nothing." She shrugged her shoulders. "Just happy I guess."

"Happy? Even though your car's dead?"

"Oh, right." Her shoulders slumped a little. "But a new battery can't be all that expensive, can it?"

"Seventy to a hundred bucks," he replied.

"Oh." That would put a dent in this month's budget. So she'd better splurge on tonight's dinner because she'd be eating Ramen noodles for the next couple of weeks.

Not for the first time, she wished she'd asked Mrs. Wyndham for a larger deposit.

CHAPTER 11

"Well, it's not the battery," Dev concluded. He stood next to her car and leaned down to talk to her through the open window.

"Are you sure?" Amanda still sat behind the wheel of her Civic, her expression forlorn. "I mean . . ."

Dev knew what she was thinking. After all, he'd been a musician, not a mechanic.

"You mean, maybe I don't know how to jump-start a car."

Amanda started to protest.

"No, no. Don't apologize. I admit automobiles are not my strong suit, but I do know how to use a set of jumper cables. So it might be your starter that's gone bad. But no matter what it is, you're going to have to get it towed into town and have a mechanic check it out."

He turned off the engine in the Land Rover and detached the cables. She still hadn't budged. He opened the door and held out his good hand.

"Come on. Let's go inside and we'll call one of the service stations. Maybe they can come get it now and work on it first thing in the morning."

She sighed heavily and regarded him with those big soulful eyes.

"Come on," he coaxed, and she put her hand in his so he could help her out. The urge to pull her into his arms was so strong he almost succumbed, but managed to step back at the last second.

The afternoon breeze had picked up and the sun was setting behind a bank of dark red and purple clouds. He could feel the temperature dropping as the wind made little whorls in the sandy soil of the parking area. He shut the car door and followed her into the house.

It was almost as chilly inside as it was outdoors. Amanda turned on the two lamps in the living room then went to the kitchen and turned on the oven.

"I'm sorry about the temperature in here. This place has very poor insulation and the windows leak like sieves. The baseboard heaters are having a real struggle trying to keep up with the drafts, especially on a day like this when it's so windy."

"You've been living here all winter like this?"

"Yeah." She shrugged. "I planned on caulking around the windows and maybe buying another baseboard heater, but I . . ." She bit her lip.

"Don't know how to caulk windows or install baseboard heaters?"

"Well, that too, of course, but . . ." She paused again.

He silently kicked himself. No money. That was her problem. And she wasn't about to tell him her situation.

"It's not all that bad really. I layer up and wear a couple of pairs of socks to bed. If it gets too cold I turn on the oven and leave the door open for a little while. That usually helps a lot."

"And jacks up your electric bill." He unconsciously rubbed his hands together.

A tiny line appeared between her brows as she worried her bottom lip. "I'm so sorry. I was hoping it wouldn't be so cold tonight, but I do understand if you don't want to stay for dinner and risk frostbite." She tried to smile but still seemed miserable.

"Don't be ridiculous. You can't get rid of me that easily. I was promised a delicious dinner and I intend to collect." He followed her over to the kitchen area. "I've spent nights in a tent in the desert that were much colder than this."

Shit. He clamped his mouth shut and cursed silently. He definitely did not want the conversation to go there.

The silence seemed to solidify into a wall between them and he was helpless to stop it.

Amanda turned from washing her hands at the sink and picked up a towel to dry them.

"It's okay. We don't have to talk about that. Believe me, I understand. My fiancé was over there. In Iraq." Her voice hitched ever so slightly. "There were lots of things he didn't want to talk about either. I imagine it's hard to find anything about war that's easy to talk about to a civilian."

Worse and worse. Nerves chilled his blood and his shiver had nothing to do with the room's temperature. He didn't want to talk about Danny, but how could he ignore a reference to a fiancé without at least making some comment?

"Your fiancé is in the Army?"

Jesus, he hated this. Lying to her was almost as bad as telling her the truth would be.

"*Was* in the Army. Danny was killed in Iraq last year."

Amanda went to the refrigerator and got out the chicken tenders for dinner. She kept her back toward him while she delivered this news as matter-of-factly as possible. He winced at the sadness in her voice.

"I'm so sorry."

The understatement of the century. Could he really have said something so mundane considering the guilt that was eating him alive? He wanted to tell her how truly terrible it was—the loss of his best friend, who also happened to be her fiancé— but couldn't even imagine the words that could accurately express the depth of his despair, let alone work up the courage it would take to say them out loud.

Amanda glanced over as she took a frying pan from the drawer below the oven. "Thank you. Danny was a wonderful man. I wish you could have met him. You would have liked him, I'm sure."

He had absolutely nothing to say to that.

She put a frying pan on the stove and drizzled some olive oil in the bottom then crushed a few cloves of garlic into the pan and turned on the burner. While it was heating, she sprinkled the chicken tenders with salt and pepper.

He could only watch her, afraid to say anything as the silence lengthened in this conversation filled with potential land mines.

She dragged a stool over to the counter that separated the kitchen from the rest of the room.

"You're welcome to sit here or"—she gave him a brief smile—"you can help, if you want."

"I'll help," he said, grateful she was not going to make a big deal out of his protracted silence. He went to the sink and washed his hands, then used the same damp towel to dry them.

"What can I do?"

"How about opening some wine? There are two bottles of Cabernet in the fridge. They both need to come out and breathe, so that would be a big help." She searched in a drawer till she found the cork pull and handed it to him.

He retrieved the bottles from the refrigerator and used his pocket knife to peel the lead foil from the top of the first one.

"What did you think of Mrs. Wyndham?" Amanda asked, obviously wanting to get their conversation back to lighter ground.

"She seems like a nice enough lady," he answered. "Younger than I expected, considering it's a seventy-fifth birthday party for her husband."

"Yeah, that surprised me too at first. She's very, um, polished."

"I'm sure she spends lots of money to keep that shine too," he agreed. He glanced over and caught the twitch of Amanda's mouth as she tried to smother her laugh.

"Between you and Jeff, I'm sure she had a hard time deciding which handsome hunk she should flirt with the most." Amanda's eyes were full of mischief. "Her eyelash flutters were on overdrive."

"Yeah, Jeff can have all of her attention as far as I'm concerned. Maybe he can talk her into becoming his patron. You know, support him until his sculptures make it big?" He smiled as he extracted the cork from the first bottle with a pop.

"You can pour that into this," she said as she reached up to get a carafe out of the cabinet by the sink.

"Here, I can get that," he offered as the sight of her on tiptoes reaching for the top shelf gave him a distracting view of her slender torso, with her ample breasts outlined nicely in the black turtleneck.

As he reached over her to get the carafe, she turned to say something and wound up plastered against his chest, her lips inches from his and those perfect orbs crushed against him. In the two nano-seconds it took before she jerked back, his blood went from chilled to full boil.

"Sorry."

"Sorry."

The simultaneity of their apologies had Amanda calling, "Jinx! You owe me a Coke," to cover the awkward moment.

Dev didn't keep the heat out of his eyes when he replied, "Let me know when you want to collect."

Her fair complexion couldn't hide the flush that climbed her neck and stained her cheeks. She turned back to the stove more than a little flustered and added the chicken to the frying pan.

Dev decanted the wine and poured two glasses, bringing one over to her at the stove. "Here, the cook should always have a glass while she's working. It's only fair."

"Oh, thanks, but I really shouldn't. By the time I have one with dinner too, I'll be too buzzed to be sensible." She sat the glass on the counter.

"Well, you don't have to drive." He winked as she gave him a rueful glare. "And the day's work is done, you're safe at home, dinner's well on its way"—he shrugged—"so you don't have to be sensible." He picked the glass up and handed it back to her.

She took it with a laugh. "Okay, but if I start acting silly, it will be your fault."

"I take full responsibility." He clinked their glasses together and held her gaze as they each sipped. The room had warmed considerably, and not from the heat the stove was giving off either.

Amanda handed him a large pot with instructions to fill it two-thirds full of water and put on the back burner. While he did that, she turned on the radio and the sound of The Beach Boys' "Wouldn't It Be Nice" filled the room. She added a little salt to the pot, covered it, and turned up the heat. When she turned from the stove to get the box of pasta on the counter, they collided again.

"This kitchen is not meant for two cooks," she said with a laugh. "Why don't you set the table while I finish getting this casserole into the oven."

As he carried place mats and silverware to the small table, there was a knock on the front door followed by Zoe's boisterous entrance.

"Hi, guys, we're here," she chirped. When she saw them, she grinned. "What a charmingly domestic scene. I see you're training him already, Mandy. Good job!"

Jeff came in behind her and stashed his helmet, gloves, and jacket in the corner by the love seat. He regarded Dev and shook his head sadly.

"Don't let her do it, man. Us guys have to stick together." He nodded at the handful of knives and forks in Dev's hand. "Zoe can do that. It's woman's work. Right, Sweet Cheeks?"

"In your dreams, Lover Boy," Zoe scoffed. "I'd advise you to watch closely and take notes."

"You wound me, Babe," Jeff put both hands over his heart. "You know I'm always willing to help out at your place."

"Yeah, as long as it involves a hammer or saw. Dishes are a whole different ballgame." She softened her criticism with a brief kiss to Jeff's cheek, then turned her attention to Dev, who had finished laying out the plates, glasses, and silver. "Could I trouble you for a glass of the red, my good man? Riding on the back of the death cycle has not only chilled me to the bone, it's given me a powerful thirst."

Dev complied, and Zoe accepted the glass, then took his hand and led him over to the love seat, tugging him down until he sat beside her.

"So, tell me, Dev, what's it like to own a radio station?" She took a big swallow of the dark ruby liquid. "I bet it must be really cool. Do you get to pick what songs everyone plays, or just the ones on your show? Do you like working the night shift? I would think that sucks because not that many people are listening to you in the middle of the night, right? Amanda really likes the music you play, but I have to admit I'm more of a country music fan, myself. You won't hold that against me, will you?"

Her questions and comments followed one after the other without leaving him a second to reply, which was fine since he wasn't prepared to answer most of them anyway. He managed to get in a, "No, of course not," as she stopped for another swallow of wine and that appeared to satisfy her.

Meanwhile, Jeff had sauntered to the kitchen and stood looking over Amanda's shoulder as she worked at the stove. "Mmm, smells delicious, Beautiful. How much longer before we can eat?"

Dev resisted the urge to go over and tell Jeff the kitchen wasn't big enough for two, when Amanda shooed him away like he was a wayward puppy.

"Twenty minutes till dinner, so go sit down and stop harassing the cook," she scolded. "Dev, would you be a sweetie and get this poor, hungry man a glass of wine while I finish up in here?"

She leaned around Jeff and gave him a conspiratorial smile and if there had been any doubt in his mind before, that smile sealed his fate. He was doomed to love her forever.

"Excuse me," he murmured to Zoe and quickly got to his feet, which probably didn't touch the floor as he crossed to the counter and poured a glass of wine for the other man.

She'd called him *sweetie*. He knew it was just a slip, not really an endearment she actually meant. Still, his heart swelled to twice its size, and he had trouble breathing with it lodged so firmly in his throat.

"Thanks, Dude." Jeff took the glass and went to sit next to Zoe.

Dev could only nod, afraid to speak and have his voice crack like a teenager's. He went over to Amanda and topped off her glass, although not much had been consumed.

"Thanks." She opened the oven door and slipped the casserole in. "Let's go sit down. We've got twenty minutes to kill before dinner." She went in ahead of him and sat in one of the armchairs that faced the love seat. He took the other.

"Cheers," she said, holding her glass out and they all followed suit, clinking happily. "Anyone have any problems they thought of since we left the Wyndham's?" She glanced from Jeff to Dev. "You two are satisfied with the electronics, the amp and speakers?"

Dev spoke up, this being his bailiwick. "As you might expect, the Admiral has a top-notch set up as far as the sound system goes. I don't foresee any problems in that area but I'll bring a spare amplifier and sub-woofer as a back-up just in case."

Jeff was nodding in agreement. "Yeah, we did a little test. Cranked up the volume and went down to the pavilion to make sure the speakers down there were still in good condition." He sat back with a very self-satisfied smile on his face.

Dev did his best to keep a straight face, but as Amanda peered from Jeff to him and back, he knew they'd have to come clean.

"Dare I ask what music you used for the test, gentlemen?" Amanda asked softly.

Jeff threw himself on the grenade, which was only fair since the song was his choice, and mumbled, "'The Boys Are Back in Town.'"

Zoe sat up as though she'd been stung by a bee. "Thin Lizzy's 'The Boys Are Back in Town'?"

"That's the one," Jeff confirmed.

"Seriously?" Amanda echoed faintly, expecting Dev to deliver the punchline to this bad joke.

He nodded, pressing his lips together to keep his grin from escaping. "We didn't play it all that loud," he added hastily, glad his voice came out in its normal timbre. "We told Mrs. Wyndham we used it because it tested the complete range of the speakers. She was fine with it, Amanda. Really."

Jeff was nodding enthusiastically. "Absolutely. That old broad's hipper than you'd think."

Zoe smacked him hard enough on his arm to cause the wine to slosh dangerously in his glass. "First, don't call any woman an 'old broad'. And second, what if she hadn't been 'hip' as you so anachronistically put it. She could have been annoyed enough to send us all packing, you idiot."

"Yeah, but she didn't. So chill, Babe. She loved us, right, Dev?"

"She did seem fairly enamored with the two of them," Amanda noted.

Zoe tsked at Dev. "And here I thought your maturity would have a stabilizing influence on Jeff, but I can see leaving you two alone together merely doubles the chance of trouble."

"No, Babe, you've got us all wrong," Jeff protested. "I think we make a pretty good team. Don't you agree, Dev?"

A quick glance and Dev caught a glimpse of the serious man Jeff tried so hard to camouflage with his flippant behavior. The jokes, the flirting, the cocky attitude were all a front to protect the sensitive soul of the artist that lived inside.

"Absolutely," Dev agreed. "As a matter of fact, we worked so well together today I wanted to ask you to give me a hand with another project I'm considering."

"Yeah? Well, hell, man, let's get together and talk about it." Jeff dug in his jeans and came up with a crumpled receipt, which he smoothed over his knee. "Babe, you got a pen in that suitcase you call a purse?"

"I'm sure I've got one in the office," Amanda offered.

"Not necessary," Zoe said, and produced a pen from her over-sized purse with the practiced ease of a magician materializing a rabbit.

"She's something else, isn't she?" Jeff threw his arm around her and hauled her up against him for a quick kiss. "Thanks, Babe."

"Stop that!" Zoe slapped at him ineffectually. "What is the matter with you!"

Jeff ignored her and scribbled his phone number down on the paper then handed it to Dev. "I tend to work late and sleep late, so afternoons are best for me. Call me anytime after eleven a.m. Will that work for you?"

"Perfectly. I'll call you in the next couple of days. This needs to get done soon."

No way was Amanda living in this cracker box without decent heat and insulation for even one more week. Danny would have killed him for letting her live like this.

Dinner went well, Amanda thought, as she sipped her second glass of wine. Dev seemed to relax and even enjoy himself once Zoe and Jeff had arrived. He and Jeff hit it off much better than she expected and Zoe had nudged her leg under the table several times—especially when Dev offered to help her clean up or poured her more wine. For the first time in several weeks, Amanda was confident enough about the preparations for the party that she could relax and enjoy the company of her friends.

She felt she could call Dev a friend now, glad the awkward moment when she told him about Danny hadn't made him retreat back into his shell. Too bad he and Danny had never met. They would have become good friends she was sure. Too bad . . . She felt the sting of tears behind her eyes and blinked rapidly to force them back. When she glanced across the table she found Dev's eyes on her, his own shadowed with pain. He appeared strangely attuned to her moods. Or maybe she'd just imagined that. After all, she certainly wasn't the only one who had reason to be sad. She forced a smile. "Who's interested in dessert?"

Jeff groaned and rubbed his stomach. "I made a complete pig of myself with that casserole. I don't have room for anything else." Zoe shook her head. "No thanks. I've had twice my allotment of calories for the week in that cheese sauce."

"Oh, right. Like you have to worry," Amanda scoffed.

"All the same, I'm going to pass on dessert."

"How about some coffee? There's always room for that." She pushed her chair back from the table. "I can have a pot ready in a couple of minutes."

"Not for me," Zoe declined. "If I have coffee this late I'll be up half the night."

"I could use some," Dev chuckled, "For the exact same reason." He stood up as well and started to clear the plates from the table.

Behind his back, Zoe gave Amanda two thumbs-up.

"I'll take you up on one cup," Jeff said. "I'll be up working for hours yet, anyway." He took his cue from Dev and began picking up dishes.

Amanda intercepted him. "I appreciate the help, Jeff, but there just isn't enough room in there for three of us. Why don't you and Zoe go sit down on the sofa, and I'll bring the coffee in there when it's ready."

"Yeah, I've pretty much got this anyway," Dev said, then promptly dropped the silverware he'd been gathering onto the floor.

For one second everyone froze. Then Zoe started back across the room. Jeff blocked her with his arm and gave a quick negative shake of his head. She watched Amanda and saw that she had ignored the incident and was busily spooning coffee grounds into the basket of the coffee maker.

"At least it wasn't anything breakable." Dev picked up the utensils and took them to the sink. "Sorry," he mumbled.

"No biggie." She turned and handed him the cream and sugar—both in ceramic containers. "Could you take these in and put them on the coffee table for me, please?"

He seemed startled but carefully slipped his left index finger through the handle of the cream pitcher and held the sugar bowl in his right.

"Thanks." She turned back to the coffee maker to fill the reservoir with water. In a few seconds, he was back. She pointed to the other cabinet. "Mugs are in there. We'll only need three since Zoe is passing."

This time he didn't move till she looked him in the eye. She would swear his eyes were lighter green than she'd ever seen them. There were little crinkles at the corners. His lips barely moved but hinted at the beginnings of a smile. She felt her own twitch in response. He held his silence for so long she finally gave in.

"What?" She threw her hands up and tried to sound exasperated. He still didn't reply, but went to the cupboard and got the mugs, then set them carefully on the counter next to the coffee maker.

"You're something else, you know that?"

He'd copied the phrase Jeff used and for a moment she thought he might follow up with the same gesture—pulling her in for a quick kiss. But instead he stood there, a pleased smile on his face, until she had to say something before she turned pink as a cooked lobster.

"Well, if you thought you'd get out of helping by dropping a few things, you're sadly mistaken. I'm expecting you to dry when I wash these dishes."

She had no intention of letting him do that, of course. She'd clean up after they'd all gone home, but she liked the real smile that turned his classically sculpted mouth into a work of art.

"I don't have a tray, so you take the mugs and I'll bring the coffee pot."

They settled back with their coffee and Dev picked up the framed photo of her and her dad that sat on the end table nearest him.

"Is this you and your dad?"

"Yeah. I think I was ten when that photo was taken."

Dev cleared his throat. "You've, um, changed so much I don't think I'd recognize you if I hadn't seen you since then."

"Yep, I was definitely ugly duckling material in junior high. Braces and glasses with lenses as thick as Coke bottle bottoms. And it got worse before it got better, too. By the time I was thirteen I had shot up to five-six but still only weighed about ninety pounds. Skinny and tall with those braces on my teeth? You could have used me for an antenna."

They all laughed.

"Nice to see you made the same transition as the Ugly Duckling," Dev commented. "I bet by the time you graduated from high school you were beating the boys off with a stick."

"Danny carried the stick back then. He was always my defender. Even during the 'Ugly Duckling' period. By graduation I couldn't think about any other guy but him."

No one spoke for a moment or two. Then Amanda set her mug down. "Listen, we have to be able to talk about Danny without worrying that I'll burst into tears. I loved him. I'll always love him. I can't let the fact that he died keep me from remembering all the wonderful things he did and what a special person he was. I don't want to forget those things that made me fall in love with him. I want to celebrate them and be able to talk about them with you. So don't walk on eggshells around me when his name comes up in conversation. I can handle it."

"OK, Beautiful, you got it," Jeff said with a wink, as Zoe nodded in agreement.

"Dev, I realize you didn't know him, and when I mentioned earlier that he was killed in Iraq I know you were uncomfortable. Sorry to drop such serious stuff on you the first time you're around us," Amanda apologized. "Don't let it scare you off. We're usually a lot more fun."

Dev gave a nod. "I think your attitude is amazing, and I can bet Danny would be proud to see how you honor his memory. It's no wonder he loved you."

You wouldn't think I was so amazing if you knew how often I've cried myself to sleep the past eight months.

"All right. I said no doom and gloom, and I meant it. Who needs a refill?" She picked up the pot.

"I can use a little more caffeine before I go," Dev said, offering his mug for more.

"Not for me, thanks." Jeff drained his mug. "What do you say, Sweet Cheeks? Time for you to say goodnight?"

Zoe nodded. "What are you going to do about transportation tomorrow, Mandy? Do you have client appointments you need to get to?"

"No. Lucky for me I have plenty of work I can do right here tomorrow." She tilted her head in Dev's direction, indicating that work belonged to him. "But, if they fix my car by tomorrow afternoon, I'll need a ride into town so I can pick it up."

"Just call me," Dev offered. "I'll be glad to give you a lift into town. I have a couple of errands I can do after I drop you off."

"Great. Thanks."

"And my earlier offer to give you a ride home still holds, Zoe. It's gotten pretty chilly outside. Do you still want to brave the cold on the back of Jeff's bike?"

Jeff's head was down as he collected his jacket and gloves from the floor beside the love seat, but his hands stilled as he waited for Zoe's reply. The scowl he gave Dev from under his brows clearly said he didn't appreciate the gesture. Amanda suppressed a smile as Jeff silently staked his "no trespassing" sign and Dev just as silently indicated he understood with a barely noticeable nod.

"Thanks, Dev, but I like to leave with the fella I came with. That's what my mom always taught me. I'll be fine, but I appreciate the offer."

"No problem." He stood and shook hands with Jeff. "It was nice to meet you, Jeff, I'll be in touch with you soon."

"Same here, Dev. See ya."

"Drive safe, you two," Armada called as the pair settled themselves on Jeff's bike. She closed the door with a shiver as they sped off into the darkness.

Dev was over at the radio turning the volume up. "I hope you don't mind. Isn't this is one of your favorite songs?"

"My Funny Valentine" was playing.

"Yeah, I requested it a few weeks ago. It was my dad's song for me when I was in the 'Ugly Duckling' stage."

"I remember." He walked over and put his arms out. "Want to dance?"

She thought she should refuse but the music and the wine made her foolish and sentimental. She stepped into his arms. He drew her in until she fit against him perfectly, then he began to move her effortlessly around the open space in the center of the room. She felt a sense of completeness and joy she hadn't felt in years. She gave herself up to the music and clung to Dev, their bodies swaying together to the familiar song.

The music ended, and she smiled up at him. "Thank you. That was lovely. You're a marvelous dancer." She deliberately stepped out of the circle of his arms.

"The pleasure was mine, Ma'am," he said very formally with a slight bow and they both laughed.

"We shall have to do it again sometime, Sir," she replied with the same formality and a mock curtsy. She tried to dial back the lingering sense of intimacy their dancing had created to something . . . friendlier, less intense. But she couldn't ignore the faint tingling that covered every inch of skin that had been in contact with his.

Then she caught sight of the kitchen clock over his shoulder.

"Oh my gosh. It's almost ten o'clock. You're not going to have time to sleep at all before you have to be at work. I'm so sorry. The time just got away from me."

"Don't worry, it's not a problem."

"Oh, but, Dev—"

"Really, I'll be fine."

He tucked a tendril of hair behind her ear and chucked her under the chin. "Believe me, there are lots of days I don't get much sleep before going on the air. I wouldn't have traded one minute of today for an hour of sleep."

"That's so sweet of you to say but I wish there was something I could do—"

"To make up for lost sleep? I don't think there's much you can do about that. I am going to have to use your bathroom before I go, though."

"Of course. Straight down the hall." She pointed to the short hallway the led to the bedrooms.

"Thanks."

She watched him all the way down the hall, aware of how well his butt filled out his pants, of how his broad shoulders tapered so nicely to slim hips and long legs. Aware of sensations she hadn't felt for a long time. Then she concentrated very hard on remembering Danny exactly as he was the last time she saw him. She took the coffee mugs to the kitchen sink, turned on the hot water, and added some liquid detergent.

A few minutes later Dev was back, offering to dry the dishes she had started to wash.

"Don't be ridiculous. You're not doing dishes."

"I distinctly remember you telling me I had to dry the dishes."

"Well, I changed my mind. I don't want you to be late for work."

He laughed. "It's not a problem. The boss and I are like this." He held up two fingers tightly together.

"Regardless. No dish drying for you." She dried her hands and led him to the door.

"You'll call me tomorrow if you need a ride?"

"I will, I promise. Thank you for rescuing me today." She leaned up and kissed him on the cheek. "You're my knight-in-shining-armor."

"Thanks for dinner." His eyes glimmered like emeralds in firelight.

She thought he was about to say something else but he turned away and crossed the porch to the steps. There he hesitated, then spun around and came back, flung open the screen door, and drew her into his arms. He gazed down at her for one endless second with such heat all she could think of was how her grill sounded when the match was struck and then—*whoosh*—they both went up in flames.

His fingers threaded through her hair and his mouth came down on hers, hot, firm, demanding. Leaving no doubt that complete possession was his goal.

She couldn't remember why she knew this was a bad idea, dangerous even. There were reasons, good reasons, that she shouldn't be doing this.

Unfortunately reasons required thought and thought was beyond her at the moment.

Right now there was only the length of Dev's body, all flat planes and hard muscle that rippled under her hands and met her softness and curves in a perfect match. The feel of his erection pressed against her belly and the heat of his tongue as he licked his way into her mouth made her knees weak. The softness of the hair at the nape of his neck under her fingers and the feel of his arms tightening around her crowded out logical thoughts. Right now there was only feeling. Sensations so heightened it was like the difference between black-and-white and color. She hung on and absorbed it all.

When oxygen starvation forced them apart, her legs were too weak to support her. If Dev hadn't had his arms wrapped around her, she would have slid to the floor in a boneless heap.

He picked her up, kicked the door closed behind him, and carried her into her bedroom. Enough light filtered down the hall from the kitchen to let him find the bed and lay her on it.

She looked up at him, his pupils wide and black, his dark hair falling over his forehead. Other than the sounds of passion, neither had said a word since he thanked her for dinner. She reached up to brush his hair back and he closed his eyes at her touch.

Then he stroked her cheek gently with a fingertip and let his head fall forward, his wayward hair hiding his eyes. In a voice harsh with regret he ground out, "I can't do this."

Ten seconds later, her front door slammed again and he was gone.

CHAPTER 12

Dev drove with all the windows down, hoping the cold air would cool him off and deflate his raging hard-on. So far that plan failed miserably.

Was he nuts? Or just a fool?

A despicable opportunist, more likely. Worse than a seventeen-year-old with no self-control.

He berated himself all the way to the radio station. Told himself he had no business starting anything like this with Amanda. Listed every reason he should back off, starting with Danny, his promise, his own shortcomings—to say nothing of the fact she worked for him, and was still in a very vulnerable place while she came to grips with Danny's death.

Every time he got to the end of that list, his mind did an instant replay of that single second that had stretched to infinity before he kissed her. Etched forever in his memory, he saw her eyes first widen in surprise then soften and dilate when she accepted what was going to happen. The soft intake of her breath when acceptance became desire and her eyes went molten silver as she watched him lower his mouth to hers.

When he carried her to her bedroom, his need to bury himself in her sweet heat blinded him to all reason. She was willing—more than willing—to let him touch her, taste her, love her—and he wanted to pleasure her until she cried his name as she exploded in his arms.

If only he hadn't seen that picture of Danny on her dresser. The one *he'd* taken. On their first tour in Iraq. Danny standing under the only tree for miles around, wanting to send Amanda a picture that didn't show any of the dirt, destruction, and desolation that surrounded them every day. Dev had told him some stupid joke to make him laugh while he snapped that picture.

He'd looked down at Amanda and felt his heart clench in despair.

If she had been surprised when he'd pulled her into his arms, she must have been astounded when he pulled out of hers.

Hurt.

Confused.

Relieved?

Maybe that too. He hadn't waited long enough to find out, knowing he couldn't explain his own reasons for going.

Christ, what a mess he'd made. Work was going to be hell tonight. *Please, God, keep the callers on the request line to a minimum.* He wasn't sure he'd be able to do mindless banter over the airwaves with his mind and heart a tangled mess of guilt and desire. He walked down the hall to the studio mentally preparing himself for the eight-hour shift ahead.

Andy was standing at the mike doing his wrap-up. A set of ear buds dangled around his neck, the cord snaking its way across his chest and into his shirt pocket where his own iPod held the music he preferred—heavy metal.

Dev entered the booth and closed the door quietly behind him. He watched Andy hit the button that started the news feed—right on time—and flip the switch that killed the mike.

"You're late tonight, Boss. Had me worried there for a few."

Dev had a reputation for arriving early for his shifts. He didn't have all that much going on in his life and oversleeping was never an issue.

"What? You were worried you'd have to stay a few extra minutes to cover for me? You got a hot date waiting for you?"

"Yeah, right. That's gonna happen." Andy snorted a laugh. "A few minutes or a few hours, it's no problem.

There's only a beer, a computer, and a few Grand Theft Auto missions waiting for me at home." He paused and added casually, "I just thought you might have been tied up with some . . . thing and lost track of time."

He finished stacking the CDs from his shift, missing Dev's scrutiny, and took them over to the bookcases to return to their assigned slots.

"Nope. Just had to stop for gas on the way in. Hadn't realized I was so low," Dev lied. At least at this point the bulge in his pants had subsided enough not to give him away.

Somehow everything that concerned Amanda required him to lie, and he hated it. It was his own fault for not telling her the truth right from the beginning. Because one lie had inevitably led to another and then another and the weight of all those lies was adding up to a giant boulder that was going to crush the life out of him when she found out the truth. He shoved his worries to the back of his mind—where they would stew until the next time he tried to sleep—and concentrated on the job at hand.

He was glad to see that his recent lecture on keeping the broadcast booth tidy was having its desired effect on Andy. Still, the kid was acting a little strange tonight. He hoped this wasn't some symptom he should recognize. Andy's PTSD seemed to be the most well-controlled of all his employees. He tended to be sloppy, though, and Dev wouldn't mind it if he upped his personal hygiene a notch or two, but those were fairly minor issues. He saw a psychologist regularly, which was more than Dev could say for himself.

He settled in front of the microphone with the first few CDs he'd use if no caller rang in on the request line.

"Thanks for cleaning up, Andy. See you tomorrow."

"Want me to bring you a cup of coffee on my way out?"

"No thanks. I've had a couple of cups already. I'm good to go."

"Okay then, good night, Boss."

Dev nodded as he flipped the switch on the mike and began his usual intro. The call-board lit up immediately with a request for "Cheek to Cheek" and as he queued it up he took two more calls.

Andy flipped open his phone and punched in Mike's number. "Mike? You listening?" he said without preamble.

"To the boss? Yeah. Been catching the request hour ever since Rosemary gave me the heads-up. Why? You got news? Something more substantial to go on than just the music the guy's been playing the past few weeks?"

"Oh yeah. Rosemary was right. Dev just got in a few minutes before he was due to go on. I thought for a minute he might actually be late," Andy marveled, recalling the numerous memos Dev had sent concerning arriving at work in plenty of time for the hand-off between announcers to go smoothly. "When he came into the booth it wasn't his after-shave I smelled. It was Amanda's perfume, or whatever she wears that makes her smell so damn good. I don't think he even realized his hair was kinda messed up either," Andy cackled.

"All right," Mike exclaimed, and Andy visualized the fist-pump that went with his tone. "That's good news. The boss deserves a dynamite lady like her."

"Yeah, you got that right. Well, keep listening. I suspect tonight's show will be even more interesting than usual. And pass the word, okay?"

"Will do. Thanks for the call."

Andy snapped his phone shut and started his pick-up, his grin widening as he left the station's parking lot. Hot damn. About time one of them got lucky around this home for the lost and unloved—and Dev deserved it more than any of them.

Dev hadn't wanted to be busy but maybe it was a good thing to be distracted from the jumble of mixed emotions ricocheting through his beleaguered brain.

Little by little, the music got to him, as it usually did. Music had always been his refuge, his inspiration in tough times, his celebration in good ones. It was an integral part of his being and even now—when he couldn't play the notes himself—it was still there, his heartbeat echoing its rhythms, the melodies every bit as vital as the air he breathed.

No wonder he loved the music of this era. The songs were actual stories, celebrating the wonder of new love, the tragedies of love lost, and everything in-between. Lyrics you could understand set to music that made your body move in spite of your best intentions to stay still. None of those three-word phrases repeated twenty times in a row and that passed for a song nowadays, or lyrics so mumbled you couldn't understand them without reading the liner notes.

His callers were building themes with their choice of songs—playing on the previous selection's words or sentiment. Whether that was intentional or just coincidence, Dev went with it, the same way he'd treated Amanda's requests in the past. He wondered if she was listening now or too angry with him to keep the radio tuned to his station.

When a caller requested "A Kiss to Build a Dream On", he cued up Louis Armstrong's version and let the raspy voice lay the groundwork for the next few selections.

His next caller was a woman who obviously knew her music and was happy to stay in theme. Very specific about the version, she asked for Vera Lynn singing "I Had the Craziest Dream," and Dev searched for the forties singer n his database. His listeners were reminding him of tunes he hadn't played for quite a while, and yet were somehow perfect for his mood tonight.

He faded Vera out and faded in Tommy Dorsey's orchestra playing "Imagination" with a young Sinatra giving the lyrics his perfect timing and impeccable phrasing.

Yep, there was no denying that dreaming, crazy, and imagination had a lot to do with Dev's feelings for Amanda.

He was not only crazy about her but crazy for imagining his dreams could go anywhere but down the drain as soon as he told her the truth. He had a hard time imagining what he was going to say to Amanda about his abrupt departure tonight when the call board lit up again.

"Thanks for calling Dev's Dream Machine. Do you have a request?"

"I have two of them actually," the slightly husky voice whispered over the phone.

He stood up abruptly, raking his hand through his hair.

"Amanda. Hi."

Stellar response, Dev.

He hadn't believed she would call, so he was completely at a loss for words—not a good thing in a deejay. Thank God he didn't take these calls 'live' on the air.

"Amanda, I'm so sorry to bolt out of there the way I did," he began, still not sure where he was going with this apology.

"Let's be honest, Dev," she murmured.

A tight fist squeezed his heart. *Honest. Yeah. Sure. That would work. Suicide by truth. But not over the telephone while he was on the air.*

"If you had kissed me one more time, we both know you would never have made it to work tonight. That wouldn't be the kind of precedent a boss should set, don't you agree?"

He did a mental double-take, afraid he had misunderstood. Ever the glib conversationalist, he replied, "Uh . . ."

"So, I repeat, I have two requests. Is it okay to have two?"

"Absolutely." There, he had actually said a real word.

"Oh, good. Well the first request is for you to play 'My Dreams Are Getting Better All the Time'."

"All right." Two words this time. He was on a roll.

"And the second request is for you to have breakfast with me tomorrow morning."

His heart started to pound. The blood rushing south left him dizzy and he fell into his chair, still struggling with speech. He took several deep breaths, then savagely squashed the small seed of hope threatening his sanity.

"You know we need to talk, Dev. You can't pretend it never happened. I'm not sure I want to pretend it never happened. So we need to talk, don't you think?"

Her voice got fainter and more hesitant with each word—like she had second thoughts about the wisdom of this call—and he finally found his own voice with the urgency to reassure her it hadn't been a mistake.

"Yes, we need to talk, and, yes, I will be at your house for breakfast this morning. And, yes, I will try my damnedest not to ravish you on your kitchen counter before we eat. But it's going to be a close thing, Amanda. A very close thing," he warned her.

"Maybe we should go out for breakfast."

The breathlessness of her response had him wishing he was with her right now to kiss her senseless and finish what he had started earlier. *Get a grip, ass-hat. You shouldn't be laying a finger on her, let alone contemplating what it would feel like to be buried inside her.*

"No. Not necessary. I'll be happy just to share another meal with you, Amanda. I'll be there at eight-thirty, is that okay?" That would give him time to go home, shower, and change after he ended his shift at seven.

"Perfect, Dev. See you then."

She hung up, and he sat, stunned, sure that the last five minutes had been a figment of his overheated imagination.

He'd fallen so hard, so fast, his conscience had deserted him. His judgment was totally overwhelmed by the warmth in her eyes, the sound of her laughter, the gentleness of her touch. He debated calling her back and canceling. He should find some excuse to stay away, because he sure as hell shouldn't be going.

The quiet finally penetrated the whirlwind of emotions spinning around in his head and he realized there had been several seconds of dead air. He'd made the worst rookie mistake in the broadcasting business, and one he constantly warned his employees against. He quickly grabbed a CD from the stack and scanned the play list as he dropped it into the player. The air left his lungs in a long, slow exhale as he dragged his hand through his hair. The music never lied. The first notes of "The Very Thought of You" floated over the airwaves toward Amanda while he got her request ready to go.

If she wanted only to talk, they'd talk. If she wanted anything more, he wouldn't hesitate and debate ethics with his better half. He knew there'd be no cottages and white picket fences in his future. No years full of good night kisses or mornings when he woke with Amanda's warm body snugged up against him.

So he'd take whatever she offered now and store the memories to warm the long, cold, lonely, rest of his life.

Amanda gave up the idea of sleep around four a.m. and opted for a shower to clear her head. She'd tossed and turned all night after her phone call to Dev, alternately berating herself for being fickle and faithless to Danny's memory then forgiving herself for succumbing to the lust that'd arced through her the moment Dev's mouth took possession of hers. She was certainly no saint but hated to think of herself as a slut either.

Standing under the hot spray, she took refuge in her normal problem-solving routine. Visualizing a white board on the tiles she began listing the pros and cons of having sex with Dev MacMurphy.

The Pros:

One. (The most important point first): It was, after all, just sex. It bore no relationship to the love she'd had—still had—always would have—for Danny.

Two. She wasn't going to give up sex for the rest of her life, just love. Her love had proved deadly to both recipients, so she wouldn't risk it again.

But she wasn't about to enter a convent either.

Three. Unrelieved sexual tension clouded one's judgment, made sleeping difficult if not impossible, and caused a certain amount of bitchiness to spill over into other unrelated activities.

Four. Dev was a smoking-hot combination of classic good looks, a body that wouldn't quit, pheromones that sent her senses reeling and kisses that rated a thousand on a scale of one to ten.

Five. He wasn't married and had no significant other (of which she was aware, anyway).

Six. He definitely wanted her.

Seven. She definitely wanted him.

Eight. See Number Six. Etc.

She squirted shampoo into the palm of her hand and began to lather her hair, the faint scent of lilacs rising on the steam surrounding her.

The Cons:

One. She still missed Danny terribly.

Two. She and Dev had a business relationship that could become awkward if they became lovers.

Three. Dev had his own issues concerning his injuries.

Four. Would he be unable to see this relationship as it really was? i.e. Two people taking what comfort they could find in each other's bodies. (See Number One under Pros) Because she could not, would not, allow him to believe there might be something more.

Five. Would he think she was too easy, leaping into bed with him so soon after her fiancé's death?

She rinsed her hair, and as she stepped out of the shower she realized this line of thought had made her wet in areas the shower spray didn't reach. It also made some parts of her body particularly sensitive to the friction of her towel. She stepped over to the sink and wiped the steam off the mirror above it, then stared somberly at her reflection.

All things considered, she would only give in to her lust if she could convince Dev there was no chance of anything more between them than a purely physical relationship. There was no possibility of love, and if he wasn't okay with that, this attraction between them would go no further. She figured he'd be pretty happy with the no emotional involvement stipulation, though, because wasn't that the fantasy all men dreamed of? A willing woman who offered sex with no strings, no commitments, just mutual pleasure with no recriminations if one—or both of them—wanted to call it quits?

A decisive nod to the woman on the other side of the mirror ended her inner debate. She brushed her teeth, toweled her hair, and began to blow it dry.

After much debate, Amanda went with a pair of gray yoga pants and a long-sleeved pink T-shirt. She didn't want to appear to be enticing him until she was sure he would agree to her terms. She gathered her hair up in a casual French twist and secured it with a tortoiseshell clip, then put on a pair of thick socks and ballet flats. This was about as un-sexy as she could get.

She put fresh sheets on the bed, not trying to kid herself about the way she hoped Dev's decision would go.

And then she picked up Danny's picture off her dresser and took it into the living room, setting it next to the one of her and her dad on the end table. No way was that photo staying in her bedroom while Dev was here. With a little sigh, she went to the kitchen to inventory the fridge for breakfast.

Great. She should have considered the state of her pantry before she offered Dev breakfast. She surveyed the meager provisions lined up on the counter. Five strips of bacon, two eggs, one container of frozen orange juice, and a bagel that was so old it might crack the tiles if she dropped it.

Okay, not enough eggs to scramble, so pancakes would have to do. She had a stick of butter but no syrup. Ah, but powdered sugar from her Christmas cookie marathon would substitute. She mixed up the orange juice and put her frying pan on the stove, then got out her recipe for pancakes and started mixing. She barely had enough milk for the recipe so she was glad Dev didn't take any in his coffee. While the bacon sizzled in the pan, she set the table for two and turned on the radio.

Neal sounded more upbeat than she had heard him in a long while as he reported high school sports scores then the marine weather report with conditions on the bay. He commiserated with the local fishermen who would be out on the water with temperatures in the low forties this morning and Amanda shivered in sympathy just thinking about it. She turned on the oven and left the door ajar to help warm up her house. She'd make the pancakes ahead of time and keep them warm in the oven till Dev arrived.

Her nerves were strung so tightly that when the phone rang she almost flipped a pancake into the sink. It had to be Dev. He was probably going to back out of breakfast after he had eight hours to think things over and come to his senses. She didn't blame him. She moved the frying pan off the hot burner and picked up the phone. "Hello?"

"Ms. Adams? This is Tom. From the service station in town?"

Relief spilled through her, leaving her legs weak. "Yes, Tom, good morning."

"I hope it wasn't too early to call you, Ms. Adams, but

you said you wanted us to come tow your car as early as possible today."

"Oh, yes, this is fine. I've been up for hours."

"Well then, I'll have Ed come by and get your car in about fifteen minutes. That be okay?"

"That would be wonderful, Tom. Thank you so much for getting started on it so early."

"No problem, Ma'am. Once I take a look at her, I'll give you a call and let you know what the problem is."

"Okay, Tom. I'll talk to you later today then."

She hung up and glanced at the clock. Eight-oh-five. Hopefully Ed would pick up her car and be gone before Dev arrived. If Dev got here first, Ed might think he had spent the night, finding his car here at such an early hour. That little tidbit of gossip would make the rounds in town before noon.

She debated calling Dev and asking him to come a bit later, but that might give him an excuse to cancel. After that brain-melting kiss last night, they needed to talk, or working together in the future would be too awkward. Drat that man. Why did he have to go and kiss her like that? One little kiss, and he had wreaked havoc with her well-ordered life.

She should never have called him last night. When he bolted out the door, leaving without a word of explanation, she should have decided to be angry and waited for him to apologize. Then she could have accepted that apology graciously and agreed to remain on friendly terms.

But no, she had to listen to him on the radio, letting his velvet voice slide over her skin the way his hands had, making her heart pound and her nipples tighten in longing. By the time he'd played half a dozen songs, she was aching to feel the solid muscles of his chest crush her into the mattress, while his mouth licked and sucked its way down her body to where the firm length of his erection cradled itself between her thighs.

So she'd called and made a bad situation worse. No way to back out now and pretend indifference.

She finished the pancakes and closed the oven door. She certainly didn't need the extra heat. Her temperature was already several degrees above normal. The sound of tires crunching on gravel brought her to the front window and, thank God, it was the tow truck to take her car away. She went out on the porch and gave her car key to Ed. A man of few words, he had the Civic on the flatbed of his truck in five minutes and, with a brisk nod, was on his way back to town in less than ten.

Amanda stood on the porch for a few more minutes letting the chilly morning air cool her heated cheeks. Just as she turned to go in, Dev's Land Rover pulled to a stop in the very spot her Civic had just vacated. He got out and climbed the steps, heat already in his eyes as they traveled down her body and back up again. He wore neatly pressed khakis and a chambray shirt under a navy CPO jacket. His thick hair curled damply over his collar and his strong jaw had no five a .m. shadow, a testimony to his trip home to shower and change before coming.

"Good morning, Amanda."

His green eyes sparked a fire in her belly that had her pulse kicking up and heat coiling low.

"Good morning, Dev," she replied, suddenly sure that any kind of physical contact between them would be a terrible mistake. "Come on in."

CHAPTER 13

"Coffee?" She took his jacket and laid it across the back of a chair, avoiding his eyes.

"Sure, thanks." He sat at the little table and watched her move about the kitchen. A few tendrils of hair had slipped from the clasp on the top of her head and curled over her shoulders drawing his attention to the graceful curve of her neck.

Amanda glanced up from pouring the coffee and caught him staring. Color washed up her neck and she caught her lower lip between her teeth. She placed the cup in front of him and retreated to the kitchen to bring glasses of juice to the table.

"It's all ready, such as it is. Are you hungry?"

He captured her eyes. "Ravenous."

She twisted her hands together, her shoulders up around her ears.

He studied the table for a second and blew out a breath. "Sorry. I don't want to make you uncomfortable." He took the napkin off his plate and dropped it in his lap. He could do this. He glanced up, keeping his smile cheerful and merely friendly. "It smells delicious. I haven't had a home-cooked breakfast in years, so this is a real treat."

Her shoulders relaxed and she brought the warm platter out of the oven and set it between them. "Careful, the plate's hot."

"Mmm," he said, leaning over the platter and inhaling. "Wow, pancakes. Now you're really taking me back."

"Oh? Did your mom make pancakes for you when you were a kid?"

Don't I wish. "Not my mother. She was a college professor so mornings were too hectic for her to cook. We had a maid when we lived in Virginia and she made me breakfast. She believed in those massive southern deals with six or seven courses. You know, eggs, pancakes or waffles, bacon or sausage, grits. Good thing I was a growing boy with a metabolism like a ditch-digger, otherwise I'd have weighed two hundred pounds by the time I hit high school." He took a swallow of orange juice. "That stopped when we moved to New York, though. The cook my parents hired there was very health oriented, so no more pancakes or French toast, just granola, yogurt, and fruit for breakfast." He wrinkled his nose. "I'm sure it was better for me, but I really missed those pancakes."

Amanda laughed. "Sorry I don't have any syrup, but here's some powdered sugar to sprinkle over them. That ought to make them sweet enough."

"Or you could just stick your finger in them, that would do it, too."

"Oh, stop, please." She rolled her eyes.

He put his knife and fork down. "You know, I can't seem to stop when I'm around you, Amanda. I can't stop thinking, I can't stop looking, and for sure, I can't stop wanting you."

She put the sugar down, a mix of anguish and longing in her eyes. Before she could form a response, he put his hand up to stop her.

"I want to apologize about last night, running out on you without any explanation. That wasn't my plan." He huffed out a breath. "The fact is, I didn't have a plan, but I couldn't resist the temptation to steal a kiss, even if it got me slapped—or worse." He looked down, unconsciously rubbing his left elbow, then back into her eyes. "After one taste of your lips, I was out of control, which doesn't say much for a thirty-year-old man, does it? I wouldn't have blamed you if you never wanted to see me again." He reached over and took her hand, turning it palm up and bringing it to his mouth, his eyes never leaving hers. "Even though we both know there is a lot of mutual attraction between us." He placed a soft kiss in the center of her palm.

Admit it. Don't tell me I imagined the way you responded to my kisses.

"There is a certain amount of . . . chemistry, between us, Dev. I won't deny it." She bit her bottom lip. "But that's all there is ever going to be."

Now it was her turn to gesture him to let her finish.

"I think I know why you left so abruptly last night, Dev. You caught a glimpse of Danny's picture on my dresser and it reminded you . . . of my recent . . . loss." She cupped the palm he had just kissed against his cheek. "And because you're such a decent man, you thought you were taking advantage of a woman grieving over her dead fiancé." She gave him a sad little smile. "I know you're the kind of man who would never exploit a woman's loneliness and grief that way, so I do understand why you left before I did something I might regret."

Part of what she said was the truth, but the altruism she ascribed to him was so far off the mark as to be laughable.

Decent?

Hardly.

Danny's picture had sent him running for sure, by reminding him of what had gotten him there in the first place—his promise. The promise he made to a man whose bravery and selflessness haunted his days and kept him sleepless most nights. For the millionth time, Dev wished he was the one who had died over there. Now he was knee-deep in a situation that was becoming more complicated by the minute.

She'd given him the perfect opening to tell her the truth.

To confess his part in Danny's death.

To tell her who he really was.

There would never be a better time, and he steeled himself for the pain he knew would follow his confession.

"Amanda, I—"

"Before you say anything, I want you to know where I'm coming from, Dev." She glanced over at the shelf where Danny's picture now resided. "I will always love Danny. I still miss him, and I'm sure this feeling of loss will stay with me forever." She returned her level gaze to Dev. "But Danny is the last man I will ever love. I won't allow that to happen again because I don't think I could survive if another man I love . . . died."

Her dove gray eyes glistened but they were wide open and unapologetic.

"But *I'm* not dead. And . . . I like you, Dev. You're charming and generous. I like the sound of your voice and the kindness in your eyes and the feel of your mouth on mine. And while my motives may be somewhat confused right now, I know I want to touch you, kiss you, and feel your hands on me. I want to make you laugh and make you groan my name when you're inside me. I want all those things, Dev, but only with the understanding that I'm never going to fall in love with you. And you can't fall in love with me, either. This is strictly a 'friends with benefits' offer."

Amanda sat back in her chair with a genuine smile on her face and, by God, a twinkle in her eye designed to take the pressure off him. "If you don't think you can handle something purely physical between us, then we'll keep what we have now. Friendship and a good working relationship. No questions asked, no apologies necessary."

Christ, this woman was amazing. He'd never met a female so open, so honest, so unafraid of laying her feelings out like cards on a table, face up and vulnerable. No wonder Danny had loved her. How could anyone know her and *not* love her?

How could he take all that she offered and not tell her the rest? Not tell her that it was already too late—he already loved her.

Easily. Oh, so easily.

Because he wasn't decent. He'd fallen for his best friend's fiancée. The fact that Danny was dead didn't make it seem any less like poaching. More like it, in fact.

But this charade wouldn't last for long. Just a few weeks, and he would tell her the truth. He'd fix up her house, deejay her party, and make sure she was financially secure. Somehow he'd convince her she *could* love again and then he'd drop the truth bomb.

He was glad she wanted to keep her emotions out of things with him. She'd be able to kick him out of her life without the slightest hesitation. The pain would be all his.

Yeah, her rules made this way too easy.

He stood, reached for her hand and pulled her up out of her seat and into his arms.

"I'll take the friendship and the physical, if that's all right with you," he whispered in her ear, breathing in her scent and trailing kisses down the soft column of her throat to the place where her pulse beat fast against his lips. Her head tipped back to allow him better access and he nipped the tender skin lightly before he covered her mouth and sank into her sweetness.

He would take his time this morning. Make up for last night's impulsive missteps.

He barely brushed her lips with his, then leaned back to gaze into her eyes. They were already smoky and heavy-lidded. He kissed her again, lightly, lingeringly. She spread her hands on his chest and leaned up to meet his lips. His arms tightened around her, holding her against him as he deepened the kiss and sought entry to her soft mouth. She opened to the thrust of his tongue and met it eagerly, stroking and sliding while she made small sounds in the back of her throat that drove him wild.

Her arms slid around his neck and she pressed herself against him while his hands found their way under her pink tee shirt to the soft skin of her back. He walked her backward two steps and pressed her up against the kitchen counter. While she buried her hands in his hair and squirmed to tease his dick into a level of rigidity rivaling a sequoia, he flicked the clasp on her bra and spilled her luscious breasts into his palms.

Rubbing his thumbs over nipples already taut brought a gasp from her and he felt her knees go weak. So he slid his hands inside her pants, and cupping the smooth cheeks of her butt, he boosted her up onto the counter and proceeded to peel her pants and panties down her long, shapely legs, stopping only to place strategic kisses on her thighs, calves, and ankles.

Not to be outdone, her hands were busy with the zipper of his pants and the brush of her fingers over his cock had him scrambling for the condom in his pocket. It was well over a year since he'd had sex with anyone other than himself, so he knew that despite his best intentions, he wouldn't be able to last much longer. While he had nothing against having sex up against walls or on kitchen counters, this was not the way he'd dreamed of making love to Amanda—at least the first time.

"Darling, wait," he groaned, his eyes almost crossing as his erection sprang free and Amanda's soft hand stroked it from base to tip. "Let's, ahhh. . ." he panted, "let's get to your bed before my knees give way."

"Mmmm . . ." Amanda replied, her breath hot in his ear, as she brought her legs up and wrapped them around his hips. She finished unbuttoning his shirt as he kicked his pants the rest of the way off and started down the short hallway to her bedroom. With his hands supporting her butt, his long fingers edged toward her center, where he felt hot, slick wetness. As soon as his knees hit the edge of the bed, he laid her on the quilt and stripped her shirt over her head, the clip from her hair coming loose and allowing it to tumble over the pillow.

The sight of her, rosy areolas with pebbled pink tips, creamy ivory skin dipping into the delicate curve of her waist, then over the gentle flare of her hips, had him speechless at her perfection. He leaned down and suckled one breast while his fingers teased the opposite nipple and she writhed beneath him gasping, "Yes . . . more . . . there . . . Oh God, don't stop, don't stop that." He was happy to oblige, slipping one finger between her lips to release a flood of wetness as he circled the tiny nub of pleasure at their apex with his thumb.

He wanted to watch her as she came, but knew he couldn't hold back from plunging into her for long. He slid a second finger inside her and felt her muscles convulse around them as her eyes went wide and her nails scored crescents across his shoulders. His thumb flicked the sensitive nub faster until with a moan she bucked against his hand, losing herself in her rclease.

He quickly covered himself with the condom then leaned down to kiss her as her eyelids fluttered open.

"Please," she begged, "I wanted to feel you inside me. Don't make me wait any longer." She trailed her fingers over the head of his cock then stroked down its length and caressed his balls. His groan put a self-satisfied smile on her lips and she leaned up and licked first one nipple then the other. "I need you inside me . . . now," she ordered him.

At her words an almost furious feeling of possession poured through him. He put the tip of his cock at the entrance to her slick heat and in one thrust, sheathed himself inside her.

Mine.

He slowly withdrew and then pushed inside again as she lifted her hips to allow him even deeper access. Again and again, he withdrew, then slowly buried himself to the hilt. The clenching of her muscles around his shaft brought him so much pleasure he could barely maintain control. He slid his hand between them and caressed her, bringing her back to the peak with him. She moaned his name and with swift, hard strokes he tumbled them both over the edge into bliss.

"Mine, please," he whispered, praying to whatever gods hadn't deserted him as he emptied himself into her.

Amanda woke up warm for the first time in months. The sensation was so soothing she almost went back to sleep until the reason for all that warmth stirred and tightened his arms around her. She couldn't stop her little wiggle of delight in response.

"Careful, lady. One more move like that and I'll consider it an invitation," Dev murmured, kissing the back of her neck.

That sent shivers down her spine and goosebumps cascading down her arms. This man brought her to a boil with barely a touch. Zoe was right in her assumption. He had very talented hands. And a mouth she couldn't seem to get enough of.

"From the feel of things, you don't need any more of an invitation," she giggled. She couldn't resist rubbing her tush against the growing evidence of his arousal. That got her a warm hand on her breast and a thumb brushing across its sensitive crest. She sighed as it pebbled and turned toward him to give him easier access to the neglected nipple.

"Guess that was an invitation, after all," he said, trailing kisses over her shoulders and licking his way to her breast where he suckled hungrily on the rosy tip.

She gasped and arched against him, threading her fingers through the thick, soft brown hair that was already unruly from their earlier lovemaking.

"Ohhh God! Please tell me we didn't use up your entire supply of condoms."

His tongue flicking back and forth across the peak was driving her mad with desire. She felt the flood of wetness between her legs and spread her thighs.

"Sorry, Honey." He kissed his way down her belly to the soft mound of curls covering her clitoris. "I didn't bring an entire box with me, I'm afraid," he said, as he spread the tender lips and blew a hot breath over the tiny nub. "We used up the second of the two I brought this morning, so this will have to do for now."

He nuzzled her and twirled his tongue around her center until she came up off the bed and moaned, her thighs quivering, her body arched tight as a bowstring. Her fingers twisted in the sheets and she realized the strange keening sound she heard was coming from her own throat.

"That's right, Darling," he crooned in that velvet voice, "just let go and come for me now. I want to watch you explode."

He lifted her legs over his shoulders and kneaded her breasts, tweaking her nipples as his mouth devoured her. And she came as he requested, shattering in a million pieces, fireworks sparkling behind her closed lids, exquisite sensation ricocheting through her body.

When the aftershocks had stopped and she was able to see straight, Dev was sitting next to her, tenderly brushing the damp tendrils of her hair out of her eyes. His expression was such a strange mix of satisfaction and longing she didn't know what to make of it, so she went for a light-hearted response. "I can't believe you didn't bring more condoms with you. We'll have to go shopping."

That got her a laugh. *Thank goodness.*

"Well, I didn't want to appear too presumptuous." He traced a finger over her lips.

She gave his fingertip a quick kiss and sat up.

In a voice so soft she barely heard him, he marveled, "Who knew I'd get so lucky?"

A little dart of fear shot straight to her heart.

He couldn't fall in love with her.

He said he wouldn't. They were only going to do the "friends with benefits" thing. There would be no love involved—on either side.

He promised.

"You're not going to get all mushy on me, are you?" she demanded, eyes narrowed.

He inspected the evidence that, although she had found release, he obviously hadn't. "I think it's safe to say I'm not getting all mushy."

Instantly contrite, she put her arms around him. "How selfish of me," she murmured, nipping at his earlobe.

"Hold that thought, darling," he chuckled. "At least until we do that shopping." He kissed her lightly on the nose. "Right now, I need sustenance, to, you know, keep up my strength." The loud rumbling of his stomach confirmed his hunger.

"I guess we're having pancakes for lunch instead of breakfast," she said, pointing to the clock radio next to the bed. She tried to remember exactly where she had lost her pants. She suppressed a smile. This man could make her forget her name with a few of his drugging kisses, let alone where her clothes had gone.

Thinking about clothes made her decide that now was as good a time as any to clear up the problem he had letting her see him naked. Although she'd managed to unbutton his shirt and get her hands on his well-muscled chest, he'd kept her from removing it completely. The man was a master at distraction.

"I think we need a shower before lunch," she said with a coy peek over her shoulder. "Come scrub my back?"

"You go ahead, I'll . . . clean up the breakfast dishes."

"Leave the dishes. I have better things for you to wash."

She slipped her hands underneath his shirt and began to slide the fabric down his arms.

He grasped her wrists, holding her hands still against his chest. "Don't. Believe me, you don't want to see anything more than you've already seen."

She could feel the tension in his shoulders and see the pain that darkened his green eyes to jade. "I'm not some faint-hearted female who swoons at the sight of a few scars, Dev. If you get to see all of me, I want to see all of you."

"Well, that's not gonna happen, darling." His tone brooked no argument.

"Really," she said, her eyes mutinous. "That's a deal-breaker, huh?" She clenched her fists and tugged them out of his grasp. "That's too bad."

She went to her closet and put on a terrycloth robe. "I'll put fresh towels out. You can shower first while I clean up the kitchen. Don't take too long, the hot water heater has a limited capacity." She left him sitting on her bed, his stubborn jaw clenched tightly enough to have a muscle jumping in his cheek.

She collected their clothing. Hers went into the hamper. His briefs and slacks she left on top, along with the towels. Then she went to her bedroom door and leaned in. "Okay, you're all set. I put your clothes in the bathroom, too."

He sat where she'd left him, left arm cradled against his chest while he rubbed the elbow with his right hand. "Amanda, honey, don't be mad. You don't want to see this, trust me," he declared.

"Dev, please don't presume to tell me what I do or don't want to see. You really don't know me well enough to make that kind of judgment call."

By the same token, if he couldn't deal with her seeing his mutilated arm, she didn't want to force the issue. So she lost the irritation that had crept into her voice and tried for sweet reason. "You don't want me to see your arm? Fine.

That's your call and I'll respect that decision. If I'm going to have an affair with you, I'm going to have it with *all* of you—or none. That's *my* decision." She took a deep breath. "So let's stick to the 'friends without benefits' model that was working pretty well for us and forget the last twenty-four hours ever happened."

"Fine." Now it was his turn to sound irritated.

"Okay, then." Amanda turned and retreated down the hall so he wouldn't see her disappointment.

She would forget the last twenty-four hours. It was better this way anyway. Her emotions were still too unstable. But the tactile memory of his body pinning hers against the kitchen counter, his erection rigid against her belly, had her nerve endings standing at attention, aching for his touch.

Oh yeah. She'd forget it ever happened.

Dev sat there, amid the rumpled sheets redolent with the scents of sex and Amanda, and wondered how he had managed to go from the luckiest guy in the world to the dumbest in the space of ten minutes. All because he couldn't bear to see the expression on her face when she got a good view of the ravages to his arm that burning Humvee had wrought.

Sure, she said she could take it, but once she saw the thick, corded scar tissue that covered his left arm from shoulder to fingertips, fish-belly white and pitted with holes still black with embedded debris, she'd change her tune.

He'd seen the expressions before, when he was first released from Walter Reed. Before he learned to wear a glove and long-sleeved shirts out in public.

Man or woman, it was pretty much the same. First came revulsion, the tightening around the eyes, the lips pressed together, the nose slightly wrinkled as though a faint but putrid odor clung to him. Then embarrassment as people realized he saw their reaction. Most folks just hurried away at that point or averted their faces, but some, the stronger ones, seemed proud of the fact that they could tolerate seeing his disfigurement. Their eyes held only pity. Strangely enough, it was kids who had the least problem with it. They usually were just curious until their mothers hurried them away.

So, no. He wasn't going to let Amanda see. Because he already knew how strong she was and pity was not something he wanted to see in those expressive gray eyes.

He went into her bathroom, took a five-minute shower and dressed, doing his best to smooth the wrinkles out of his shirt.

He hadn't expected this to be an issue. He'd assumed Amanda would be glad not to have to deal with a part of him that would put a serious damper on the smoking-hot sex they were both anticipating. Now that wouldn't be a problem.

Could they both pretend the past twenty-four hours hadn't happened?

Un-ring that bell?

Not a chance in hell, but he'd try his damnedest to *act* that way. Because the satin of her skin, the faint fragrance of lilacs in her hair, the softness of her mouth, and the sexy sounds she made coming undone under him—those things he'd never forget. He'd treasure them forever.

He studied himself in the mirror and straightened his shoulders. Tried on a friendly smile. Shit. He'd have to work on that. He felt like a mannequin, his face stiff and wooden.

Screw it. He couldn't hide in here forever. He headed for the kitchen.

Funny how cool the little cottage felt to him now, without his overheated libido to keep him warm. Amanda leaned against the sink and gazed out the window. The draft around it was strong enough to stir the curtain on one side. The day was overcast and windy. The sky matched her eyes when she turned to face him, her smile as strained as his.

"I made a fresh pot of coffee. Want some?"

"Sure. Thanks."

She set it on the counter rather than handing it to him, and avoided staring at his left hand.

Nice going, idiot-boy. You've taken the best day of your life and totally trashed it. Try to salvage something out of this disaster. Talk to her, for god's sake. Your imitation of a statue won't help anything.

"How about letting me help you get these windows caulked? It wouldn't take very long and you'll be surprised at the difference cutting out these drafts will make."

Could he possibly sound any more lame?

"Thank you, but you don't have to do that."

"I know." He went from window to window, examining the casings, then went over to the back door that led out to the dock. He tried on the smile again, hoping it improved with practice. "But that's what friends do for each other." He hunkered down and opened the door a crack, then closed it again. "Weather-stripping's gone from the bottom of this door, too. I can put a new piece on for you."

"Listen, Dev, I really appreciate the offer—"

"But I don't have to do it," he interrupted her. "I know. I'd feel a lot better if you'd let me, though."

He stood up but stayed by the door, giving her as much space as he could in the cramped kitchen. Knowing she was naked under that terrycloth robe made it difficult to concentrate and he prayed his body wouldn't betray him.

She started to say something, stopped, then tried again. "All right. Thank you, that would be very nice." She folded her arms across her body. "When would you, um . . .?" She caught her bottom lip between her teeth and he had to look away, pretending to check the lock on the door.

He'd need to check with Jeff to see when he'd be available to help, then they'd have to go into Easton to buy supplies. He tried to remember what he had on his calendar at the studio for the coming week.

"This week? Thursday, Friday?" he suggested. "You don't have to be here if you have other things to do. Let me know what time's good for you."

"Dev, you already work so hard at the radio station. I really hate to take up more of your time."

We would have been taking up my time with much more enjoyable endeavors if . . . things had been different. He stifled a sigh.

"Don't worry, it won't take me long." He'd recruit Jeff to help him install new baseboard heaters, and maybe a tankless water heater while he was at it. They could knock those jobs out in a few hours. It would be better if she didn't know about those plans until he was finished. Then even if she stayed mad, she'd at least be *warm* and mad.

The microwave dinged and Amanda gestured toward the table she'd reset with clean plates. "Come sit down. I reheated last night's casserole. I hope you don't mind leftovers." She brought the warmed dish over to the table.

He hesitated, wishing she would get dressed if he was going to sit across from her at the small table.

"I'm sorry. I don't have anything else but this," she apologized.

"Oh no. This is fine." He picked up his cup and went to the table, carefully avoiding brushing against her as he navigated the narrow space.

"I planned on going to the store today, but . . ."

But we spent the morning in bed together, instead.

Yeah, they were both on the same wavelength now. He could tell from the flush staining her cheeks.

"I'm, uh, going to . . . um . . ." She made a vague gesture toward the robe she wore. "Get dressed."

Thank God.

"I'll be right back."

He nodded.

She bolted for the bedroom.

He blew out a breath. This was torture. He had to get out of here.

His stomach growled again, his hunger not diminished one whit by the emotional upheaval going on in his head. He spooned a generous portion of the leftover casserole onto his plate and began to eat.

Amanda was back in a few minutes wearing jeans and an Army sweatshirt, her face freshly washed, her hair secured in a ponytail low on her neck. Even without a hint of makeup, she was lovely.

Before she could sit down, the phone rang.

She answered it and he couldn't help but hear her side of the conversation.

"It's not the battery?" Pause. "It's the starter. I see." She turned away and lowered her voice. "How much will that cost, Mr. Evers?" She listened again. "That much? There's nothing else . . .?" Pause. "Oh, could you? That would be wonderful, Mr. Evers. How long do you think it would take to find one?" Pause. "Oh. Well. Of course. I understand." Pause. "No. No, one from a junkyard will be fine, Mr. Evers." Pause. "Yes. Call me as soon as you know how much. Yes. Thank you. Goodbye."

She sat down, dejection apparent in the slump of her shoulders. "It appears I'll be without a car for a little longer than I expected."

"The starter, hmm?"

She nodded. "Mr. Evers is going to try to find a used one in a junkyard. He's sending Ed over to Easton to see if he can find one." She put a spoonful of the casserole on her plate but showed no interest in eating it.

"I'm sure he'll find one for you," Dev said.

"Do you think so?"

"Yeah, I do. Your car was a very popular model. There must be hundreds of them in the junkyards. Chances are good they'll find one for you in Easton." *And if they don't, I'll find one for you myself.*

She gave him a genuine smile. "Thanks, that makes me feel a lot better." She took a bite of food and chewed thoughtfully. "I'm going to have to ask you for another favor."

He met her gaze and smiled. The practice was helping. His face didn't feel like a block of wood. "Sure. That's what friends are for."

Yep, he could do this. It might require countless cold showers, and large quantities of Jack Daniels, but he'd pretend the last twenty-four hours had never happened.

CHAPTER 14

Why in God's name did she have to be so stubborn—and stupid? Amanda took her self-recriminations out on the casserole dish, scrubbing it and everything else within reach till the kitchen sparkled.

Then she took a second cup of coffee into her office. She'd already stripped the bed and had the sheets in the washer—except for one pillowcase. The one that had been under Dev's head and still bore that wonderful, woodsy fragrance she found so irresistible. She couldn't bear to remove all traces of a morning spent having the best sex she could remember.

She refused to compare it to the lovemaking she'd shared with Danny. That would be like comparing apples to oranges. She was in love with Danny. Sex with Dev was fueled by pure lust. It had been a long while since she and Danny had shared a bed, so she was sure that played some part in the intensity of her responses to Dev's kisses. His broad chest, sculpted abs and powerful thighs did things to her that turned lust into rocket fuel and had sent her to the moon—twice. And Dev's mouth? The mere thought made the very tender parts between her legs clench.

So what did she do with all that hot, wonderful male in her bed? She got on her high horse, picked a fight, and ruined it all. Stupid, stupid, woman! Was it so important to prove to him that she cared more about what was on the inside instead of a person than outward appearances?

Disgusted with herself, she plopped down in her desk chair, winced, and booted up her laptop. She had to make calls to set up interviews on Friday for bartenders, wait staff, caterers, and what she referred to as "muscle"—college kids to park cars, help set up and then tear down all the props.

What caught her eye immediately was the little blinking icon on her desktop that indicated she had a new entry from one of the clipping services. Job interviews flew out of her mind at the thought she might learn something that could relate to her dad's disappearance.

She clicked on the icon and opened an article from a Virginia newspaper about the apprehension of a serial killer whose MO was to hitch a ride, usually along an interstate highway, then kill the driver and take the car south into another state. Once the cash he'd taken from the driver ran out, he dumped the car in a lake or quarry. Eventually he'd hitchhiked back north, killing another motorist to finance his trip. Apparently the man had done this so many times he "couldn't remember" all the people he'd murdered, but he'd told the police about some of the drop spots he'd used to hide the vehicles. The FBI was sending divers into one quarry in Alabama to see if they could recover anything. Her heart rate sped up as her blood chilled. Could her dad have been one of this man's victims?

Amanda found the number for the police in the town where the newspaper article had been published and with shaking fingers dialed. She told the sergeant who answered that she feared her father may have been one of the killer's victims. He took down her information and told her that the FBI would probably get in touch with her in a day or so. It appeared that a lot of folks thought a missing friend or relative might have picked up the "Highway Hijacker". Every report would be investigated, he assured her, but she'd best be patient as it may take quite a while. Still, she hung up with renewed hope.

Back to work, she reminded herself, and opened the spreadsheet she had created with the names, addresses, and phone numbers of all those who had answered her ads in the local papers, or responded to bulletins she had tacked up at community colleges and supermarkets. In two hours, she had enough interviews lined up to keep her busy all day Friday. She was glad Zoe would be there to help and share her opinions of the candidates.

Dev offered to give her a ride into town and then come back here and caulk her windows while she did the interviews. In an effort to revert to pre-sex friendship mode, she'd accepted. She didn't want to be indebted to him for anything but he was so insistent about getting rid of the drafts she'd finally given in. It would be nice to have a warmer house and safer to have him do the work while she was away, because she didn't trust herself to be alone with him—especially in such close proximity to her bed. One smoldering glance, and she'd tell him he could keep all his clothes on if he would just kiss her.

Mr. Evers had better find a starter for her car soon. She didn't want to rent one but she was not going to ask Dev to chauffeur her around town. She sighed. Somehow ever since she'd met that man, her life had become more and more complicated.

Her last call of the day was to Zoe. It was after five so the gallery should be closed. The phone rang so long she was about to hang up when Zoe finally picked up.

"Did I drag you away from your painting?"

"Painting, yes. Art? No. I'm gilding the Styrofoam urns we're using to hold the amaryllis. A little antiquing and they'll look authentic enough to fool anybody."

"I ordered five dozen amaryllis. You're sure that will be enough, right?"

"Yep. We're doing ten tables, so that will take thirty of them. The rest we'll use along the walkway to the pavilion and on the buffet table. I'm more worried about the ivy. Needlepoint ivy is so delicate we'll need a lot to make sure the arrangements are full enough. I wouldn't want Mrs. Wyndham to think they're skimpy."

"I agree. Once I get my car back we can ride over to the nursery and see the actual size of the plants I ordered. Buying plants in six-inch or eight-inch pots didn't really give me a good idea of how full they'll be."

"Which reminds me, how goes the car situation?"

"Not good. It wasn't the battery, it was the starter."

"Oh no."

"Yeah. Mr. Evers is trying to find a used one in a junkyard to keep the cost down. Otherwise I may have to go with a new one, which will completely exhaust my emergency fund—and then some." Amanda rubbed her forehead. "I should have asked Mrs. Wyndham for a bigger initial payment, Zoe. That was a mistake I won't make again."

"Considering this is our first foray into event planning, I think you're doing a fantastic job. There's bound to be a few things we have to learn from experience. Your car's breakdown was just bad luck."

"I'll go along with that."

"I'm sure Dev would be glad to help you out if you need to borrow a car," Zoe teased. "He was very helpful at dinner the other night. I think the guy is really into you, Mandy."

Into me? Oh yes, he was certainly into me. Heat flooded her face. Good thing Zoe couldn't see her right now. She wouldn't need to keep fishing for details.

"Mandy? Are you still there?"

"Yes. Of course I'm still here."

"You were so quiet there, I thought you . . . Wait a minute. Is there something you're not telling me?" Zoe asked shrewdly.

Amanda didn't want to lie to her friend, but if she told the truth, Zoe would have her ordering wedding invitations before she blinked. She paused too long while she debated how to avoid full disclosure.

"Oh my God, he kissed you!"

Damn. Her friend was worse than a bloodhound after a bone. Maybe if she confessed to the kissing, she could stop this interrogation. "Yes. He kissed me. Okay? Are you happy now?

"What's more important is—are you happy now?"

If Zoe had asked her this when she woke up in Dev's arms, her answer would have been a resounding "Yes!" Now? Not so much. "Um, it's a little complicated, Zoe."

"Oh, Lord. What did you do?"

"Why do you immediately assume it's something *I* did?" Amanda griped.

"Okay. What did he do?"

"Well, it's—"

"Complicated. I can see that. Why don't you just tell me the whole deal, so I can stop dragging it out of you inch by inch? Yeesh. I feel like a dentist here, pulling teeth."

"Zoe, I just don't want you to leap to the wrong conclusions."

"You mean just because you slept with him I'm not supposed to assume you're having a June wedding?"

Amanda choked. Her friend was too smart by half. "Exactly."

"No problem," Zoe continued equitably, "I can wait until September. I love fall weddings."

"See? This is why I didn't want to say anything. There will be no wedding. Not in June. Not in September. Not ever. Am I making myself clear?"

"Yes. Foolishly, stupidly clear." Zoe's sigh came over the line. "On the other hand, there is a lot to be said for a smokin'-hot, torrid affair. Let it not be said that I am too narrow-minded to embrace that plan."

"Well, you needn't worry, there isn't going to be an affair either. We had a . . . disagreement. And mutually decided to remain just friends."

Silence. Amanda waited, not willing to give out any more information on their "disagreement".

"Wow. The sex was that bad?"

If only.

"Cause I would have thought, you know, that he'd be hotter than a blowtorch in the sack."

"He is. Was. Listen, I don't want to talk about this right now, okay? I've got more important things on my mind. I saw an article in the newspaper about a serial killer who traveled up and down the East Coast hitchhiking then killing the drivers and taking their cars and money. My dad might have been one of his victims. I'll show you the article on Friday. In the meantime, I need some time to . . . think."

"Sure thing. Doing this on the phone sucks. We can talk more after the interviews on Friday."

"Yeah, thanks, Zoe. Bye."

Amanda hung up and sat with her chin in her hand, staring out the window at the tall beach grass bending in the wind. She had no doubt her life was about to change. She felt like a passenger on a runaway train, careening toward a future that was out of her control.

Dev parked in front of the end unit of the Blue Point Motor Court and gave the horn two short blasts. A minute later Jeff stuck his head out the door of the next unit down, wiping his hands on a piece of terrycloth that may have once been a beach towel.

"Be right there." The door slammed shut.

Dev inspected the nineteen-fifties motel, comprised of nine units in an L-shaped, single-story building, tucked back among the trees. Once the only public lodging in Blue Point Cove, it was clear that the newer motel chains had won the competition for vacationers. Jeff had given him a short history when he'd called to set up this meeting.

As the run-down motel settled ever more deeply into obscurity, its owner sought other ways to turn a profit. George Pennypacker, seventy-eight years old, arthritic, and well acquainted with the joint-easing properties of bourbon, converted the units into "studio" apartments by simply adding a small refrigerator and hot plate to the existing amenities. These he now rented on a month-to-month basis. The income thus produced went directly into George's stomach, courtesy of Jim Beam, which left him little time for, and no interest in, the maintenance the aging building required. George solved that problem by letting Jeff use three units at one end of the L in return for his services as caretaker and handyman. Like they say on Wall Street, it was a win-win situation.

A few minutes later, Jeff came out of the end unit and climbed into the passenger seat.

"'Sup, Dude?" he asked, pulling an Orioles baseball cap down over his unruly hair.

"Don't call me dude." Dev scowled as he threw the Land Rover into reverse and backed away from the building. Gravel spewed from under the tires as he hit the gas and pulled out onto the highway.

"Wow. What bit you in the ass today? Last time I saw you, you seemed pretty happy," Jeff commented.

"Not what. *Who*."

"Oh. Say no more. I get the picture."

"I doubt that, it's pretty complicated. And I don't want to talk about it," Dev groused, cutting off Jeff's reply.

Jeff gave him a sympathetic smile. "It's not *that* complicated, Dude. You've got it bad for Amanda and she's not ready for the kind of hot monkey sex you have in mind." Jeff shrugged as though any idiot could see what the problem was.

"It's not that at all," Dev ground out. *We already had the hot monkey sex. Then I effed it up.* "And I don't want to talk about it," he repeated. He tried to relax the death grip he had on the steering wheel, which only made him more aware of the glove he wore on his left hand. He flexed his fingers. Thought about taking it off. *Goddamn it.* "And don't call me dude."

"Well, it beats calling you *Prick*, which is what you're acting like." Jeff settled back and put one foot up on the dash. He ignored the scowl from Dev and started humming Queen's "Another One Bites the Dust".

Dev drove in silence for a few minutes. He finally shook his head in disgust. "Sorry, Jeff. You're right. On both counts."

Jeff slapped him on the shoulder. "Believe me, I feel for you, D. Women are the worst kind of trouble. I've been there myself." He tilted his head and quirked his mouth.

"Jesus, she's going to put me in an early grave." *Which I deserve.* "But that's not your problem. I'll figure it out somehow."

"Hey, great, D. When you do, you'll tell me how, too, right?"

"Don't push it, *J*," Dev warned, accenting the initial.

"Okay." Jeff held up his hands in surrender. "So. You going to tell me where we're going?"

"To the Home Depot in Easton. I want you to help me pick up new heaters for Amanda's place. And some caulk. And maybe one of those tank-less water heaters." Dev stopped at the only stop sign between Blue Point Cove and Cambridge and glanced over at Jeff. "I'm willing to pay you to help me install them, and I need your advice on what kind to buy."

The silence lasted long enough to get Dev's attention.

"In the interest of not getting slugged by you, I will confine my response to one word. Sure."

Dev caught the smirk on Jeff's face out of the corner of his eye, but he wasn't going to argue with success. "Thanks. I owe you one."

"Wait till you hear what I'm going to charge you." Jeff chuckled.

"Doesn't matter. I'll still owe you."

It was past six o'clock by the time they were back at Jeff's, the back of the Land Rover crammed full of heaters, caulk, electrical tape, battery-operated drills, screw drivers, putty knives, and anything else Jeff thought might come in handy.

"I need to stash all this stuff here until I drop Amanda off at the gallery Friday morning. I don't want her to see it and start asking questions. She's going to be over there interviewing candidates for the party jobs all day. That should give us plenty of time to get this all installed, don't you think?"

Jeff squinted as he did some mental calculations. "Yeah, I think with the two of us working on it we can have everything done in a day. Part of that depends on whether there's an empty slot in the breaker box at Amanda's place for the new baseboard heaters and part depends on how much help you can give me, D."

"Don't worry about me. I can handle my share. You just make sure you sack out early enough the night before to be ready to go by nine. I don't think I'll get over to her place in the next two days to check out that breaker panel, so we'll just have to play it by ear."

"We can always come back in a day or two and put a new panel in, if we need to," Jeff said.

"Don't count on it. I figure I'll only get one shot at this. Once she sees what we've done, I expect I'll be *persona non grata* at her place."

"You really haven't talked to her about any of this?"

"I told her I'd caulk the windows. That'll get me in the front door. I haven't mentioned the rest." Dev opened the back of the truck and picked up the carton holding the new tank-less water heater.

"Why not, D? The lady should be falling all over you with gratitude." Jeff hefted one of the heaters and a coil of 14-gauge copper wire over his shoulder. "I figured that was your grand plan. You get her nice and toasty warm, she'll be much more . . . pliable."

He unlocked the door to his studio and flipped on the light. Except for the bathroom, the unit had been gutted. Several tables held half-finished sculptures and there was a potters' wheel in one corner. A large piece of black soapstone was covered with a sheet, obscuring whatever it was that Jeff was carving out of it. Paintings covered the paneled walls and a work-in-progress sat on an easel in the corner.

Dev whistled. "You paint *and* sculpt? You're a regular Michelangelo, Jeff." He went over to study the closest one. How come these aren't for sale in Zoe's gallery?"

"Some of them are. It's kind of complicated." Jeff brushed off Dev's interest. "Let's concentrate on fixing up Amanda's place." He indicated an empty spot along the front wall under the window. "Stack the stuff over there."

"As independent and stubborn as that woman is, she'll be pissed as hell that I did this without asking her first. I know she doesn't have the money to do it and she'd rather freeze that cute little butt of hers off than ask for help."

They went back to the truck for the remainder of their equipment. Dev had no trouble handling the largest heater while Jeff grabbed the tools.

"So that's why you want her out of the way while we do this. You're taking a big risk, Du—D. Women are damned unpredictable about stuff like this. You think they should be all happy and then they turn around and kick your butt out the door."

"Yeah. I expect the butt-kicking," Dev acknowledged. "But I figure it's better to beg forgiveness than ask permission. That way, even if she never speaks to me again, I'll feel better knowing that little place is a lot more comfortable." He surveyed everything he'd bought with satisfaction. "Come on. Let me buy you some dinner down at the diner."

"No, thanks, D. You don't have to do that."

"I know. But let me do it anyway. I have to put something in my stomach before I go to work and I hate to eat alone."

"Okay, if you insist. Far be it from me to turn down a free meal. I'll ride over on my bike, though. That way you don't have to bring me back."

"Suit yourself, but I don't mind bringing you back here."

"Nah, I'll take the bike. Who knows? I may not want to come straight home," Jeff added with a sly wink.

Dev nodded. He envied the other man his prospects for the rest of the night. He'd be training his newest employee, Lance Fisher, while visions of a certain blond, gray-eyed beauty paraded through his head, keeping him aching and annoyed until dawn.

Dev got to the station at eight p.m. and found Lance Fisher in the control room with Ed Santone, who was going over the equipment with the new announcer. Lance was dressed neatly in khaki slacks and a polo shirt. He listened intently to Ed and jotted a few things down in a notepad. Dev didn't see any visible signs of injury but caught the slight limp as the man moved around the room.

He waved to Andy as he passed the broadcast booth and got a big grin in return, something so unusual he would have gone in to make sure the kid wasn't high if he didn't have the new guy on his mind. In the past week it seemed most of his employees were acting a bit strange and it was starting to worry him.

"Ed, thanks for staying late this week," he said when he entered the control room.

"No problem, Boss. Glad I could help."

"You do more than help, Ed. You damn near run the place. I've got to find another engineer so we can give you some of that comp time you've accrued." He turned to the new man. “Lance. How are you making out? Starting to get the hang of things?”

“Sir. Yes, Sir. Mr. Santone has been very patient with me.”

Consciously or not, the ex-sergeant stood at ease as he answered Dev. They’d have to work on changing habits the Army had ingrained in Lance Fisher, but Dev was sure his disparate crew was up to the task.

“No need to call me sir, Lance. Dev is fine. We run a pretty relaxed show around here, as I’m sure you’ll find out quickly enough once we get you on a regular shift. Chris Majewski tells me you’d prefer to work nights, is that right?”

Lance looked quickly at Ed then at the floor. Ed picked up on his discomfort, and immediately said, “I’m done here for tonight, Dev, so if you don’t mind, I’ll be heading home.”

Dev nodded. “Thanks again, Ed. I’ll catch up with you tomorrow.” He motioned to Lance. “Let’s go to my office and we’ll get the rest of the paperwork out of the way.”

“Yes, sir.”

“Want some coffee?” Dev nodded to the break room as they passed it.

“No sir, I’m good, sir.” Lance winced at the second sir. “Sorry, S— Dev. Hard to break the habit.”

“Don’t sweat it, Lance. You’re a few years older and several ranks higher than I was, so just try to envision me as a new recruit and we’ll get along fine.”

“Don’t think I could do that, S— Dev. I gave new recruits a pretty hard time.”

A brief flash of pain in the man’s hazel eyes stopped Dev from following that line of conversation. He recognized the signs.

“Just so you’re aware, most of the guys here are trying to lose their military baggage, but that doesn’t mean there still isn’t plenty left. Since we all have our ‘problems’, you’ll find everyone is pretty tolerant of each other’s idiosyncrasies. If something bothers you, it’s best to point it out right away.

Don't let it eat at you, or eventually there'll be an explosion that will be much harder to recover from. No one will take offense as long as you're not a smart ass about it. If you have a problem you don't want to talk about with the rest of the staff you can always come to me. If it's something I can't handle, I'll kick it up the ladder to Chris. He stops by every couple of weeks to give me a hard time—and check on the guys he's sent over here."

Dev pointed to a chair. "Have a seat, Lance. There are a few papers you have to fill out. This one is your W-4. If you're not sure about deductions you can speak with our accountant, Ms. Adams. She can point you in the right direction on most matters that have to do with money. Did Mike find you a place to stay?"

"Yes, at least temporarily. It's in a . . . boarding house, I guess you'd call it. A private home that has another fellow and myself using a couple of spare bedrooms." He hesitated. "I'll try to find something else as soon as I get a few paychecks in the bank. I really need a place all to myself, sir, Dev."

Lance squared his shoulders, although his back was already so stiff it couldn't get any straighter. Dev recognized the stance. Admitting weakness to a virtual stranger sucked, and he appreciated the direct gaze and non-apologetic delivery.

"You asked me about working nights. I'm sure Captain Majewski told you I have flashbacks. They're worse in the daytime, or when there's a lot of noise. I, uh, can get kind of loud myself, you see, so it's better if I live where I can't disturb other folks." The man looked miserable, but determined to make sure Dev knew the worst. "I do better when it's quiet and dark—that's why I want to work nights. I take some medication that helps but I can't promise I won't have one when I'm on duty. Will that be a problem, sir?"

"We'll talk to Chris together about what to do if you have a flashback when you're on the air. I won't bullshit you, Lance, that could be a real problem."

Dev sat back and considered possible alternatives. "You were going to take over half of my shift, from three a.m. to seven a.m. That would be a big relief to me, so I hoped it would work out for you, too. Now I'm not so sure that would be the best fit for you."

Lance didn't try to hide his disappointment. "I understand, sir. I'll call Captain Majewski in the morning and thank him for the opportunity. There was a night watchman opening at a warehouse in Salisbury that might still be available."

"Hold on, Lance. Let's not jump to conclusions." Dev studied the man's paperwork for a few minutes. "It says here that you quit college at the end of your junior year to enlist in the military. Also says you were on the football team and had a chance at being recruited by some professional scouts if you'd stayed to play in your senior year. So I have two questions. Did you make it to college on a football scholarship and was that your plan for the future—playing professional ball?"

"I did get a partial athletic scholarship. That was the only thing that made it possible for my folks to send me to college in the first place. My major was engineering, though. I got the football scholarship mostly because I was big and pretty fast on my feet, but believe me, sir, I was in no danger of being drafted by the NFL. I just wasn't that good. I won't say I didn't fantasize about going to the pros and making the big bucks," he said, remembering. "But in the cold, hard light of day I had a good GPA and knew if I kept at it I'd make a nice enough living as an EE."

"What made you quit, then?"

"My dad was in construction. Hurt his back and couldn't do it anymore." Lance shrugged. "With two other kids in high school they needed financial help. The Army was the quickest way to a steady paycheck. I figured I could finish college while I was in and start my career a little later than I planned." He rubbed his right leg and stretched it out in front of him. "Didn't work out that way."

Oh, yeah. Dev could relate to that. He liked this guy. Life had given him some crappy choices and he'd made the best of them, then got the shit kicked out of him again in Iraq as a reward. He made a decision and kissed his dreams of a four-hour shift goodbye.

"Being an on-air personality is not a good idea for you, Lance, at least not right now. But how would you feel about an engineering slot? The two men I have are each doing twelve-hour shifts and I've been searching for a third guy to share the load."

"I'd like that, sir, but don't I need an EE degree to do that kind of job?"

Dev caught the flare of hope in the man's eyes. "Let's have you talk to Mike Kovak in the morning and see how long it would take you to get a Class A Radio license. I'm pretty sure that's all you'd need to get started. While you study to take the exam, you can work here as a trainee under Johnny Miller. He's our seven p.m. to seven a.m. engineer. We'll see how you do and if you have a flashback there will be someone close by to take over if that's necessary. It may take a bit longer to solve your housing problem but we'll find a more suitable place. Think you can hang in at that rooming house for a while?"

"I'll try my best, sir."

"Can't ask for more than that." Dev checked his watch and stood. "Let's get back to the control room. I'll introduce you to Johnny and you can get an idea of what the job is like before you commit to it. We'll talk salary later, but I have to tell you that until you're licensed I'll have to cut your pay by twenty percent. Think it over while you're here tonight and give me your decision in the morning."

“I don’t have to wait till morning, sir—Dev. I’ll take the job.”

They shook hands, and Dev clapped him on the shoulder. “Let’s get you settled, then. I’ve got to be in the booth in a few minutes to start my shift. The first rule around here is to be on time. That means announcers should be in the booth ten minutes before they’re due on the air so the hand-off goes smoothly.”

He was happy with his solution to Lance Fisher’s situation even though it didn’t shorten his own workday. He’d had visions of three a.m. visits to Amanda’s little bungalow. No need to fantasize about that anymore. Too bad he couldn’t solve his own problems as easily as Lance’s. He entered the booth quietly and got another broad grin and thumbs-up signal from Andy.

What was with this kid lately? He sniffed the air. No telltale scent of cannabis. Dev was glad to see Andy hadn’t relapsed. Which made his unusual good humor all the more puzzling.

His own mood could stand some improvement. Not likely to happen anytime soon, though. He’d keep one eye on the control room tonight to see how things went with Lance. It would keep his mind off Amanda.

CHAPTER 15

The call came Friday morning at eight forty-five, catching Amanda just before Dev was due to pick her up.

"Good morning, Ms. Adams. I'm Agent Charles Thorndyke from the FBI. I'm sorry to call you so early in the morning but I understand you spoke to the Police in Winston two days ago about Brian Donlevy, the man they're calling the 'Highway Hijacker'. Is that correct?"

"Yes, Mr. Thorndyke. I saw the news article and thought my father might have been one of this man's victims."

"Yes, Ma'am. I'd like to get some basic information from you over the phone if I could. We're trying to put together a timeline on this suspect to see if we can determine what part of the country he was in month by month. Do you have a few minutes to answer a couple of questions right now?"

Nothing was as important as the possibility she could clear up the mystery of her dad's disappearance once and for all. If she was a bit late for the interviews, Zoe would have to start without her.

"Yes, sir. What would you like to know?"

"Let's start with the name and address of the person you think may have been the victim."

"That would be my father, Frank Adams. We lived in Annapolis, Maryland, On Porterville Road."

"Thank you, Ms. Adams. And what was the date of his disappearance?"

"It was Sunday, June nineteenth, nineteen-ninety-four," Amanda said, her throat getting tight as she recounted the details. As long ago as it had been, the particulars of the next two days were burned into her memory. "He left work at two-thirty a.m. on Sunday morn—"

"Was that the normal time he finished work?" the agent interrupted her.

"Yes, he was a musician and played with a jazz quintet in Annapolis and Washington, D.C. They usually finished up around two a.m. He was supposed to drive down to Blue Point Cove and open up our summer cottage to get it ready for my mom and I to come down here the next weekend."

Amanda glanced around the room, visualizing her father coming through the front door, tired but happy to be here, opening the windows, turning on lights, then popping the top on a beer from the cooler he always brought with him. The scene was so vivid in her imagination, she barely heard the FBI agent ask his next question. "I'm sorry. Could you repeat that, please?" she asked, closing her eyes as though that would block out the scene her imagination had conjured up.

"When did you know he was missing?"

"We, my mother and I, didn't know he was missing until the next evening. He usually called sometime Sunday morning to let my Mom know the phone service was turned on and that everything was all right. When she hadn't heard from him by late afternoon, she called the sheriff in Cambridge and asked him to check our cottage. They didn't find him or any indication that he had been there at all." Her eyes burned and the effort to maintain control of her voice roughened her breathing.

The agent summarized, "So, after your father left work at approximately two-thirty a.m. on Sunday, June nineteenth, no one saw or heard from him again. Is that correct?"

"Yes, sir."

"What kind of car was he driving when he disappeared?"

"We had a nineteen-eighty-eight Pontiac Grand Prix. It was a gray, two-door model." She rattled off the license plate number from memory.

"You're positive of the make and model of the car? And the license plate?"

"Yes, Agent Thorndyke, I'm positive. I've been searching for my father for fifteen years. I can even tell you what he was wearing the night he disappeared."

"Thank you, Ma'am. I wasn't doubting your accuracy, just double-checking to make sure I had all the information you gave me correctly. I'll enter all of this in the file we have on Brian Donlevy. The car may be the best chance of finding out if your father was one of his victims. This sociopath was more interested in talking about the cars of his victims than the victims themselves. I want you to understand that this investigation may take quite a while, so if you don't hear back from us right away, don't think we've forgotten about you. Be prepared to wait a month or so. It will take us at least that long to check out all the places this guy dumped the cars or their drivers."

"Yes, I understand. Will someone be coming here? I'm living in the cottage I told you about, where my dad was headed that night."

"Possibly, Ma'am. If your father was killed by Mr. Donlevy, it probably would have happened before he got that far. If we need more information, or if we discover remains that need to be identified, we'll be in touch by phone. Thank you for taking the time to speak with me, Ma'am."

"You're welcome, Agent Thorndyke." She didn't want to hang up and end the only link she'd had in fifteen years to someone who might know something about her dad's fate. But, really, what more could she ask? At a knock on her front door, she reluctantly dropped the phone into its cradle and answered it.

"Hi. I beeped but I guess you didn't hear me . . ." Dev stopped and studied Amanda's face. "What's wrong? Are you okay?" He opened the screen door and came in, not waiting for an invitation.

Amanda swallowed twice to ease the tightness in her throat from unshed tears. “I’m . . . I’m not quite ready to go, Dev. Sorry,” she croaked.

The tenderness and concern in his eyes almost undid her and she turned away so he wouldn’t see the two escaping tears slide down her cheeks. She needed to get to the bathroom, splash some cold water on her face, and get herself together.

His hands on her shoulders stopped her and turned her around to face him. He tipped her chin up with a finger.

“Tell me.”

That voice of his always was irresistible.

“The FBI called. About my dad. They caught a serial killer in Virginia.” Tears welled up again and she couldn’t fight them back this time. “He might have . . . murdered . . . my dad,” she said on a sob.

Dev put his arms around her and she buried her face against his chest and let the tears come, hot and fierce. She held on to him so tightly he probably couldn’t breathe, but he wrapped his arms around her and rubbed slow, soothing circles across her back until the torrent of tears lessened to a few shaky gasps. He brushed her hair back from her face and stood there, rocking her gently from side-to-side, and she thought how wonderful it would be if she could just stand here like this forever. Warmed and cherished and comforted, while Dev kept reality at bay outside the circle of his arms.

She sighed and released him and he instantly responded, dropping his arms and backing away a step. Reality rushed back to fill the void and she shivered.

“I’ve gotten your shirt all wet,” she apologized as she plucked the dampened material away from his chest, avoiding his eyes.

“It’ll dry.”

He cupped her face with his hands and wiped her tears away with his thumbs, the thin cotton glove on his left one soaking up the wetness more efficiently than his bare right one. She put her hands over his and squeezed gently.

"Thanks. You arrived at just the wrong time to witness my melt down. My emotions are all over the place lately, and the call took me back to when . . . my dad . . . went missing."

You don't need to apologize, darling," he said.

The endearment slipped out so naturally she wondered if he realized he'd used it.

"I gather the FBI arrested someone who may have been involved in your father's disappearance."

She nodded and took a deep breath. "Apparently this man—Brian Donlevy—hitchhiked up and down the East Coast. He'd kill the driver, put the body in the trunk, take his money, and drive a few states away before he dumped the car, usually in a lake or a quarry. When the money ran out he'd hitch another ride and do it again."

She realized her hands were trembling and crossed her arms, tucking her hands in her armpits to warm them. She shivered again.

"Maybe you should sit down for a few minutes," Dev suggested. Her eyes still held hints of horror, and he knew she was thinking of her father stuffed in the trunk of his car. He didn't blame her for her meltdown. It was a pretty grim thought to deal with, no matter how long ago it may have happened.

"How about a glass of water? Or coffee? Would you like me to get you some coffee?" he asked, acting as if he was at his own place instead of hers.

The irony of it struck Amanda, too, and she managed a brief smile. "Thanks, Dev. You don't have to take care of me, really. Despite my reaction a few minutes ago, I'm a big girl. I can take care of myself." She sniffled and took a deep breath. "Let me go wash my face and we can go. I'm already late for my first interview. Zoe must be wondering what happened to us, uh, me."

"If you want I can call her while you go wash your face," he offered. "Let her know we're on our way."

She caressed the side of his face. "I know men hate to hear things like this, but you are so sweet, and thoughtful and . . . kind."

He winced. "You're right, we hate that." He fought to keep his hands away from her.

"But it's true, you know." Her eyes still held the glimmer of tears.

"No, it's not," he said so emphatically she dropped her hand and stared at him. "I'm only doing what friends do for each other when one of them is hurting. And we're friends, right?"

"Right," she agreed.

A second ticked by.

Two seconds.

She stepped up to him and kissed him softly on the mouth. "I think I want those benefits back, Dev."

Thank God.

He slipped his hand behind her neck and cradled her head, holding the perfect angle to match his lips to hers. Much as he wanted to kiss her senseless, this was not the time. In a few hours, when she was over the shock of the news of this serial killer, she might regret the weakness that walked her into his arms and let him comfort her, hold her, kiss her. He returned her kiss gently then grasped her shoulders and stepped away again.

"I want to talk to you about this some more, but you've got things to do today, and so do I. Can I see you later? For dinner, maybe?"

"That would be . . . nice. Can you pick me up at Zoe's about six o'clock? I should be done by then."

"I'll be there. Now you go wash the tear tracks away and I'll call Zoe and tell her you'll be there in fifteen minutes, okay?"

"Yes, thanks. I'll be right out." She went down the hall and her voice echoed back. "Hate it all you want, you're still a kind, sweet man."

Dev grimaced. Once she knew the truth, she was going to hate having said this sweet crap all the more. He dialed the Silvercreek Gallery and Zoe picked up on the second ring.

"Silvercreek Gallery, may I help you?"

"It's Dev, Zoe. Amanda's running a little late. I'll drop her off in about fifteen minutes. Are any of her appointments there yet?"

"One just got here a minute ago. I'll get him some coffee and chat with him till you get here. Thanks for the call, though."

"No problem. Bye."

He scanned the room. He and Jeff had better not waste any time today. He hadn't planned on having dinner with Amanda. He thought he would be dropping her off after a silent and tense ride back from Zoe's. He planned on hightailing it out of there before she even got inside, fully expecting her to be furious when she realized all he had done. Now he was back to clueless as far as what would be going on between them by tonight.

Amanda came back carrying her briefcase, her eyes a little puffy but still beautiful. He helped her on with her coat. "Ready?"

"All set." She led the way out the door. "Are you still going to caulk the windows today?"

"Yes, that's the plan." He opened the car door and she climbed in, then he went around, got in, and started the engine.

"I guess you'll want this then." She handed him a key.

"Right. Thanks." He put his hand out and she dropped the key into his palm. He slipped it into his jacket pocket, wishing he never had to give it back.

On the drive into town, Amanda informed him that she had to stop by the station on Monday. She had filed his corporate tax return on the fifteenth. Now she was working on his personal return. That was due in two weeks.

"I have to admit I haven't done a return for a veteran before, so I want to make sure I've got all the details right. You paid yourself so little since your discharge from the Army that there is no doubt you won't owe the government anything. In fact, you should be getting a refund."

Delivering good news put a smile on her lips and some sparkle back in her eyes. He, on the other hand, felt like he was walking on eggshells. As soon as he dropped her off at the gallery, he bee-lined to Jeff's place, backed the SUV in, and pounded on the studio door.

"Easy, D. You don't have to break the door down, I'm up and ready to go," Jeff said.

"Sorry. I'm anxious to get started. I want us finished by five-thirty, so I can get cleaned up before I pick Amanda up. We're going out to dinner." He delivered this news with all the nonchalance he could muster, but he didn't fool Jeff for a second.

"Dinner, huh? What got you back in Amanda's good graces?"

Jeff gathered tools and joined Dev in loading the Land Rover. Together they had the equipment and supplies packed in five minutes and Dev was barreling down the two-lane road a minute later.

"Dude, we have to live in order to do the work. Slow down to mach two, will you?" Jeff had his foot braced against the dashboard but he grinned as they sped down the road.

"I'm not going any faster than you do on this stretch," Dev shot back. "And don't call me Dude."

"Yeah, but I'm on my bike. It takes corners a lot better than this hunk of—" He revised his description at Dev's dark scowl, "—metal. The center of gravity is a lot lower."

Dev slowed as they went back through town, then sped up again, passing the turn-off to Mrs. Wyndham's in a record three minutes. Still, it was almost ten o'clock when they reached Amanda's bungalow. Dev was out of the truck and up the stairs to the porch before Jeff had unfolded himself from the front seat.

"Hmm, she gave you a key, huh? You never did tell me what turned things around." Jeff followed him inside and went over to the small alcove off the kitchen that held the washer and dryer. Above them was the circuit breaker box. He opened it and gave Dev a thumbs-up. "We're golden, D. Enough breakers in here to hook up the new heaters."

"You're sure you know what you're doing with that electrical panel? I don't want to worry about burning this place down just for the sake of a little hot water."

"No worries, D. My dad was a general contractor. Used to help him out on jobs a lot during my summers in high school. Now I'm a licensed electrician. I got this." He flipped a couple of breakers. "I'm going to kill the power to the baseboard heaters, then you can get them out of here."

The two men worked together with a minimum of conversation for several hours, during which time Dev gained considerable admiration for Jeff's skills as a jack-of-all-trades. While Jeff installed the new water-heater, Dev removed the old baseboard heaters and, after Jeff showed him how to connect the new ones, began installing them. Meanwhile, Jeff tackled the plumbing connections and by one o'clock they had the heat and hot water issues licked. Dev made a quick run to the diner in town and brought back sandwiches and sodas. They took a break to eat and admire their handiwork.

"Once we get the caulking done to block all the drafts, this will be one cozy little cottage," Jeff said.

Dev surveyed the results of their labor so far and nodded. "Wish we could insulate the walls and floor, too," he said, then added quickly when he saw the expression on Jeff's face, "but I know that would be a major remodeling project."

"You got that right. Major with a capital M. It would be easier to knock this place down and start all over again. Be happy with what we're doing. It's going to make a big difference for Amanda. That was the point of this little adventure, right, D?"

"Yeah. I want her safe, comfortable and happy before—" Dev clamped his mouth shut. He caught Jeff studying him, curious to hear the rest of that sentence.

When Amanda had introduced them, he'd found Jeff to be irritating and immature, but after being in close proximity with the man for the past couple of days, he began to see the banter and devil-may-care attitude for the camouflage they were. Underneath all the trash talk and teenage jargon was an intelligent—even sensitive—guy. Not that it meant Dev would share his innermost secrets with him. He didn't trust him that much. The language still got on his nerves, but Dev felt that if he could get past the façade, he and Jeff might just become friends.

"Before . . .?" Jeff prompted.

"Before I'll be satisfied with what we've done." Dev drained his soda, crushed the can, and tossed it into the trash. "Let's finish up. Do you want to caulk the windows or put new weather stripping on the doors?"

Jeff gathered up the remains of his lunch and put them into the garbage. "I'll do the weather stripping. There's only two doors." He grinned, slapping Dev on the back. "You can do the windows."

His smug grin faded a little when Dev reminded him he'd have to take the doors off their hinges to do the job. He tossed Jeff the roll of weather stripping and picked up the caulking gun. Again they fell into a rhythm and worked in companionable silence until Jeff was ready to re-hang the doors.

"I'm gonna need a little help here, D," he called to Dev who was in the bathroom finishing the window over the toilet. "I can't get this sucker back on its hinges by myself. I think it's a little warped."

Dev joined him at the door, a fair amount of caulk decorating his shirt and pants. The glove on his left hand was sticky with the white goo and he hesitated to grab a hold of the door and get caulk all over it.

"Dude, just take the damn glove off," Jeff said, exasperated, as he tried to hold the door in place while Dev vacillated. "I don't give a shit what your hand looks like. It's not going to bother me any."

Dev hesitated, and Jeff blew out a breath.

"Jesus Christ, you treat that thing like it's Medusa's head. I'm not going to faint or go blind if I see it, you know. But if you grab this door and get that caulk all over it, you're cleaning it up. So make up your mind before I drop the damn door on your foot and fuck that up, too."

Dev striped the glove off and dropped it into the sink, then gripped the top half of the door and steadied it while Jeff banged the hinge pins into place.

"Thanks. Now help me with the other door, and we can call it a day."

When they finished, Jeff made it a point to examine Dev's injured hand. He shrugged and said, "Well, it won't win any beauty pageants, but I've seen worse."

"The hell you have," Dev countered as he tried to identify the strange sensation in the pit of his stomach.

"God's truth," Jeff swore. "A guy on my dad's crew got his sleeve caught in a cement mixer. Sucked his arm right into the thing. Now, that was one bloody mess."

He wasn't into one-upmanship when it came to mangled hands, so Dev just nodded. "Yeah, I bet it was."

He went over to the sink to wash out his glove. While he worked, he diagnosed the funny feeling in his gut. It was relief. Not unlike the ability to take a deep breath after being in a strait jacket for eight months. To talk about the 'elephant in the room' that he carried around twenty-four hours a day, seven days a week with the same amount of attention one would give the weather was liberating. Jeff's matter-of-fact appraisal shrunk that elephant to a much less intimidating size. His indebtedness to this guy was growing exponentially.

Jeff started to pick up the debris from their work. He tossed what he called 'salvage' into a cardboard box, the rest went into Amanda's biggest trashcan. Dev joined in the clean up and Jeff watched him stack the old heaters by the front door, and remarked, "Your hand is pretty flexible. Too bad they didn't do some skin grafts to make it look a little better."

"They offered to, but I didn't want to spend any more time in the hospital. I'd been in for weeks and I just wanted out, you know?"

That was partly true. Mostly, though, he didn't feel like he deserved the cosmetic repairs to remove the scars. The nerve damage was too severe to allow him to play the piano again but that wasn't bad enough. He'd wanted to punish himself as much as possible for being alive when Danny wasn't. That was the main sticking point he and Chris Majewski had spent hours debating.

"I guess you could go back and have them do it anytime," Jeff said. "The Army would still pay for it, right? I mean, if you wanted to, that is." Jeff tossed off the comment as he started taking the old heaters out to Dev's truck.

Dev followed him out with some more of them. "Hey, why are you putting them in my truck? Won't the trash collectors pick them up? Or do we have to take them to a local dump?"

"Neither. I'm going to use these in some of the units over at the motel. The ones in there are even older than these and a few don't work at all. These may not be new but they're better than what we've got, and I know George will never spring for new ones. You don't mind if I take 'em, do you?"

"Hell, no. If you can use them, take them."

By five o'clock Amanda's little cottage was neat and tidy and, best of all, warm. Dev turned on one of the lamps in the living room and the one next to her bed, then locked the doors and drove Jeff back to the Blue Point Motor Court. They unloaded everything into one of the currently vacant units. The clouds that had been gathering all day finally reached critical mass and a fine rain started to fall.

Dev stuck out his hand, and Jeff slapped it. "Thanks for all the help, Jeff. I never could have done it without you."

"That's true," Jeff agreed with a grin. He shook his head when Dev peeled off several Ben Franklins from his money clip. "No need for that, Dude. I'll sell these heaters to George and have him pay me to put 'em in. That'll be payment enough."

"No way, guy. You take this. You earned it, and I don't have time to argue." He stuffed the bills into Jeff's shirt pocket. "I have to run. Got to get cleaned up for my dinner date with Amanda."

"You never did tell me how you fixed things with her, Dude."

"Let me get through dinner and the great unveiling tonight before we declare things 'fixed' between me and Amanda. She still might kick me out when she sees what we did today." He climbed into the truck and stuck his head out the window. "And don't call me dude," he said, this time with smile.

He studied his left hand, still without a glove. Should he leave it like this when he picked her up? Wearing a glove was safer. But she wanted to see him, so she said. Might as well get all the shocks over with in one evening.

CHAPTER 16

"Thanks for coming in, Bill," Amanda said. She stood and walked the young man to the door of the gallery. "We'll be in touch with you the week before the party to tell you when to arrive. We're going to have all the staff meet at the little house on Admiral and Mrs. Wyndham's property about two hours before the guests are due, just to go over all the last-minute details. You will be wearing a long-sleeved, white dress shirt with a black bow tie and black slacks. You can change when you get here, and remember, your shirt needs to be starched and ironed, okay?"

"I've got it, Ms. Adams. Don't worry, I'll be here in plenty of time." He hurried to his car through the fine drizzle that had begun to fall.

Amanda heaved a sigh and rubbed the back of her neck. She felt as though she had been talking nonstop since morning. She'd made a big dent in hiring staff today, but she still needed waitresses to circulate with trays of champagne and hors d'oeurves. She went into the back room and sat at Zoe's desk, meticulously adding Bill Leonetti's name to her staffing spreadsheet.

Between the two of them, she and Zoe had interviewed fifteen people today. That had kept her so busy she didn't have time to think about the FBI agent, the serial killer, or Dev. As soon as she closed her laptop, those things popped to the front of her mind.

Her brain was overloaded juggling so many problems. Her car would be ready tomorrow, thank goodness, but the bill had to be paid when she picked it up. Her emergency fund was gone and her checking account was down to double digits. There was no hope for it, she would have to ask Mrs. Wyndham for another advance. She hoped the woman didn't give her a hard time about it. It was her own fault for underestimating the amount of money they needed up front as deposits for all the supplies she had ordered. Mrs. Wyndham knew it was their first event so maybe she would understand.

Amanda propped her elbow on the desk and rested her forehead in the palm of her hand. There were times, like today, when she just wanted to run away from the responsibilities of adulthood.

Zoe came down the back stairs from her apartment carefully balancing two glasses of white wine. She handed one to Amanda and slid a chair next to the desk for herself.

"I don't know about you, but I need to unwind after all that talking. How many did we wind up hiring? I lost track after lunch." She took a big gulp and smacked her lips. "Oh yes, that's much better."

"We hired two bartenders, a caterer, three college boys for valet parking, five more for the clean-up service, and one waitress. We need at least two more to help with set-up in the few hours we'll have to prepare."

Amanda sampled her wine and pinched the bridge of her nose. She'd had a headache dancing behind her eyes all day in spite of the two aspirin she'd taken at lunch. She tugged the elastic band off her hair and ran her fingers through it. Maybe the ponytail she wore was too tight. She suspected the morning's events were the main reason, though.

Zoe watched her over the rim of her glass. "So, talk to me about what held you up this morning. You seemed a little shaken when you finally got here. Did you have a problem with Dev?"

"No. The poor man arrived to pick me up just in time to see me lose it. I got a phone call from an FBI agent. He wanted to know the details about the night Dad went missing."

"Have they come up with something?"

"No. They're still getting information from anyone who's contacted them about a missing person who might have been one of this guy's victims. I'm sure the list is enormous and it will take them months to go through it and try to match up any of the . . . remains they find."

She took another swallow of wine.

"I was so into recalling that night, remembering every little detail and standing in the very room my dad was heading for when he left work, I got pretty emotional." Amanda rolled her eyes. "The moment I hung up from the call, Dev was at the door and I guess I must have looked terrible because he got all concerned. He was so sweet I rewarded him by bursting into tears and sobbing all over his shirt."

"Good thing he was there," Zoe said. "It sounds as though you needed a shoulder to cry on."

"I sure picked a lousy time to have a meltdown though. Leaving you stuck here by yourself with the first interview. He wanted to know what set me off, but I didn't want to take the time to go through it all then, so he's going to pick me up here and take me to dinner. Let's hope I can give him the gist of the past few days without any more histrionics."

"Dinner, hmm? He is being awfully considerate. Especially after that disagreement you were going to tell me about. I'm still waiting for all the details, Mandy." She sipped her wine and watched Amanda expectantly.

"Uh, Zoe, I don't think there's time to talk about this right now. Dev's going to be here any minute and I need to at least run a comb through my hair." She got up to get her purse.

"Of course. I understand completely." She snagged Amanda's arm and tugged her back down into her chair.

"Just give me the *Reader's Digest* version," she said firmly. "I'll get all the juicy details later."

"Zoe, come on, I . . ." She rubbed her forehead at Zoe's raised eyebrow and implacable stare. "Okay, here's the condensed version. We had sex. It was off the charts." She finished her wine in one gulp. "Then I decided I wanted to see his injured arm, which he had managed to keep covered up till then. I suggested we take a shower. He told me in no uncertain terms that I didn't want to see that part of him." She got indignant just thinking about it again. "So I said if I couldn't see all of him we should forget the whole sex thing and just go back to being friends."

Both of Zoe's eyebrows were up to her hairline as she nodded sagely. "Uh, huh."

"Yeah. Stupid move on my part. Especially since he didn't give in and I didn't back down, so our affair lasted roughly four hours. After mulling my decision over for a day, it took about two minutes for me to change my mind when he put his arms around me and let me cry all over him this morning."

"In which case you'd better get freshened up," Zoe said. "Why are you sitting here talking to me?'

Amanda narrowed her eyes. "You're the one who—" She stood up again and headed for the stairs to Zoe's apartment, shaking her head in disgust at her friend's laughter.

She barely had time to wash her face, comb her hair, and put on a bit of lip-gloss when she heard the door to the gallery open and close. That had to be Dev and she wasn't sure how safe it was to leave him alone with Zoe, knowing she'd be trying to wheedle more info out of him—and not very subtly either. Amanda hurried down the stairs.

"Hi." She smiled brightly and picked up her coat.

"Hi." He smiled in return and the heat in his gaze wasn't missed by Amanda—or Zoe.

"I'm all ready to go." She gave Zoe a hug. "I'll talk to you tomorrow, okay?"

Zoe confined her reply to, "Oh yeah." But the twinkle in her eye was unmistakable. Amanda ignored it and put her arm through Dev's as they walked to the door.

Only then did she notice he didn't have a glove on his left hand. Her surprise was so great she almost stopped mid-stride. Instead, she slid her hand down to lace her fingers with his and kept walking. She beamed a smile up at him and tossed a goodbye over her shoulder to Zoe as he opened the door for her. The rain had changed to a fine mist, but the temperature had dropped since sunset. The damp cold was chilling so she leaned closer to Dev, whose body gave off heat like a banked furnace.

"I've been told the little Italian restaurant a couple of blocks from here is pretty good," he said. "Is that okay with you?"

"Yes, it's fine. Donatelli's is one of my favorites. During the summer, it's jammed every night. Even now, in the off season, it's usually pretty busy on a Friday night."

He headed toward his truck but Amanda resisted and suggested they walk since the restaurant was so close. She didn't want to let go of his hand. His decision not to wear a glove was huge, and she wanted him to know she had no problem holding it. He had to be nervous about displaying his injured hand in public. She sent a silent prayer heavenward. *Please God, don't let some jerk make a stupid comment.*

"I hope it's not too busy. I didn't think we'd need reservations, so I didn't call ahead." He slowed down and scanned the few blocks that comprised most of Blue Point Cove's downtown. "If you'd rather we went somewhere else, it's okay with me."

She winked up at him. "Never fear. I've got a little 'in' at Donatelli's. We should be good." She urged him along the sidewalk to the cheerful red and white striped awning that covered a few outdoor tables, deserted in this weather, and preceded him inside.

A hostess stand was just to the left of the door and ten or twelve tables filled the center of the room, with cozy booths marching along one wall. They all had the typical red and white checkered cloths with flickering candles in Chianti bottles as centerpieces, and most appeared to be occupied. The aroma wafting from the kitchen was mouth-watering, and Amanda inhaled deeply.

Dev spoke to the hostess and Amanda had to smile as his voice worked its magic. Pretty and petite, with long dark hair and skin kissed by a Mediterranean sun, the woman allowed her dark brown eyes to rove over Dev with obvious appreciation. A quick glance at her seating chart had her shaking her head regretfully. "I'm so sorry, sir. We've nothing available right now. If you could wait, a table should be free in twenty minutes or so."

Even the fact that Dev and Amanda's hands were still clasped together didn't deter the woman from giving him a radiant smile.

Dev turned to Amanda. "Want to wait or try a different restaurant?"

A waiter had just finished serving diners at a nearby table. The young man caught sight of Amanda and hurried over.

"Ah, *bella*! How good to see you." He hugged her and kissed her on each cheek, then scolded, "You have not been here for too long, Amanda. Let me tell Antonio you are here. He will want to say hello."

"Hello, Mario, it is good to see you, too." Amanda laughed. "I've been so busy, I haven't had time to stop in. But I've brought someone who hasn't had the opportunity to sample Antonio's wonderful crab ravioli. Do you think you could squeeze us in somewhere?"

Young and darkly handsome, the waiter turned to Dev. "Please give us a moment, sir, and we'll have a table ready for you." He spoke in a low voice to the hostess, obviously new on the job. "We always have room for Amanda, Maria." He gave Dev a once-over. "And her beau." He winked at Amanda and headed toward the kitchen.

Maria ignored Amanda completely and concentrated her attention on Dev, her cheeks flushed with embarrassment and her full lips pouting prettily. She apologized so profusely that Amanda would have been annoyed had it not been obvious that all the woman's wiles had zero effect on the man still holding her hand. She couldn't keep a smug smile from her own lips as they waited for the waiter's return.

In a few minutes Mario was back and led them to a table for two near the kitchen. "I hope you don't mind the noise, *bella*," he said over the clatter of plates and pots coming from the back room.

"All the better to smell Antonio's creations," she replied. "Thanks for finding us a spot."

"Do not thank me." He flashed white teeth in a grin. "If Antonio found out we had turned you away, I would have been on a ship back to Italy the next day." He lit the candle in the center of the table and disappeared.

"I can see why you weren't worried about reservations," Dev said.

"I took over doing their books last fall," Amanda explained. "I saved them a lot of money, so Antonio loves me now." The sharp look Dev shot her had her laughing again. "Not like that, you silly man. He loves me like a daughter. Wait till you meet him. He's shorter than I am and twice as wide, but his heart is bigger than the moon."

"And the waiter? He seemed pretty smitten—not that I blame him." Dev picked up his menu and opened it. "He's certainly not old enough to be your father, and given the chance, I think he'd be happy to do much more than serve you food."

"Really? You think he might like to date me?" She had to bite the inside of her cheek to keep a straight face when Dev scowled at her over the top of his menu.

"Well, I'd have to ask Anna if she would mind if I went out with her husband, but she's pretty busy with their two kids, so maybe she'd like him out of the house once in a while." She picked up her own menu and used it to hide her grin.

"You think you're pretty smart, don't you?"

"Not really, but I am thinking you might be just a tiny bit jealous."

"Not at all. I was just commenting on his enthusiastic greeting."

"He's Italian, Dev. European men are very demonstrative. It doesn't mean anything." She perused the menu and added as an afterthought, "Unlike the hostess, who would have scribbled her phone number on your shirt sleeve if you'd have given her half a chance." She kept her eyes on the menu until the long silence made her peek over the top.

"Now who's sounding jealous?" he said, grinning. "Believe me, no one's scribbling anything on my sleeve but you," he said with that voice that sent heat spiraling through her. He reached across the table and clasped her hand with his damaged one. "Thanks for being so cool about this."

She deliberately studied his hand as she laced her fingers between his, then brought his hand to her lips. She kissed each knuckle lightly. "I am sorry for your injury, because it's stopped you from becoming the great jazz pianist I know you would have been. But it hasn't kept you from being a wonderful man." She gripped his hand more tightly as he tried to break away. "And it certainly hasn't kept me from seeing you as one very sexy guy."

Mario's return to take their order finally made her let go. Dev ordered a bottle of Chianti and Mario quickly brought a basket of crusty Italian bread and a large plate of antipasto.

After he poured them each a glass of the dark red wine, he left with their order—the house special of crab ravioli in lobster sauce.

"Tell me about the FBI," Dev said.

She went through the past few days from the initial newspaper story that had appeared in the report from her clipping service, to her phone call to the police in Winston, Virginia, and finally to the conversation with Agent Thorndyke. Luckily the intervening hours and her busy day provided enough distance to keep her from dissolving into an emotional mess during the telling. By the time she was done, their dinners had arrived and both of them were hungry enough to give their full attention to Antonio's delicious food.

"It's not that I think he might still be alive." She picked up their conversation over a second glass of wine as their plates were removed. "I gave up that hope years ago. My dad would never willingly abandon us. But I always thought the reality of what happened to him couldn't be as bad as some of the things I imagined. Now I'm not so sure."

The somber tone of their conversation was dispelled as a short, rotund man in chef's whites barreled through the kitchen door, carrying two plates holding large portions of tiramisu. He set them in front of Amanda and Dev, then leaned down to buss Amanda on each cheek.

"You stay away too long, bella," he boomed. "See how skinny you are? You should come here more often. I would not let you get so thin."

She laughed. "I'm sure you wouldn't, Antonio. If I came by more often I would weigh as much as you." She poked him playfully in his belly. "I want to introduce you to my friend, Dev. Antonio Donatelli, Devlyn MacMurphy."

Dev started to get up.

"No. No. Don't get up. We are not so formal here, *si*? More like *famiglia*, eh?" He looked to Amanda for confirmation.

"Yes. Like *famiglia*." She smiled fondly.

"I am glad to meet you," Dev said. "You are a superb chef, Antonio. The food was delicious."

Antonio beamed at the praise. "Ah, a nice man, Amanda. You have good taste." He gestured to the plates. "Now, *mangia, mangia tutto*!"

"You brought us too much, Antonio." Amanda patted her stomach. "I am stuffed full of ravioli and antipasto. Can we take it home to eat later?"

Antonio was disappointed but resigned. "*Si*. You eat later. You come back again soon," he ordered as he returned to the kitchen.

They left the restaurant with boxes full of the sweet Italian dessert. Amanda's stomach was full but her hunger for Dev grew with every passing minute.

CHAPTER 17

The ride to Amanda's place took longer than Dev expected. The rain started again after they left the restaurant and he drove slowly in the pitch dark with the rain coming down so hard the wipers could barely keep up. Amanda slid over so that their shoulders touched and balanced the dessert boxes on her lap. They passed Crooked Neck Road, the turn-off that led to the Wyndham's place, and Dev began to tense up. His initial plan had been to drop Amanda off and leave, letting her find the changes to her little cottage on her own. That way there would be time for her to calm down before she saw him the next morning.

He now viewed that plan as cowardly. But, shit, they'd had such a nice dinner together he hated the thought of ruining it with a fight. Maybe she wouldn't be angry. Jeff thought she'd be grateful, but Dev wasn't so sure. She was so damned independent—which was a good thing, as far as his promise to Danny went. Not such a good thing when he'd done a whole bunch of stuff to her property without her permission.

Their reconciliation this morning might be over before it began and he could be going home sad, horny, and covered in tiramisu.

"You're awfully quiet. Is something wrong?"

It was uncanny the way this woman could read him. "Just concentrating on staying on the road. I wouldn't want to put us in a ditch in a storm like this."

"Not like some other crazy driver might," she teased.

He had to smile at that. "Let the record show that you brought up bad drivers, not me."

"So noted, Mr. MacMurphy." She sighed and leaned her head on his shoulder. "Too bad you have to go to work tonight."

He ordered his little head to stand down. That one simple comment from Amanda had it up and exploring the possibility of escape.

"Yeah."

"Don't you ever get a night off?" she asked, sounding wistful.

His pants got tighter.

Up until he met Amanda he relished having to work every night. It gave him something to do besides think of what happened in Iraq—and what he wasn't getting done here, now that he was out of the hospital. The beautiful blond with the mesmerizing gray eyes had changed all that.

"Not so far. I've got to hire another announcer first. I thought I was set when Lance Fisher applied for a job, but it turns out he's a much better fit as an engineer than an on-air personality."

He stopped in front of Amanda's bungalow and the headlights caught reflections from a pair of eyes under the porch.

"What's that?" She pointed to the twin green dots.

"Probably just a raccoon or a possum trying to stay out of the rain. Nothing to worry about." He cut the motor and the green reflections disappeared. "You stay here. I'll go open the door. Do you have an umbrella?"

"Yes, it's in the closet off the kitchen."

"Good. I'll get it and come back to get you. No sense in both of us getting soaked."

"Okay. I'm leaving one of these desserts here for you. Lord knows I don't need two of them."

"Yeah," he agreed. When she swung around in the seat, her face indignant in the glow from the porch light, he smiled to himself. "You're sweet enough already."

"You like living close to the edge, do you?"

We'll see just how close in a few minutes.

"Keeps the blood pumping, you know?"

He slid out of the seat and ran for the door. He was inside in seconds and went to find the umbrella. The place was warm and cozy—a nice contrast to the cold rain outside. He went out the door and opened the umbrella. What was that sound coming from under the porch? He hoped to God whatever animal it was wasn't hurt. Amanda was so soft-hearted she'd have him crawling around under there trying to rescue the damned thing.

He opened the car door and helped her out, tiramisu in one hand, laptop in the other. Keeping her sheltered under the umbrella required him to stay very close as they made their way up the steps. Just as they reached the door, a black streak shot by them into the house. Amanda shrieked and stumbled over the threshold, glancing around wildly. He snapped the umbrella closed and followed her in, slamming the door behind him.

No chance of a fast getaway now.

"Did you see where it went?" She stood in the center of the room, still clutching her laptop and the dessert box.

"I think it went down the hall. I'll see if I can find it. You stand by the door. If it runs back this way, open it fast and maybe it'll run back out."

Amanda nodded. She set the laptop and box on the table, then went to stand by the door.

A few minutes later he called out, "Found it. It ran under the bed in your office."

There was the sound of a brief scuffle.

"You can forget the door. It's not dangerous. In fact, I don't think you're going to toss it back out in the rain."

He came back down the hall, carrying a little bundle of wet, black fur. A pitiful meow identified it as a coal-black kitten, soaked and shivering in Dev's arms.

"Ohhh," Amanda cried, scooping up the soggy kitten and cuddling it against her chest. "Oh, you poor baby. What were you doing out on a night like this?"

The kitten nuzzled under her neck and started to purr. She turned surprised eyes to him and he shrugged. He knew nothing about cats, but he'd be purring too if she held him like that.

She went back to the bathroom and got a towel then handed cat and towel to Dev. "Hold her a second while I get my coat off."

She hung up her coat then came back and relieved Dev of the kitten who was doing its best to burrow under the folds of the towel.

"Okay, your turn. Take that wet coat off before you catch a cold."

He did as he was told, watching her tenderly rub the towel over the kitten's face. So far she hadn't seemed to notice how warm the room was. When she did, he hoped the kitten would provide him some protection. How furious could she get while she held a bedraggled cat? This might work out better than he'd hoped.

"The poor little thing is so skinny. I wonder if she's lost or abandoned." Amanda sat at her kitchen counter and continued to dry the stray. "She's probably hungry, Dev. There's a can of tuna in the cabinet over there. Would you be a dear and open it for me?"

He brought the can and a saucer over to the counter and rummaged through the drawers to find an opener. Once he got it open the little cat lost all interest in being dried off and struggled to get out of Amanda's arms and over to the dish.

"Okay, okay, you little spook, here you go." Amanda put the saucer on the floor and the kitten attacked the tuna. "It's a good thing it's nice and warm in here or the poor . . ." She stopped mid-sentence and peered around the room.

Here we go.

"Wow. I didn't realize how much difference caulking the windows would make." She wandered around the room, put her hand up to the kitchen window, and brushed the curtain back. "No drafts." A pleased smile lit her face. "Dev, thank you. Your work made this place so much warmer. I'm amazed." She came over and kissed him on the cheek. "I owe you one."

He put his arms around her. "Doesn't all my hard work deserve more than just a kiss on the cheek?" Without waiting for an answer, he captured her lips and kissed her soundly. When he released her, her eyes had already gotten hazy.

"Hold that thought," she said. "I'm going to get a dry towel and make a place for Spook to sleep tonight. Then we'll see about thanking you properly for what you did."

While she was gone, he considered making a run for it. Any second now, she'd stop thinking about that cat long enough to take a good look around. At that point he doubted that thanking him properly would include any intimate contact.

She brought a dry towel back, then went over to the alcove that held the washer/dryer to put the damp one in the laundry pile.

"I wish I had a cardboard box or something to—"

There was the pause he'd been expecting.

She leaned around the corner with a puzzled frown. "Dev, what's this . . . thing . . . on the wall over here?"

"It's a hot water heater. One of those tank-less kind that heats the water instantly as you need it."

"But—"

"I saw it in the store when I bought the caulk and remembered you saying how your hot water supply was kind of limited, so I figured, what the heck . . .?"

"Dev." She shook her head. "Listen, I appreciate the gesture, but I can't afford this right now. You shouldn't have bought it without asking me first."

"It's not that big a deal, Amanda. The thing didn't cost all that much."

"However much it cost was more than I have."

She got another saucer out and put some water down next to the tuna. When she didn't straighten up right away, he knew the other shoe had dropped. She finally straightened up and without a word, walked slowly around the main room, then went down the hall and checked both bedrooms and the bath. By the time she came back, her cheeks were pink and her eyes snapped with anger.

"Are there any more little surprises for me to find, Dev?"

He grimaced. "Nope. I think you've seen everything."

"What could possibly have led you to believe that I would be okay with all this?"

She strode up to him and poked him repeatedly in the chest, emphasizing her points.

"One, I don't have the money to pay for it. Two, I don't know you well enough to accept it as a gift. And three, you didn't even ask me if I wanted a, a tank-less water . . . thingy."

She was so mad she was sputtering. Well, he knew it was going to be bad. It was time to apologize. To grovel, and beg forgiveness. But she was so damn cute all fired up like this, he made the mistake of smiling.

Her eyes went wide. "You think this is funny?" she exploded. "You think you can just waltz into my life and do whatever you damn well please to it? Or is it that since I slept with you once you thought you needed to pay me somehow?"

"Oh for Christ's sake, of course it's not payment of any kind for anything," he shot back, angry himself now. "I simply hated the thought of you here, cold and uncomfortable, when I could so easily fix things."

She spun around and stalked to the sink. He watched her shoulders rise and fall as she took deep breaths. When she turned back to him, her gray eyes held more than a hint of frost. "This stunt of yours was completely unacceptable, Dev. The only reason I haven't beaned you with my frying pan and thrown you out in the rain is because I'm giving you points for your kindness and generosity."

He opened his mouth to speak and she threw up her hand, an imperious queen addressing her miscreant vassal. "I'm not finished. I will pay you back for this."

He tried to get a word in, and again he got cut off.

"Don't. Argue. I will repay you. That's non-negotiable. *You—*" Her pointed finger shot invisible bullets. "—will promise never to do anything like this ever again, or we will call our friendship off."

Her back was a ramrod, and her chin angled up in challenge as she delivered her ultimatum. Again he was tempted to smile, but had the good sense to restrain himself. They regarded each other in silence as seconds ticked away.

"Well?" she demanded.

"Am I permitted to speak now?" he asked politely.

Her eyes flared briefly, then narrowed. "Yes."

"I apologize. You are absolutely right. I should not have done this without asking you first. It was rude and overbearing and I am very, very sorry."

Her eyes softened minutely. Good. Groveling was working. And he should grovel. She was right after all, and would be even more outraged if she ever found out the starter the mechanic was putting in her car wasn't from a junker, but a new one purchased by him. He'd sworn Mr. Evers to secrecy and he wasn't about to divulge any more of his devious deeds to Amanda.

Even when he finally told her about his friendship with Danny, he wouldn't mention his promise. There'd be more than a flying frying pan in his future if she knew he had done any of this to fulfill a promise to her dead fiancé.

He sighed, doing his best to appear as pitiful as a homeless kitty. “I don’t want you to pay me back, but if that is the price of keeping our friendship, I’ll accept your terms.”

“It is.” She caught her bottom lip between her teeth. “It . . . may take me a while.”

He shrugged. “I’m not going anywhere. In fact, why don’t we do this? Let’s put off your repayment for six months. That will give you time to get your new business off to a good start and pick up a few more accounting clients. Then we’ll talk about a plan to pay me back that you can handle.” *Assuming you’ll even speak to me by then.*

“Fine. I’ll need the receipts for everything that you bought. I’ll figure a reasonable cost for your labor on top of that.” She went over to her briefcase and got out her Day-Timer. “Six months from today will be September twentieth. I intend to repay you the total amount on that day.”

Dev threw his hands up in defeat. “As you wish.”

She came over and sat next to him at the counter. “I don’t mean to sound so ungrateful. It was awfully kind of you to go to so much trouble for me. I can’t imagine how you managed to get so much accomplished in a few short hours. You did an awesome amount of work. But that’s nothing compared to this,” she said, picking up his left hand and lacing her fingers through his. “It makes me feel I’m getting to know the real you. The one behind the smooth-talking radio host who takes me on a sentimental journey every Friday night.”

“You’re tougher than I thought, Ms. Adams,” he said, studying her smooth, graceful fingers intertwined with his scarred, twisted ones. “Not even a flinch when you first noticed the glove was off.” He leaned over and kissed her. “Thanks for that. But, in the interest of full disclosure, I have to tell you that Jeff helped me do all this. In fact, without his expertise, I never would have been able to do anything more than the caulking.”

"Oh my. So now I owe Jeff, too? The luxury of all this warmth is really going to cost me."

"I've already compensated him financially, but I'm sure he'd appreciate your thanks. No way would I cut him out of the massive amount of credit he deserves for helping me with this little project." Dev paused, thinking back over the day's work. "He's a pretty complex character, you know?"

"Yes, he is, and I'm so glad you can see that in him too. He puts up such an annoying façade to most people that they don't take the time to get to know him. Underneath all that attitude, he's smart and actually quite sweet."

"So I'm finding out."

He pointed down at the kitten. "Better find a place for her to sleep. Now that she's warm and dry, with a full belly, she'll want to take a nap." Amanda picked up the sleepy kitten and set it in the towel she'd formed into a bed. It blinked slowly and yawned, then collapsed into a small furry heap and was instantly asleep.

"I hope no one claims her. I haven't had a cat since I was a kid in school. It would be nice to have her here for company." Amanda stroked the soft fur for a minute. "I couldn't have a cat . . . before."

"Yeah, Danny's allergies would have gone ballistic," Dev said, then wanted to kick himself.

"How did you know Danny was allergic to cats?" she asked in surprise.

He scrambled for some plausible explanation, then spied Danny's picture on the bookshelf. He nodded in that direction. "Are you kidding? With that red hair and fair skin? I've never met anyone with that kind of coloring who wasn't allergic to damn near everything. I . . . guess I just . . . assumed he would be, too."

"Well, you assumed correctly. Put him in the same room with a cat and in five minutes his eyes would water and the sneezing would start. It was such a shame, too, because he really loved animals."

Nice going, Dev. You keep sticking your foot in your mouth like that and this little charade you've got going will be over before you're ready.

Silence settled around them and Amanda seemed lost in her memories. Dev stroked a finger down her cheek to bring her back to the present.

"Listen, you've had a very busy day and I have to get to work." He tipped her chin up and kissed her lightly. "Call me at the station tomorrow when you're ready to get your car and I'll come by and pick you up."

"Okay. Thank you again for all that you've done. I'll be even more grateful tomorrow morning when I can get out of bed without getting frostbite," she said. "Drive carefully, now."

"No worries. All the crazy drivers around here are home in bed by now," he teased.

She gave him a punch on his shoulder and walked him to the door. He leaned down and captured her mouth one last time in a kiss that was way more than friendly. This one was hot enough to remind her that she had wanted those 'benefits' back—and so did he.

CHAPTER 18

Amanda brought the makeshift bed and the sleeping kitten back to her bedroom. Tomorrow she'd print some fliers to put up around town when she went to pick up her car. The little stray didn't have a collar on, so she hoped that meant she wasn't already someone's pet. It would be nice to have company, and a cat would be perfect.

Funny how Dev had figured out Danny's allergy, just from seeing his picture. That was one smart man.

Her lips still tingled from his kiss and her body ached for his mouth to work its magic elsewhere too. The next time they made love she intended to touch, taste, and savor every inch of Dev MacMurphy, including those parts he'd been so reluctant to show her.

This 'friends with benefits' arrangement could become a problem, though. It seemed she got more benefits than a super hot man in her bed. She didn't want anything else. Certainly not home improvements. All the work he did just made her nervous. Did he think he owed her something in exchange for sex? He'd better not or she would be seriously pissed off. But if not, whatever had prompted him to go out and buy all that stuff? It couldn't be solely because he wanted to sleep with her. He already knew that was going to happen after they made up this morning.

They were good together, that first time. Before her stubbornness had ruined things.

Good? Okay, the sex was great, Amanda, stop kidding yourself.

But with looks like his and a voice that could melt ice at twenty paces, he surely could find other willing partners who didn't come with so much emotional baggage. Women for whom home remodeling wasn't necessary.

But you don't want him to, do you?

Her conscience sat on her shoulder, smug and superior, forcing her to face the truth. *That cute hostess at Donatelli's got under your skin a little, didn't she? Tried to poach on your preserve right in front of you, and if Dev had shown the least little bit of interest you would have had to . . . what? Tell her to back off, he was already taken?*

No, no, that is *not* the way their arrangement was supposed to work, she argued back. Mutual physical attraction, yes. Lots of sexual satisfaction, hell, yes. Emotional involvement, definitely not. She silenced the annoying voice in her head, temporarily at least.

Slipping into a set of satin boy shorts and tank top, Amanda delighted in the sensuous slide of the fabric over her skin. A definite improvement compared to the flannel PJs she'd worn last night.

She turned on the radio. Since she'd first tuned in, listening to his request hour had become a habit. She slid beneath the sheets and snuggled against the pillow, still faintly scented with Dev's woodsy cologne. Should she call in and request something? What would he be expecting?

She dialed.

"What would the most gorgeous woman in Somerset County like to hear tonight?"

The deep rumble of his sexy voice caused an automatic clenching between her legs.

"How'd you know it was me?"

"Had to be. The hair on the back of my neck stands up when you call."

"That's a lie."

"No, it does," he insisted. "I also have caller ID, so that helps, too."

She smirked to herself. "I have a request."

"Shoot."

"'Let's Call the Whole Thing Off'."

"What?"

"You heard me." She waited a few seconds while silence reigned on the other end. "The song, you fool," she finally said and chuckled. "Fred Astaire? Ginger Rogers? 'Shall We Dance'? You have heard of it, haven't you?"

"Yes. Yes, of course I've heard of it," he replied, sounding a bit put out. "I just thought, for a minute there . . ."

She heard him exhale, and felt a stab of guilt.

"Okay, I guess I deserved that," he said.

"Um, yeah, but I'm not one to hold a grudge. Want to try breakfast again? We might actually eat it this time."

"Better make something we can eat cold. We won't be getting to it right away," he said, his voice dropping down into the heart-pounding, thigh-dampening register.

"Right," she agreed. "See you in the morning." She set the phone back in the cradle.

The next song after her request was "You're the Top".

She was really getting to like this guy.

Eight a.m. on Saturday had Amanda cooking an old-fashioned Southern breakfast for Dev and herself. Ever since their first aborted breakfast together, she'd wanted to make the meal he had reminisced so fondly about. Sausages, bacon, and waffles were being kept warm in the oven while she made home fried potatoes, a substitution for grits, which she hated and couldn't bring herself to cook. As soon as Dev arrived she would slip the eggs into the waiting pan and put the toast in the toaster. She was no gourmet cook but this hearty meal was one even she could handle.

She hoped it might put him in a good enough mood to take her to the daffodil festival in Princess Ann. The April sky was robin's egg blue without a cloud in sight. The temperature was predicted to climb into the mid-sixties, warm for this early in the spring, and Amanda saw that as a sign that she should take one whole day to ignore Mrs. Wyndham's party and the two remaining tax returns she had to finish for her clients. It would be nice to get out into the sunshine and fresh air. She might have to use some other incentives besides breakfast to get Dev to go to a flower show. She smiled to herself at the thought.

There was just one thing related to the party she had to do. She needed Dev's measurements for the tux she would rent. Once that was taken care of they'd have the rest of the day for themselves.

The sound of tires on gravel alerted her. She glanced at the clock. Eight-thirty-one. The man was amazingly punctual. She met him at the door and he swept her into his arms for a lingering kiss.

"Good morning, gorgeous," he said as he tucked a stray lock of hair behind her ear.

"Good morning to you too. Could I have another one of those, please?"

"Anything my lady wishes."

He kissed her again, long and deep. She slid her arms around his neck and felt the hair curling over his collar still damp from his shower. A warm hand slid under her tee shirt and inched its way upward. She danced back out of his embrace, and slapped his hand.

"Nope. We're having breakfast this morning, not brunch after you've had your way with me. Come sit down and have some juice."

She took his hand and tugged him toward the table.

"Are you sure, honey? I could be quick. We could be quick."

He hauled her in the opposite direction—toward the bedroom. She dug in her heels.

"You lie. Once we get in that bedroom we won't come out for hours and you know it. I've made you a special breakfast this morning and I'm not letting it get dried up and cold. Now sit," she commanded.

Dev sighed deeply. "You're getting awfully bossy, you know that?" He sat but didn't release her hand.

"I am not," she declared.

"Am I?" She bit her lip.

He tugged her down for another quick kiss. "No, darling. You're perfect."

"Well, now, I know that's a fib." She tried to remove her hand from his grip but he held her fast. "Let me get the food on the table, mister, or we'll never get to . . . anything else."

He released her instantly and she rolled her eyes skyward. By the time all the food was set out, he could only stare at the platters, plates, and bowls. "Good Lord, woman, how long did it take you to cook all this? And when are the other ten people coming to help us eat it all?"

"I wanted it to be like those breakfasts you told me about when you were a kid," she said with some hesitation.

He merely gazed at her with enough warmth in his eyes to start an answering heat in her heart. "Thank you, darling, it smells delicious." He began to pile his plate with some of everything. "Seriously, though, you made enough food to feed an army. We should be inviting the homeless in for a meal."

"I did get a bit carried away," she admitted. "Why don't we wrap up what's left and take in to the studio? Your crew always acts half-starved. Surely some of them would eat it."

"We could," he agreed. "But that would mean we'd have to go out." He looked wistfully down the hall toward the bedroom.

"True." She kept her eyes on her plate. "I, ah, thought we might go out today, anyway." She glanced up quickly then back at her plate where she pushed home fries and sausage around without taking a bite. "There's a festival in Princess Ann. It's not very far and the weather is supposed to be beautiful . . ." She chanced a peek at Dev's face.

"I knew from that first day in my office you were a conniver. I just never realized the depths to which you would sink to get your way." His gaze roved over the table full of food and settled back on her.

"I am not a conniver. I wanted to cook you a nice breakfast. The festival just happened to fall on the same day." Her bottom lip pushed out in a pout. "We don't have to go. We can just take the food to the studio and you can go home and get some decent rest for a change."

"Not a conniver, huh?" He chuckled. "Did I detect a not-so-veiled threat that I would sleep alone if we didn't go to this festival thing?"

"It was not a threat. I don't know how you get by on so little sleep as it is. I simply figured you would do well to catch up a little." She had to bite the inside of her lip to keep from laughing.

"Once again it seems you've made me an offer I can't refuse. The festival it is."

He sat back and sipped his coffee.

She smiled brilliantly.

"What kind of festival is it, anyway?"

The smile wavered the slightest bit. "Daffodil. It's the Annual Daffodil Festival."

"Conniver," he mumbled into his coffee cup.

"What did you say?"

"Nothing, darling."

Amanda started packing up the leftovers. "I have one other thing on my to-do list for today. I need your measurements for the tuxedo I'm renting for the party."

"You don't need to rent a tuxedo for me."

"Oh, please don't be one of those men who hate to wear formal clothes," she said. She snapped the lid onto a plastic container of sausages and gave an exasperated shake of her head.

"I'm not. I—"

"You know, I never could figure out why so many men moan and groan over getting dressed in formal wear," Amanda interrupted. "You all like it when women wear something sexy, don't you? Plunging necklines, thigh-high slits in our skirts, rhinestone-encrusted bustiers? Right?"

Both eyebrows heading north, Dev could only nod.

"Well, here's a newsflash. Put a man in a tuxedo, dinner jacket, or military dress uniform and you're more than halfway to success in the seduction department. We women loooove to see our men in formal wear."

"That's good to know. But I wasn't trying to get out of wearing a tux."

"Oh."

"I was trying to explain that you don't need to rent one. I own several sets of formal clothes. Everything from white tie and tails to dinner jackets."

"Wow. I had no idea."

"Yeah, well, you don't graduate from the New England Conservatory without acquiring at least one tuxedo. Especially if you've trained in classical piano. My family was more generous along those lines, since they expected I would be going on the concert circuit after graduation."

"And they still fit you?"

"Probably. I bulked up in the Army but after all that time in the hospital, I'm back to my old size. I'll call Mom and ask her to send them down. What do you want me to wear?"

Visions of him in white tie and tails danced in her head. She'd love to see him like that, but no one else would be dressed that formally.

"A regular tuxedo will be fine. You'll be absolutely dashing."

“I’m going to wear white gloves, too. I don’t want any of Mrs. W’s guests freaking out and ruining your party.”

He put a finger over her lips when she tried to protest. “Don’t argue with me this time, Amanda. Think about it and you’ll realize I’m right.”

She kissed the finger, then nodded. “All right. You can have your way this time.”

Dev went to the pantry where she stashed grocery bags and retrieved a couple to pack the containers in while she finished clearing the dishes. She piled them in the sink to wash after they came back from the festival. Spook was curled up in a square of sunshine on the floor. She’d be fine till they came home.

“Okay, darlin’, let’s get a move on,” Dev urged her.

“I had no idea you’d be so anxious to get to the festival,” she teased as she got her blazer out of the closet. Dev helped her slip it on and nuzzled her neck in the process.

“I’m not. It’s what comes after the festival I’m anticipating,” he whispered in her ear. The resulting quiver of delight arced its way to all of her erogenous zones. This was going to be one wonderful day.

“No! Don’t! Get back. Get—”

Amanda woke to the sound of panic. Dev thrashed his right arm and groaned as if in pain. She caught at his arm and grabbed his shoulder.

“Dev, wake up. You’re dreaming.” She switched on the bedside lamp, then shook his shoulder a little harder. He was bathed in sweat, his face contorted in a grimace that was frightening to see. “Wake up, Honey. It’s just a nightmare.” She stroked his damp hair off his forehead and he jerked away from her touch, opening his eyes but obviously not seeing the bedroom or her. “Honey, it’s me, Amanda. Please wake up,” she begged.

He jerked out of her grasp, put the flat of his hand against her chest, and shoved with all his might. She flew backward across the bed and off the side, knocking the clock radio off the table and cracking her elbow against its edge. She landed with a resounding thump and the alarm went off, loud enough to scare Spook and send her running for cover.

Dev sat up and leaned over the side.

Amanda scooted backward at the sudden move. "Are you awake?"

"Yeah."

He scanned the room, still a little disoriented. She went to get up but her elbow protested and she sat down hard. "Ow."

Dev was on the floor next to her in seconds. Gathering her into his arms, he picked her up and sat on the bed with her in his lap.

"Oh, baby, I'm so sorry. Show me where it hurts." He examined her arm, squeezing gently along its length until she reacted with another "ouch." Her skin was intact but a bruise was already beginning over the outside of her elbow. "Can you bend it?"

"I could, but I don't want to."

"Shit. I'll get some ice. It'll help to keep the swelling down." He went to slide her off his lap onto the bed.

"Wait." She could feel the pounding of his heart where her arm rested against his chest. The sheen of perspiration on his face gleamed in the lamplight. "Are you all right?" She searched his eyes for reassurance that the Dev she knew was back in control.

"I'm fine. Let me get the ice, baby, I'll be right back."

He maneuvered her onto the bed and put a pillow behind her back. Aching elbow or no, she enjoyed the rear view of her totally naked lover as he hustled toward the kitchen. A few seconds later the sound of ice being smashed by a very heavy object was followed by drawers being opened and closed.

"I need a—"

"Bottom right-hand drawer," she called down the hall.

He came back with the ice wrapped in a dishtowel. He laid it against the bruise and wrapped a second towel around her arm to hold it in place.

"You could at least wait until I finish the question before you answer it, smarty." He kissed her lightly on the tip of her nose.

"Why? I always know what you want." She patted the mattress next to her. "Come on over here and give me something to lean against." When he settled at her side, she snuggled against him, arranging the covers up over their laps.

"That must have been some nightmare." She felt his whole body tense. "You want to talk about it?"

"No."

She sighed. "Okay. But if you ever do, I'll be glad to listen."

"Thank you. If I ever do, you'll be first on my list of listeners."

She smiled and kissed his chest. She loved the feel of him, the play of his muscles under her lips. The light dusting of hair across his chest, arrowing down his flat belly to the darker nest of hair surrounding his manhood drew her eyes like a magnet. And where her eyes went, her mouth longed to follow. Her own heart rate kicked up and despite the ice against her elbow, she felt her hands warm.

For the past two weeks they had spent every non-working moment together—most of them right here, in this bed. Some days it was in the evening before he went in to work, some days in the morning as soon as he was off the air. She'd finally gotten him to take his shirt off and while the sight of his damaged arm broke her heart, it didn't repel her or diminish her attraction one little bit. The rest of his body was everything any woman could want and she'd enjoyed every inch of it thoroughly. She'd like to know him on the inside just as well.

"Maybe I shouldn't sleep here anymore."

"What?" She pushed away from him so she could look him in the eye. "That's it? You've had enough of me already?"

"Don't try to twist my words, woman. You know I haven't had enough of you." He brushed a finger over her cheek. "I'm not sure I'll ever have enough, but that's not what I'm saying. I don't want to take the chance I might hurt you again."

"Oh for Pete's sake," she huffed, "you didn't hurt me."

"I did. I don't want it to happen again, Amanda, but I never know when I'm going to have a nightmare."

"Are they always the same dream?"

"Pretty much, yeah."

She reached down and held his left hand, then brought it to her lips and kissed each finger. "It's about how you got hurt over in Iraq, isn't it?" He didn't answer, but his hand curled into a fist. "Well, maybe if you talked to somebody about them they would stop happening."

"No." He snatched his hand away.

"I didn't mean me, Dev. You should talk to someone who could help you."

"I've already talked to people. They couldn't help me. No one can help me."

"I don't believe that." She smoothed her hand over his solid abs, stopping tantalizingly short of her goal.

"I." She leaned down and kissed his chest.

"Only know." She kissed his neck.

"One way." She kissed his ear.

"To help." She kissed his cheek.

"You." She laid claim to his mouth and slid her leg over his, gratified to feel the evidence that her plan was working poke her in the belly.

"Your arm," he growled when she broke the kiss, his words harsh.

Amanda put her lips against the pounding pulse point at the base of his neck. His breathing became ragged, but he kept his hands at his sides. She smiled like a vixen, her eyes heavy-lidded. "The only way we can be sure it won't get hurt again," she whispered, sitting back to straddle his hips, "is to let me have full control." She reached over to the drawer in the nightstand, aware that the movement slid her along the rigid length of him, coating his shaft with her slick warmth. She held up a foil packet.

He reached for it but she held it away and shook her head. "Oh no." She paused to adjust her position and slide her clit to the tip of his erection, again applying the hot juices now flooding between her legs. His pupils dilated until the jade green was but a thin circle around them. "My idea of full control means you cannot use your hands at all. Only your mouth." She leaned forward to bring her breasts close to his face and he groaned as he nipped, licked, and finally suckled one peak, then the other.

Amanda writhed in delight as sounds of approval escaped her. She wiggled her tush in slow circles, the friction releasing even more of her honeyed sweetness.

"Enough of this torture, minx. If you don't open that packet soon it may be too late." Dev's hands were fisted in the sheets, his knuckles white with the tightness of his grip.

Knowing how close she was to her own release, Amanda acquiesced to his demand and quickly covered him. She intended to impale herself on his cock slowly, to savor the sensation as he stretched her, then filled her completely. But she'd waited too long, allowed herself to get too close to the precipice. So when Dev thrust into her, seating himself deeply, she felt her climax begin.

"Oh, yes!" she shouted as it crescendoed through two more deep, rapid strokes and burst upon her with the force of a thunder clap, lights pinwheeling behind her closed lids, sensation pulsing outward from her center as wave after wave of ecstasy cascaded along her nerve endings, leaving her nearly senseless in the aftermath. She collapsed onto his chest, every muscle in her body turned to liquid from the heat of their joining. Dev followed, scarcely a beat behind, her 'no hands' rule forgotten as he gripped her hips and buried himself to the hilt again and again.

Once their breathing had returned to near normal, he gently turned her over, still careful of her bruised arm, and got up to dispose of the condom. She protested, his absence for even a few seconds leaving her feeling strangely bereft. He was back in less than a minute, tucking her against him spoon-fashion, his arm around her with her breast cradled in his hand and his breath warm on her neck. Amanda smiled to herself, his plan not to sleep with her again vanquished by post-coital bliss.

His nightmare still worried her and she debated talking to Chris Majewski about it, but discarded that idea as being too meddlesome.

"How is your new employee working out? The one Chris sent over?"

"What brought that up? You're supposed to be drifting off to a satisfied nap or I'm not performing as well as I should be."

Amanda twisted in his arms to face him and kissed him lightly. "Your 'performance' was spectacular, as always. But I just had a nap and I'm not tired anymore. Besides, I hate to waste any of the time we're together sleeping."

"I second that motion." He drifted a finger across the slope of her breast and smiled as her nipple peaked in response.

Amanda held his hand to prevent further exploration. "There are other things two people can do together besides . . ." She almost said 'make love' but caught herself. "Have sex."

"Yeah, but they're not nearly as much fun." He tried to tug his hand free but Amanda held on. He sighed. "Okay, let's talk, since that seems what you're so determined to do."

"I don't get to the station as much anymore now that I have your books in order and I miss seeing everyone. Catch me up on what's been going on."

"There isn't a whole lot new. Lance, the guy you asked about, is making progress toward getting his license. I think he'll make a good engineer."

"I know Chris is grateful to you for taking him on. Has he been by to see how Lance is doing?"

"Just who is it you're more interested in? Lance or Chris?" Dev's voice took on a bit of an edge.

Amanda's eyes slid away from his penetrating stare. "Well, you mentioned that Lance has PTSD and I merely wondered how often Chris checked in on him, that's all."

Dev tilted her chin up till she met his gaze. "And as long as he came all that way, I might as well talk to him about my nightmares, hmm?"

She bit her lip.

"Darling, don't ever try to be devious. You're about as transparent as a pane of glass." He kissed the tip of her nose. "Believe me, Chris and I have had many talks about my nightmares and, as I said before, it hasn't helped."

Amanda pushed the sheet-covered furniture against one wall in the living room. The party was barely two weeks away and props and supplies were piling up. She lugged the cardboard boxes filled with tablecloths and toppers in from her car and stacked them against one wall. They'd need ironing. Folding chairs were lined up on the other side of the room and boxes of 'slipcovers' for them had already arrived. They'd have to be unpacked and checked for wrinkles. There'd be a lot of ironing in her future.

She checked the two bedrooms. Each had a double bed, a chest of drawers, and a single chair. They would do nicely as changing rooms on the night of the big event. The bartenders and wait staff would all be in the uniforms she dictated. Only the three parking valets would be allowed to wear their own clothes. They had all sworn to own dark slacks and white polo shirts. She and Zoe would be working right up until the guests were due to arrive and would have to change into their own dress clothes at the last minute.

Mrs. Wyndham wanted them on site during the entire event to deal with unexpected emergencies, but she wanted them to 'blend in' with the guests and be as inconspicuous as possible. That meant formal attire for both of them. Zoe had been complaining about it for weeks. They'd decided on black in case they should need them again for another affair and made a trip to Annapolis to scout the consignment shops. Luckily they managed to get two suitable second-hand gowns at reasonable prices.

This little house on the Wyndham's property was working out perfectly as a staging area. Amanda opened both front and back doors in the hope that she could get rid of the musty, closed-up odor with a little cross-ventilation. The windows hadn't been opened in so long they appeared to be swollen shut. Maybe she could ask Jeff to see if he could work on that.

Once she harangued him for his participation in Dev's remodeling scheme—then thanked him for his help—he'd been offering his services for any odd job the party required. Zoe suspected there would be IOUs he intended to collect when all was said and done, and complained every time Amanda put another 'Jeff job' on their to do list. Jeff had borrowed Mr. Pennypacker's pick-up and he and Zoe were bringing the painted urns and ivy garlands over here after the gallery closed.

Amanda was silently congratulating herself on how well the plans were moving along when an imperious Mrs. Wyndham strolled through the open front door.

"I see you're making good use of my property," she said, taking in the supplies stacked in boxes.

"Mrs. Wyndham, how nice to see you. I didn't know you'd be back in town this week." Amanda smiled and started to walk over when she realized the matron's expression was not a happy one.

"Yes, I can see you didn't expect me."

Amanda's eyebrows shot up in surprise.

The social maven of Blue Point Cove was dressed to the nines as usual. She glanced askance at the covered sofa as if to decide whether her Donna Karan pantsuit would suffer permanent damage by coming into contact with it. Apparently unwilling to risk it, she walked slowly through the living room toward the kitchen, murmuring to herself, "Such a long time since I've been in here. It seems much smaller than I remembered—" She broke off and turned back to Amanda.

"Everything is coming along nicely for the party, Mrs. Wyndham. As you could see when you came in, we've had the area in front of this house cleared and leveled. The mulch will arrive next week so it will be ready for us to park cars here." She smiled brightly to compensate for the unease she felt building in the pit of her stomach.

"I attended an engagement party in Annapolis last week," Mrs. Wyndham began, totally ignoring Amanda's remarks. "The Michaelson's daughter is marrying some lawyer fresh from Harvard." She waved her hand, dismissing the details as unimportant. "She had a singer there. Someone from New York City. I've never heard of him but the guests were very impressed." She fixed Amanda with a stare. "I want you to find a singer for my party."

Amanda's stomach did a triple flip and nosedived to her feet. "Mrs. Wyndham, we never discussed having entertainment other than the band, and it's kind of late to arrange for that now."

"I don't want to hear excuses, Ms. Adams. You touted yourselves as event planners and I gave you a chance. Now I expect you to be a professional and able to deal with unexpected. Find me a singer. It doesn't have to be Michael Bublé, just someone who knows the songs the band will be playing."

"Ma'am, this is terribly short notice. I doubt if I can find anyone with that kind of talent that isn't already booked at this late date."

"Well, you'd better find someone. Otherwise I may have to call that other planner. See if she can be up to speed on *short notice*." Mrs. Wyndham emphasized the final two words with a heavy dose of sarcasm. "Remember, my dear, in this business, like any other, the customer is always right." She gave one last look around the room, shivered slightly, then headed out the front door. "I expect to hear from you by day after tomorrow, Ms. Adams. Please don't disappoint me."

Amanda heard the smooth purr of the BMW as it left the driveway, then collapsed onto the sheeted sofa, a little dust on her jeans the least of her worries.

Holy cow. She'd never be able to find a singer in time. Heck, she couldn't find one if she had a month. Mrs. Wyndham was being completely unreasonable.

Besides she couldn't just cancel A to Z Event Planning and go with another company at the last minute.

Could she?

With a sinking feeling, Amanda realized she'd not put a cancellation clause into their contract. She'd never even considered the possibility. An amateur's mistake. One that could end their business before it even got started. Visions of unpaid student loan bills danced before her eyes. She pictured a FOR SALE sign on the door of Silvercreek Gallery. Oh God. When she told her partner about this, she'd lose it. Zoe had depended on her for all the business details.

And I've dropped the ball completely.

CHAPTER 19

Rosemary buzzed the intercom. "Captain Majewski is here, Dev."

Dev cursed under his breath. "Send him on back, Rosemary."

He saved the file he had been working on and stood up. As Chris appeared at the doorway, Dev came around his desk and went to meet him. He'd been expecting this visit.

"How about some coffee?" he suggested as he pointed to the employee lounge.

"Sounds good. I don't suppose there are any of Rosemary's muffins back there, too?"

"You'd better ease up on the muffins, Freud. They're starting to accumulate above your belt. Pretty soon you'll have your very own muffin-top."

Dev went to the counter and poured two cups. He set one in front of Chris and waited for the interrogation.

Never one to do the anticipated, Chris sat back and stirred sugar into the dark liquid, happy to let Dev take the conversational lead.

"I gather you're here to see how well Lance is making out," Dev began.

Let's pretend that's the only reason you're here. Maybe the world will end and we won't have to get around to my problems. "I'll tell you right up front that I didn't hire him as an announcer."

"Job placement is your bailiwick, Marconi. I just send 'em over in the hopes they'll fit in somewhere." Chris took a cautious sip of the hot coffee. "You know I like to see how all of my former patients are making out." He shot Dev a look that clearly indicated he wasn't getting out of the cross-hairs that easily. "You seemed to be working harder than anyone else here and since Lance needed night work I thought he might give you some relief."

"Yeah, I thought of that possibility myself, but much as I wish I could split my shift with someone, Lance wouldn't work there. He's still too worried about flashbacks to be on the air—especially at night with no backup."

"So? What's your plan, then?"

"How do you know I have a plan?"

"You always have a plan, Marconi. It's one of the things that intrigues me about you. You seem to know exactly what should happen for everyone else." He leaned across the table to get a napkin. "But you won't plan your own life further than a week down the road."

"Let's just confine our conversation to Lance," Dev said, but he knew it was only a matter of time before he was the duck in the shooting gallery.

"Fine. Tell me about your plan for Lance."

Dev saw the faint smile lurking at the corners of Chris's mouth and chose to ignore it.

"I think he'll make a fine engineer. I had Mike run him through the basics. Now he's reading some engineering handbooks and shadowing one of the other guys at night. The control booth is a much safer place for him until he's more comfortable with us. If he wants to try for a first-class radio license, I'll see what I can do to make it happen."

"Do you think he'll go for that?"

"He'd be a fool not to. He's a smart guy, Chris. He'd be a college graduate if he hadn't had to drop out to support his parents. He could make a decent living at this. Move on to a bigger city if he wanted to, once he gets a little experience under his belt."

"Don't expect too much too soon, Marconi. I'm not sure he'll ever want to *go* to a big city, let alone live in one. As long as you're willing to give him time, I think he'll work out well right here."

Chris got up, went to the refrigerator, then picked up the round metal tin on the top. "Mind if I have one of these?" he asked before he even opened the tin.

"It's your call." Dev smirked, staring pointedly at the other man's waistline.

"I don't weigh a pound more than I did ten years ago," Chris retorted. He opened the tin.

"True, but some of your chest muscles have moved south and disguised themselves as a paunch."

Dev wanted to get a rise out of Chris, who was determined to remain as fit as he had been in boot camp. There was no evidence to support Dev's taunt. Chris's physique was the envy of Hank and Neal, both of whom had indeed allowed their pecs to migrate toe-ward.

"The hell you say." But Chris sucked in his gut and put the lid back on the tin without taking a muffin. He refilled his mug and offered to do the same for Dev, who refused, so he sat back down and stirred two packets of sugar into his.

"So, what else is new?" Chris asked casually, continuing to stir his coffee. "I see you've lost the glove."

Here we go.

"Not completely. Just around friends, and here, where everyone's used to me."

"What made you change your mind?" Shrewd eyes examined Dev over the rim of his coffee cup.

"Jeff started it. He's a friend of Amanda and Zoe. He got me to take it off when he was helping me with some repairs at her house. Then Amanda didn't seem to have a problem with it, so I leave it off most of the time now."

"How are things going with Amanda? I noticed she wasn't here today."

"Pretty well."

Really well, if you considered the fact that he could count on one hand the number of days he hadn't slept at her place over the past five weeks.

Or the fact that he could accurately locate, with his eyes closed, the scar on her left knee she got at age eight when she knelt on a piece of broken glass.

Or that he could kiss the little mole just below her navel and know she'd squirm with delight.

The only thing that wasn't going really well was his reluctance to continue lying about who he really was.

"Pretty well? Does that mean you've told her about being Danny's friend—or that you haven't?"

"Haven't."

He bristled at Chris's disappointed expression. "Listen, I'm not telling her until after this big party she's handling. She won't take the news well and we have to work together that night, so I don't want to throw a monkey wrench into the works."

"So you're sleeping with her under false pretenses?"

Dev's mug clattered to the table as he choked on his last mouthful of coffee.

"See, that's the thing. We psych docs are supposed to be observant." Chris tilted his chair back on two legs. "Did you really think I wouldn't notice any difference in you?

Yeah, he had. He'd tried to act normal, especially around the station where it seemed the other guys were acting strangely enough around him as it was. Thought he was doing a pretty good job, too.

"Well, I—"

"You haven't rubbed your left elbow once since I've been here. You actually made a joke about me getting fat. A joke, Dev. When was the last time you made a joke?"

Last night in bed with Amanda he'd joked about Spook, her black cat, being his good luck charm. Now he crossed his arms and clamped his mouth shut, too stubborn to admit Chris had him nailed.

"I bet it was with Amanda. I bet when anyone says her name, your eyes light up like traffic signals. Just like they did a moment ago when I asked about her."

"Okay, okay, Freud, you got me."

Damned shrinks think they know everything.

Dev stood and began to pace. "I know I shouldn't sleep with her. Believe me, she was the one who instigated our affair, if you could call it that. I mean, I kissed her one time and we both kind of lost control. But I managed to back off before things went too far." *As in, I ran like a scared rabbit.* "The next day Amanda wanted to talk about it and I expected at least a verbal slap in the face. Instead she explained that she wasn't going to fall in love again—but she didn't plan on being celibate forever either. She was okay with the physical attraction as long as I realized it wasn't going any further than that. She calls it as 'friends with benefits'."

He raked his hand through his hair and dropped back into the chair. "But I fell for her, Chris. And now that I love her it's killing me to lie to her every day, but I have to wait till this party is over before I drop this on her."

"When is this big event?"

"Saturday, May ninth."

Less than two weeks away. Ten days before his world imploded and left his heart broken and bleeding amid the ruins.

"So, after this party, you're going to tell her all about you and Danny?"

Dev nodded.

"And are you going to mention that you're in love with her too?"

"Hell, no. I won't get the chance anyway. Once she knows I'm the reason Danny's dead, she'll drop me like the festering leper I am and run so fast in the other direction there'll probably be a sonic boom. Besides, we're supposed to be just friends getting together to relieve a little sexual tension. She made me promise not to fall in love with her. Telling her I love her will only be one more thing I've been lying to her about these past few months."

Chris sat silently sipping his coffee for a few minutes. "Lying tends to cause more problems than it fixes. The longer you wait, the harder it will get. Amanda might surprise you. What will you do if she doesn't run screaming into the sunset?" He got up and took his mug over to the sink and rinsed it.

"She'll run," Dev said, his certainty evident in the slump of his shoulders. "She may be civil and even try to be understanding, but in the end, she'll go. And I won't blame her."

Chris nodded, not agreeing with Dev's opinion, but acknowledging it. "Keep me in the loop about Lance and let me know if he has any problems you can't handle." He walked to the door.

"Yeah, I'll do that," Dev said.

"You might want to talk to Danny's mother soon too. It may take some of the pressure off. Give you a bit of practice accepting all the blame and hate you expect to have dumped on you." Chris shrugged. "You're so sure you know how everyone will react, but what if you're wrong? Apparently Amanda isn't repelled by the sight of your damaged arm. If she's willing to ignore a physical defect in favor of having an intimate relationship with you, there must be something in you she finds worthwhile." He slipped around the doorway and whistled as he walked down the hall.

Dev sat until he heard Chris say goodbye to Rosemary. *You're wrong this time, Freud. And I'll prove it to you on May the tenth.*

Dev was mulling over Chris's parting remarks when Rosemary announced Amanda's arrival. He'd not expected her at the studio today but planned to see her at her house around dinnertime so her unexpected visit seemed oddly coincidental with Chris Majewski's.

Generally any time he got to see her was good, but after the conversation with Freud, he found himself unsettled. On the one hand, the time they spent together in what Dev thought of as his fantasyland trickled away faster and faster and he wanted to slow it down. On the other, the strain of keeping the truth from Amanda was increasing with every passing minute and he almost wished the party was over so he could finally confess.

He stood up as she barreled through his office doorway, a worried expression on her face.

"I'm sorry to barge in on you like this, Dev, but I've got a problem and don't know what to do." Rather than sit in the visitor's chair by his desk, she paced the length of the room and back again.

"Tell me. Maybe I can help."

"I was at the old Wyndham place this morning, accepting a delivery for the party, and much to my surprise, Mrs. Wyndham showed up."

"Okay, first, sit down and take a breath. The pacing back and forth is wearing us both out." Obediently she sat on the very edge of the chair, still wringing her hands and biting her lip. He came around from behind the desk and cocked his hip on the corner. He didn't think he'd ever seen her so upset, except— "Is it something about your dad?"

"Dad? No. No. Nothing like that." She took a deep breath. "Mrs. Wyndham wants me to hire a singer for the party. She went to some big shindig in Annapolis given by one of her *friends*"—Amanda put air quotes around the word—"who had a singer from New York performing, so now *she* wants a singer. I told her it was too late to find someone but she got all huffy and lady of the manor on me. Told me if I couldn't find a singer she might cancel and go with a different event planner."

"That's ridiculous. The invitations have gone out and she won't find another event planner able to put together a party of this size on such short notice. To say nothing of the fact that she'd still have to pay you the cancellation fee as well as pay the new planner. She won't want to spend that kind of money. Relax. She's bluffing."

"She didn't sound like she was bluffing. And I, uh . . ." Amanda hung her head, blew out a long breath then looked up. "I didn't write a cancellation clause into the contract."

"Ah." Dev rubbed his chin.

"Yeah. I am so stupid. I can't believe I made such a terrible mistake. I called the band and asked if they knew anyone who might perform . . ."

"And?"

"They gave me a couple of names but they were all booked for the weekend of May ninth."

"Not unexpected. As you said, this is very short notice."

"Oh, Dev, what am I going to do? Zoe counted on me to take care of the business side of our partnership. If she loses the gallery it will be all my fault. And I'll probably go to jail for defaulting on my student loan."

"I don't think they put people in jail for that. And besides, I still think the old biddy is bluffing."

"Easy for you to say. Your world isn't about to come tumbling down around your ears in two weeks."

The irony almost made him laugh. "Let me try to find a couple of the guys from my old band and see if they know anyone who could help you out. Don't get your hopes up, because this will be a long shot, but I'll see what I can do."

Amanda leapt out of the chair and threw her arms around his neck. "Oh, thank you. You are a wonderful person," she exclaimed. Her exuberance almost knocked him over and his arms came around her to steady them both. Before he could say anything, a discreet cough from the doorway had them both springing apart like two teenagers on a couch when Dad turns on the light.

"Sorry, Boss. Didn't mean to interrupt," Mike said, doing his best to hide his smile but failing. He had some papers in his hand, but stayed at the door, waiting for Dev to invite him in.

Amanda's face was pink as a peony as she sat down again. Dev signaled for Mike to bring him the paperwork.

"Just needs your signature, Boss. Then I'll be out of your hair." He allowed his grin to escape and Dev's scowl only made it get broader. Dev sat back behind his desk and quickly scanned the papers before he signed them. Mike turned to Amanda and asked, "How are you, Amanda? We haven't seen you around here for a few weeks."

"I, um, I'm good, Mike, thanks. How's everyone here? Are you all doing okay?"

"Yes, ma'am. We're all happy as clams. Especially now that the boss is, uh"—he paused to give her a knowing look—"um, happy, too."

Dev quickly scrawled his signature. He noted that Amanda's face was an even deeper shade of pink and Mike was grinning like a fool. "Mike," he barked to get the man's attention and thrust the papers back into his hands.

Not one to be rushed, Mike tapped the papers on the desk until they were perfectly even, then clipped them together. "Thanks, Boss. Nice to see you, Amanda." He did an about-face and left, whistling.

Dev and Amanda exchanged glances.

"Do you think he knows there's something going on between us?" He'd been trying to keep their affair a secret, knowing that in a few weeks it would be history.

Amanda nodded. "I'm pretty sure he knows. You must have let something slip. I know I haven't said anything."

"Neither have I," he retorted.

"I don't have time to worry about that now," Amanda said. "Let's get back to the possibility you might be able to find me a singer."

"I'll make some calls and let you know," he said, getting up and coming around to walk her to the door. He scanned the hallway, then took her in his arms and kissed her soundly. Pleased that he had erased the frown line between her brows, he kissed her once more for good measure. "When will you be home this afternoon?"

"By four o'clock at the latest. What would you like for dinner?"

He said nothing, just looked at her like a starving man staring at a banquet.

She rolled her eyes. "If you look like that every time you think of me, no wonder people are suspecting things." She crossed her fingers. "Good luck with the search. I've got to go tell Zoe about Mrs. Wyndham's new demands."

Dev sat at his desk and stared at his phone. *Time's up, buddy. Just bite the damn bullet and do it.* He dialed.

"Hi, Mom, remember me?"

"Oh, Dev, is it really you? How are you? Is everything all right?" With just those few words, the voice on the other end ran through a gamut of emotions—surprise, delight, worry, and finally caution.

"I'm fine, Mom. I know I should have called before now, but—"

"That's all right, dear. I understand. I'm happy to hear from you now. Tell me everything. What are you doing? How's your arm? Where are you?"

They hadn't spoken since she and his father had come to see him at Walter Reed. That had been a disaster. She had kissed him and cried, patting his good arm and stroking his forehead while his dad had stood, grim and unbending, at the foot of his bed, saying little other than a terse version of "I told you so". Mom had offered her condolences for Danny, knowing how close the two had become during their two tours together, but his father had stared at his bandaged arm as if Danny's sacrifice was doubly tragic since Dev's career was gone and his talent as a pianist only a memory, now.

"Slow down, Mom. Are you alone? Can you talk?"

"Your father's not here, if that's what you mean," she said sadly. "He'll be sorry he missed your call."

"Yeah, right, Mom. Let's not get into that, okay? I have a couple of favors to ask you."

"Anything, son. You know that. What do you need?"

"I'm working at a little independent radio station out on Maryland's Eastern Shore. I own it, actually."

"A . . . radio station?"

"Yes, Mom. At least I'm still involved with music in some way. I used part of Aunt Edith's bequest to buy it and I've hired a few other guys from the Army to help out. I work the night shift and get to play the music I love, but all of this is beside the point right now."

His mother sounded puzzled but her usual sense of optimism prevailed. "As long as you're happy, dear. That's what's important."

His happiness would end in about two weeks but he wasn't going to share that with her now.

"I'm helping out Danny's fiancée, Mom. We, uh, Danny and I, that is, had a pact that if anything happened to him, I would watch over Amanda and make sure she was okay."

"That's a fine thing, dear. How is she doing? These past months must have been so hard on her."

"She's holding up well, Mom. Amanda's an exceptional woman. Smart and kind and generous. I can see why Danny loved her."

Images of her laughing, playing with Spook, sleeping next to him with her arm draped across his waist, brought the usual tightness to his chest. A longing for something he knew he could never have. He squeezed his eyes shut to banish the pictures.

"At any rate, she is having some financial difficulties that I'm helping her work through. She has started a new event planning business and her first client is very influential in the town where she lives. Also very demanding. I'm, uh, acting as a deejay for her at this party and since it is a formal affair, I need a tux. Can you get mine out of mothballs and send it down here?"

"Of course, dear. It's still hanging in your closet. I haven't changed a thing in your room since you . . . left."

"Thanks, Mom. I appreciate it."

It wasn't right that he should punish her for the separation between his father and himself. He vowed to keep in touch with her more often.

"I don't suppose you're coming up this way any time soon?"

Her wistfulness came clearly over the phone line, and he grimaced.

"Not in the near future. Are you teaching at the university this semester?"

"I am. Only two courses. Enough to keep me occupied. Your father has been out of town a lot, doing those financial seminars, so I'd go stir crazy here without something to do."

Another shaft of guilt lanced through him at the thought of her alone in the sterile high-rise overlooking Central Park. He seemed to let everyone down.

"I'll try to call more often. And I'll email you, too. Do you have the same address at the university as . . . before?"

Everything in their relationship was divided into the time before or after his enlistment in the Army. The demarcation point that changed his life forever. No doubt it was a milestone for his parents as well.

"Yes. Same address."

"I have one more favor to ask. Do you still see Mrs. Katzenbach?"

"Sylvia? Yes, we meet for lunch occasionally. Why?"

"I need to get in touch with Arnold. Do you know if he still lives at home?"

"I believe he does, but he travels around the northeast quite a bit. He's making a good living singing at weddings and bar mitzvahs, so he's often out of town on the weekends. Not the Hollywood star he'd hoped to be but you know how difficult it is to break into show business."

"I need to get his cell phone number so I can call him. I'm trying to find a singer for this shindig Amanda's coordinating. Her client dumped this request on her at the last minute, so we're sort of under the gun here."

"I'll call Sylvia and get it for you, then call you back. Is this number you're calling from a cell phone?"

"No, Mom, this is my office, but here's my cell phone number."

He rattled it off.

"Don't give these to Dad, okay?" He doubted his father would call him, but he wasn't about to take the chance he might have to listen to another lecture on how he had ruined his life.

"All right, dear. But I do wish you two would talk. He's not as heartless as you think, Dev. He worried more than you have any idea while you were in Iraq."

"Let's not go there, Mother, please. Try to get that phone number for me as soon as you can."

"I'll phone Sylvia right away, Dev. I'm so glad you called, darling. Take care of yourself."

Dev sat back and blew out a long breath. That went better than he expected, especially since his father wasn't home to complicate matters. Now if he could reach Arnold and do a little arm-twisting, he might just get lucky.

This morning's conversation with Chris stirred his resolve to tie up more loose ends. The past weeks with

Amanda had been a bright and beautiful bubble of time that he would treasure always. He'd put off doing things he knew would smash that fragile envelope. But it was time to man up. Tomorrow he would visit Danny's mom. Then he would stop by Arlington and have a long talk with Danny.

CHAPTER 20

Amanda parked in front of the Silvercreek Gallery and noted a new sign in the window.

'Sale! Twenty-percent Off All Art and Sculpture'.

She sighed and steeled herself to break the bad news to Zoe. Today the cheery tinkling of the bell as she opened the door sounded mocking rather than welcoming. There were two browsers inside, no doubt attracted by the sign. She hoped they would buy something to counteract the depression Zoe would feel upon discovering that her business partner was not so business savvy after all.

Zoe was at the counter, putting some jewelry into the display case. Amanda caught her eye and signaled that she was going to the back room, but Zoe waved her over.

"Come see these new pieces Marjorie just brought," Zoe said.

Amanda pasted a smile on her face and greeted the woman dressed in a long peasant skirt and embroidered tunic.

"Hi, Marjorie. I haven't seen you in ages. How's the B and B doing?"

"Business is slow this time of the year, as usual. We get a little bump around the holidays, but then things die down until spring break. Gives me time to work on the fun stuff though," she said, pointing to the array of earrings and necklaces laid out on velvet-covered boards.

Amanda didn't have to feign enthusiasm once she saw the display.

"Oh, Marjorie, these are beautiful. I envy you your talent. You and Zoe are both so creative."

"Yeah, but you're the business brain, Amanda. Without you to crunch the numbers, all of our creativity would be in vain," Zoe said as she ducked down to put the new jewelry into the display case. "I think it's your jewelry that brings the customers in, Marjorie, then I can sometimes snag them with one of Jeff's sculptures or a painting." She picked up a necklace of finely wrought gold in the shape of a vine with tiny blue topaz cabochons sprinkled like water droplets on the leaves. "This one goes in the front window. I know it will catch the eye of anyone who strolls by."

Marjorie beamed with pleasure at the compliments. "I'll be on my way, then, Zoe. Let me know if anything sells and I'll bring a replacement. And don't forget, if anyone at the big party has a little too much to drink to drive home, point them in my direction. I'll be ready to welcome them no matter how late the hour." She turned to Amanda and lowered her voice. "I'd like to make an appointment with you in the near future. I'm beginning to feel that Mr. Coghill is not giving my business the amount of attention it deserves."

"Certainly, Marjorie. I'll call you next week and see what time works best for you." The normal elation she would feel at the prospect of a new client didn't materialize. The possibility that Mrs. Wyndham could cancel and leave them with all the rental bills completely outweighed the potential of one new client. Doing her best to look pleased with Marjorie's request, she watched the owner of the Blue Point Inn leave in a flurry of silk scarves and softly chiming bangle bracelets.

The other woman browsing left shortly afterward without making a purchase and Amanda saw the disappointment on Zoe's face as she watched her leave.

"It's a good thing you came up with the event-planning idea, Mandy. That money will have to tide me over until the tourists arrive this summer." Zoe led the way back to her office and offered Amanda a cup of coffee. "What brings you here so full of gloom and doom?" She put her hand on Amanda's arm sympathetically. "Don't tell me you heard something about your dad?"

"No. Nothing new on that front, but I, uh, have some other news to talk to you about."

"Oh, Lord, with a face like that, it must be bad. Just spit it out. I can deal with anything, knowing that I'll get a big paycheck in two weeks."

Amanda's stomach coiled into a knot so tight she thought she might lose her lunch all over Zoe's desk.

"Yes, well, that's what I have to talk to you about. Mrs. Wyndham stopped by her old house while I was unpacking the supplies we had delivered there. She dropped a bomb on me about wanting us to find a singer for the party, because she went to some affair held by one of her friends and she had a singer. They're playing a game of social one-upmanship I guess."

"That is ridiculous. We can't find a singer this late in the game. Is she nuts?" Coffee splashed over the rim of her cup as Zoe banged it down on her desk. "Damn!" She moved her paperwork out of the path of the spill and rummaged through the bottom drawer for paper towels.

While they blotted up the mess, Zoe kept up her tirade.

"She's going to have to get over her duel with this other lady about who can throw the best party. You told her that, right? It wasn't in the contract, and we're not going to pull a singer out of our ass like a magician." Zoe's rant wound down and she studied Amanda through narrowed eyes. "There's something else, isn't there?"

"Yeah. She sort of threatened to cancel our contract if I couldn't come up with someone and I, um, didn't put a cancellation clause in the contract. I'm so sorry, Zoe. It was a stupid, rookie mistake. I'm sure we could sue her for breach of contract, but that would take months plus lawyer's fees, and she knows we don't have the money for that."

"Still, how can she cancel a party this big? The invitations are out, half the stuff is in her old house already. Surely she wouldn't just call everyone up and tell them not to come."

"I agree. She threatened to talk to that other planner who put the bid in before us. Theirs is a more experienced organization. Maybe they can actually get up to speed on this that quickly."

Zoe digested this news in silence for a few minutes. "So . . . now what?"

"I've been on the phone ever since Mrs. W walked out this morning, trying to find someone, but so far, no luck. I finally went over to the station and talked to Dev. He's checking with his contacts to see what he can come up with. If he saves my butt on this, I'll owe him big time."

Amanda's eyes filled with tears. "I'm just so sorry I let you down, Zoe. You trusted me to take care of the business end and I made a mistake that may cost you the gallery. I wouldn't blame you for throwing me out on my ear."

"Oh, be serious. We'll think of something. You're the one who always says never give up. Practice what you've been preaching to me, kid."

Amanda had always had someone to lean on when things got tough. After her dad disappeared, Danny had stepped in and become her rock. She'd never realized how much she leaned on him until he was killed. The fear that she was too much a weakling to stand on her own two feet and succeed had haunted her dreams and intensified her grief over Danny's death. The mistake she'd made with this contract was about to make that fear come true. Not only would she fail, but Zoe could lose everything as well.

No! She could not let that happen. Would not let that happen.

Amanda straightened her shoulders and blinked back her tears. "You're right. She's being unreasonable, but I'm not losing this battle. Even if we can't find someone to sing,

I'm going to tell her that I have. We'll go ahead with the party and if the singer doesn't show, it will be too late for her to do anything about it."

"Except not pay us," Zoe commented with a shrug, as though that were an insignificant detail.

"Listen, if this party goes as well as we think it will, she should be delighted, singer or no. I think she'll pay us. And if she doesn't, well, she's not the only one who can bluff. I can threaten to sue for breach of contract every bit as convincingly as she can threaten to cancel." Amanda finished with a determined set to her jaw and a decisive nod.

"Yeah, and who knows? Maybe Dev will come to your rescue—again. He does seem to be doing the knight-in-shining-armor routine lately." Zoe arched a brow. "I trust you're rewarding him appropriately?"

"I'm . . . We're . . ."

Amanda searched for the words to describe their relationship, another problem she was having trouble coming to grips with. Somehow the ground rules she had laid down weeks ago had shifted under her feet, leaving her floundering in the unstable sands between friendship and something deeper. Not love. She was still resolved not to give her heart into another man's keeping again. The pain that would inevitably follow was more than she could bear. Where that left her relationship with Dev she would figure out once this godforsaken party was past.

"He's, um, such a really nice guy, Zoe," she stammered, "though he hates it when I tell him that." She smiled briefly, then her expression turned serious. "I've been feeling kind of guilty, Zo. He should find some wonderful girl to settle down with, instead of spending all his time in a dead-end relationship with me. Now that he's gotten over his shyness about his arm, I know he could get any woman he wanted with his looks and charm."

"It hasn't occurred to you that he's already found the woman he wants? Whenever I see the two of you together he seems pretty serious. He floats about a foot off the ground and you act as though you've been happily married for months."

"I like him a lot, Zoe. But we went into this in total agreement. Nobody is falling in love. I told him right up front that I was not going there again and he promised he wouldn't either."

"Uh huh," Zoe said, nodding. "Once we get past this party, you need to have your head examined, because I think you're kidding yourself. Promises or no, you're falling for this guy. And he's just standing by, waiting for you to wake up and smell the icing on the wedding cake."

Amanda hoped Zoe was wrong. She didn't want to be responsible for disappointing anyone else, let along breaking their heart.

By the time Amanda got home she felt as though her brain had been dipped in glue. She couldn't seem to resolve any of the problems that plagued her and worrying about them was exhausting. She made herself a cup of tea and went into her office, booted up her laptop, and checked her email.

An email from her mom boosted her spirits a bit and she wrote back, leaving out the difficulties with Mrs. Wyndham. She missed her mom's support and affection but she was twenty-eight and much too old to run to her parents when things got tough. She did include an invitation for her mom and step-dad to visit this summer and hoped they would take her up on the offer.

Spook came in and jumped up on the desk, the smell of salt and sea grass clinging to her sleek black coat. An adolescent now, she spent a good deal of time outdoors stalking critters in the long grass by the water and generally working off some of her boundless energy. Amanda stroked her, wishing she could absorb some of that vitality from the contact.

A knock on her door sent Spook diving for cover. "Don't be such a scaredy cat, Spook." She hurried to the door. She seldom had visitors she wasn't expecting, so she peered through the peephole Jeff had recently put in. It wasn't Dev's SUV parked in front of her house. A man she didn't recognize peered directly into the lens, no doubt anticipating her examination.

"Who is it?" she called through the door.

"Agent Gallagher, FBI," he replied and held his badge up so she could see it.

She opened the door, dread knotting her stomach.

"Come in, Agent Gallagher. Are you here about my father?" She took in the neat dark suit, nondescript tie, and polished wing-tip shoes. Maybe the standard FBI uniform on the TV shows was the real thing.

"Are you Amanda Adams, ma'am?"

Her throat became so dry she could barely swallow and her heart began to pound. She nodded.

"Have you found him?"

"No, ma'am. I'm sorry to say I have no news about your father. I'm one of the agents from the regional office who's been tasked with visiting the site of any disappearance that may be connected with Brian Donlevy."

Her breath came out in a *whoosh* that made her realize she'd been holding it.

"Oh." She gestured toward a chair. "Would you like to sit down?"

"No, ma'am. Thank you. I won't be here long. Since I was in the area I just thought I'd touch base with you, so you'd know we were exploring all the possibilities related to your father's disappearance."

"I guess there's not much for you to see, considering how long ago he went missing. The local police investigation didn't turn up any leads down here. They seemed to think he never made it to Blue Point Cove at all."

"Yes, ma'am. I've reviewed the file on your father and you're right, there wasn't much to go on. The other band members said he left as usual around two-thirty. After that"—he spread his hands—"the possibilities of whatever route he took are too numerous to follow. He may have never even made it out of Annapolis. He gave her an apologetic smile. "I'm only here to see if there is anywhere Mr. Donlevy could have dumped a car. You know that's his MO, right?"

She nodded again.

"Well, other than the five million little coves and backwaters along the bay, I'd say we're out of luck."

Amanda caught the sarcasm and realized the enormity of the search the FBI was conducting. Her resurrected hopes of a resolution to the mystery surrounding her dad hit a new low.

"I'll leave you my card, Ms. Adams. If you think of anything new that might help, call me. I've explored pretty much every possibility around here, so now I'm going to work my way back to the bridge. I don't expect to find anything, but you never know." He put his hand on the doorknob.

"Thank you for stopping to see me, Agent Gallagher. I appreciate the effort the FBI is going through." There seemed nothing more to say and she watched as he climbed into his dark gray sedan and drove away.

A new wave of depression settled over Amanda. She would never find out what happened to her dad. She might as well stop thinking she would. Every time she had the slightest hope, it was crushed.

The only bright point in her entire life right now was the fact that Dev would be coming over for dinner.

Dev sat back from the mike. He was halfway through his shift and from now until seven a.m. he would remain pretty much on autopilot, interjecting a few comments or facts about a particular performer to break up the musical stream and remind his listeners that there was indeed a live person behind the mike.

Over in the control booth, Lance was handling the engineering duties under the watchful eye of Jerry Gardner. Reports indicated that Lance was learning fast and Dev could see the Certification Handbook for Radio Operators open on the table next to the control board. Everything seemed to be going well in that department with no signs of PTSD flashbacks so far.

He'd had no good news to share with Amanda at dinner. Arnie Katzenbach had not returned his calls and all of his other contacts came up empty. He had even asked the announcers and engineers at work if they might know of anyone who could fill the bill, but no luck there either.

Amanda was in a rare mood when he arrived for dinner. One minute she was dejected, the next annoyed in the extreme over Mrs. Wyndham's ridiculous request. By the end of the meal, though, she'd become more philosophical.

"I'll do my best to make this party everything I promised in our contract," she'd said. "But if she thinks she can use this last-minute requirement to produce a singer as a deal-breaker, she's got another think coming. As far as I'm concerned, we have found someone. If it turns out that he is unavoidably detained and doesn't arrive on time, well, that's show biz, right?"

"So, you're going to tell her you have someone lined up to perform?"

"I am going to be as evasive as possible and lead her to believe that, yes."

She got the bottle of wine Dev had brought out of the fridge and handed it to him to open.

"I am not going to let some other planner step in at the last minute and steal our contract out from under us."

She accepted the glass Dev handed her, the worry line between her brows deepening briefly.

"I can't let Zoe down, Dev. Too much is riding on this party. We both worked hard for this money and I'm damn well going to get it. Legally I know we're on the winning side, I just hope she doesn't make me go to court to prove it."

She's going to be fine, Danny, he thought. *She's strong and self-sufficient. Once she gets paid for this job, her financial worries will be significantly reduced, too. Then all I'll have to do is convince her to open her heart to someone new.*

Well, two out of three ain't bad.

By unspoken agreement, they'd gone to bed after cleaning up the dishes, letting the time-honored method of crazy monkey-sex replace their anxiety with exhaustion. A few hours of sleep and he was back behind the mike, hoping Arnie would call him in the morning and let him come to Amanda's rescue one last time.

Not sure what his own frame of mind would be after his visit with Danny's mom, he'd begged off getting together with Amanda tomorrow night. No, tonight, he corrected himself, eying the clock, then staring at the calendar on the wall.

The good times were fast coming to a close.

CHAPTER 21

Dev crossed the front porch and raised his hand to knock. A soft breeze blew around the corner of the modest clapboard house. It ruffled the new leaves on the big maple tree in the front yard and carried with it the moist scent of damp earth and tulips, released after a brief morning shower.

He rapped on the frame of the aluminum screen door. After a minute, the main door opened to reveal a plump woman with salt and pepper hair, a faded flowered apron covering her T-shirt and jeans.

"Yes? Can I help you?"

"Mrs. Miller?" he asked, though he recognized her from another of Danny's pictures. He swallowed twice in an attempt to wet his suddenly dry throat.

"Yes, I'm Madeline Miller. I hope you're not selling insurance or magazines, young man, because this stop would be a waste of your time."

"No, Ma'am. My name is Dev. Devlyn MacMurphy." He took a deep breath. "I was in the Army with your son Danny."

He watched the shadow of sorrow fall across her face. Then she forced a smile and opened the screen door.

"Please, come in. I'm sorry, I don't remember Danny mentioning you in his letters home, but I'm always happy to talk to anyone who knew him over there."

"Thank you, Mrs. Miller." He stepped inside and offered a handshake. His left hand stayed tucked in the pocket of his jeans, his long-sleeved green jacket still bearing the faint outline of military patches that had been removed. "Everyone pretty much called me Mac in the Army, Ma'am."

"Oh, Mac." Her smile turned genuine. "Of course I remember that name." She grasped his hand in both of hers. "How nice to meet you at last. Danny wrote about you often. Please, come sit down. Can I get you some coffee?"

Dev had expected this meeting would be hard, but even so, he could barely breathe around the massive amount of guilt clogging his throat and tightening his chest. He could have called on the phone, but since he was the one responsible for her son's death, he felt honor-bound to make a personal visit. The punishment of watching her hospitality turn to hostility would be nothing more than he deserved.

"No, thank you, Ma'am. That's very nice of you, but I can't stay long."

The bright smile dimmed a little. When she knew he was the one responsible for the death of her son, it would vanish completely. She'd regret spending even these few minutes in his company.

They stood awkwardly by the front door, while she searched his eyes for some clue to his visit. Then, in the straightforward manner that reminded him so much of Danny, she put her hand on his sleeve and asked, "What can I do for you, Mac?"

He moved back an infinitesimal amount, and she took her hand away. Not too quickly, but Dev could tell she'd felt the ridges of scar tissue that covered his arm. She waited, her expression expectant and curious.

"Danny and I got pretty tight over in Iraq, Mrs. Miller. A year together serving in Fallujah brings you closer than most stateside buddies ever get. He was my best friend."

His voice almost broke and he paused long enough to get it under control.

"You were with him when he got hit, weren't you?" She pursed her lips. "That must have been hard."

Hard?

Not the word he would have chosen.

The memory unrolled like a horror movie he'd watched a thousand times and never wanted to see again.

He didn't remember the explosion that blew their Humvee ten feet in the air and flipped it like a giant metal pancake. His memory began with the burning vehicle pinning his left arm, his ears ringing from the blast so that the destruction and death around him proceeded in eerie silence. He didn't hear the screams from the other members of his patrol, didn't hear the sniper fire, or the crackling of the flames as they ate his arm.

He didn't hear himself screaming.

He saw Danny come to. He'd been thrown fifteen feet by the blast, knocked unconscious, but miraculously had no major injury. It took him barely ten seconds to assess the situation, then, staying in a crouch, Danny ran over and tried to drag him from under the burning wreckage.

Dev squeezed his eyes closed to halt the memory, then opened them to see sympathy in Mrs. Miller's blue ones.

"I told him to leave me. There was gasoline all over the ground and I knew it would go up any second. I tried to make him go, Mrs. Miller, but he wouldn't listen. I tried to push him away." His voice got harsher as the damning words scraped their way up his throat and out of his mouth.

A part of his brain stood aside, stunned that he was blurting all this out within minutes of meeting Danny's mother, yet strangely satisfied that now he would get the punishment he deserved.

"He just kept searching until he found a piece of the wreck he could use as a lever to get me out. The gas tank blew before he had dragged me very far and, and a piece of metal caught him across the back." He finally shut up, like a wind-up toy that had run down.

When he could bear to meet her eyes again, they were filled with tears. She closed the distance between them and put her arms around him, hugging him tightly and rocking him a little back and forth.

"Thank you so much for coming here to share that memory with me. I always knew my Danny was a fine man. The Army gave him a bronze star and the Purple Heart, but medals don't mean much to a mother." Her voice quavered a little. "Hearing how brave he was in saving another man's life makes his death a little easier to bear." She let go of him and used her apron to dab at her eyes.

"No. You don't understand." He shook his head, his words vehement in his anger. "Don't *thank* me, for god's sake. I was the reason he died. It should have been me coming back in that box. He had everything to live for—his family, his fiancée—everything. I should have died. Not him. *Me*." He slammed his fist into his chest, outraged she wouldn't blame him, hate him the way he hated himself.

Now it was her turn to take a step back in surprise at his impassioned speech. She shook her head slowly, her gaze filled with sympathy.

"Mac, you can't take responsibility for Danny's actions. You both volunteered to join the Army and fight for our country, knowing what the risks were. Enlisting was a heroic act all by itself. I hate this war that takes the lives of our finest young men and women. I hate that Danny died over there. But your life is worth every bit as much as his, and I would be a terrible person if I believed you should have died in his place."

She took his right hand in hers again. "Please, come sit down. Tell me about some of the good times you had with Danny. Those are the memories you should keep, and share, with those of us who loved him."

He let her draw him into the comfortable living room and sit him in an overstuffed armchair covered in flowered chintz. When he took his left hand out of his pocket, she glanced once at the dark cotton glove covering it, but made no comment.

"I've just made a batch of brownies. I'll get us both a glass of milk and we can make sure they came out right."

He tried to refuse but she wouldn't hear it. "It was serendipity that I made those brownies this morning, so let's not ignore it." She hurried from the room before he could get in a second protest.

While she was gone he wandered around the comfortable sitting room, so much warmer and friendlier than the upscale sterility of his parents' condo. He stood there, envying a dead man for the childhood he must have had. Christ, what was wrong with him?

His survey of the room stopped at the fireplace where the mantel held an assortment of family photos, Danny's induction picture holding pride of place in the center. Next to it was a picture of Danny and Amanda, and Dev had to close his eyes as shame washed over him.

"That's Danny's girl. Amanda," Mrs. Miller said, as she set down a tray holding a plate of brownies and two glasses of milk. "She used to live a few houses down the street, so she and Danny practically grew up together."

Dev nodded. "Danny talked about her a lot."

He accepted the glass Mrs. Miller offered.

Mothers were amazing women. By all rights she should show him the door and slam it behind him. How did she find the strength, the compassion, to spend time with the man responsible for her son's death? He couldn't fathom it, but if she could go to this much trouble to put him at ease, the least he could do was participate in the farce.

He took a large brownie and bit into it. The rich chocolate flavor and chewy texture elicited an appreciative hum and nod. Once he swallowed, he said, "No worries, Mrs. Miller. These came out perfect."

She beamed at the praise.

He looked over at the picture of Danny and Amanda. Time to get back to the confession of his other sins. "He was full of plans for when he got home and they got married."

Mrs. Miller smiled fondly at the photo. "Danny loved Amanda from the time he was twelve. They were such good friends. If he hadn't been there for her the year after her father disappeared I don't know how she would have made it at school."

"Danny told me she took a lot of abuse from some of the other kids in her classes."

"Oh, indeed. Teenage girls can be so mean, and Amanda was the perfect target, poor thing. At eleven she was already five-seven but weighed only about a hundred pounds. They called her The Bean Pole, and Wired for Sound, because she had braces. She was such a smart girl, but she didn't realize she should have kept that a secret. Math was her special passion. She was the kind of student every good teacher longs for." Mrs. Miller sighed. "That pretty much sealed her fate. But what really hurt her was the rumor those nasty girls spread that her dad had run off with a waitress from the club where he worked." She frowned. "That was nonsense, of course. Her dad worshiped Amanda's mom." Mrs. Miller shook her head as though to dispel old memories. "I haven't seen her since we held the service for Danny last June. I know my son's death hit her hard, poor girl. First losing her dad and now Danny."

"Yes, Ma'am." Dev squirmed a little in the chair. "I've, uh, met Amanda."

"You have? Oh how lovely. Then you already know what a wonderful girl she is."

Oh yeah, he knew all right.

"I made a promise to Danny while we were in Iraq. He wanted me to make sure Amanda was okay if anything ever happened to him over there."

Mrs. Miller nodded. "That sounds just like my boy. He was always concerned about others more than himself—Amanda most of all, of course."

"You'll never know how much I admired Danny, Mrs. Miller. He was the most honorable, courageous man I've ever known. He watched out for everyone in our platoon. Mine wasn't the only life he saved." *Just the last. Which got him killed for his trouble. I'll never forgive him for that.*

"I can see you didn't escape without some injuries of your own," Mrs. Miller said, glancing at his glove-covered hand. "Danny wrote that you were a piano player before you enlisted." Sadness took up residence in her blue eyes again. "What are you doing now?"

"I own an indie radio station over on the Eastern Shore. Since I can't perform anymore I decided to get a job playing the music I love for others. My preference isn't exactly the top forty hits of today, so the only way I could do that was to buy my own radio station."

Unable to meet Mrs. Miller's gaze, he stared at the plate of brownies as he continued.

"I didn't have the nerve to find Amanda when I first got out of the hospital. Didn't have the courage to tell her I was the reason Danny got killed. I knew she'd hate me, which was only right, I deserved that. But then how could I make sure she was okay, like Danny asked me to?" He rubbed his elbow. "Turns out when I did find her, she'd moved to Blue Point Cove, just a few miles from the radio station I bought."

Mrs. Miller nodded sagely. "The Lord works in mysterious ways."

She leaned forward and put her hand on his arm, forcing him to meet her eyes and read the intensity there. "You've got to get over the guilt you feel, Mac. I know Danny would never want you to repay his sacrifice with years of remorse. He did what he did because he cared about you. Don't throw that gift back at him. It demeans you and his memory."

"But—"

"There are no buts, Mac." She sat back and picked up another brownie. "Now tell me how Amanda is doing. You've become friends, I'm sure."

Ah, hell. He couldn't lie to her. She would know. Mothers always knew.

This day was taking more out of him than a year's deployment in that godforsaken desert. "She is working as a CPA. Just getting started but already she has quite a few customers—including me. She's also joined with one of her client friends to open a local event-planning service. That's how we met actually. She came to hire a deejay to work at her first big job." A smile flitted across his face at the memory of her that first morning at his radio station.

Mrs. Miller sipped her milk and smiled. "So you've managed to find a way to keep your promise. And, knowing Amanda as I do, I'm sure she doesn't hate you or blame you for Danny's death."

"I haven't told her who I am. Exactly."

Mrs. Miller's eyebrows rose, and Dev flinched at the unspoken criticism.

"At first I couldn't seem to find the right time and then the more I got to know her, the more I didn't want to take the chance she'd . . ." *Blame me. Hate me. Leave me.*

For the first time this afternoon, Mrs. Miller regarded him with annoyance.

"Surely by now you've realized she would never think badly of you because of your part in Danny's death? When he failed to answer her question, she continued testily, "I guess you don't know her very well at all, then."

"I do know her, Mrs. Miller," he protested. "I know why Danny loved her. Why everyone who meets her loves her. Because I've fallen in love with her, too."

"Ahhh," Mrs. Miller said as understanding dawned. She didn't smile but that twinkle was back in her eyes. "I guess you've got quite a problem then, young man. What's your plan?"

Why did everyone assume he had a plan? He had no plan. He certainly hadn't *planned* on blurting out his love for Amanda to Danny's mom. If having a plan meant putting off the bad news until the last possible moment like a coward, then, yeah, he had a plan. If having a plan meant he knew a way to fix the situation he'd gotten himself into, then, sorry, folks, he was clueless.

Mrs. Miller sat patiently waiting for an answer to her question. Dev might as well have been a grade-schooler caught by the teacher with no homework to turn in. Excuses never worked in that situation either.

"Amanda's under a lot of pressure right now with this big party coming up," he said, trying an excuse on Mrs. Miller anyway. "I plan to tell her who I am as soon as it's over. That way she won't have to work with me when she . . . doesn't want to."

"You think she'll be angry with you? Hate you, even, after you tell her the truth?"

He nodded.

"You're right. She will," Danny's mom agreed, a little spark of anger turning those blue eyes into lasers.

Finally, someone who agreed with him. He should feel vindicated but instead he felt even worse.

"Oh, Amanda will be angry all right, but not because of your misplaced guilt over Danny's death. She'll be mad that you lied to her all these weeks. Because my guess is that if you've fallen in love with her, she must be feeling something too. Or she would have said goodbye to you already. This stupid game of hide and seek you've been playing will piss her off royally. I wouldn't blame her if she drop-kicked you right into the bay."

Perfect, Dev thought. He'd managed to put himself into a no-win position. Amanda would either hate him for letting Danny die or hate him for lying about himself. Either way, he'd lose. Which was, after all, exactly what he'd known from the start. Any ridiculous dreams of winning Amanda for himself had a half-life of about thirty seconds.

The white markers stood in orderly rows, stretching across the gently rolling acres of well-manicured grass with only the occasional tree to mar their symmetry.

In the distance, Dev could see the small gathering that marked the interment site of another fallen hero. They were all heroes in his opinion and he saluted them, grieved for them, wished he were one of them. The sad notes of "Taps" sounded faintly in the distance, carried on the warm spring breeze.

He stood at Danny's marker and made his confession to the man he had so admired and now mocked every time he held Amanda in his arms.

I'm keeping my promise, Dan. I know it's taken me a while to get my act together, but I'm taking care of Amanda—the best I can. She's stronger than you might have thought. Maybe tragedy brought her strength to the surface. God knows she's had plenty of it. She still loves you and misses you but she handles her loss with grace and dignity—you'd be proud of her.

The financial road's been a little bumpy but I'm giving her a hand with that and after this damn party she's organizing is over, I think she'll be on her way in that department.

There's only one problem, Dan. She doesn't want to find someone else. She swears that she won't fall in love again and I'm not trying to change her mind, because I don't want her to. We've been together for the past couple of months. I've fallen in love with her, Dan, and I know that makes me the worst kind of bastard to betray your trust like this. But don't worry. For her, our relationship means nothing more than friends. When I tell her who I really am, this strange and wonderful friendship will be over and I'll be out of her life forever.

Sometimes I wonder if you anticipated that should the worst happen, Amanda and I would get together. But I know that's just wishful thinking. Before I go, I'll do my best to convince her to find a love to replace yours.

I miss you, buddy, and if I'd known how hard it would be to keep this promise, I don't think I'd have given you my word on it.

The ceremony a few hilltops away had concluded, the mourners dispersing, a woman in black clutching the folded flag to her breast as a man and woman helped her to a waiting limousine.

His confession over, Dev started the long walk back to the parking lot. He'd made no request for absolution. He didn't deserve his friend's forgiveness.

CHAPTER 22

The day had finally arrived. After all the weeks of preparation, Amanda could hardly believe the event that had taken over her life would be over in less than twenty-four hours. She threw back the covers and stretched.

Spook jumped onto the bed and purred mightily as she rubbed against her mistress, an unspoken request for breakfast. As soon as Amanda stood, the black cat raced for the kitchen.

The weather gods had smiled upon her. The cloudless sky was a sign the unusual warmth of the past few days would continue. Although they had made contingency plans in case of rain, she was glad the party would remain outdoors under the moonlight.

She padded to the kitchen in her bare feet, her furry slippers a thing of the past, ever since Dev and Jeff had installed the new heaters. She put on coffee, fed Spook, then dialed Zoe as she scanned the timeline she'd drawn up for the day's preparations.

"Yes, yes, I'm up," Zoe answered. "You didn't have to worry about me oversleeping, even after you kept me up until midnight going over every last detail for today."

Amanda could hear her yawn and responded with one of her own. "I wasn't worried about you sleeping in this morning, partner. I'm sure we both have enough adrenaline circulating in our bloodstreams to kick-start Rip Van Winkle."

"I'm heading to Mrs. Wyndham's place as soon as I get a cup of coffee in me. Jeff's recruits will be arriving early to move furniture and set up the tables."

"Yes and I'll be right behind you to finish steaming the chair covers. The flower arrangements need to be carried from the little house up to the deck as soon as we have the tents set up."

"Yeah, Mandy, we've got it all covered, I think. You excited?"

"Terrified, more likely," she said with a chuckle. "I hope the singer Dev said he got gets here in time. That's the only little glitch we can't control, and the one Mrs. W will be the most pissed off about if we don't come through."

"Oh pooh on her. She should be so wowed with this party she should give us a big fat bonus. I refuse to worry about it anymore. Listen, I've got to go, I hear Jeff's bike out back and I haven't gotten dressed yet."

"That ought to make Jeff a happy camper."

"Humpf," Zoe snorted. "Which is why I haven't gotten dressed yet."

"Of course." Amanda laughed. "Okay, Zo. See you soon."

Amanda heard Jeff's wolf whistle before the connection was cut and smiled. How long had Zoe refused to see Jeff's attentions as anything other than sexual overtures? She hadn't wanted to believe his interest was fueled by admiration and true affection for her as a person, not simply a sexual partner.

Zoe had been saying essentially the same thing about her relationship with Dev but there was no comparison.

Was there?

Since she'd laid down the rules at the beginning of their affair, she had continued blithely along, not really examining her feelings. She liked Dev—a lot. True. She certainly was sexually attracted to him. Admittedly. But now that she studied her emotions more closely, she realized they had deepened into something much more than friendship. Every good thing that happened she wanted to share with him. Every distressing event had her seeking him out for solace. If she didn't see him for twenty-four hours, she missed him.

Everything she used to want to share with Danny, she now shared with Dev.

She glanced across the room at Danny's photograph. The familiar heartache blossomed at the thought that she would never see his smile or hear his laughter again. That pain would never go away. But it was beginning to hurt a tiny bit less every day.

She set her coffee cup down carefully. Her hands were shaking as the full force of the truth hit her. She was in love with Dev. She wasn't sure how that had happened exactly, but there was no denying it. She loved that man.

A tiny bubble of happiness that had been lurking unnoticed in a hidden corner of her heart expanded, pushing aside her sorrow over Danny as it grew. At first she smiled a little, then she sat back and grinned like a fool. Finally she laughed out loud.

Spook came over at the sound and twined about her feet. She scooped her up and giggled like a schoolgirl. "I'm in love with Dev, Spook. Isn't that wonderful?"

The cat licked her nose then squirmed to get down, not sure what all this fuss was about.

Amanda could hardly wait to tell Zoe. She wouldn't even mind all the "I told you so's" she'd hear from her. She'd—

Abruptly her rosy little bubble turned to lead and plummeted to her stomach.

What if Dev didn't love her back?

He said he was fine with their 'friends with benefits' arrangement.

She'd made him promise not to fall in love with her, hadn't she? She could hardly blame him for keeping to his promise.

Contemplating Dev's behavior the last couple of weeks, he had seemed different. She'd not been able to put her finger on the change in his attitude. They still made love frequently and with passion, though often his caresses were more lingering, more tender than ever before—as though he was memorizing her body, imprinting her face in his heart and mind. He'd said several times that he'd never get enough of her. That certainly sounded like he loved her.

Or did it sound like he knew their time together was finite? That someday he would leave her—or she, him?

She would have to let him know how she felt. Tonight, after this party that had been occupying every spare moment of her time was over, after they had made love, as she knew they would, she would tell Dev she loved him. She was ninety-percent sure he would say he loved her too.

It was that other ten-percent that would add an extra little fillip to tonight's stress level.

"This is it," Zoe said.

The little house that had been a hotbed of activity all afternoon was quiet now. The main room held only empty boxes and a few pieces of furniture they moved down from the "big house". The hired staff had changed into their uniforms and left to take their assigned places before the guests began to arrive.

Amanda slipped into her dress, a deceptively plain black matte jersey number with a high neck, long sleeves, and a bodice that hugged her curves then fell to her feet in a soft drape of fabric that allowed her legs the freedom to move quickly should she need to attend to any emergency. Prim and proper from the front, the dress turned seductive when viewed from behind, where her back was bare almost to her waist. She hoped she wouldn't be too chilly later tonight. Her hair was up in a neat French twist, *a la* Grace Kelly, with a few tendrils left free to float around her face. Her only jewelry was the pair of diamond studs her stepfather had given her at graduation.

"My nerves are strung so tight I think I may twang if anyone brushes up against me," Amanda said.

She made a circling motion with her finger for Zoe to turn around so she could zip up her dress. The strapless black sheath with an empire waist added inches to Zoe's petite frame and the bolero jacket she wore over it was studded with tiny jet beads that didn't sparkle so much as shimmer where they caught the light.

"You look wonderful, Zoe. Wait until Jeff sees you in this. I'm not sure he'll be able to keep his mind on his duties tonight."

Jeff was their "outside man", in charge of the valet service, emergency supplies, and overall security. They doubted that anyone would try to crash the party but Amanda felt safer knowing someone was on the lookout just in case. He'd also made an ice sculpture for the main buffet table.

Commissioned by Mrs. Wyndham, it was a miniature replica of the new boat she was giving her husband as a birthday gift. Once she saw it, Amanda no longer felt the slightest concern over the amount they would make from this party. By now she realized they had not charged nearly enough for their services. Although she doubted they would ever manage another event as large as this one, the experience would be invaluable for future jobs.

The band was here, finally. One member had taken a wrong turn and wound up in Salisbury before he realized his mistake, but they were all here now, setting up in the white tent at the opposite end of the deck from the bar.

Amanda's only worry was Dev's job. He'd come by early in the afternoon to set up his equipment then left to drive to BWI airport to pick up THE SINGER. She thought of the man in capital letters because he was the one person she had not personally hired and the one person Mrs. Wyndham was so insistent about. Until Dev arrived with the mystery man safely in tow, she would be one isotope short of a total nuclear meltdown.

Jeff came back to report that all the outside staff were at their assigned places.

“Okay, Beautiful, we’re all set. You look like a million bucks.” He winked. “Better watch out for gropers. You don’t want to be stealing the show from Mrs. W. She’ll be expecting the major portion of attention from the male half of this shindig.”

“She can have all the attention as far as I’m concerned. Most of these men are too old and too elite to hit on the hired help,” Amanda replied. *Besides, there’s only one man I’m longing to see. Please, God, let him get here soon.*

“Don’t count them safe because of their age, Beautiful. That puts them right into the dirty old man category. They’ll think feeling up the hired help is not only allowed, but expected. If you—” Jeff stopped mid-sentence, mouth open. He clutched his chest, then fell to his knees.

Amanda rushed over to him. “What’s wrong? Don’t you feel well?” *Please don’t let him be having a heart attack.* “Zoe get Jeff some water. We may need to call a doctor.”

Jeff brushed her aside, his eyes fixed on Zoe. “My sea goddess,” he said with reverence bordering on awe.

When Zoe realized she was the cause of all the commotion, her cheeks pinked up and she gave Amanda a surprised shrug of her shoulders. She marched across the few feet that separated them. “Get up from there, you idiot. You scared me to death.”

“No more than you do to me,” he said. “Promise to marry me and be my muse forever, my beautiful sea nymph.” He clasped his hands in supplication.

Grinning from ear-to-ear, Amanda turned to go somewhere, anywhere, that would give the two of them some privacy. She’d never heard Jeff so eloquent.

Zoe reached out and grabbed her wrist to stop her exit. "No need for you to go, Mandy. Jeff has obviously been sampling the champagne fountain up at the big house. It's not water he needs, it's coffee."

Amanda saw the flash of defeat cross Jeff's face, before his usual flippant mask slid into place and he bounced up off the floor.

"No need for coffee, ladies. I'm fine. I'll just go back to my duties. Call me if you need me." He directed his last comment to Amanda and without another glance at Zoe, he left.

"He was being so sweet." Amanda threw up her arms in exasperation. "Did you have to crush him so completely?"

"What do you mean, crush him? He was just kidding around like he always does. And I'm too nervous to put up with his little games tonight."

"That wasn't a game, girl. That man's eyes nearly popped out of his head when he saw you. It was his way of telling you how beautiful he thinks you are. And I'm not so sure that proposal was just a throwaway line either."

"There was no proposal," Zoe scoffed. "You were standing right here the whole time."

"Oh, I see. The whole 'marry me and be my muse forever' thing didn't count because I was standing here to hear it?" Amanda crossed her arms to keep from giving her friend a good shake. "Let me give you a little bulletin, my dear. That man is in love with you. Has been in love with you for as long as I've known you. I would think proposing to you in front of a witness would make you take it more seriously rather than less."

Amanda wasn't sure if the surprise on Zoe's face was for the content of her little bulletin or the forcefulness of the delivery, but she was on a roll and couldn't seem to stop.

"You know how you've been telling me for weeks that Dev's in love with me? Well, it took me a while, I agree, to see the light. But now that I know I'm in love with him, I sure hope you're right, because I don't think I could stand it if he walked away from me now. So take a good look in the mirror, Zoe, and realize you're in the same boat as I am. Don't let Jeff get away, he's—"

The strange expression on Zoe's face finally penetrated. Amanda glanced over her shoulder to see what she was staring at. Dev and another man dressed in jeans and polo shirt stood in the doorway. Amanda could feel the heat of her blush all the way to her hairline.

There were twenty seconds of dead silence, then the stranger stepped forward and put out his hand.

"Hi. I'm Arnold Katzenbaum. It's nice to meet you. I hear you're in need of a singer."

Only the good manners her mother had drilled into her growing up allowed Amanda to respond in a reasonably normal voice.

"Hello, Arnold, I'm Amanda. It's a pleasure to meet you, too."

Another brief silence followed before Zoe stepped up beside Amanda and offered her hand to the newcomer. "Hi, I'm Zoe, Amanda's partner. We are sooo glad you could make it tonight."

"Thanks. Glad I could help you out. Sorry to cut it so tight but I had a wedding reception this afternoon." He slipped the garment bag from his shoulder. "Is there someplace I could change?"

"Oh, of course. I'm so sorry. I'm . . . a little . . . tense, tonight." Amanda heard Zoe snort a laugh, and closed her eyes briefly. "You can use the bedroom to the right. Can I get you something to drink? Soda, coffee, water?" *I'm getting a cup of hemlock for myself. Or a shot of tequila. Whatever's handiest.*

She debated apologizing for her rant but that would only magnify the mortification she was doing her best to ignore. Talk about making declarations of love in front of bystanders! This was not exactly the way she had planned on telling Dev her feelings. If only The Road Runner would zip by with one of those portable holes, she could sink right through the floor.

"Cold water would be great, thanks."

Arnold did his best to keep a straight face, but Amanda could see his lips twitching up at the corners. No doubt he thought she was hilarious. Or a ditz. Or both. Meanwhile, Dev had not said a word since they'd walked through the door. Was he totally dismayed by what he overheard? Oh God.

Arnold looked back and forth between the two of them, then said to Dev, "Yeah, I understand where you're coming from now, buddy. No wonder you were so persuasive. Come on, let's get these monkey suits on. It's almost show time."

Dev followed him toward the bedroom saying, "I have it on good authority that these monkey suits are very attractive to the opposite sex." He winked at Amanda.

"No kidding, pal. Why do you think I went into this line of work? Weddings, bar mitzvahs—the dames practically stuff their phone numbers in my pockets. It's a gold—" The bedroom door shut, cutting off the rest of Arnold's sentence.

Amanda and Zoe stared wordlessly at each other. There had been too much information and too little time to process it. For either of them.

"You could have told me they were here," Amanda groused.

"I, I couldn't seem to get a word in." Zoe sounded apologetic but the mischievous sparkle was back in her eyes. She started to laugh. "You were just tooo good. I had to let you run with it."

Amanda tried to maintain her cool, but in seconds she broke, joining in the laughter as they went into the kitchen and hunted for glasses and ice. They had brought a bag of ice earlier and stashed it in the freezer. The old fridge was so small it barely held the water and soda bottles. Amanda rummaged through the drawers to find an implement capable of cracking the now-solid bag of cubes. She found a wooden crab mallet, a few paring knives, and a tea strainer in a drawer. Way in the back was a solitary key on a chain with a plastic fob designed to float, usually used for boat keys.

"Hey, look, Zoe. This key chain is from my junior high school. We sold a ton of these to raise money for band uniforms. Nice to know Mrs. Wyndham supported my school way back then. It was designed for boats, but since we didn't have one, my dad used ours for the key to The Last Call." She rubbed it fondly, remembering the way she'd had to "talk" her dad into buying one. She tossed the key back in the drawer and began to attack the bag of ice with the crab mallet. A few good whacks and she had enough broken off to use for their drinks.

It was only water but instinctively she and Zoe turned to each other and clinked glasses.

"To A to Z Enterprises," Amanda said.

"Hear, hear," Zoe responded with a grin.

Amanda glanced at the wall clock. "Oh my, look at the time. We'd better get up to the big house before guests begin to arrive. I've got a final checklist to run through."

"Of course you do." Zoe laughed. "You are *such* a Girl Scout."

"I try to be prepared."

Yet she hadn't been prepared when she realized she was in love with Dev. That reality was still sending shock waves through her system.

She called through the bedroom door. "Guys, we're going on over to the big house. We've left your drinks on the kitchen counter. See you over there."

Dev's voice came faintly through the door. "Right. See you there. We won't be long."

Neither she nor Zoe were wearing stilettos, but the walk over didn't do their shoes any good. They picked their way through the mulch and gravel, trying not to sink too deeply into the soft, sandy soil.

Jeff met them at the front door, and Zoe motioned Amanda to go in without her while she stopped to talk to him. Once inside, Amanda did a quick walk-through of the spaces set up for the party. She had to admit it had come together every bit as beautifully as they had envisioned. Snowy linens with black toppers added elegance to the tables, where the candles in the centerpieces cast warm, flickering light. The fairy lights in the garlands made all the pricked fingertips worthwhile. The effect was truly magical.

She went over to the band, checked to make sure the microphones were working, and thanked them again for coming. The tall metal heaters were scattered around the area, but so far the evening was still balmy enough to leave them unlit.

"Well, Ms. Adams, you and Ms. Silvercreek seem to have exceeded even my expectations," Mrs. Wyndham said from behind her.

Amanda turned with a satisfied smile on her lips, the butterflies in her stomach no longer in frantic flight.

"I'm glad you're pleased, Ma'am. I know this party means a lot to you and the Admiral."

"Yes. Well. The Admiral would have been just as happy to get his boat and skip the party, but I told him it was a package deal." She chuckled. "The ice sculpture your handsome artist friend did will be the highlight of the party for Henry. That young man is very talented."

"Yes, he is. You should come by the gallery soon. Zoe is displaying an entire collection of his works."

"Perhaps I shall. Right now I'm interested in the mystery singer you've hired. Has he arrived yet?"

"He has. Dev drove him here from the airport. They're changing at your old house right now. They'll be along any minute. Can I get you a glass of champagne while you wait to greet your guests?"

"How kind of you, dear, thank you."

Amanda went over to the bar. On a round table next to it a champagne fountain was burbling cheerfully. She held a flute under the stream of pale gold liquid and took the filled glass over the Mrs. Wyndham. As usual, the woman appeared as though she had just left a salon—hair and makeup perfect, nails manicured, a fragrant gardenia tucked behind one ear. She wore a stunning red sheath, which bared one shoulder and outlined her figure. There was no doubt about it; for a woman in her sixties, Mrs. Wyndham was still a knockout.

"Come on, man, I can already hear the band tuning up."

Dev adjusted his bow tie one last time. He paced the living room, thinking about what Amanda had said to Zoe. She loved him? Sweet Jesus, that revelation blew him right out of the water. He'd been rehearsing his entire speech on the drive to the airport. Explaining his friendship with Danny, his guilt over causing Danny's death, his promise to watch over her till she got over his loss.

Actually he wasn't sure he'd even get to those other parts. When she found out how Danny died, she may well show him the door and politely, but firmly erase him from her life. But if she loved him? That would make things so much worse.

He checked the clock again. Arnold had insisted he needed a quick shower before he changed into his tux. He'd come straight from the wedding reception, where he had time only to swap his tux for street clothes and grab a cab to the airport.

"I get pretty hot under those lights. I'm not going out there all sweaty like I've been working on a chain gang. Chill, buddy. I won't need more than five minutes in the shower.

Besides I'm not singing for the band's first set. We decided to wait until most of the guests had arrived to do the vocals. They're going to be playing background music for the first hour. People will be eating and drinking, chatting with friends. The band will break, you'll do your thing for thirty minutes or so, then I'll come on and get the party going." Arnold clapped Dev on the back and headed for the bathroom.

Dev did his best to wear a path in the ancient shag carpeting while he waited. He'd planned on dancing with Amanda one time tonight. One magical dance under the stars with the most beautiful woman in the world. It might be selfish but he didn't care. He wanted those few minutes with her in his arms to remember after his world came crashing down around his ears.

He'd almost swallowed his tongue when he got to the door and saw her in that dress. All that creamy skin waiting for his touch when he put his arms around her. Tall and slender, her glorious hair captured in a sleek twist that left her neck bare, she was a vision in black. His fingers itched to trace the graceful line of her neck, to plant tender kisses from her hairline to her waist following the delicate curve of her spine.

Then her words managed to penetrate the haze of desire that had him hard as stone, standing on the doorstep.

She loved him. And she'd been berating Zoe for something. He didn't know what. After she'd said those words, he didn't really listen to anything else. He felt a little lightheaded as what little blood remained above his neck rushed south. Thank God Arnold had stepped up to the plate and introduced himself. Now that he had thought about it, he understood the definition of tragedy. The truth would hurt so much more now that she cared for him. The betrayal would be deeper, and he could only hope that her anger with him would help to cushion the blow when he left. He thought he'd been doing what was best for her, but Chris was right. The longer you, lied the worse things got.

Dev took a deep breath. For the next five hours he would ignore the future. He would do his part to make this night a resounding success and insure Amanda's financial stability. Her emotional stability? Well, he *had* convinced her to move on, to open her heart to someone new. Hopefully she could do it again.

He groaned. He cursed himself. But in the end, there was nothing to do but play his final part in her life tonight. He donned his gloves, shot his cuffs, put a smile on his face, and walked through the door to the Wyndham's Cottage, Arnold Katzenbaum at his side.

Guests had already begun to arrive and the Wyndham's stood by the door, greeting each couple as they entered. Dev took Arnold's arm and sidestepped them past the receiving line. Zoe stood unobtrusively near the fireplace, checking the crowd for trouble spots. She noticed them and immediately made her way over.

"I'm glad you're here. Maybe now Amanda can relax a little."

"Where is she?"

Dev scanned the room and discovered why Amanda and Zoe had chosen to wear black. It was the choice of over half the women here. But if Amanda thought it would make her blend in with the crowd, she was sadly mistaken. Her beauty and grace drew the eyes of more than a few male guests. He scowled and wished there was a way to brand her as 'taken'. As his. Something . . . like a wedding ring. If only he'd done everything differently.

CHAPTER 23

The party was in full swing and Amanda was so full of mixed emotions she felt barely able to maintain her composure. There was no doubt she and Zoe had produced an affair that would be the talk of Mrs. Wyndham's social circle for months.

She could hardly believe it herself. Not one glitch. The food was excellent, the champagne flowed like a river, and she overheard so many compliments about the décor, she knew they had scored a home run in that department. The band's repertoire was wonderful and their selections had more couples out on the dance floor than Amanda had anticipated. The partygoers obviously loved it.

When Arnold Katzenbaum took his place in front of the band, Amanda was in the kitchen checking with the caterer to make sure there was plenty of food left. She'd lost track of Zoe as they split up to keep tabs on different areas—moving unobtrusively through the crowd in a fairly continuous circle.

At first she thought Dev was still playing recorded songs, because the voice sounded like Frank Sinatra. But when applause followed his first song and he tossed out a one-liner that had a wave of laughter rippling through the crowd, Amanda made her way to the French doors.

He began "Polka Dots and Moonbeams" and the guests quieted so there was barely a murmur to compete with him. Arnold was not a particularly imposing entertainer. Medium height, average build, brown hair, brown eyes—there was nothing remarkable about him. Until he opened his mouth and let his voice transform that average persona into a reincarnation of Sinatra in his early years.

Amanda realized her mouth was agape and snapped her jaw shut. She searched the deck and caught Zoe coming up the walkway from the pavilion. Their eyes met and mirrored each other's amazement. Zoe broke into a big grin and gave her a surreptitious thumbs-up, to which she could only nod.

Amanda scanned the crowd. She had to find Dev and thank him for pulling such a fantastic rabbit out of his hat. Where was he? Most of the couples who had been dancing in the pavilion had thronged the walkway to get a better view of the singer causing such a stir up on the deck. She couldn't see past them to the small area where Dev had been spinning his CDs while the band took a break. She stretched her neck in an attempt see over the press of bodies.

"Looking for someone?"

The warm breath on the back of her neck at his whispered words sent a wave of heat through her that had every erogenous zone in her body tingling with desire. Only the fact that they were in full view of the guests kept her from turning and wrapping her arms around him.

Instead, she leaned back against his broad chest and tilted her head to whisper, "You are an amazing man, Dev of the Dream Machine. It appears you can make all my dreams come true tonight."

Dev didn't reply but she swore she felt the heat from his body ratchet up several degrees.

Finally, his voice rough with emotion, Dev whispered, "Your wish is my command, darling. Remember that."

She nodded, smiling to herself at the wishes she intended to make later tonight. His warm breath in her ear peaked her nipples and sent a flash of heat over her skin. She was glad the audience was so taken with Arnold's singing that they wouldn't notice her body's reaction to Dev's nearness.

"Sometime tonight I am going to dance with you, so make sure you're down by the dance floor during the band's final set," he continued sotto voce.

She shook her head. "I don't think that's a good idea, Dev. Mrs. Wyndham won't be pleased with the idea of the hired help behaving like guests."

"By then she'll have had so much champagne I don't think she'll be in any shape to notice. In fact, she's been flirting with the sax player outrageously since they began playing, so I expect she'll be too busy to pay any attention to us." He dropped a tender kiss on the back of her neck. "Surely I deserve one dance for bringing Arnold to this shindig."

She sighed. He deserved more than a dance, but that could wait till later. Arnold encouraged the guests to get up and dance then began "Let's Do It" to scattered applause. Following his advice, the dance floor filled. Amanda turned to face him. "You're irresistible, Mr. MacMurphy. I'll meet you in the pavilion at midnight."

For a minute she was afraid he might kiss her, the heat in his eyes was so intense, so she backed away a step and ducked around him to escape to the relative coolness of the deck.

Automatically scanning the area for potential trouble spots, Amanda stayed by the deck railing inhaling the sharp, salty scent of the bay carried by a light breeze. The full moon banished all but the brightest stars from the cloudless sky and the temperature had dropped enough to send a little shiver up her bare back. Better have one of the waiters light the heaters. She swept the room but didn't see any of the wait staff. Instead she found the Admiral bearing down on her like a schooner under full sail.

"Ms. Adams, good evening."

"Good evening, Admiral. I hope you're enjoying your birthday party."

"You and your partner have done a first-rate job, Ms. Adams. The guests all seem to be having a wonderful time."

He surveyed the crowd, his eyes lingering on his wife dancing with someone up near the bandstand. Amanda sensed he wasn't happy about something.

"And you, sir, are you having a good time?"

"Well, these parties aren't my type of thing. This is really more Mrs. Wyndham's cup of tea." He tore his eyes away from the lady in question. "I wanted to thank you for your efforts. Caroline is quite happy, especially with the band and the singer you found. She has always been a big fan of live music and dragged me to more concerts than I can remember."

"I'm so glad we were able to find someone so talented for tonight, Admiral. I suppose you know it was not until the last minute that your wife requested a singer, so it was quite a challenge."

"Yes, once she gets an idea in her head she's harder to turn around than an aircraft carrier." He gave a brief chuckle. "I was curious where you found the combo. They remind me of another group that used to be one of Caroline's particular favorites."

"Actually I asked one of the men from the quintet my dad used to play with. He gave me the names of this group and a couple of others to check out. Mrs. Wyndham did mention that you and she had seen the Alex Carr Quintet on a number of occasions, back when my dad was playing saxophone."

The sharp look the Admiral shot her took her by surprise. But seconds later his genial smile was back in place, forcing her to wonder if she'd imagined it. He certainly was a strange bird. She decided to switch to a topic more to his liking.

"I understand your birthday present is a new boat, Admiral. If the ice sculpture is any indication, it will be beautiful. Will she be delivered soon?"

"Can't deliver her till the channel to the dock is dredged. Right now the water isn't deep enough to float her. I wanted to start that weeks ago but Caroline was afraid the machinery would ruin the 'atmosphere' for this party."

He sounded a little disgruntled but resigned to his wife's priorities. No doubt he would have been happier to have his boat sooner and skip the party altogether.

Amanda hid her smile at the idea the Admiral ordered hundreds of sailors around but couldn't overrule Mrs. Wyndham's plans.

"Well, I hope it doesn't take long to do the dredging. I know you must be anxious to take the helm."

He gave her another sideways glance and Amanda ordered herself to shut up. She knew little about boats and the Admiral's aura of command intimidated her. Did captains 'take the helm' on anything less grand than ocean liners? She had no idea. This conversation was uncomfortable on a number of levels. She was about to come up with an invented task to use as an escape mechanism when he nodded abruptly, thanked her again, and headed toward the bar. Relieved, she went to find Zoe. After checking that there were no problems, she headed for the bandstand. She needed to speak to Arnold.

Dev surveyed the couples that crowded the dance floor and congratulated himself for his part in making this party the fantastic success it was. Standing behind the small table on the landing that led from the pavilion down to the dock, he stacked his CDs in the order he intended to play them—barring requests from the party goers. They loved this music and asked for any of the big hits from the forties the live band and Arnold hadn't already performed. Arnold was a smash and even though most of the women here were a good deal older, he was still getting phone numbers tucked into his pockets from a few cougars in the crowd.

Dev put “Let’s Face the Music and Dance” on and searched the group for Amanda. The band was about due back from their break to start their last set and he intended to have his dance while he wasn’t needed to man the recorded music desk.

Both Zoe and Amanda had checked in with him several times as the evening wore on, each barely able to contain their delight that everything was going so well. What a great kick-off for their new event-planning business. Word would be all over town by tomorrow considering how many of the locals they had hired to help out tonight.

He caught the column of red that was Mrs. Wyndham chatting with friends up by the bar. She appeared to be enjoying herself, though she wasn’t spending much time on the Admiral’s arm. He saw her glance over at the band’s empty chairs as though anxious for them to return. They had been gone for a little over thirty minutes now, and sharp as that lady was, she probably had a stopwatch on their break time. She broke into a wide smile and excused herself from the group she was with to make her way over as the band members returned. She whispered something in the ear of the sax player—probably a request for some favorite song—and he nodded. Dev faded out his music as Arnold stepped up to the microphone. He checked his watch. Five minutes to midnight. Time to find Amanda and claim his dance.

The crowd on the dance floor thinned as couples headed toward the main deck for the band and Arnold’s final set. He opened with “Taking a Chance on Love” and Dev watched Amanda come down the walkway, her slender form and the graceful sway of her hips taking his breath away as usual. He met her at the edge of the dance floor. The fairy lights seemed to put twinkling stars in her eyes and her tender smile had his heart pounding double-time.

"I believe we have a date," she said with a sigh, giving him her hand.

"We do, darling."

With impeccable timing, Arnold began the pre-arranged song as he swept her into his arms. "Moonlight Becomes You" floated over the deck. His hand found the smooth skin of her back and his arm tightened around her, drawing her close. Their bodies melded and they moved so perfectly in sync they glided across the floor as a single being.

He concentrated on capturing the scent of her hair, the softness of her cheek against his, the feel of her body pressed against his from shoulders to hips. His senses were heightened with the knowledge this would be the last time he held her in his arms and he burned those sensations into his memory. They would have to last him a lifetime.

The music ended and he steeled himself to release her. To his surprise, her arm slid around his neck and her fingers tangled in his hair as she whispered in his ear, "I'm afraid I'll need one more dance before I can bear to let you go."

He leaned back to see such love shining in her eyes that his knees almost buckled as his heart broke. He refused to let the crushing pain of losing her reach his eyes. He would not ruin her night. Instead, he folded her back into his arms as the band began "The Nearness of You" and Arnold sang the words he would remember later with such clarity.

It was four a.m. The last of the guests had departed around two o'clock, some to drive back to Annapolis, a few to stay at Marjorie's bed and breakfast. Several couples had been offered guest rooms at the Wyndham's Cottage. Without exception, they all had raved about the party, congratulating Mrs. Wyndham for hosting such a remarkable affair. On several occasions, Amanda overheard her graciously giving credit to Amanda and Zoe for the entire event from concept to completion. That put a satisfied glow in her mid-section.

The caterers had packed up their gear and left. What food remained was offered to the staff. Tomorrow they would come back and take down the tables, the tents, the lighted garlands, and centerpieces and return the "Cottage" to its pre-party state.

Tonight, Amanda would bask in the glory of a job well done and the satisfaction of a final check—including a hefty bonus—from Mrs. Wyndham. More importantly, she would share the success with the man she loved, who had had no small part in contributing to that success. The man, who after those incredible dances at midnight, had left no doubt in her mind about his feelings for her. He loved her.

Amanda's heart swelled with joy. The sorrow of losing Danny was tucked away in a corner of her heart, never to be completely vanquished, but overlaid by the happiness of her love for Dev. She was sure that if Danny had only known him, he would be happy for her too.

She'd changed out of her long black dress, a smile twitching her lips as she remembered the heat in Dev's eyes every time he caught sight of her in it at the party. Comfortable in soft sweatpants and an ancient tee shirt, she snuggled next to him on the ride home. He was unusually quiet, no doubt as exhausted as she, but without the thrill of their success to buoy his spirits. She imagined his enthusiasm would return as soon as they slid between the sheets.

As soon as she stepped through the door, Spook twined around her legs meowing loudly.

"Oh, poor baby, you must be starved."

The black cat agreed, dogging her footsteps to the kitchen, keeping up her complaint as Amanda opened a can of cat food. She put the dish down and Spook fell on it like a ravening beast, much to Amanda's chagrin.

She turned to find Dev making a fresh pot of coffee. "Honey, it's almost four-thirty. You want a cup of coffee now?"

"Yeah. I'm too keyed up to go to sleep. I thought we could talk a bit."

He avoided her eyes and her stomach began a slow roll. Something was wrong. She thought back over the evening, trying to find something, anything, that might be the cause of his troubled expression. Anything except the very first thought that had leapt to mind. She'd said she loved him. He'd had several opportunities, but he hadn't said he loved her back.

Her stomach bunched itself into a fist and slammed against her heart.

Now he was going to remind her gently that she had made him promise not to fall in love. He was only following the rules. *Her* rules. She slid heavily into a chair at the table. She tried to concentrate but her thoughts skittered away in a hundred different directions, like insects running from the light, leaving her mind blank. She watched the thin stream of dark liquid begin to fill the coffee pot.

Dev set cream and sugar on the table with two spoons. "Would you like a cup?"

She shook her head, sure the coffee would never stay down. When he brought his cup over and sat down opposite her, she said calmly, without a hint of the despair that filled her heart, "You don't love me. I understand. It's okay. After all, I'm the one who made the rules. So don't feel obligated because of what you overheard me tell Zoe. There's no reason for you to feel badly."

She had to close her own eyes against the regret in his.

"There are plenty of reasons for me to feel badly, but that certainly isn't one of them." He took a deep breath and squared his shoulders. Then he pointed to the picture of Danny on the table by the love seat. "You know, that was the only tree within a mile of the dusty, half-destroyed village we stopped at that day. Danny wanted you to think the areas we patrolled were . . . nicer . . . than the usual collection of five or six hovels with a well and a couple of goats trying to find something to eat. He always wanted the best for you."

Amanda studied at the picture and frowned. "What are you talking about? That picture was taken by his best friend, Mac."

"Yeah, that was me." He kept his eyes locked on hers. "In the Army everybody called me Mac."

"But . . . but . . ." She shook her head slowly, struggling with this unexpected piece of information. "When he was killed in that roadside bombing, I thought there were only two survivors, and those men were critically wounded and not expected to survive . . . When I never heard from him, I thought Mac had . . . died . . . too."

Her gaze went to his arm and the hand, now gloveless, that rested on the table next to his coffee cup. She looked up. "You were one of them? But why didn't you tell me before?"

"Because I'm the reason Danny didn't make it. He got killed because he came back to get me out of the wreckage. I tried to make him stay back but he wouldn't listen. So you see, if it hadn't been for me, Danny would be here with you right now."

It must be because she was so tired that this conversation didn't make any sense. The man sitting across from her said he was Danny's best friend, the man he'd mentioned in dozens of letters during his five years in Iraq. Dev was Mac.

"Danny made me promise that if anything should happen to him, I'd find you and, well, make sure you were okay." He grimaced. "It should never have taken me that long to contact you, but I was a coward. I figured you'd hate me for coming back alive instead of Danny, and I wouldn't blame you. Most days I hate myself for it." He dragged a hand through his hair, leaving an unruly tangle in its wake. "After all the things that Danny told me about you, I felt like I already knew you. Knew how devastating his death would be for you. That's the reason it took me so long to . . . Believe me, Amanda, I'd give anything to change places with him."

"Wait. Wait just a minute." She held her hands up. "You're telling me that *you're* the Mac Danny mentioned in his letters to me?"

"That's right."

"So that's how you knew he was allergic to cats," she said, rubbing Spook's ears while she purred.

"Yes."

"And the nightmares? They're about the bombing? When he . . . When you were wounded.

"Yes."

"All these weeks we've . . . been together, you've been fulfilling this, this . . . *promise* . . . to Danny to take care of me?"

"Yes. No. Sort of. Well, it started out that way but th—"

"So the repairs to my house, the new hot water heater, that was all part of the *promise*?" She made air quotes around the word.

He nodded, not even trying to interrupt her now.

"And hiring me to do your company's books?"

She had her arms crossed in front of her, and her eyes had gone from smoke to steel. This was rapidly turning out to be the worst day of her life since the day she got the news about Danny.

"Well you must really have loved it when I tumbled right into bed with you. That was part of making sure I was all right too, no doubt." Her voice dripped acid.

"No. That . . . that was all me. It was wrong. I should never have—"

"Lied to me? For weeks? Pretended to be my friend while you treated me like a helpless child who couldn't take care of herself? Slept with me under false pretenses?" *Made me fall in love with you?*

She stood up, fury coursing through her body like molten lava. She wanted to scream at him, throw things, hurt him as badly as he had hurt her. Instead, she gathered contempt around herself like armor and said icily, “Get out. Consider your ‘promise’ kept. Find a new accountant, because we won’t be speaking to each other again—ever. The money I owe you will be in the mail tomorrow.”

Thank God for that bonus check from Mrs. Wyndham. It had been earmarked to provide a nice cushion while she grew her business, but using it to erase the debt to Dev would allow her to cut him out of her life completely. The pain and anger she tried so hard to control got the better of her, and even though she knew she would hate herself for it later, she couldn’t stop herself from lying, “All those times we made love? It was Danny’s face I saw.”

The flash of pain in Dev’s eyes didn’t give her the satisfaction she’d hoped for. With a last disdainful glance, she picked up Spook and walked to her bedroom, closing the door softly to prove to herself that she hadn’t lost all control. A minute later she heard the front door open and close.

CHAPTER 24

Eighteen hours A.A. That's how Dev measured time now. After Amanda. Knowing for weeks that this pain was coming still hadn't prepared him to deal with it. He felt hollow. All the good things in his life were gone, leaving behind a shell filled with regrets and recriminations. He'd called the dependable Ed Santone and asked him to cover his Sunday night shift. He couldn't face the mike and pretend to be fine. Not yet.

He went to the tiny cove he and Amanda had found weeks ago. Sitting on a sliver of sand too narrow to deserve the term beach, he watched the moon fall into the bay, its silver trail snuffed out like a burned down candle. By the time the dawn was casting a golden glow on the electric blue horizon, his clothes were damp with dew and his eyes gritty with unshed tears. He drove home, showered, and threw himself across his bed in an attempt to lose his pain in sleep.

Visions of Amanda played across the inside of his eyelids. Sitting at the conference table, her bottom lip caught between her teeth as she worked on the company's books. Her eyes full of mischief as she pushed back the shower curtain to join him in a soapy prelude to lovemaking. Her face relaxed in sleep with her hair spread across the pillow like pale silk.

Eventually he gave up on sleep, dressed, and went into work.

"Hey, Boss. I hear Saturday night's party was the bomb," Mike greeted him with double thumbs-up.

Unable to reconcile Mike's sunny greeting with the gloom that had taken up residence in his head, Dev frowned. "Who told you that?"

"Are you kidding? It's all over town. Some of the people Amanda and Zoe hired were in the diner this morning sharing all the juicy details. The food, the swanky clothes on all those hoity-toity big wigs, the band—and your music, too. That guy you got to sing? Wow, did he ever create a sensation. The ladies were all swooning about his voice." He nudged Dev with an elbow. "I hear Amanda was a knock-out too. A few of the waiters were taking bets on who could score a date with her first." He chuckled. "I didn't have the heart to tell them she was already taken," he finished with a sly wink.

Dev rewarded his enthusiasm with a stony stare that had Mike's smile shrinking like a punctured balloon. "Yeah. It went well. What are you doing this afternoon?"

"I was running a couple of tests on the back-up transmitter."

"I'd like you to do me a favor, if you don't mind."

"Sure, boss. What do you need?"

"Would you drive over to the Wyndham place and pick up the equipment and CDs I left there? It was too late to pack everything up on Saturday night, but I imagine the cleanup crew Amanda hired will have it all ready to go by now."

If he was confused by Dev's strange lack of animation, Mike hid it well. "Absolutely, boss. Let me put these data sheets in my office and I'll get right over there."

"Thanks, Mike. I appreciate it." Dev went into his office and left Mike staring after him. No way was he going over there himself and take the chance of running into Amanda. The paperwork in his inbox had piled up since he'd been spending so much time at her place. Time to get back to business. He slid a stack of correspondence over and started in on it.

At five-thirty, Rosemary brought him a sandwich and a mug of coffee before she left for the day. She set the food on the edge of his desk. "I've retyped those letters you wrote today, boss. I have to say your spelling has taken a nosedive since Friday."

"Oh. Bad, huh?"

"My third-grade nephew can do better. What's got you so distracted?"

"Nothing you need to worry about, Rosemary. I've not been sleeping very well and I'm just tired." He nodded toward the plate she had brought him. "Thanks for the sandwich."

"You haven't eaten anything all day. Are you sure you're not coming down with something? I don't remember you ever skipping lunch before."

"I'm fine, Rosemary. You don't need to mother me."

He tossed his pen on the desk and scrubbed his hands over his face. "Sorry, Rosemary. That didn't come out the way I meant it. I've just . . . got a lot on my mind right now. I appreciate all that you do for me, especially things above and beyond what I pay you for." He slid the plate and mug in front of him. "Mmm, corned beef on rye. Smells delicious. Thank you again, Rosemary."

"You're welcome, boss. I'll be heading home now, unless you have anything else for me?"

"No. Nothing else tonight, Rosemary. I'll see you tomorrow. Have a good evening." He picked up the sandwich.

"Okay. See you tomorrow."

As soon as she was through the door, he put the sandwich back untouched, then got up and closed his office door. He was in no mood to swap idle chitchat with any of his employees. He'd already made Rosemary look at him like a kicked puppy, God knew what would have come out of his mouth if Andy gave him a hard time. Better to hole up in here and try to get some more work done before he was due to go on the air.

At ten-forty-five he'd consumed five cups of coffee and had damn little in his out-box to show for the hours he'd worked. Not surprising since the image of a beautiful gray-eyed blond kept coming between him and his computer screen.

Would she be in bed by now? The thought of her in the skimpy tank top and satin boxers she'd taken to wearing to bed when he was there had him instantly hard as steel. Would she listen to his show? Probably not. Why would she listen to someone she hated? So, no more calls on his request line from Amanda Adams.

Nevertheless, when he took over the mike after the eleven o'clock news, he couldn't stop himself from playing "Someone to Watch Over Me".

Amanda sat in the back room of Silvercreek Gallery sharing a lunch of coffee and a day-old scone, which she was slowly reducing to crumbs on her plate. Zoe, meanwhile, wolfed down a chicken salad sandwich, a glass of iced tea, and two cookies.

Amanda squeezed her eyes shut. She was done with crying. She'd cried enough over the past three days to make it worthwhile to buy stock in Kimberly-Clark. She inhaled deeply then exhaled slowly.

Someday she would be able to relive the triumph of their first event without thinking about the personal disaster that had followed. But that day wasn't here yet. She didn't want to think about the Wyndham's party now. Today they had finally finished removing the last few items from the Wyndham's old cottage. They'd cleaned up, taken out the trash, and recovered the furniture with white sheeting. But when she closed the door behind her, Amanda had an overwhelming sense of sadness and loss.

She had held the answer to her life in her hands right there in that living room. She admitted her love for Dev and even though she was talking to Zoe, she was glad he had overheard, because when she turned and found him standing behind her, dumbstruck, she was sure he loved her too. And for the space of a few short hours she was the happiest of women.

Now that joy had turned to ashes, her happiness burned to the ground by Dev's revelation. How could she have been so careless? After Danny, she had sworn she'd never fall in love again. She knew what a risk it was to give her heart into another's keeping. Her father . . . gone. Danny . . . gone. And now, Dev.

Zoe gave her arm a little shake. "Mandy? Come back, honey."

"Sorry."

"Don't apologize. It'll take a while to get past all this. But you will, honey, you will."

Amanda nodded. "You are so right." She set her jaw and angled her chin. "We never did go out and celebrate the way we should have." *I was too busy crying into my pillow or cursing the man who'd broken my heart.* "Why don't we go out for dinner tonight and drown my sorrows while we toast our success with a few Margaritas?"

"Fabulous idea! It's great to have enough money in the bank to be able to splurge without worrying about next month's rent. Where shall we go? Donatelli's?"

"No. Bad choice." She could only imagine how Mario would greet her—with lots of questions about Dev, no doubt. "Want to check out that new seafood place that just opened down at the end of First Street by the public dock?"

"Okay, why not? It's got to be better than Joe's Cheeseburgers and Fries," Zoe agreed, referring to the burger joint the new restaurant had replaced. "That place was the pits."

"Lord, yes. How can you mess up a hamburger?"

"I don't know, but they did." Zoe grimaced. "Let's hope Belle's Shells is an improvement."

Amanda dumped her pile of shredded scone into the trash and grabbed her purse. "I'm sure you have lots to do getting ready for Jeff's show, so I'll be back around six to pick you up for dinner, okay?"

"I'll be ready. And, Amanda? Bring your appetite, for Pete's sake. Pretty soon you'll weigh less than me, and that's not good."

"Don't worry. I'll eat. See you at six."

Back home, Amanda wandered around her property thinking about planting some flowers now that the weather had warmed up. She sat at the end of her dock and savored the last few weeks of peace and quiet. Memorial Day weekend was only two weeks away when the floodgates would open and the summer tourists would descend upon Blue Point Cove. While most of the merchants in town happily anticipated the deluge of thick-walleted visitors, Amanda's income was little different summer or winter.

And, unlike Zoe, she didn't have the financial cushion the bonus from Mrs. Wyndham provided. She'd used her share to pay Dev back for the work he had done to her house, not wanting to wait until September as their original agreement stipulated.

She was still furious every time she thought about all he had done. She'd thought he'd helped her because he liked her. No, because he loved her. These past few months they'd done everything together. Even chores as mundane as grocery shopping had seemed fun when Dev was with her. They had found that tiny cove, so secluded that they were sure no one knew of it but them. It'd become their go-to place to talk and dream and kiss.

She got up and stomped back up the dock. The check she had mailed him on Monday hadn't hit her bank account yet, but it was only a matter of time. Lucky for her, the news of her party's success had quickly spread throughout their bayside community and she had already received two inquiries about family reunion parties on the fourth of July weekend.

She rounded the corner of the house as a delivery truck stopped in front. She frowned as the driver hopped out and opened the rear doors to retrieve an arrangement of long-stemmed red roses in a crystal vase. If Dev thought that was all it would take to get back in her good graces, he was a bigger fool than she thought.

"Miss Adams?"

At her nod, he presented her with the bouquet. "Then these are for you, ma'am." He touched the bill of his ball cap.

"Well you can take these right back to the man who sent them. I don't want them." Amanda clasped her hands behind her back.

"But, Ma'am, I can't do that. If I bring these back, my boss will skin me. You can throw them away if you don't want them, but you gotta take 'em." He held them out to her again.

Feeling foolish to take her anger out on the hapless deliveryman, she finally took the vase. "Wait here and I'll get you a tip."

"Oh, no, ma'am. That's okay." He slammed the rear doors and headed for the driver's seat. In thirty seconds he was back on the road, leaving her standing in a cloud of dust holding a dozen roses.

"He was probably afraid I'd throw them at him," she muttered to herself as she went inside.

The card on its little plastic stick was too much for her to resist. Cursing her weakness, she slipped it from the envelope and read aloud, "It was great working with you. Next time you need a bartender, please call me. In fact, next time you need anything, please call me. Bill Leonetti." The word *anything* was underlined.

Well, that'd teach her to be so sure of herself. Had the expectation that the flowers were from Dev been wishful thinking? Or had she merely wanted the opportunity to spurn another gift from Dev? She wanted to throw something at him, that's for sure. The man had the gall to play "Someone to Watch Over Me" last night. Granted, it was the song she'd wanted to hear, but how annoying was it that he could read her so well? She wasn't sure which made her more angry—the fact that she did listen, or the fact that he knew she'd listen.

Dev lay in bed, his hands stacked behind his head. He wondered if today would be the day when complete exhaustion claimed him. It had to be soon. What was the Guinness record for hours without sleep? He ought to find out—he might be getting close to breaking it. Since last Saturday night, the sandman sat in a shadowy corner of his apartment sporting an evil grin and mocking him.

The endless debate circled around in his head. If he had told Amanda who he was from the start, would she have accepted his role in Danny's death and still been willing to get to know him, at least long enough for him to have fulfilled his promise to Danny? Or would she have politely told him to never darken her doorstep again?

And if she didn't brush him off, would she still have asked him to do her party? Agreed to be his accountant? Got to know him well enough to act on the sizzling attraction that had crackled between them from the first moment they met? Maybe there wouldn't have been any attraction—on her part at least—if she'd known who he was from the get-go. It could have all been one-sided in that alternate universe.

Of course the way he'd played it hadn't worked out well, either. The blame was all his, due in large part to his selfish inability to give up knowing the beautiful, funny, charming Amanda Adams. No matter how superficial their relationship might be, it was better than none at all. Or so he had thought all those weeks ago, the first time she sat in his office and completely enchanted him.

The debate was strictly academic at this point. He'd fucked up—and hurt her in the process. Something he'd never envisioned happening. Accepting his own pain at their inevitable break up was no problem. Those weeks of bliss were worth the payment. But more than his regret over Danny, it was having been the cause of Amanda's pain that ate at him now.

When he walked into the broadcast booth to take over from Andy, Dev began to think he really had entered an alternate universe. Andy signed off and cued in the eleven o'clock news feed. He swung around from the mike. "It's all yours, boss. Anything you need before I bug out of here?"

Dev frowned. "Did you get a haircut?"

"Yeah. Well, it was kinda gettin' in my way, you know?" Andy rubbed his hand over the one-inch stubble, all that remained of the style that had earned him the nickname Andy J., for Jesus.

Dev glanced around the studio. "Okay, who are you and what did you do with Andy Phelps?"

"Cute, boss. You're a barrel of laughs lately." He coiled up his ear buds and stuck them in his shirt pocket.

"Hey, sorry, Andy. No offense meant." Dev scanned the room again, still expecting a gremlin to hop up on the table and yell "surprise!" "You just threw me a curve here. The haircut is great. And I really appreciate you keeping the studio so clean. Guess my comments haven't been falling on deaf ears after all."

"Yeah, you'd be surprised at how much attention we pay around here." Andy nodded at the control booth. "You're on in thirty seconds, boss. I'll see you tomorrow night." He squeezed Dev's shoulder on the way by. "Have a good one."

Bemused, Dev watched him go. He glanced into the control room to see if Lance was still the man he remembered. He was, thank God. Although he was gesturing urgently for Dev to step up to the mike and say *something*.

Dev hit the switch and did his regular introduction. No calls lit up the phone lines immediately so he slid "Stormy Weather" into the player and let Billie Holiday's distinctive voice fill the studio.

Soon the call lights did light up, one after the other, and he was on a roll. He fielded three more in the same ballpark, before a caller asked him if his girl had just dumped him.

Dev denied even having a 'girl' in keeping with his usual method of withholding personal information. But it gave him pause. Seemed like a lot of folks out there were feeling the blues tonight. Or had he unconsciously been fueling the airwaves with his own troubles? He slipped in "Thou Swell" and "Night and Day" to break the mood and his listeners responded with some more cheerful requests. He worked at sounding upbeat all through his show—right up till it was time for the last song. He doubted Amanda listened any more, but he always dedicated the final play to her. Tonight it was "Nevertheless".

He flipped the call lines over to the canned answering machine. "We're sorry. The request hour is over. Please call in again next Friday night . . ." yada, yada, yada. For the remainder of his shift he kept his comments to a minimum and let the music float him along while the earth spun toward dawn.

By the following Wednesday, the normal easygoing atmosphere around the studio was history and his crew walked on eggshells and spoke in hushed voices around him. His desk was clear of paperwork. He'd written employee evaluations on every one of his employees, met with each of them to discuss their strengths and weaknesses, and bestowed raises where he felt they were deserved. He'd started a three-year business plan aimed at increasing revenues enough to make the station self-supporting. He'd jotted down the numbers for accountants, but had yet to call any of them.

Tonight Andy had ducked out of the studio as soon as he signed off. Dev marveled again at the change in the kid. Andy and Lance were having a conversation in the control room and Andy kept glancing over his shoulder at Dev. Normally he would have wondered what was going on but tonight he was too tired to give a damn.

He checked the clock. Ten-fifty-seven. He slipped the CD into the player, closed his eyes, and took a deep breath, trying to settle into the right frame of mind to respond to his callers.

He opened his eyes to find Lance and Andy watching him closely from the control booth. Sitting here with his eyes closed, they probably worried that he'd fallen asleep. Fat chance.

By the time seven a.m. rolled around, Dev was more than glad to hand off to Neal. Today was officially fourteen days A.A. He was bone-weary and aching. Chris Majewski was due for a visit and for the first time in months Dev would actually be glad to see him. He needed to talk to someone who might help him get through the despair-filled desert his life had become.

CHAPTER 25

Dinner had been a surprise in a couple of ways. Amanda was determined to enjoy their celebration, so she dressed with care, going with casual chic, and used makeup to camouflage the dark circles that had taken up residence under her eyes. The bright colors of her softly draping tropical blouse were perfect against her white jeans. So what if she was jumping the gun by wearing white before Memorial Day? That rule was for her mother's generation anyway. They cheered her up and the strappy sandals on wedges added to her good humor. She left her hair long and loose and slipped a pair of big gold hoops in her ears.

The new restaurant had open-air seating by the waterfront, a nice dining room with the expected nautical décor, a small bar up front, and a separate room furnished with picnic tables covered with brown paper where patrons used wooden mallets to beat steamed crabs into submission. The smell of Old Bay seasoning and beer combined to produce a distinctive aroma, and piles of empty crab shells were dumped into large trash bins at the end of each table. It was community dining at its finest and everyone seemed to be having a grand time.

Amanda and Zoe opted for a booth in the main dining room and had barely had time to glance at the menu before their waitress brought over a pair of margaritas.

"Oh, there must be some mistake," Amanda told her. "We haven't ordered drinks yet."

"These are compliments of our bartender," the waitress replied, pointing to the bar. "He said if you preferred something else, he'd be happy to exchange these for whatever you'd like."

Zoe looked over Amanda's shoulder to see Bill Leonetti wiping the bar and grinning. "It's the guy you hired to work the Wyndham's party. This is pretty nice of him," she said, raising her glass in salute.

Amanda turned and smiled. "Please tell him thank you," she told the waitress. "I, for one, am perfectly happy with a margarita. How about you, Zoe?"

"Oh yeah, I'm happy. This is the best margarita I've ever had. Tell the man to keep 'em coming. We're celebrating."

By the time they left, three margaritas and a delicious dinner later, they both had a nice buzz and a case of the giggles. On their way out, Amanda stopped at the bar to thank Bill for the drinks and the flowers.

"No thanks necessary. That party helped me get this job for the summer. I hope that means I'll be seeing you around often, Amanda," he added quietly.

"I'm sure we'll be back," she replied, dodging the unspoken meaning his words conveyed.

At home later, she sat at the end of her dock hugging herself and gazing up at the stars. Far from the lights of a big city, they sprinkled the heavens with thousands of bright pinpoints, the fainter ones fading with the rising of the waning moon.

That moon had seemed so magical a few nights ago.

I know you meant well, Danny, but sending Dev to watch over me was a terrible mistake. I was doing fine. Missing you like crazy, but dealing with it. Standing on my own two feet without your help or anybody else's. I didn't need to be 'looking after'.

It was a particular one of those ways Dev 'looked after' her that so angered her.

The repairs to her house were needed, true, but she would have taken care of them herself—eventually. She was coping with the cold weather just fine before she met Dev. A few more months would have been uncomfortable but not intolerable.

The financial support was helpful, she had to admit. Especially with her car problems. But she came up with the event-planning idea on her own and had gotten Zoe to go along with it. That would have solved her money problems without Dev's help.

Even the pretense of friendship she might be able to accept, someday. But the pity fucks? No, she was never going to forgive him for that. It was too humiliating, the way she believed Dev actually cared about her, found her sexy and desirable. All the tenderness, all the passion—faked.

Now my house is full of memories of Dad and you and Dev. Everywhere I turn there's something that reminds me of one of you. It's just not fair. It's not fair that I loved all of you and here I am, alone.

Spook came padding silently down the dock and rubbed against her. She picked the cat up and snuggled her in her lap. Purring rumbled into the night. "Well, I guess I'm not all alone, kitty. Come on, let's go inside. I'll make tea, and you can have a little milk, okay?" Spook jumped out of her embrace and led the way.

Inside, she put the kettle on for tea and turned on the radio. It was torture to hear Dev's voice but she couldn't seem to break the habit.

"Welcome to the tonight's edition of Dev's Dream Machine. For those who are new to the show tonight, prepare yourselves to listen to some of the great music from the thirties, forties, and early fifties. If you like the Big Band sound, I have it all and I'm willing to play whatever you want to hear. Just give me a call at 888-555-WMES."

Funny, his voice sounded different tonight. Still smooth and deep, but there was no animation, no excitement. Usually his enthusiasm for the music he loved came right over the air. She stared at the radio as if she could see into the studio if she concentrated hard enough.

The music started. She recognized Billie Holiday instantly.

She closed her eyes. The man was uncanny. Even if he wasn't here, he could rip out her heart and stomp it to pieces. She sat at the kitchen counter and wallowed in self-pity while the next few songs played. By the time "You Made Me Love You" came on, she was knee-deep in tissues and cursing the day Dev MacMurphy came into her life. But she couldn't turn the damn radio off. She just couldn't. Because she couldn't turn off her love for Dev either, the jerk.

A few days later, she was planting petunias by her porch when a black sedan pulled up in front of the house. A man dressed in a suit and tie and wearing dark sunglasses got out and walked over to her. She recognized the FBI uniform. Slowly she got up off her knees and stripped off her gardening gloves.

"Miss Adams? I'm Agent Baley, FBI." He flipped open his credentials.

"Agent Baley." She held out her hand.

He shook it. "I have some news for you concerning your father."

The breath she had been holding whooshed out. She gestured toward the door. "Why don't we go inside?"

She offered him a seat in the small living room. "Can I get you something to drink? Iced tea? Water?"

He pocketed his sunglasses, his face appearing much younger without them.

"Nothing for me, ma'am, thank you."

No formalities then, to delay the news. She sat across from him, hands in her lap.

"We believe we've found the remains of your father, Miss Adams."

The news, not entirely unexpected at this point, still hit her in the chest with the force of a physical object.

"He was one of the Highway Hijacker's victims, then?"

"We're not sure about that yet. You see, his car was found not far from here, by the dredging company that is working at the Wyndham's dock."

"Here. In Blue Point Cove?" He'd been this close all these years? "H . . . How . . .?"

"The dredging company discovered the vehicle by accident. They were about to have it hauled out of their way when their diver saw the remains in the driver's seat. They called the police and gave them the vehicle's make, model, and license number. When the police realized it might be a dump from the Highway Hijacker, they called us."

Amanda opened her mouth. Closed it. Tried again. "I guess I don't understand."

"I know it's a lot to take in and I don't have any more information than that right now. I'm on my way to the Wyndham's to talk with them, but I wanted to let you know first."

"Thank you."

He seemed a nice enough man. Very formal, no-nonsense personality on the outside, but that was tempered by a certain amount of kindness and consideration for the news he had to share.

"Would it be all right if I went to the Wyndham's home with you? I'd like to see where they found . . . the car."

"I don't see why not."

She brushed at her dirt-stained jeans. "Just let me change and I'll be ready to go." She hurried to the bathroom and washed her face and hands then changed into slacks and a short-sleeved shirt.

A short while later, Mrs. Wyndham answered their knock, dressed impeccably as always. Her husband came out of the library at the sound of their voices.

"Hello, Amanda, dear." Mrs. Wyndham greeted her first. "And you must be . . . Agent Baley?"

"Yes, ma'am. I spoke with your husband on the phone earlier. Would you mind if I asked you a few questions?"

"Not at all, Agent Baley. Please, come in." She led the group through the great room to the deck and settled them around a table. "Can I offer you anything? Agent Baley? Amanda?"

Agent Baley declined with a shake of his head, but Amanda asked for water, her throat suddenly parched. She couldn't stop her eyes from straying toward the pavilion and beyond to the dock where the huge dredging equipment hulked in the water.

The Admiral brought her a cold bottle of water from the outdoor bar and served his wife and himself with gin and tonic. "I'm not sure we can help you much in your investigation, Agent Baley. While we know Amanda's father went missing fifteen years ago, we weren't living here at that time."

"So I understand." Agent Baley took out a notebook and flipped through some pages. "County records show that you did own this property at the time. Including the house next door."

"Yes, that's correct," Mrs. Wyndham agreed. "We bought both lots because they were such a steal." She turned her attention to Amanda. "Did I tell you that we first found out about this place from your father, dear? I overheard him talking to the bartender one night when my friends and I went to hear his quintet play. He was so happy to find such an undiscovered gem like Blue Point where he could afford to buy a summer home for your family." She smiled fondly at the reminiscence. "The very next time Hal's ship was in port we came down here and snapped up these two lots."

"That's enough, dear. I'm sure Agent Baley doesn't need to hear the entire history." He patted his wife's hand.

"Oh, well, of course. I was just . . ." She shot the Admiral a frown. "Sometimes I talk too much. Forgive me."

Agent Baley consulted his notes again. "So in June of nineteen ninety-two you owned these parcels, but weren't living here?"

The Admiral answered. "By then we had demolished the old house on this lot and this house was under construction. We left the other house intact to use when we came down to see how the contractors were doing. You've got to keep an eye on them or they'll rob you blind, you know. Especially if you don't live close enough to monitor their progress regularly." He took a long swig of his drink. "I was at sea much of that time, so I had Caroline come down from time to time and take pictures to send to me. She got to be a right good little photographer." He patted Mrs. Wyndham's hand again.

"So, on the night of the disappearance, were you here on one of your photographic forays, Mrs. Wyndham?"

"No. I was back in Annapolis. Belinda Hopps had a party that night and I attended." She rolled her eyes heavenward. "Terribly boring, as I recall."

"There was no evidence of a break-in at the other house? Nothing out of the ordinary that you noticed the next time you came down?"

"No, Agent Baley, nothing that I recall. It has been seventeen years, so I will admit my recollection of that time is not crystal clear. The police had me drive over and open up the house, but all I remember was that it had been raining for days and there were muddy footprints from the policemen all through that house by the time they were done."

Agent Baley closed his notebook. "Thank you for your time. I'm sorry for the interruption but the Crime Scene Investigators will have to collect evidence before your dredging can proceed."

The Admiral heaved a sigh. “I’ve been waiting for a month to get that boat up here, what’s a few more days?”

This time it was Mrs. Wyndham’s turn to pat his hand. “I’m so sorry, dear. It won’t be much longer, will it, Agent Baley?”

“The team will be over from Salisbury in the morning. I don’t expect it to take them more than a day to process the scene. After that, the dredging company can move right along.” He stood and everyone else stood with him.

“I’ll show you out, though no doubt you can find your way, Amanda.”

“If you don’t mind, Mrs. Wyndham, I’d like to come back tomorrow when they . . . when they . . . recover . . .”

Mrs. Wyndham put her arm around Amanda’s shoulder and gave her a hug. “Of course, dear. We’ll see you tomorrow.”

Rosemary looked up from her keyboard as the office door opened. Relief washed across her face when she saw the familiar uniform.

“Good morning, Captain Majewski. It’s good to see you. Let me tell Dev you’re here.” She reached for the intercom button but stopped when he shook his head.

“Don’t bother with the announcement, Rosemary. I’ll just go on back.”

Rosemary gave him a grateful smile and returned to her typing.

Chris stood quietly in the doorway of Dev’s office and studied the man behind the desk. Neatly dressed in his usual white long-sleeved shirt and jeans, a casual observer would see nothing more than a businessman at work. The eyes a little red-rimmed, perhaps, but after all he had just finished an eight-hour stint behind the microphone.

Chris noticed the less obvious signs and knew better. Faintly hollowed cheeks. Slumped shoulders. Strain lines at the corners of the mouth. Hair that had been rearranged by fingers dragged through it—more than once. The sightless stare at the glowing computer screen was the final giveaway.

"How's it going, Marconi?" He sauntered in and sat, crossed his legs and gave no indication he'd been doing a quick psych eval. Now that he had Dev's attention, he got an even better read on how bad things really were. Damn. He had hoped . . . He made sure nothing of his own regret showed on his face.

Dev started at the sound of Chris' voice, but disguised it with a stretch. If he'd been that oblivious in Fallujah, he'd be dead. Not for the first time, he wished he were.

"Hey, Freud. If you're here to ask about Lance, he's coming along nicely." He doubted this mis-direction would work, but anything to deflect Majewski from his own problems was worth a shot. He knew that conversation was going to be painful.

No luck. The Army doc merely sat and waited. Dev did his best to hide the bleakness in his eyes with a business-like brusqueness. "If you're short on time you don't have to waste any talking with me."

"Talking to an old friend is never a waste of time."

"Is that what we are? Old friends?" Dev leaned back in his chair.

"I'd like to think that. Now that there isn't any doctor-patient relationship, there's no reason we can't be friends." He settled himself more comfortably.

The silence stretched.

Unreasonably irritated, Dev asked, "So, what's new with you? Been out on the water yet this season?" *You want to play friends, Chris? I can do that.*

"Nope, not yet. Hopefully this weekend, though. Want to come along? Unless you have other plans, of course."

"If I liked boats, I'd have joined the Navy," he snapped, thoughtlessly parroting a phrase used often by Danny. He winced at the memory.

On second thought, he couldn't play games. He needed to talk and the fact that Chris knew that made his already crappy mood even worse. Dev flicked his monitor off and stood. "Let's get coffee since I can see you're not leaving until I spill my guts." He stormed out of his office and Chris trailed him down the hall to the lounge.

Dev set a mug of steaming coffee in front of Chris and dropped into a chair across the table. Without preamble, like ripping a Band-Aid off an unhealed wound, he said, "You were right. I made a mess of everything by lying. Amanda was furious. Kicked me out and told me she never wanted to see my sorry ass again." He took a gulp of coffee and cursed as it scalded his tongue.

"How about we start at the beginning," Chris suggested amicably. "You worked the party?"

"Yeah. I have to hand it to them. Amanda and Zoe did a fantastic job." He got lost remembering his first sight of Amanda in that black dress. The haze of desire generated by the expanse of creamy skin from neck to waist was abruptly shattered when she'd confessed to Zoe that she loved him. He looked over at Chris. "She, uh, said she was in love with me." He dropped his gaze to his coffee cup and contemplated the damage drinking the whole mug of molten liquid would do to his throat.

"She told you she loved you?" Chris leaned forward in his chair.

"Actually, no. She told Zoe. I just happened to walk in behind her and overhear."

"And?"

"And nothing. I kept up the charade during the entire evening, just like I had planned to. When I took her home, I told her the whole story."

Chris nodded.

"She didn't take it well. From her point of view I not only lied to her and treated her like a child, but sleeping with her was apparently the ultimate insult, since she assumed it was all part of the promise I made to Danny."

"And when you told her you loved her, did that make any difference?" Chris attempted a sip from his mug and watched Dev over the rim.

"I didn't tell her," Dev mumbled.

"Why not?"

"At that point I don't think she'd have believed me."

Silence settled like a shroud as Chris simply stared across the table. Unable to meet Chris' gaze, Dev's shoulders slumped and he examined his hands clenched together on the table.

"So that's it? You're just going to let her go?" Chris got up and dumped his coffee into the sink, then turned around and leaned against it. "You know, I really thought you had more in you, than to give up so easily."

"Apparently you were wrong this time, Freud."

Chris shrugged and headed for the door. Halfway there, he pivoted and faced Dev again, his frustration so palpable Dev felt the force of it from across the room. During his weeks of recovery in Walter Reed, he'd had numerous sessions with this man, yet he had never provoked him to anger. Until now.

"Quit living your life as though you don't deserve to be happy. That's bullshit anyway. Your friend made a decision that cost him his life. Of course that's sad, but it was *his* decision—not yours. Instead of wishing every day that you could change places with him, how about thanking him every day for the gift of life he gave you? Then think about the fact that you had the love of an amazing woman, but you dropped her off a cliff and didn't even hang around long enough to watch her hit bottom. What did she do to deserve that kind of treatment? Wake up, Marconi, and get your head out of your ass. You wish you were dead? Let me clue you in. Living is much harder than dying. You want to do penance for being alive? Try to make sure at least one other person on the planet has a good life, a happy life—no matter what it costs you." He shot Dev one last annoyed look and left.

A few minutes later Rosemary stood in the doorway. "Boss, you okay?"

Brought back from a deep analysis of his recent choices by the sound of her voice, Dev decided it was past time to get his act together. "I'm fine, Rosemary. Is there a problem?"

She eyed him closely. "No, I guess not. Captain Majewski left in a hurry and he didn't seem his usual self. I thought maybe . . ."

"I had pissed him off? Yeah, I'm pretty sure I did. Royally."

He accepted Rosemary's eye roll and exasperated sigh as his due. "Don't worry, I'll fix it. But I've something else to fix first." He shoved his chair back. "Call Andy and ask him if he can cover my shift tonight—the first half of it anyway. Then get Neal to come in at three a.m. for the second half. I'm not sure how long this will take. If you get static from either of them, call me on my cell and we'll work out something else."

With the faintest hint of a smile lurking at the corners of her mouth, Rosemary clicked her heels together and saluted. "Yes, sir. Right away, sir."

"You mocking me, Rosemary?"

"No way, boss." But her eyes twinkled and the smile got harder to hide.

He dumped his own coffee in the sink. "You should be. God knows I deserve it." He squeezed her shoulder on the way out the door. "Thanks, Rosemary. I don't know what I'd do without you. Call me if the building catches fire, okay?"

"Will do, boss. Keep me posted."

Dev stopped and shot her a questioning look.

"Sorry, sir, I can't help it, I'm just . . . nosy, I guess." Despite the words, she didn't appear the least bit apologetic.

Now it was Dev's turn to hide a smile. "Ahh, I see. For a minute there I thought you were the captain of the phone tree for radio station gossip."

"No, sir. That would be Andy. Sir."

Incredulous, he could only shake his head as he left.

His first order of business, a shower and shave, then clean clothes. Then he had to track Amanda down. Phone calls were useless, it was too easy for her to hang up. No, this had to be done in person. Should he bring flowers? Nah, too cheesy a cliché.

He didn't know how he would convince her to take him back. But he would convince her. This time he made the promise to himself.

CHAPTER 26

Amanda had to park on the roadside and walk up to the Wyndham's. The long drive was clogged with several large black SUVs, two panel trucks with police emblems on their sides, and an ambulance. Men and women wearing jackets with CSI on their backs were carrying cases back down the driveway toward her.

A few steps behind them she saw Agent Baley talking on his cell phone. When he spotted her, he started walking her way. His clipped responses to whoever was on the other end still held a hint of excitement.

"Yes, we've sent two divers down already. We should be raising it out of the water in a few moments." Pause. "Yes, sir. The team is here." He looked at Amanda. "Yes. His daughter just arrived. There's no doubt it's Mr. Adams though. The license plates match and so does the car make and model." Pause. "I'll let you know as soon as we get results back. They're going to have to take the body to Salisbury to do the autopsy." He caught the anguish on her face and ended his call abruptly.

"You're sure it's my dad?" She blinked rapidly and took a couple of deep breaths.

"Yes, ma'am. Everything matches the description you gave me." He pointed down the road toward the old house they had used to stage the party. "The car was fairly far away from the Wyndham's dock. It was pure luck the dredging company discovered it when they deepened the channel for the Wyndham's new boat." He put his hand on her back and they walked down the road together. "It will actually be easier to get to it from the old lot. It appears the car went into the bay from there."

She nodded, a shiver snaking up her spine when she realized how close she had been when they had spent so many hours at the old house. The ambulance passed them and turned into the area they had cleared for parking. Agent Baley put his hand on her arm to slow their progress.

"Are you going to be okay with this? You don't have to be here, you know. The divers have already confirmed it's your dad's car and that there is a body in the driver's seat. They'll put your father's remains in a bag underwater to keep any evidence that might be left intact. There won't be much for you to see."

"No. I want to stay. I've been searching for him for so long . . ." She cleared her throat and squared her shoulders. "I'll stay."

"All right. Mrs. Wyndham gave me the key to the old place. I know you used it last week, so if you have to . . ."

Sit down? Throw up? She nodded in understanding. "I'll be fine, Agent Baley. Let's go." They walked past the house toward the water. The undergrowth hadn't been trimmed along this far edge of the lot for a long time. Loblolly pines twenty feet or more high towered along the property line. Large clumps of blue flag with grass-like leaves three feet tall hindered their progress, their violet-blue flowers just coming into bloom. Vines snaked along the ground and curled around any vertical surface, transforming wires, poles, and trees into shrouded, semi-human likenesses.

As they neared the water's edge, she heard her name called and turned to see Zoe, Jeff, and . . . she squinted against the bright sunlight from her place in the shade . . . Dev. Her stomach added another half hitch to its string of knots. A double-whammy of a day. How did he even know about all this?

Zoe sprinted ahead of the other two and threw her arms around Amanda. "Oh, hon, are you okay? I had Jeff drop everything and pick me up right after you called. We thought you might need some moral support."

Amanda hugged her back and whispered in her ear as the others caught up, "And Dev? You called him, too? Why would you do that?"

"I didn't," she whispered back. "He passed us coming from your house and turned around. Said he's been looking for you." She shrugged. "I figured he might as well know. By tonight the news will be all over town anyway."

Jeff came over and gave her shoulders a squeeze. "Hi, Beautiful. You hangin' in there okay?"

She forced a smile. "I'm doing fine, Jeff. Thanks for coming."

Dev came up and attempted to take her hand but she tucked both behind her back.

"I'm sure I'm the last person you want to see right now," he began.

"True. What are you doing here?" She held up her hand to stop his reply. "You know, I don't care why you came, but I don't need you here." She turned away and waked to the waterline just as the car was lifted from the bay about fifteen feet off shore. Water cascaded off the vehicle, now slimy green over most of its surface. Huge collections of eelgrass and wild celery clung to it, dripping brackish water that smelled foul. Involuntarily, Amanda backed away, catching her foot on a clump of trout lilies. Strong arms grabbed her from behind and kept her from going down in the soft ground.

"Thanks. It's treacherous under foot out here. I—" She turned to face her rescuer and angrily shoved his arms away when she saw it was Dev. "I thought I told you I didn't need you here."

He held his hands up to stave off any more angry words. "I can see you don't."

Her chin came up and her eyes narrowed. Her hands curled into tight fists.

"I was on my way to see you . . . I have to talk to you, darli— Amanda," he amended hastily. He backed up to give her more space. "I realize this is a terrible time to ask you, but it's important, Amanda. I need to talk to you. Please, can I see you later when you're finished here?"

"You're right again, Dev. This is a terrible time. I can't imagine anything that we need to discuss at this point. Just go away, please." She turned pointedly away and concentrated on the car she remembered from childhood.

For a while it just hung there, suspended about ten feet in the air. About twenty feet further along the shoreline two divers emerged from the inlet carrying a black bag. She was certain that she didn't want to see what fifteen years in the Chesapeake Bay had done to her father's handsome face. Much better to remember him as he had been the last time she saw him.

Tears burned the back of her eyes and she couldn't seem to get any air into her lungs. A faint ringing began in her ears and her hands turned to ice. She squeezed her eyes shut. "Zoe." She put her arm out—away from Dev, who still stood behind her—and groped feebly for her friend's hand.

"I'm here, hon." Zoe clasped her hand, at the same time throwing a 'get lost' signal to Dev with a jerk of her head.

"I think I'll go back to the house and, and . . . get some water." Amanda loosened her grip on Zoe and her knees buckled.

Dev caught her and swung her up in his arms. Her head lolled against his chest. Too dizzy to complain that he'd picked her up, she kept her eyes closed and prayed for the ground to stop spinning beneath them.

"Is the house unlocked?"

The soft rumble of his voice made her want to snuggle her cheek into his chest. She fought off the temptation and pushed weakly against him, the feel of his muscles so familiar it made her already aching heart twice as painful.

Agent Baley's voice sounded far away and Amanda couldn't seem to get her eyes open.

"I was afraid this might be tough on her. Should I get someone from the ambulance crew?"

"I don't think she needs that." Zoe took the key from Agent Baley. "Let's get her up to the house and let her lay down. She's been under a lot of strain lately. I think she's just a bit lightheaded. If she doesn't come round in a few minutes, we'll get one of the paramedics."

Zoe trotted ahead to unlock the back door and Jeff followed behind Dev, who laid her on the sheet-covered sofa. Amanda's eyes fluttered open and she struggled to sit up.

Jeff brought in a glass of water, and Zoe got a chair and settled next to her.

A rapid knocking on the front door made them all jump.

"I'll get it," Jeff said, handing the water to Dev.

Dev was next to her in an instant, supporting her back and holding the glass to her lips. "Here, dar— Amanda. Drink this."

She took a sip and focused on the one who held the glass. Her color came back in a rush. "You! Didn't I ask you to leave? Why are you still here?"

Amanda pushed Dev's hand away. "I don't want any more of that." She wrinkled her nose at the water.

"I don't blame you, my dear. Brandy would be much more the thing."

Mrs. Wyndham stood in the doorway, her hands on her hips. As the older woman came over to the sofa, she issued orders over her shoulder. "Mr. Petrosky, please go up to the big house and bring back a bottle of brandy. There should be an open one on the bar in the library." She glared down at Amanda and tsked. "Poor girl. This must be a terrible shock to you." She smiled at Zoe and Dev. "It's good that you have people who care about you on hand."

Realizing she had unconsciously been leaning against Dev, Amanda sat bolt upright. In her most forbidding Ice Princess voice, she dismissed him. "Thank you for your help. I'm sure I'll be fine now. Please go, I don't want to keep you . . ."

Mrs. Wyndham looked between the two of them. Disappointment followed surprise on her face.

Dev set the glass on the table and stood. "I'm glad I could be of service," he said, just as formally. "If there is anything else that I can do—"

"There isn't."

Dev nodded and left.

At the sound of the door closing, Mrs. Wyndham wagged her finger at Amanda. "I don't know what's happened between the two of you, but that was foolish, my dear. It's plain to see that man loves you. No matter what he's done, he doesn't deserve such poor treatment."

"I beg to differ with your assessment of Dev's feelings, Mrs. Wyndham. He doesn't love me. He's merely keeping a promise he made to a dead man."

She drew her knees up and locked her arms around them, burying her face against them.

Mrs. Wyndham sighed deeply, cocking her head then shaking it sadly. "My dear, you are just like your father. Stubborn, both of you." She opened her mouth the say something more, then snapped it closed. She went to the front door. "Where is that young man? Must I do everything myself? Ah, thank goodness, here he comes."

Jeff hurried through the door, the bottle of brandy tucked under one arm. At her imperious gesture, he handed it over. She rewarded him with a beatific smile and a pat on the cheek. "Thank you, dear."

"I have one more request, Jeff," she said with a coy smile. "Will you bring in a glass from the kitchen, please?"

When he returned with it, she splashed two fingers of the dark gold liquid in the bottom and handed it to Amanda. "Now, I want you to drink this, my girl. All of it. Don't worry about driving home. I'll have one of those nice FBI men take you. You've had a very trying day, and this will help you relax. Go on, now." She stood over Amanda until she took a sip.

The brandy left a fiery trail down her throat but settled comfortably in her stomach. She took another sip. The second one didn't burn quite so much. Over the next few minutes the warmth spread, slowly thawing her icy hands. Emotional upheaval was certainly tiring. Mrs. Wyndham's idea to have someone drive her home sounded better with each passing minute.

Agent Baley poked his head through the doorway. "Ms. Adams? How are you feeling?"

"Much better, Agent Baley. I'm sorry to have been so much trouble." She took another sip of brandy.

"Think nothing of it, ma'am. I've seen much worse reactions in similar situations." He studied her then glanced at Zoe and Jeff.

"If you have something to tell me, you can speak freely in front of my friends, Agent Baley. They all know the circumstances surrounding my dad's disappearance."

"All right. Your father's remains have been removed from the car and are on their way to Salisbury for autopsy. The vehicle will follow as soon as we can get it on a lift. The forensic folks are taking photographs and attempting to get prints."

At Amanda's raised brows, he nodded. "Not likely, I agree, but we don't want to miss anything. Your father may have been one of the Highway Hijacker's first victims. Or it could just be that he didn't get to use this dumpsite again for any number of reasons. The divers have searched widely enough to be certain that your father's car was the only one out there. They collected most of the evidence underwater but there are still things that need to be done before we remove the vehicle. You don't need to be here for any of that. I'll have one of my men drive you home," he finished with a nod toward the glass Amanda still held. It was almost empty now. "Do you have someone who can stay with you tonight?"

"I'm sure I'll be fine, Agent Ba—"

"I'll stay with her," Zoe interrupted. "Don't argue, Mandy. You should have someone around tonight."

Agent Baley flipped open his cell phone. "Good. Ms. Adams, I'll be in touch with you as soon as we know anything." He dialed and started talking as he left.

"Listen, Zoe, I'll be fine. I'll have some soup and climb into bed. A good night's rest is all I need, and there's no point in you sitting around watching me sleep." She held out her hand to Jeff. "Thanks for being such a good friend, Jeff. Take Zoe home, and I'll check in with her in the morning."

"Anything for you, Beautiful." He winked. "Do you want to take the rest of this bottle of brandy home, or should I take it back up to the big house?"

"Oh, I don't think I should—"

"Yeah, she'll take it," Zoe said and picked up the bottle. "I'm sure Mrs. W had lots more. She won't miss this."

In a few minutes a young man with FBI stenciled on his jacket knocked at the front door. "Someone in here need a ride?"

"That would be me." Amanda stood up, doing her best to appear calm and composed. The brandy made her a little unsteady, but the warmth was blurring the sharp edges of pain that sliced at her heart.

"Thank you so much for the ride. It won't take long, my house isn't very far."

"No problem, ma'am. Right this way."

He ushered her out and into one of the black SUVs. She rolled down the window. "I'll call you in the morning, Zo. Thanks again."

"If you need anything tonight, I don't care what time it is, you call me, okay?"

"Okay." Amanda leaned back in the seat and closed her eyes as the car backed down the driveway.

Dev sat in his truck in front of Amanda's house. Between her father's discovery and what he'd put her through on that fateful Saturday, she must be having a hard time finding her balance. When her knees buckled and he'd caught her up in his arms, he never wanted to let her go. If he hadn't been so stupid, *he'd* be the one comforting her now instead of Zoe and Jeff. But she'd made it perfectly clear at the Wyndham's that she didn't want to see him, talk to him, even be within half a mile of him. So given those restrictions, how could he convince her that he loved her? He smacked the steering wheel and swore. The timing couldn't be worse.

He toyed with the idea of hiding the truck and walking back here to wait for her. He still had the key. He could go inside and when she came home, she'd have to talk to him.

Yeah, idiot, don't give her a choice, just treat her like a child who can't make an intelligent decision on her own. That worked really well last time. No, the trick was to get her to want to listen to what he had to say. He could write her a letter, but pouring his heart out on paper wasn't his strong suit.

Plan B began to take shape in his head. He put the truck in gear and drove back into town, parked behind the Silvercreek Gallery, and waited for Zoe to return.

Amanda picked up the phone and dialed her mother's number. "Hi, Mom. It's me."

"Amanda? Is something wrong?"

"Not wrong, exactly. I have some news, though. You might want to sit down."

"Oh God. What is it, Amanda?"

In the background, she heard Jack ask what was going on and her mother reply, "Something with Amanda."

"Mom, they found Dad's body." What was left of it anyway. She had to clear her throat to go on. "His car was in the bay near the Wyndham's old place."

"Oh my God. Do they know what happened? How did it get there?" Not quite out of earshot, she repeated Amanda's message to Jack.

"I just came back from there, but we don't know anything yet. The FBI are investigating to see if he was killed by that Highway Hijacker I emailed you about a few weeks ago."

"Jack and I will be on the next plane, dear. Are you managing all right?"

"Mom, I'm . . . fine." A bald-faced lie. "You guys don't have to come all the way from California for this."

"Don't be ridiculous, Amanda. You're not fine. Don't try to fool me. How could you be fine? I think we should come."

Damn those psychic Mom vibes. She hadn't told her about Dev yet and once she and Jack arrived there'd be no avoiding it. She couldn't handle that right now.

"Mom, really, I'm okay. Of course it was a shock but ever since I heard about the Hijacker guy I've been preparing myself for this. Why don't you and Jack wait until I know more before you come? The FBI agent said it would take at least a week for the forensic team to finish going through the . . . remains."

"Honey, are you sure? You don't sound okay to me."

"Mom, I'm sure. I sound a little weird because Mrs. Wyndham made me drink some brandy. Everyone seems to think I need to be wrapped in cotton batting and tucked into bed. But I'm fine. Really."

"Is your friend Zoe close by? In case you need something? I hate to think of you alone in that cottage, dear."

No sooner had the words left her mother's mouth than the sound of Jeff's motorcycle made her look out the window. Zoe jumped off, gave Jeff her helmet and a peck on the cheek, and waved good-bye.

"Actually, she's right here," Amanda said, opening the front door before her friend could knock. She pointed to the phone and mouthed, "My mom."

"Oh, good."

"Mom, are *you* okay?"

"Dear, I have Jack right here for support. I'll be fine. You'll call as soon as you know anything?"

"Of course, Mom. Give my love to Jack. I'll talk to you again soon."

"All right. Good-bye dear."

Amanda hung up, glad to have that conversation taken care of. She turned to her friend and asked, "What are you doing here? I told you I'd be fine."

"Yeah, I know. But after you left I couldn't help feeling you should have some company tonight. So much baggage to deal with, I thought you might want to talk about . . . things. I know it must have been difficult today but at least now you'll have some closure about your dad."

"There is that", Amanda agreed, "but I still think it's kind of spooky to find him so close to where we've been working for the past few weeks. The FBI agent told me they think Dad might have been one of the Hijacker's earliest victims. Maybe even his first one, before he found better places to ditch the cars and the . . . the bodies." Amanda shivered and rubbed her arms to quell the sudden goose bumps. "I'm glad you and Jeff were there today. I really thought I'd be fine but I guess I was wrong." Again.

"You didn't cut Dev much slack, though," Zoe commented. "Mandy, I have to agree with Mrs. W on this one. That man loves you. He may have messed up but if you could've seen the way looked at you when he carried you back to the house . . ." She shrugged as though the conclusion were obvious.

It had felt so good to be in his arms. Amanda shook her head to banish the memory. "I don't want to talk about Dev, Zoe. He was keeping a promise, and I mistook his attentions for the real thing. That was a mistake and I'll get over it—eventually."

"But—" Zoe objected.

"Drop it, partner"—Amanda held up her hands in protest—"what I need now is a distraction not a lecture."

"Right." Zoe acquiesced with a sly smile. "I have just the thing."

CHAPTER 27

Zoe held up a DVD. "*Momma Mia*. I know it's one of your favorites."

She did love ABBA's music, and Meryl Streep *was* her favorite actress. "Great idea. How about I order us a pizza?"

Zoe nodded.

Amanda dialed Donatelli's and raised a brow at Zoe. "The usual?"

"Everything but anchovies and green peppers," Zoe confirmed. She plopped onto the love seat and patted the cushion next to her. "Come sit down and put your feet up. You're still looking a bit pale and wan, sweetie."

Amanda joined her friend and tucked her legs under her. She leaned against Zoe and put her head on her shoulder. "It is a wonderful thing to have friends like you and Jeff. I'm not sure how I would have made it through this past week without you." She sighed, then frowned.

"Something's still bugging you about today?"

"Yeah, I still can't help wondering how he wound up in the bay by the Wyndham's old place. If their new house was being built I wouldn't think the Highway Hijacker guy would have dumped the car where it might be found so easily. Of course they hadn't started building the dock and pavilion yet, so maybe he didn't realize there would be crews driving pilings in just fifty yards away in a few months."

"Probably. I wonder if he knew your dad lived down the road. The whole thing seems very strange."

"I know. It could just be that Dad told him about our place before . . . before . . ." Her eyes filled and her breath caught on a sob.

Zoe put her arms around Amanda's shoulders. "Oh, honey, don't even think about that. Maybe I should get you another glass of brandy."

"No. No more brandy. I've already got a headache from the first glass. Besides, more liquor will only make me maudlin."

What she needed was distraction. And the very best distraction she could think of right now would involve Dev's arms around her, his lips kissing their way down her body . . . Damn that man! What had he needed to speak to her so urgently about today? Probably some tax problem. She heaved another sigh.

"Let's get that movie going, Zo. I need to get my mind off everything in my life right now."

"Sure. Pizza should be here any minute, too." Zoe turned on the TV. "Mandy, where'd you stash the remote for this thing?"

"The drawer in the coffee table. Dev always puts it in there so he won't . . ." *Have to search for it. Does everything in this house have to remind me of you, you jerk?* Amanda went to the kitchen. "I'm getting a glass of iced tea. Do you want some?"

"Sure. Extra sugar in mine, please. You never add enough sugar," Zoe grumped. "Too worried about losing your gorgeous figure."

"Not at all. There's plenty of sugar in my tea. You just have a sweet tooth bigger than Mount Rushmore."

The doorbell cut short their debate.

"Yes! Pizza! I'm starving." Zoe sprang up and opened the door. She offered the delivery boy a couple of dollars as a tip, but he refused, saying, "No tip necessary, miss. Just meeting you was worth the trip." He winked. "If you could just write your number on the back of this receipt . . ." Zoe gaped, and closed the door firmly in his smiling face.

"They just drool all over you, don't they?"

"Who? Delivery boys? *Boy* being the operative term here." Zoe put the box on the coffee table and went in search of napkins.

"No, men."

Zoe raised a brow.

"Okay, males, then. Even the ones ten years younger than you." Amanda brought in the tea. "Actually, age doesn't matter. Old, young, they follow you around like little puppy dogs."

"Only they're the ones with the bones." Zoe sounded less than enthused. "Don't think it's such a great thing. Ninety-nine percent of them only want one thing, and once they get it, they're gone, faster than a Houdini disappearing act." She took a huge bite out of her pizza slice and mumbled around it, "At least your men fall head over heels in love with you—" She closed her eyes and winced. "Sorry. I'll keep my mouth full of pizza to stop the truth from escaping."

"Zoe, I told you, Dev does not love me. He was keeping a promise he made to Danny, whom he loved like a brother. He has all kinds of guilt that he shouldn't have about Danny's death and that made him even more determined to go to ridiculous lengths to satisfy that debt."

"Well, you didn't see his face when he heard you tell me you were in love with him. Because Christmas, birthdays, Fourth of July, and winning the lottery all rolled into one couldn't compare to it. He was so dumbstruck I was afraid he'd need CPR."

"I thought we weren't going to talk about Dev," Amanda reminded her.

Zoe took another bite and shrugged. "Just sayin', is all." She clicked the remote to start the movie.

Ten minutes into the movie and Amanda realized it was a colossal mistake. There was Pierce Brosnan on the screen looking like Dev would in about twenty years. Same untamed shock of brown hair across his forehead, same sexy body, same handsome face—with a few extra laugh lines perhaps, but close enough to make all her feminine parts sit up and beg. She should have gone for the brandy after all. Anything to dull the ache that spread from her heart to the increasingly damp spot between her legs.

She sneaked a glance at Zoe, who appeared engrossed in the film, but whom, she suspected, had chosen this movie with an ulterior motive. The movie's little lesson about the miscommunication that cost two people years of potential bliss wasn't lost on her.

But there was no miscommunication between her and Dev—there was no communication at all. All those weeks they were together he'd kept his stupid little secrets. Then, *after* she falls in love, he drops the truth bomb on her. After she admitted to loving him, he fesses up, gets all that angst off his chest. But did he mention that, oh, by the way, he loved her too? Heck, no.

So no happy ending for her, no touching scene in a church where he asks her to marry him. Crap. She hit the stop button in the middle of Pierce Brosnan's proposal.

"That is enough of that," she snapped. She ignored Zoe's whine of protest, and turned on the radio. The smirk on her friend's face had alarm bells going off in Amanda's head.

"Zoe Silvercreek, are you up to something?" At Zoe's wide-eyed denial, Amanda crossed her arms and tapped her foot until her silence broke Zoe's resistance.

She glanced pointedly at her wristwatch. "Isn't it about time for Dev's show? You do still listen to it, don't you?" Zoe had that archly superior attitude of a talk-show host who had discovered a delicious tidbit of scandal about a hapless guest.

"Not always. I—" Amanda bit her lower lip. "Okay, yeah. I still listen. I should stop, I know, but I just can't seem to quit."

A dieter whose secret stash of M&M's had just been discovered couldn't have looked more guilty.

Dev arrived at the studio at ten-thirty and went straight to the back wall, taking CD after CD from the shelves. He ignored the questions in Andy's eyes as the other man continued his on-air patter.

When he'd cued up a song, Andy turned from the mike. "Hey, boss, what's up? Rosemary told me I was supposed to cover the first half of your shift tonight."

"Well, plans have changed." Dev set the stack of CDs on the table. "Thanks for being willing to sub for me, Andy. I appreciate it. Things haven't gone exactly the way I'd hoped today, so I'll be able to do my shift after all."

"Does that mean you don't want Neal to come in at three a.m. either?"

"Yeah, I guess it does. Could you give him a call when you're off the air and tell him he's off the hook for tonight? I'll catch up with him later to thank him."

"You're sure you're not going to need either of us?"

The way things went this afternoon, he was more than sure. He was one hundred percent positive he'd be right here, alone, for the next eight hours. Instead of being wrapped in Amanda's arms like he'd hoped. "Yeah, I'm good for tonight."

Andy switched the mike back on, did his sign-off, and signaled Lance in the control booth to start the eleven p.m. news feed. He and Dev switched places and Andy left the studio, stopping to talk to Lance on his way out.

Okay, Zoe, don't let me down. Dev got the nod from Lance and clicked the mike on.

"Good evening, ladies and gentlemen. Welcome to the Friday night edition of Dev's Dream Machine. For those of you who are new listeners, the first hour of my show is normally a by request hour where we open up the phone lines and let the audience choose the music we broadcast." He paused and took a slow breath in. "But tonight the format is going to be a bit different. All the songs you'll hear are dedicated to a wonderful woman named Amanda. A woman I happen to be madly in love with. Unfortunately, I made a colossal mistake in our relationship and this smart, kind, fascinating woman doesn't want to hear from me ever again."

He paused and wished he'd brought a glass of Jack into the booth instead of going cold turkey. "Now I'm sure there are a number of my male listeners who've been in a similar situation—maybe even a few ladies too. Since I'm not so good at writing love letters or making speeches, there's only one thing I could think of that has a prayer of making my lady change her mind. I'm going to let a few of the greatest singers and songwriters of all time speak for me. I hope you're listening, Amanda. These songs are for you."

He opened with "All of Me".

He stacked the next few selections back to back: "You Made Me Love You", You'll Never Know", and "Darling, *Je Vous Aime Beaucoup*".

Dev checked the control room and saw Lance staring at him in amazement while Andy talked on the phone—no doubt telling Neal he didn't have to show up at three a.m. Then again, there seemed to be way too much gesturing and animation for such a simple message. He didn't have time to figure out what was going on with Andy because the phone lines were all blinking furiously. Didn't these callers hear his lead-in?

He answered the first one. "Dev's Dream Machine, I'm sorry I'm not taking requests tonight—"

"Yeah, I heard, man. You go for it. Just wanted to say I've been there too and hope this works for you."

"Ahhh, thanks."

The caller hung up, and Dev punched the next button. "Dev's Doc—"

"No worries, mate. I'm not calling to request a song. Let us know how it works out though, would you?" *Click.*

Dev tried the next line. "Dev's Dream Machine." This time the caller didn't leap right in, so he said, "I'm afraid I'm not taking any requests tonight."

A sultry female voice responded. "I hope she doesn't fall for this ploy, lover boy, though she'd be a fool not to. Any man with a voice like yours has to be hotter than a rocket. If it doesn't work out, call me." She reeled off a phone number and hung up.

Dev took off his headset and sat. The reflection of light on the studio glass produced the same ghostly image he'd seen before. Danny, laughing at him. The image faded away as light from the open door to the break room washed across the glass.

Dev put on the next CD in his stack. Bing Crosby's mellow baritone filled the studio.

Dev closed his eyes and let the memory of their dance torture him. The feel of her skin beneath his fingers had them twitching and he took a deep breath, reliving the sweet scent of her perfume. By the time the song ended, he was hard as stone and aching with need.

He opened his eyes. What the—? Was that Rosemary walking down the hall to the break room? What was she doing here at this hour? He waved to get Lance's attention, then once he had it he pointed toward the break room and spread his hands in question. Lance just shook his head and shrugged.

Damn. Dev turned his attention back to the show. He'd figure this out later. Right now nothing was going to interfere with Plan B. Too much depended on it. He slid the next disc into the player.

"Amanda, I hope you're still listening out there. The Mills Brothers can say how I feel much better than I can, but if you'll only give me a chance I'll spend the rest of my life making up for my stupidity."

The Mills Brothers harmonized "You Always Hurt the One You Love" and Dev willed Amanda to keep her radio on.

Amanda sat curled in a chair, a pillow clutched to her chest as Bing Crosby and the Andrews Sisters asked, "Have I told You Lately that I Love You?" A single tear slipped down her cheek.

Zoe sat across from her, a smug I-told-you-so look on her face. She was enjoying this, Amanda could tell.

When Dev's voice had come on the radio at the beginning of his show, she started to go over and turn it off. Just to prove to Zoe that she could get along without hearing his voice every day. But Zoe had grabbed her arm and tugged her back down on the couch with a single command. "Listen."

So for the past thirty minutes she'd listened. Dev had admitted he was a fool. He'd apologized for everything he'd done. And he'd used some of the greatest songs she knew to tell her how much he loved her. She racked her brain trying to decide why he was making such a public spectacle of himself and came to the only possible conclusion—he really did love her. For the first time in days, she began to smile.

"At last," Zoe exclaimed, noting the beatific grin on her friend's face. "For a while there, I thought you'd never see the light."

"Oh, and you saw it all along, right?"

"Yep. But like Mrs. Wyndham said today, you were stubborn where Dev was concerned."

Amanda made a face at her friend. "You've got a few blind spots yourself, missy. But we'll have to address them some other time." She jumped up and grabbed the phone.

She dialed, waited a minute, then her face fell. "They're sending the calls on the request line to a canned message. He's not taking any requests." She dialed the office number out of desperation.

"Rosemary? I'm sorry to bother you. I thought I dialed the office." Amanda ran her hand through her hair. "You're there? At the office? What are you doing there at this hour?" She frowned, then rolled her eyes in disbelief. "I'll be there in ten, no, fifteen, minutes. Don't tell him I'm coming, okay?' She smiled and nodded. "Can you get a special request to him? Give it fifteen minutes and then tell him you got a request on the office line for 'The Man I Love.' You're an angel. Bye." She ran for her room. "I have to change my clothes and get to the radio station. I'll drop you off at the gallery on my way."

"Oh no, my friend. I'm not gonna miss this. I'm coming with you." Zoe picked up her own cell phone and dialed.

Fifteen minutes later, Amanda blew through the front door of the radio station and skidded to a stop. Zoe plowed into her from behind.

"Hey, don't stop so sudden. I almost broke my nose on your shoulder blade." Zoe stopped complaining at the unexpected sound of applause.

Amanda looked from face to face in astonishment. Rosemary, she'd expected. But Andy, Mike, Neal, Ed Santone? What were they all doing here? Rosemary beamed at her, and even Neal appeared happy. "What—?"

"Oh honey, we figured you'd be here as soon as we heard Dev's opening tonight. We didn't want to miss this."

Andy sidled up to her and said, "We had faith in you, Mandy, but for a while there we were afraid the boss would never get his act together."

Amanda felt her jaw drop.

"Yeah," Neal chimed in, "we listened to Dev's show every night, once Andy figured out that he was sending you love letters over the air. After the party, though, we knew something bad happened."

They all nodded in agreement. Andy continued, "We almost called Captain Majewski, but Rosemary said the boss needed to figure this out on his own." He winked. "Seems like it worked out okay, though."

Rosemary went to the door. "I'm going to tell him about your request, Amanda. Are you ready?"

She nodded. "Oh yeah, I'm ready." She had a lot of moisture in her eyes so they glistened as she scanned the group. "I'm so glad I had so many people here to watch over me. You're the best."

There was a knock on the front door, and Zoe opened it. "About time. You almost missed the best part."

Jeff took off his helmet and shut the door behind him. "Got here as fast as I could, babe." He eyed Zoe up and down. "We don't all sit around being beautiful and waiting for phone calls, you know."

The song playing was "I Could Write a Book" and everyone in the room quieted down as Frank Sinatra sang.

When he finished, Dev's voice came on and Amanda looked up at the sound coming through the overhead speakers. "Ladies and gentlemen, I've just been given a request, and due to its very special nature, I'll have to make an exception to tonight's rules and play it."

Sophie Tucker's rendition of "The Man I Love" began and Amanda walked down the hall to the broadcast booth.

She stood on the other side of the glass and smiled at Dev, then walked around to the door. Andy caught up with her before she entered.

"Allow me, Amanda." He opened the door. "I think I may have an extra shift ahead of me after all."

But Amanda wasn't listening to him. She only had eyes for Dev and she suspected they sparkled like stars. She walked into his arms and the heat and promise in his eyes sent her heart fluttering. "I love you, Devlyn MacMurphy."

"And I love you, Amanda Adams." He kissed her tenderly. "But I'm tired of the friends with benefits routine." He kissed her again. "How about something more permanent, like husband and wife?"

She brushed the lock of dark hair off his brow. "Just what I had in mind, Dev of the Dream Machine. You're making all my dreams come true tonight."

The rest of the spectators lined the window outside of the booth and cheered, whistled, and stomped. Since the broadcast booth was soundproof, it played like an old time silent movie from inside. Dev and Amanda broke their embrace and bowed like actors on a stage.

"All this commotion over a few kisses?" Dev grinned into Amanda's eyes. "Not that they aren't worth it."

"I think they're celebrating your engagement, boss." Andy smirked, leaning against the door. "The mike was open during your proposal."

Amanda gasped. "You mean everyone listening in heard us?"

"Sounds like it," Dev said, a wicked gleam in his eyes. "No way you can back out now."

Andy leaned over and spoke into the mike. "You heard it here first, ladies and gents. I believe Dev will be unable to finish his show tonight, but don't worry, he'll be back tomorrow night."

Dev went to the table and picked up one last CD. "Play this for me, will you, Andy?"

"Sure, boss." He slipped it in the player, and 'Time After Time' serenaded the audience.

One more lingering kiss, and the couple left the broadcast booth.

The happy group offered congratulations and Amanda was touched to see such a display of good wishes from them all. Zoe hugged her and gave Dev a smacking kiss on the mouth.

"About time you two got your act together. For a while there I thought I was going to have to lock you both in a closet until you discovered you couldn't live without each other."

"And I'm beginning to understand all the strange behavior going on around here the last week or so," Dev said.

"I hate to be the one to say this, boss, but sometimes you can be a little slow on the uptake," Rosemary scolded. "You two go along now. The rest of us have everything here under control." She made shooing motions and the group parted to let them leave.

CHAPTER 28

Amanda woke with the weight of Dev's arm across her ribs, his left hand cupping her breast, and his breath warm against her neck. She'd never known such a sense of utter contentment that loving Dev brought to her every waking moment. She sighed and pressed closer to her sleeping soon-to-be husband.

"Careful. You know what happens when you move like that."

The hand tightened around her breast as the bud puckered against his palm. She couldn't resist and pressed her bottom against his erection. Her reward was a string of kisses on her neck with special attention to the sensitive spot behind her ear. She reached back and stroked the velvety head of his shaft, smiling at the audible intake of breath.

Dev flipped her onto her back and reached across her to grab the last of their supply of condoms, not missing the opportunity to lick and suckle her other breast, then kiss her until her muscles went liquid with desire.

"Hurry," she demanded, reaching for the foil packet he held just out of her reach.

"My, my, aren't we the greedy one this morning?" he teased.

She arched her body so he could feel the moisture as she rubbed against him.

He ripped open the packet with his teeth and covered himself in record time. With a single thrust, he buried himself to the hilt, and Amanda wrapped her legs around him and began to move.

They'd made love dozens of times over the past week. Slow and sensuously, fast and furiously, and every way in-between. She still couldn't seem to get enough of this wonderful man with his fantastic body, talented mouth, and a heart that was hers alone. This morning he took her from comfortable to crazy in a matter of seconds and she scraped her nails across his back and shouted her pleasure when she disintegrated into tingling nerve endings and ragged breathing. A few more quick thrusts, and Dev followed her.

As her pulse slowed, she languidly followed the latticework of sunshine moving across the bedroom wall. This was heaven. This was bliss. She'd be happy to stay in this bed another month or so—assuming someone would send them food from time to time to keep their strength up. She glanced at the clock radio.

"Oh, crap. Dev, get up." She pushed at his shoulders but he didn't budge. "Dev." She smacked his backside for emphasis. "My parents' plane lands at BWI in ninety minutes. We have to hurry."

She pushed against his shoulders and managed to lift him an inch.

"Can't we stay like this a little longer? I love being inside you, babe."

He nuzzled her neck and she could feel him begin to harden again. No. No. Definitely not. They had to get going. She pushed against him again. "Nope, we're out of time, honey," she whispered in his ear. "I'll take a rain-check, though."

Dev propped himself up on his elbows, kissed the tip of her nose, and rolled off her.

She scrambled out of bed and ran for the shower. "Make a pot of coffee, will you, dear? Please?"

"Yeah, sure." He ambled down the hall.

She had to get into—and out of—the shower before he came back. If he got in with her, there would be another half-hour delay, and they didn't have time for that. She was towel drying her hair when Dev came through the door.

"Wow, you're fast this morning." He tugged on the towel wrapped around her torso and she grabbed it to prevent total exposure. "Why don't you hop back in there with me? I'm sure you must have missed a spot or two and I could, you know, help you with that."

She evaded his arms and shook her head. "We don't have time. Get in there. We have to leave the house in ten minutes." He kissed her anyway, but got in the shower.

Good thing her parents weren't staying here. She'd kind of let housekeeping slip this past week. Laundry was piled up in front of the washer and dirty dishes from yesterday were still in the sink. What would her mother think?

That she'd given up the trappings of civilization to spend all her time in bed with her lover? Amanda grinned and shrugged. Guilty.

Thank God for Marjorie's bed and breakfast. Her mom and Jack would be far more comfortable there, especially after she told them Dev had moved in with her. She'd ask them to stay an extra week so they could be here for the wedding.

Since neither she nor Dev wanted a big wedding, they'd decided to marry as soon as possible. Dev's parents were flying in from New York for the ceremony. She would be nervous meeting Dev's dad, knowing they weren't on the best of terms, but she hoped that seeing him happy and healthy would ease the tension between them.

Tomorrow Agent Baley would meet with her mom, Jack, she and Dev and tell them the results of the autopsy. Then, Saturday after the medical examiner had released her dad's body, they would have a short memorial service and Amanda could gratefully close the book on that chapter of her life.

Dev parked in front of the Blue Point Inn. Amanda's mother, Marian, and her husband, Jack, sat holding hands in two of the wicker rocking chairs on the big porch. Agent

Baley had asked to speak to Amanda and Marian so he was playing chauffeur. No way was he letting Amanda face whatever news the FBI agent had alone. He saw that Jack had the same idea as he walked Marian to the car, opened the door, and settled her in the back seat.

As he got in the other side, Jack clapped him on the shoulder. "Thanks for the ride, Dev. I assume Amanda is every bit as anxious about this as Marian."

"She is, though she doesn't want to admit it. She's been working off her nerves with a cleaning frenzy ever since Agent Baley called this morning."

"Even knowing what he's going to say doesn't make it any better," Marian said. "Every time I think about that Highway Hijacker, it gives me chills. Amanda and Frank were so close I know it must be terribly hard for her."

Dev saw the couple clasp hands in the rearview mirror and knew where Amanda's penchant for handholding had come from. Marian was an older, but still lovely, version of her daughter, with the same gray eyes and fine skin. Her light hair was touched with frost but warmth radiated from her face.

"I'm so glad you'll be here for this, Dev. It's good that Amanda will have someone she loves close by. She'll try to be brave but . . ."

"Don't worry, Mrs. Harris, I plan to stay right by her side today—and always." Another glance in the rearview mirror showed him Marian's smile.

After they arrived at Amanda's house, they settled in the living room and Marian studied the room with interest. It was a warm spring day and Amanda had opened all the windows to let in the fresh air with a salty tang from the bay. "You've made your mark on this place, Amanda. It looks lovely."

"Thanks, Mom. Dev, ah, gave me a little help with the hard stuff." Her eyes twinkled as she slanted a smile at him.

"I just did the basics. The beautification all came from your daughter." He winked at her and saw the color begin to stain her cheeks. He loved that she blushed as the slightest provocation. "Can I get you two something to drink? We have wine and beer and maybe some of that brandy left, too, don't we, darling?"

"Wine would be lovely, Dev. Thank you," Marion replied.

"If you've got cold beer stashed somewhere, I can take one off your hands," Jack offered.

No sooner had he pulled the cork from the wine than the FBI agent appeared at the front door. Amanda went to let him in as Dev handed beer and wine to Jack and Marian.

"Can I get you something to drink, Agent Baley? We have iced tea and soda if alcohol isn't on your agenda this afternoon."

"Thanks, but nothing for me," the agent said. He sat in one of the armchairs while Jack joined Marian on the love seat and Dev perched somewhat precariously on the arm of Amanda's chair.

"First let me say that a lot has happened in the past couple of days but I wanted to wait to talk with you until I had all the pieces put together."

Amanda slipped her hand into his and laced their fingers together. Dev gave her a reassuring little squeeze and felt the tension in her shoulders lessen the slightest bit.

"We have determined that Mr. Adams was not a victim of the Highway Hijacker. We weren't sure at first because we considered the possibility that the Highway Hijacker may have changed his MO over the years. Mr. Adams was not stabbed to death as were all of the other known victims of the Highway Hijacker. At least all that we have recovered to date. He was shot in the neck at close range with a 32-caliber pistol. The gun was found on the passenger seat and the bullet recovered from Mr. Adams' body was matched to that gun."

"But if it wasn't the Hijacker, then who shot my dad?"

"The gun was registered to Admiral Wyndham and considering where we found the vehicle, he became our number one suspect."

Amanda snapped her mouth shut. "The Admiral? I can't believe he would shoot my dad." She frowned. "Wait. Wasn't he at sea when my dad was . . . murdered?"

Agent Baley nodded. "He was. An airtight alibi."

"Then . . .?" Marian said.

"When I went to question Admiral Wyndham he indicated that he had purchased the gun for his wife since she was often down here alone while he was at sea. When I asked to speak with his wife, he told me she had gone back to Annapolis the night before to attend some society luncheon the next day. But there was no luncheon. We caught her at the airport before she managed to get on a flight to Rio."

This time Dev felt his own jaw drop. The flirtatious Mrs. Wyndham? Seriously? He traded astounded looks with Amanda.

"But why? I don't understand this at all," Marian said.

"It appears that Mrs. Wyndham had a serious obsession with your husband, Ma'am. She often frequented the clubs where he played, usually sending him a drink. In fact, she heard about this town by listening to his conversations with the bartender. That was partly the reason she convinced her husband to buy property here. That night, she apparently overheard him chatting with the bartender about opening up this cottage for the summer so she drove down ahead of him, engineered a flat tire, and waited for him to drive by. It was pouring rain so rather than fixing the flat, your husband offered her a ride home and said he would fix it the next day. Unfortunately, when she attempted to seduce him, your husband not only refused her invitation but laughed in her face." He shrugged. "In a fit of rage, she took the gun out of her purse and threatened to shoot him. She said she never actually meant to pull the trigger but he grabbed the gun and it just went off. Apparently the bullet hit his carotid artery and he bled to death in a matter of minutes."

"Oh my god, I cannot believe this. This woman, who hired me to produce her party, killed my father? This is absurd. I mean she's a little wonky, true. And she obviously enjoys men . . ." Amanda's voice trailed off.

The color drained from her cheeks and Dev picked up her glass. "Here, drink some of this. You look like you're about to pass out."

"That's what she meant, Dev." She grasped his arm, her eyes wide with shock. "The day they got dad's car out of the bay and I, uh, got a little lightheaded? After you left, she said something about how I was stubborn—just like him." She clapped her hand over her mouth as her eyes filled with tears.

Dev reached in his pocket for his handkerchief, handing it to her as the tears spilled over.

"That woman murdered my husband? And all these years she's lived scot-free and spent her summers not a mile away from us?" Marian's eyes snapped with anger. "That bitch!" She clutched at Jack's arm. "And she had the gall to hire you? The daughter of the man she murdered? She must be sick. She must be crazy."

She turned to Agent Baley. "She won't get away with this because she's crazy, will she? Please tell me she's going to jail." Tears spilled unheeded down her cheeks. "I want to strangle her myself, for taking Frank away from me." She buried her head against Jack's chest and sobbed. Jack wrapped his arms around her.

"No, Ma'am, she won't get away with murder. Crazy she may be but her intent to flee the country proves she knew what she did was wrong. She'll spend the rest of her life in prison." He stood up to leave.

Amanda stood also, using Dev's handkerchief to blot her cheeks. Dev snugged her against his side and held out his hand to the FBI agent. "Thank you for all of your hard work, Agent Baley."

"If it weren't for Miss Adam's persistence we never would have found her father, so she gets a big part of the credit," he said. "Even though he didn't turn out to be one of the Highway Hijacker's victims, I'm glad we were able to finally resolve the mystery of his disappearance for you."

That night, after slow and tender lovemaking had drained the last of the tension from Amanda's shoulders, she lay cuddled against him, her breathing slowly deepening toward sleep. Dev brushed a kiss in her hair and sent a prayer heavenward to thank his best friend for the gift of life and the chance to live his with Amanda Adams.

Coming soon from Karen Ann Dell

and Soul Mate Publishing:

HIS BY DESIGN

Zoe Silvercreek was determined to make Blue Point Cove a haven for local artisans and her gallery a showcase for their works. She'd begged, borrowed, and bet her future on her ability to make her dream a reality. She'd better succeed because she wasn't about to forfeit what she used as collateral for the loan.

Jeff Petrosky was a sculptor, currently making ends meet as a handyman. His sister was the real artist in the family, but he'd sworn to keep her secret—at least until the day he'd saved up enough money to pay for the surgery that would repair the damage to her pretty face.

The renovation of Zoe Silvercreek's gallery was a godsend. In exchange for his labor, he'd get Zoe to display 'his' paintings. He knew they'd bring in the money he needed for Jenny's surgery. Once she was healed, and willing to be seen in public, they could drop the ruse and she could claim the paintings as her own.

Working with the luscious Ms. Silvercreek would test any man's willpower, but he'd keep his hands, and his heart, to himself. Nothing would interfere with this chance to save his sister.

CPSIA information can be obtained
at www.ICGtesting.com
Printed in the USA
BVOW11s2216191117
500247BV00030B/91/P